The Fated Six
Who Am I Really?

H.K. Walker

Copyright © 2021 Walker Publishing

Publisher's Cataloging-in-Publication data

Names: Walker, H.K., author.
Title: Who am I really? / H.K. Walker.
Series: The Fated Six.
Description: Elm Springs, AR: Walker Publishing, 2021.

Identifiers: LCCN: 2021919067 | ISBN: 978-1-7379203-3-5
(hardback) | 978-1-7379203-0-4 (paperback) | 978-1-7379203-1-1
(ebook) | 978-1-7379203-2-8 (audio)
Subjects: LCSH Animals, Mythical--Fiction. | Supernatural--
Fiction. | Romance fiction. | Fantasy Fiction. | BISAC FICTION
/ Fantasy / Action & Adventure | FICTION / Romance /
Fantasy | FICTION / Romance / Erotica
Classification: LCC PS3623.A35928 W46 2021 | DDC 813.6--
dc23

Cover design by: H.K. Walker

Walker Publishing
PO Box 152
Elm Springs, AR
72728

Introduction

With multiple point of views (POV) throughout the story. The books in this series does not have to be read in a certain order.

My name is Amara Stone. Six years ago, I woke up only knowing my name and that I was not human. After joining the Marines for five years, I am recruited by The Company. They protect the secret of the existence of supernaturals as well as protects everyone from one another. I am second in command of a team that includes a shifter, an energy vampire, a magician, and a huldra. My team's job is to hunt down the beings that kill the innocent and that no one else can. I had no clue that one of our assignments was going to turn my world upside down. Changing it forever.

CONTENTS

Chapter 1: Ominous Forest

Amara's POV

"Alright ladies and gentlemen its show time.", Captain announces.

The pilot turns the status light to green notifying us that we are over the drop zone. I slide my jumpsuit up over my tactical gear, step to the edge of the plane, take a deep breath and casually fall out of the plane following Captain. I love the rush you get from free falling. There really is nothing like it. It is a sensory overload as you feel the intense wind all around you and the adrenaline pulsing through every nerve of your body. It feels like my brain is still on the plane looking down at the ground, but my body is already falling.

It is a beautiful spring day. The sun is glistening in a cloudless cotton candy blue sky. As it starts to rise for the day. The air is light and breezy with just a trace of salt and humidity. As we descend closer to our destination, an island comes into view. It is breathtakingly beautiful. The shore is outlined with sand that looks like the dark of night, the thick forest is full of various types of plants that are painted with numerous colors, and four mountains with their snowy peaks that reach up trying to touch the stars.

Once Ace's altimeter reads 2000 feet, he gives us the signal and we pull the cord to release our parachutes. By the time, all six of our feet touch the ground and we unclip our harnesses to release the parachutes. The crate with our weapons and backpacks full of gear that we will need on this journey lands a few feet from us. I pull my company issued black HK416 and black Glock 45 out of the crate. Checking to make sure both clips and both replacement clips are fully loaded. I pop one clip into place in both guns and then strap the other two to the holsters. Then I holster the Glock on my left thigh and sling the HK416 over my right shoulder. After I get them in place, I grab my black Vulcan Gear Medieval ages sword. Then sheath it on my back, which is also company issued. Finally, I grab my 6" black tactical combat boot knife sheathing it in my left boot and my 8" black tactical combat knife sheathing it to my right thigh. I look around at the rest of my team as I scan our surroundings with every one of my senses on alert. Grabbing one of the backpacks I sling it over my shoulders. Once everyone else has their same company issued weapons strapped and their backpacks on, we get down to business.

"This assignment is capture only! Our target is the Collector of Souls. He could be the strongest being we have or will ever face.", Captain informs us. "The plan is simple it's an all-day hike through the forest. We will make camp a little way in from the clearing so that we have some coverage. Then we have a two-hour hike to the first mountain where our target lives. From there we will climb up the side of the mountain almost to the top. Since Amara is our most experienced climber, she will take the lead. Once the target is captured, I will radio for our ride.", Captain lays out the plan.

When my active-duty contract with the Marines was up, I was hired by The Company. They are probably the most powerful and richest company in America. I mean they have their own personal army of beings including some humans that know about our existence. Nobody can touch them. Since I joined a year ago, I have come across countless creatures that were supposed to just be myths. The Company is in charge with keeping everyone safe from one another while keeping the existence of supernatural beings a secret. I wonder what the Collector of Souls did to get on their radar.

"The higher ups aren't even sure what all he is capable of, but they do know he has necromancy powers and is one of the Ancients. Once up the mountain we will be branching out into two teams. The castle is built into the mountain so there is only one way in and one way out.", Captain adds.

The island is said to be a myth as well as the Collector of Souls. The myth says that the Collector of Soul's castle is guarding the gate to the Underworld. It also says that if you are even lucky enough to make it to the island you will never survive whatever lives in the forest. I cannot shake how this place oddly feels like home. Hearing my name in Captain's deep voice pulls me from my thoughts.

We all enter the forest in tow behind him. I have never seen anything like it. There are so many plants that I have never even heard of and several I have only read about. It is so thick with vegetation it makes it seem like it is dusk already, giving off an ominous feeling. It is starting to feel like we have been walking for days even though it has only been maybe four hours. Something moves in my right peripheral. I swear I just saw a tree move. I watch for a minute while we continue to march forward, but there is no other movement. Dismissing it but staying on high alert I continue to follow Captain deeper into the forest.

I cannot shake the feeling that we are being watched. Also, I have a weird feeling when it comes to the Collector of Souls. I always do research on our targets before we accept the assignment. I do not like going into a job blind. Not to mention we do not have the strength or numbers to complete this assignment. The Collector of Souls is also known as the God of Death. He does not just have the usual abilities of a god, like healing himself, immortality, super strength, and speed. The God of Death can also control winter and death doors as well as other rare abilities. He is not only old but super powerful. The higher ups are stupid if they are underestimating him. Thinking that he has weakened over the years enough that my team alone could bring him in. I have read the stories about him. Even though he is also known as the Harbinger of Peaceful Deaths. He is not one to fuck with or known to be forgiving. Why the hell do they have us going after a god anyways? I heard they existed but that we stay clear of them because they are too powerful and wise. Its unheard of for them to even pop up on The Company's radar. It just does not make sense. I wonder how much the Captain knows.

"Amara your team will flank from the right while my team flanks from the left. Remember we don't branch out until the top of the mountain.", Captain informs us. "Let's move out."

"I hope we get to fight some zoms.", Ace whispers to Willa.

"Keep your mouths shut and all your senses on high alert. We don't know what all is on this island.", Captain orders as he looks back at Ace with a smirk on his face. It is no secret that Captain has been dying to fight some zombies as well.

We have been walking for a few more hours when I look back behind me making sure the others are keeping up. Malan and Ace are no longer walking with us. Willa and Aspen notice they are gone a few seconds after I do. Searching the woods around us I see no sign of them. Shit! Turning around I make sure Captain is still in front of me. I notice him walking off the trail into the forest. As I motion for them to follow me, I sprint after Captain. Where the hell is he going? Quietly I rush up behind him then peek around his body to see where he is heading. There is a sexy naked woman walking deeper into the woods. It seems that she has Captain in a trance. She looks back to make sure he is still following her. When she notices me, she transforms into a gigantic spider. She looks like a massive blue-black Missulena spider. Once it is completely transformed, it shoots a strand of its web at Captain. I am not able to draw my sword and cut the strand in time. The web strand wraps around Captain then the spider reels him in. I take off after them. Hoping Willa and Aspen are following behind me. If I kill it now, I will not know where its den is, and we will not be able to save Malan and Ace. With no other choice I continue to follow it deeper into the woods.

The spider's den comes into view after chasing it for at least ten minutes. Piled up between three trees are bones stacked on bones. They had to have been accumulated at least twelve feet high. I motion for the girls to go into the den to save the boys while I distract the spider. Reaching in I summon my flame. As heat spreads through my arms and out my hands I form a blue ball of fire. I toss it at the spider to get its attention. Ignoring me it keeps running as it tries to get its prize home. So, I throw two more. That gets the spider's attention. It turns around and charges at me. Forming two bigger balls of blue flames I throw them at it. That did not stop the spider it continued to charge at me. I barely had enough time to jump out of the way. Then instead of balls of fire I engulf the spider in two streams of blue flames. Letting out a bloodcurdling scream it pounces on me. Knocking me to the ground on my back. As the massive spider sinks its fangs into my chest it pumps me full of venom. Slipping my knife out of my boot I embed it in the side of the spider's head. The massive spider falls onto its side still engulfed in flames. Slowly it is reducing to ash. Feeling like I am about to black out I sit on the ground. Just as my whole body starts to ache. It hurts so bad I want to curl into a ball.

One minute I am so hot I am sweating so much my shirt is soaked. The next I am so cold I am shivering. Aspen comes up out of the spider's borrow in the den then pulls Ace out and lays him on the ground. Then rushes over to cut Captain free. Malan and Willa climb out next before grabbing Ace and carrying him over to where I am. He looks like he is at Death's feet. In my current state I am no help to anyone. Not until the venom is out of my system. Fifteen minutes later enough venom has been processed out that I can heal Ace. The spider had almost drained him but did not pump any venom into him. I am not sure how much longer he could have held on. Malan was drained a little and did not have any venom in his system either. It did not have time to taste Captain. Once Ace is healed and all the venom is out of my system we head towards where we came from. Back on the trail we continue our hike in silence and on high alert.

We decide to rest for a few minutes after we have been walking for an hour or so. Trying to cover as much distance as we can since we are now behind on time. Captain sits down on a log. A branch snaps to my left. I scan the area to see what made the sound and lock eyes with a creature. Letting me know of its presence, it charges at us. A tree is attacking us. I am not kidding a fucking tree!

"Enemy at nine o'clock.", I announce making sure the whole team is aware of the situation at hand.

The closer the creature gets the more it looks like a human, animal, tree hybrid. I know that sounds ridiculous, but it is the only way I can think to describe it. The creature keeps charging at us with a god like speed. As soon as it is in range we aim, click off the safeties of our HK416s and wait for the Captain to give the order.

"Fire!", Captain commands as we all unload our clips at the creature.

The creature is unfazed by the shower of bullets annealed with

Haemorrhois venom and is gaining even more ground. The bullets fall to the ground like they are hitting an invisible shield. Haemorrhois is one of the many Saharan snakes also called Bleeder. As the venom spreads through the victim's body every opening starts pouring out blood. Causing the victim's whole body to become a massive bleeding wound. Until they bleed out and die. Since the bullets are not working, we change tactics. Captain moves to my right. His usual blue eyes are a golden brown letting me know he is ready. Ace and Willa are to the side of him. To my left is Aspen and Malan. We all slip out of our backpacks letting them hit the ground.

Before any of us can draw our Vulcan Gear swords, we are all knocked on our asses by a magical force. Sliding all six of us through the grass and mud, then slamming us into different tree trunks. Damn, as far as I can remember I have not been hit that hard. What the hell is this thing? I have never heard of any creature this strong. Other than the old gods and goddesses.

The creature stood at least seven feet tall, its face looks like a moose skull with massive antlers, eyes that are glowing like the fury of the sun on a scorching summer day and the body of the creature looks like a combination of man and tree. There is dark green moss growing over its shoulders and chest like armor. With branch like arms that extend into talons in place of fingers. It is neat looking in a menacing way. Thorny, monstrous, dark green vines are shooting up out of the ground by the time we are all back on our feet. Four of us are able to draw our swords and start slashing at the vines. Stopping them from twisting their way up our legs. Willa and Ace are not fast enough causing them to be engulfed by the vines.

The thing about our team is we are a very unusual team even for living in the supernatural world. Every one of us brings something special to this team, not just our abilities. We are a family!

Aspen who is my sister, not by blood, is also what they call an energy vamp. She is so beautiful! She is about 5'4" with deep brown pixie styled hair and sea green eyes. With one touch she can absorb your abilities. The more powerful the being the more of her own energy is burnt up. Which would take a toll on anyone. She used to have to juice up before every mission, but she has gotten stronger. Now she can store up to four different abilities at a time for however long she wants them. Aspen can also siphon all of someone's energy knocking them out cold even killing them.

Then there is Malan whose full name is Malanior. He is 5'11", has silver hair with sky blue eyes. He is athletically built with a very enchanting aura about him. Malan is a Llewyrr which is a race of High Elves that were isolated for a millennium on the isle of Gwynneth in the Moonshaes. He has a keen intellect, superhuman physical agility and senses, natural magical talents and is the most talented swordsmen I know. We also have a sibling bond. Aspen, Malan, and I have been together since boot camp. While all three of us were hiding the fact that we are not human with spells and other techniques.

Ace is a magician, yes that means he is human but a human that has magical abilities. He can cast spells, has astral projection abilities, and can perform some illusion magic. He is a little nerdy looking compared to the other two men and is one of The Company's tech guys. Do not get me wrong he is a looker. Ace is slim, standing about 5'9" with a pretty boy face, sandy brown colored shaggy hair, onyx-colored eyes, and has a good heart. His glasses finish off his nerdy but hot vibe.

There is also Willa who is a huldra which is a Lady of the Forest. She is 5'6" with straight medium blonde hair and sparkling hazel eyes like her charming personality. She can call upon the forest's magic giving her the power over the elements of earth and water, as well as communicate with the forest animals. Willa also has the normal supernatural abilities. She is amazing with a sword almost as good as Malan. As well as the stealthiest person I know. We are starting to become close friends.

Captain is a shifter. When he shifts his ocean blue eyes turn to a golden brown. He can shift into any animal, creature, or being. As long as he can picture them in his mind. He can only transform into their physical form. We have been dating for about two years now. He is good to me, and I cannot picture life without him. I only call the Captain, Kaden outside of work. It helps me keep our personal and professional lives separate. Only the team knows about our relationship and that is how it must stay. He is 6 ft. tall, has light brown almost buzzed hair with a strong jaw covered by a beard and has a muscular build.

As for me, we have no clue what I am. The Company has run every test they can think of and ended up coming up with more questions than answers. I do have some impressive abilities though. The Company rates my power level close to a demigod. I stand at 5'8" with blue-raven black ringlets flowing along my heart shaped face almost to my waist. Anytime I am on the clock it is thrown up into a messy bun. Keeping it out of my dark, violet-colored eyes. I am blessed with curves with a thin waist as well as size D boobs and a nice plump ass. I woke up one morning with no memories. The only memories I have are from a couple of days before I joined the Marines until today. I knew my name and knew I was in my own bed but nothing of where I came from or who my family is. That was six years ago, and I still have no idea what happened or how to find out. We have tried hypnosis and different memory spells. Nothing was strong enough to fixed whatever had happened to me.

I am putting too much focus on slashing the vines that are twisting up my legs. That I did not see the creature charging at me. It slashes its' razor-sharp talons ripping four huge gashes deep in my stomach. I double over dropping my sword as the creature swings its other arm of talons causing it to miss me by seconds. Blood is oozing out from between my fingers as I try to keep as much of my guts inside my stomach as I can with both hands. I inhale and exhale through clenched teeth as the pain worsens. I can feel the warmth of my healing powers spread through my stomach as it starts to stitch my insides back together. Captain, Aspen, and Malan have their swords out aiming for the creature's head as they encircle it quickly.

With a lift of a single talon the creature sends Malan flying through a few trees before slamming into a huge tree trunk and then crashing to the ground with a nasty crunch. Some more monstrous vines are engulfing aspen before she can get to me. Captain is throwing punch after punch keeping the creature too busy to use its magical powers. The creature is landing more hits on Captain than he is landing on the creature. I get to Aspen as quickly as I can. As I reach her, I glance over at Captain who is nowhere in sight. My heart sinks as I force myself to focus on freeing Aspen. If I can give her the right opening, she can end this. I hope. Sending heat exploding out of my palms in a blaze of fire I burn the vines to a crisp. Then help Aspen onto her feet.

As we look towards the creature it is battling its doppelganger. Good move Captain, I just wish I knew which one he is. In a split second after they went a few rounds one of the creatures snatches the other above its head. With a magical force growing tighter and tighter around the other creature's neck. The one dangling has to be Captain seeing how his only magical ability is shifting. The creature tosses Captain to the right like a rag doll, slamming him to the ground with a hard thud. Aspen and I lock eyes having the same plan. As the creature sees me charging for it, the creature lifts a talon engulfing Captain with more of those monstrous vines. The creature only seems a little fazed by our attacks.

Charging upon the creature I throw a right then a left hook. Following with a strong kick to the creature's chest. The creature dodges both of my punches but is not quite fast enough to dodge my kick as well. The force from the kick sends the creature flying back. Causing the creature to slide through the various kinds of plants and mud. Then lands on its ass. The creature is stunned for a few minutes. Quickly recovering the creature gets to its knees. That is all the time I need to reach it. Dodging the right, left, right combo the creature tries to land on my face, I come up with a wicked right hook. Ripping the wound on my stomach open more. Blood once again starts gushing out over my tactical gear. "Shhiittt.", I hiss through clenched teeth.

With a bam and a crunch my head is thrown back. Blood is oozing out of my top and bottom lips. They are swelling instantly as blood fills my mouth. I recover quicker from that blow than ripping my stomach back open. Allowing me time to land a strong kick to the creature's stomach. The creature is thrown back through the air slamming into a tree trunk. Almost cracking it in half right by Aspen. He really could not have landed in a better spot. Aspen reaches down placing her palm on the creature's shoulder and starts siphoning. Not just its power, but its energy as well. You can see the creature getting weaker. Fighting with everything it has left the creature gets to its knees.

With her left-hand Aspen is able to knock the creature back down using a magical force. Then shooting thorny, monstrous, dark green vines from the ground, she engulfs the creature's legs. Using its own ability against it. The creature is not going to go without a fight as he pushes back with his powers. She lifts her right hand off the creature causing a stronger magical hold on the vines having them slowly crawl up the creature's waist. Sweat is dripping profusely off her face and she is starting to look worse than the creature. Even though it is starting to look defeated. She will not be able to hold it much longer. The creature is strong and fighting back the vines. Which are at a standstill until one overpowers the other.

Knowing I must think quickly I charge as fast as I can at the creature. I am not fast enough. Aspen's body goes limp and is being engulfed in vines. Just high enough up her body to pin her arms to her side. As the creature is about to rip out her heart, I tear open the shadow of the tree that is behind the creature. Tackling the creature, we plow into the shadow.

Tuatha De' Danann which is a rare race of beings is said to have been casted down from the heavens on a cloud of mist for knowing too much. They were thought to be and were worshipped as a Celtic God. Whose worship ended with the rise of Christianity. They have a similar ability to mine. Instead of opening shadows the have their own pocket-dimension that is between this world and what they call hell. They call their pocket-dimension their hoard. They can store whatever or whoever they want with no way for them to escape. As well as use it to travel through. Well, I use shadows in a similar way. I can stretch or manipulate the shadow and can also travel through them.

I throw up a magical barrier as soon as I am on my feet. The inside of a shadow is a blacked-out area as big as the object creating the shadow. The creature looks around confused before beating wildly at the barrier. My barrier is taking everything it can. It is holding for now, but I am not sure how much more it can take.

It hisses out, "Trespassers will die!" Threatening us in its native tongue.

Yep, I am an aligist, and I have not come across a language I could not understand and communicate.

"Listen!", I voice to the creature in its native tongue. The creature stops beating wildly on the barrier and looks at me all wide eyed. Its eyes are no longer glowing like the furry of the sun.

"Ancient One?", the creature mumbles. I am not sure if I had heard the creature right, so I shove the thought out of my head and I get down to business.

"We apologize for trespassing. We had no idea this forest is yours. We are just passing through to the mountains. If you agree to let us pass unharmed,

I will release you and I promise no more harm will come to you or the forest. If not, you can learn how fun it is to live in this shadow.", I explain in the creature's native tongue.

"Just like you let the juarogunna go freely?", the creature questions.

"If you are talking about that massive shapeshifting spider. That thing stole my team members and when I tried to keep it nonlethal it about killed me.", I state.

"That was quite interesting to watch.", he says with a chuckle. "For my freedom I will grant you passage out of my forest without my interference. But to grant you access through unharmed I will need a favor.", the creature offers after standing there quietly for a few minutes.

I did not trust this creature. What did it have up its sleeve? "And what is this favor?", I ask suspiciously.

"The Collector of Souls lives up in the first mountain.", the creature responds eyeing me curiously. "I need you to acquire a golden ring from him."

"So, let me get this right. You want me to steal a ring from the Collector of Souls?", I question.

"How you acquire it is up to you.", the creature informs me.

I thought about it for a while. Whatever this creature has up its sleeve we are no match for it. However, it oddly seems a little wary of me.

"Why do you want this ring?", I inquire.

"It has a certain ability that I find myself in need of.", is the creature's response.

Well, that is not vague at all I thought. I stand there silently already knowing we have no other choice.

"If you do this favor for me, I will grant you and your team free access to my forest any time unharmed as well as owe you a favor in return. Which you will need sooner than you realize.", the creature continues as it eyes the silver chain with a charm that is hiding under my tactical gear.

Wow the creature must really want to get a hold of this ring. I agreed to the deal. Before reopening the shadow that closed as soon as we plowed into it. I usher for the creature to go first as I hop out of the shadow behind it.

"If anything happens to anyone on my team. I will not stop until I find a way to end your existence!", I promise the creature.

Once out of the tree's shadow I am brought back to the bloody battle scene. Nothing around us is left standing or whole. I run over to where the Captain is engulfed in vine still in the form of the creature. I set the vine a blaze pulling Captain out as it is turning to ash. He shifts back into his own form. I stand there a few minutes getting a good view of Kaden's model like naked body. Shit he is good looking. Keep it together we are on an assignment, I internally slap myself. He snatches me up into a tight bear hug then kisses me to roughly on my swollen lips. I lean in for more returning the kiss. Remembering the situation at hand, he sits me down and we pull away from each other reluctantly. I grab his sword that is on the ground to the left of me then hand it to him.

"Go free Willa and Ace. I'll go check on Aspen and Malan.", I direct. Captain nods in response before heading towards them.

I look around for the creature as a whisper floats along the wind, "Don't forget about our deal."

I notice that the creature is long gone, and the forest looks like it did before the battle. No busted or broken trees and plants. As well as no skid marks in the grass and mud. I know what you are thinking burning the vines is faster than slashing through them. I have another talent that is extremely useful for this job. I rush over to Aspen and burn the vines off. When I tackled the creature into the shadow she dropped to the ground. She is out cold, bleeding from her head, her breathing is shallow, and she has deep thick bleeding holes from the thorns on the vines. This creature is by far the most powerful being we have encountered. I place my hand just a few inches above her body. How much more powerful is the Collector of Souls going to be than that creature? The thought crosses my mind as I look down at Aspen limp in my arms. This time I push warmth out of my palm instead of a blazing heat. As I slowly move my hand along her body all her wounds and ribs that punctured her lung are healing. The creature must have squeezed the shit out of her with those vines. With a single touch I can not only heal. I can also know what is wrong with the being or creature, from wounds to illnesses. After healing Aspen completely, her breathing returns to normal. But she still has not opened her eyes. Realizing she almost depleted her energy completely. I place my hand on her forehead pushing a good portion of my own energy into her. We do not have time to let her body build its own energy levels back up.

A couple of minutes after her eyes open, I help her upon her feet. Slowly everything comes back to her as she looks around wide eyed for the creature.

Placing my hands on her shoulders, I make her look me in the eyes. "You are safe, I'll explain everything. First, we must make sure everyone else is okay.", I express.

Nodding her head, she follows me to where Malan struck the tree then slammed to the ground. Once Malan comes into sight, I feel all the blood rush out of my face. While I am rushing over to him as fast as I can. Aspen lets a big gasp following not too far behind. Malan is leaning with his back against a tree. Above his head a way up is the imprint of his body smashed into the big tree trunk. Malan's left leg is bent at an unnatural angle with the bone sticking out, blood is pouring out of the back of his head, and his spine is broken in several places. He has also lost consciousness and is losing too much blood.

"Aspen, find a piece of bark or stick that Malan can bite on. I'm going to have to reset his leg before I can heal it.", I direct. Returning with a considerable size piece of bark Aspen opens his mouth, places it between his teeth, and then grabs his hands. With a crunch I reset his leg.

"Okay now we need to gently place him to where he is laying straight on the ground. It's the best position to heal his spine.", I instruct Aspen as I take the bark out of his mouth.

We both put one arm around his back under his shoulders and our other arm under each of his knees. Aspen places her hand on my arm siphoning some of my strength as we lift him. Then gently we lower Malan to the ground placing him on his back. I kneel beside him, starting with the wound at the back of his head that is pouring out blood. Slowly I inch my hand down his unconscious body making sure the wounds are completely healed before moving on. As I am finish healing his spine, I make my way down to his other leg. The others are making their way to us. I did a quick scan of the three of them. Captain who is limping this way is beat to hell with a few deep gashes as well as holes all over from the thorns on the vines. But no life-threatening injuries. Willa and Ace are giggling uncontrollably as they drunkenly make their way over. They have deep, thick, bloody holes all over their bodies. They are obviously trippin balls off a hallucinogen from the thorns.

It did not take long at all for Malan to gain consciousness. I heal Willa then Ace, trying hard to hold the laughter in. Hey, do not judge I cannot help it. I can heal their wounds, but I am not able to remove the effects of the hallucinogen. When I heal it has this warm tingling sensation that whoever I am healing feels. With them tripping it is magnified by who knows how much. I slowly move my hand down hovering just inches above their bodies as they moan, hiss, and squirm. Both sinking limply to the ground from multiple orgasms as I finish healing them. Lastly, I heal Captain since he always insists, he goes last. I start at his forehead slowly moving my hand down over his delicious ocean blue eyes. As my hand moves down over his nose, lips, and beard I stare deeply into his eyes almost touching his soul. Trying so hard to push back all the naughty thoughts. I cannot help but bite my bottom lip, this man is sexy.

My hand keeps moving down his body with my eyes following. As my hand is moving down over his bulge, I run my tongue along my lips and try to force myself to continue. A little disappointed that he is dressed now. I am unable to stop the flood of images of me taking him deep in my mouth, him with his mouth between my legs, and me riding him. Pushing in the image of how Malan was all limp against that tree with blood running down the back of his head, and his leg being bent at an unnatural angle with the bone sticking out in the front of my mind. In turn pushes out the dirty thoughts I was having about Kaden. I mean Captain out of my head. Malan is like the big brother I never had or the one I do not remember. It kills me seeing him like that.

"What kind of naughty thoughts were you just having?", Kaden leans in my ear whispering in a deep sexual voice with a naughty smirk curving up his lips. "I can smell your arousal."

I wonder what he is thinking. He has never acted this way while on an assignment. I really, really need a cold shower right now! A blush runs through both my cheeks as I walk over to have a seat against the nearest tree. The more people I heal and the more serious the wound, injury, or illness the more of my energy is needed to be able to heal. Not to mention my body has already healed itself for the most part while I was in the shadow with the creature. Which it takes less energy to heal myself than to heal others.

"Amara.", was the last thing I hear before I slump to the side hitting my head on the ground. Everything goes black as blood oozes out my nose and ears.

Slowly my eyes open adjusting to the brightness of the blazing fire dancing before them. Lifting my head off the pillow I sit up on my sleeping bag. The parts of the sky that is peeking through the trees is slowly being painted with different hues of pinks and oranges. Which meant we have about an hour and a half until the sun sets completely. As well as the fact that we have lost half a day. I cannot help but smile at how sweet Captain can be. Looking around for my team I spot Malan who is the closest to me cutting up a deer. It has already been skinned and cleaned. Aspen and Willa are just making it back from harvesting different edible fruits and vegetables they found throughout the forest.

Ace is helping Captain set up our Tentsiles. Which they only have two more of the tree tents to hang. The effects of the hallucinogen produced by the thorns from those monstrous vines has seemed to have faded in both Willa and Ace. It must have slowly seeped into their blood stream. Aspen and Captain were not engulfed in the vines as long, so they barely felt the effects. If they felt any at all. It appears both Ace and Willa have bathed in a body of water nearby as well. Wanting to do my part I place two logs parallel from each other on the logs already in the fire and walk over to Malan grabbing the plate of cut venison.

"How are you feeling?", Malan ask with a worried look on his face. "You really scared us! Why don't you rest some more?"

"I feel a lot better.", I try to reassure him. "I promise."

"Why do you always have to push yourself so hard?", he questions me while rubbing his hands on his face.

"Malan, I don't know how to explain it. I have this nagging gut feeling I have not really tapped into my true strength and power. Hell, I do not even know who or what I really am. I thought The Company would be able to give me answers but they have only brought new questions. How else am I supposed to learn my limits? Plus, I was only out for a few hours. You guys were hurt bad! What good is this power if I cannot help the ones I love?", I try to explain to him.

With that being said, I walk back to the fire. I search the ground for decent sticks on my way. After I collect a handful sticks and am back at the fire I skewer the meat on the sticks. Then place them perpendicular on the logs to cook. Every five minutes or so I turn them letting them cook evenly. Once Malan has finish cutting the rest of the meat, he brings it to me. As I skewer the last of the meat on the remaining stick, Malan places his hand on my shoulder.

"Please promise me you will be more careful and smarter about it. Do not push too hard even for me. I do not know what I would do without my Lil Sis.", he pleads with a smile before walking over to dispose of what remained of the deer's carcass and all the guts that were cleaned out of it. He really did have a beautiful smile.

"I promise to be more careful and smarter.", I vow. I am not going to promise I will not push myself to save him. If it were not for him and Aspen, I do not know if I would have been able to make it through everything without being completely broken. It is really frustrating not remembering a thing and not being able to find a single answer. As well as the fact that not a single person from my past has cared enough to come find me. I quit searching for answers almost seven months ago. That is when I began trying to accept that I may never have the answers I feel I need. I am also working on accepting that even though I do not have any memories except the last six years. I know who I am and what kind of person I want to be. It is a lot easier said than done though.

Before Malan can respond, Captain comes up behind me picking me up off my feet before I can place the last stick of meat on the logs. He nuzzles his nose in my neck breathing deeply as he inhales my scent.

"Don't you ever scare me like that again!", Captain demands before setting me back down.

Spinning me around he kisses me with his hands cupped around my cheeks. It is such a loving kiss that ends way to soon. He squeezes me tight one more time before letting me go. He then lets everyone know that most of the meat is done. Malan is just making it back as the other three are making their way over to the fire. Ace and Aspen are carrying the fruit and vegies. They all make their plates as I put the last stick of meat on the fire before making my own plate. We all eat in silence most likely because we are all starving. I know I am. Captain motions for us all to huddle around as I am making my third plate.

"Amara fill us in on what happened with the creature. After you freed me there was no sign of it or that a battle even had happened.", Captain demands as I am taking a big bite of venison. It takes me a little bit to chew and swallow. They are not going to like this. We have turned down jobs because the assignment was to steal or reclaim various artifacts and magically infused items. We are not thieves.

"After the creature engulfed you in the vines, I was able to knock it down. Where Aspen was able to weaken it. But it still was able to overpower her. Before it could rip her heart out, I tackled it into a shadow. We have no idea if the creature would remain in the shadow. Or if it would only trap the creature while the object that is creating the shadow has a shadow. So, I had to make a deal.", I report. I would always get this really strong bad feeling every time they wanted to test it out that would cause be to back out last second.

"What kind of deal?", Captain asks in his worried tone, eyeing me suspiciously.

"For his freedom he is letting us pass through to the mountains. But to get through unharmed I must do the creature a favor and we cannot harm another being in this forest. In return he will give us free access to the forest and owe me a favor.", I continue. Leaving out the part where it said I am going to need that favor sooner than I thought or had called me Ancient One. There is no way I am older than that creature.

"Amara what kind of deal?", Malan inquires in his big brother tone. Catching on to the fact that I am avoiding bringing up this tidbit of information for as long as I can.

"I have to acquire a golden ring from the Collector of Souls anyway necessary. I know what you guys are going to say. I had no choice but to make the deal. We are no match for whatever that creature is. I have never come across a language even close to this creature's native tongue. Which means it is probably as old as the old goddesses and gods.", I convey. As I let it all sink in, I take the last few bites finishing my food.

"We aren't thieves Amara, that's one of our main rules. But I trust you.", Ace is the first to speak up.

"No, we are not. But as my second in command, I trust your judgement. However, you are not doing this alone.", Captain replies as everyone nods in agreement. "We are going to need a new plan."

"There is only one way in and out of the castle so we will need a distraction.", Malan notes.

"And we don't know whether the Collector of Souls has it on him or has it put up. The castle is a big place. We will need to split up into two groups.", Aspen comments.

"I have an idea.", Willa chimes in.

By the time Willa fills us in on her plan, we come up with a plan B and run through them both several times the sun has completely set. Everyone turns in for bed except Malan and me.

"Hey Malan, I'll take first watch while you get the four hours of rest you need. I won't be able to sleep anyways.", I try to persuade him.

He nods my way as he sits down Indian style by the fire going into his trance like state. The next four hours are peaceful. Occasionally an owl can be heard hooting. Wolves are howling to their pack mates and the katydids are crooning a tune in synchrony calling out to their mates. I can barely see the moonless sky through the trees. I walk the perimeter a few times and before I knew it Malan is coming out of his trance like state. I had not notice how tired I was starting to get. I climb up into my Tentsile and get my sleeping bag stretched out. Then slipping into it I pull my sleeping bag up to my chin. Sleep overtook me as soon as my head hit my pillow.

"Good morning.", Captain greets me while he is shaking me gently trying to wake me up.

"Good morning.", I respond. After stretching I change into a new pair of black shorts and blue tank top. Before putting all my tactical gear on over it then slipping on my boots. I jump out of the Tentsile to grab something to eat before brushing my teeth and pulling my hair into a messy bun. Then I start packing my bag. The sun is painting the sky with pinks and oranges as it rises. The birds are chirping and the scents of all the plants around us are swirling in the light breeze.

For some reason I am not able to shake the feeling that someone is watching me. I have had this feeling ever since we entered the forest. I roll my sleeping bag up as tight and little as I can. Before taking down my Tentsile rolling it tight and small. Then arranging everything to fit in my military grade backpack. As I am zipping it up, I hear leaves crunching to my right. Looking the direction of the sound I get a glimpse of a light green figure halfway hidden behind a tree. The being takes off running when it notices I spotted it. Following suit, I am close in on it. As soon as I reach the being, I tackle it to the ground. Pulling my knife from my boot I put it to her throat. I am taking in this being's gorgeous appearance. When two branches from the tree above us grabs me by my shoulder. Dangling me a good several feet above the ground. The being smirks at me before she starts to dash off.

She is so stunning! With her parakeet green skin and hunter green moss that covered her like a spaghetti strapped mini dress, long straight hair that was the same color as the moss like dress that flows to the middle of her back. Her eyes are a beautiful brown-green color, and she is about 5'5" in height. She is definitely a Celtic Dryad. They are known as Goddesses of the Forests. I have only heard about them and their beauty until now. They are said to be loving, kind beings that never attack. Unless you are trying to harm them or their forest, including anything that lives in the forest. Then they are a force to be reckoned with.

"Wait!", I plead to her in her native tongue. "I'm sorry I thought you were a danger to my team."

"Princess?", she whispers as she walks closer to me.

"I think you have the wrong person. There is no way I'm a princess.", I try explaining to her. A lot of people would notice a princess missing. Where no one from my past has noticed I am gone.

"My mistake.", she replies eyeing me like she is not sure she has gotten the wrong person. She waves her hand commanding the branches to gently set me on the ground next to her.

"May I ask why you were spying on us?", I question her.

"My apologies, my curiosity got the best of me when I saw you enter the forest. You resemble my best friend so much. She died several years ago.", she responds as a few tears escapes out of her eyes. Before I can ask her what her name is, she vanishes. Captain and Malan are running towards me as fast as they can.

"Are you okay? You can't just take off like that.", Captain expresses as he transforms out of a wolf. Pulling on the shorts he has tide to his leg.

"What happened? I looked up from packing my bag and there was no sign of you.", Malan questions me.

"I caught someone watching us, if they were such a big threat they would have attacked and would not have been hiding behind a tree.", I respond as I roll my eyes, they can be too overprotective at times. I did not think about that fact of her not being a threat since she did not attack us until after I had tackled her.

"I did not see anyone. Did you Malan?", Captain asks him. Malan shakes his head no as they both just look at me like I have lost my mind.

"That is because you guys spooked her.", I comment.

On the way back to camp I tell them about the stunning Celtic Dryad. Leaving out the part about her thinking I am her dead best friend that happens to be a princess. They fill me in on how they had found all our weapons while I was sleeping this morning. As well as the fact that we have enough fruit and vegies left for us all to have a couple for a snack later. When we get back to camp, Aspen, Willa, and Ace have already finished packing it up. We strap on our weapons and backpacks. Then start our hike out the forest.

The forest is so alluring! It has varieties of plants you see every day to plants I have only heard or read about. It is painted with the white blossoms and black roots of Molly. Not the drug but a magical herb as well as other herbs like Valerian, Chamomile, and many others. The forest is also painted with the blood red delicate flower of Anemone, and the blue, purple, pink flowers of Aconite or Wolfsbane. There are also different hues of green from the evergreens, fruit trees with their white blossoms and diverse kinds of shrubs. In the middle of the forest there is a group of Ashes, which are small deciduous trees that produce a sweet sap harvested by the Ancients. There is also a couple of yellow and green Lotus trees with its yellow-brown, red, and black oblong fruit. We stop at the middle of the forest allowing Malan to collect some sweet sap from one of the Ashes trees and one of the black fruits from the Lotus tree. While Willa collects some Valerian, Chamomile, and other herbs needed for a strong sleeping potion. Once the potion is finished, we continue our hike through the forest.

It is a four-hour hike out and will take us two more hours to get to the mountain which is a hell of a climb. We have been hiking for an hour now. To my left I hear the crunch of a twig snapping in half. Looking through my scope I scan our surroundings. Not too far from us is a foxlike creature. It is so cute I cannot help but to slowly walk over and pet it. The men except for Malan are getting impatient with us. As we pet and gush over this creature. It looks like a fox with dark grey undercoat and the top of its fur looks and feels like lime green moss. From its head and ear to its tree root looking tail. Returning to the trail we continue our hike out of the forest. The little creature follows at my feet. Looks like I made a new friend.

As we reach the clearing, we all sit down to rest while we still have some coverage from the forest. I pull out my snacks and water. Ace refilled everyone's canister with this morning after he made sure the fire was out. I munch on the left-over vegies and fruit from last night while sharing with my new little friend. As well as share my water with him. This has been a crazy assignment even for us. Hopefully, the rest of the hike will be peaceful. After resting for about half an hour we pack up and began our hike to the mountain. The little fox creature is running circles around me as I packed my bag. Just as we all step out of the coverage of the trees we are surrounded. A dryad and several different plant humanoids are surrounding us with spears. Some of the plant people look like bare trees. With a human shaped body, branches coming out of their backs and skin that looks like it is made of bark. Others look like their light green skin of their human shaped bodies are made of the same components as a flower stem. These plant people's heads are in the middle of different flower petals. Not one has the same petals or color, and the colors are so vibrant.

The dryad has an elegant beauty. She has jade green hair with little purple flowers throughout it and two deep brown branches for horns. The tree bark on her body looks like a turtleneck sweater dress that has a tear drop opening showing off some of her cleavage. Even her fingers, legs, and feet are made of tree bark. The bark on her legs looks like knee knee-high boots with emerald vines twisting up both legs. Captain has us lower our weapons to the ground then put our hands up. To show them we are not a threat. She says something angrily that only I can understand.

"She demands we give back what we have stolen from the forest.", I translate for my team.

I take the vile of sleeping potion out of my backpack and have Malan do the same with the sap. We set both items at her feet which seem too only anger her even more. I explain we gathered the plants for that potion. She commands for some of the plant people to capture and tie us up. While others go through our backpacks. As we are being bound, I look around noticing that my little friend has ran off. I am sad that he left. At that thought.

"May I ask what exactly it is that you think we have stolen?", I ask in her language.

"Koda is my children's pet, and they will be heartbroken if you don't return him. A couple of squirrels seen him with you.", she replies.

If my assumption is right Koda is the little foxlike creature. I explain how we did come across a creature that looks like a fox but that he ran off sometime around or after they showed up. I offer for us to help them find him. She accepts our offer and has her people untie us. Little did we know we all would be playing hide and seek with Koda for twenty minutes. Once he is finally captured and back with the dryad we head back to where we left our stuff. When we reach it, I pack the vile back into my backpack and hand the sap to Malan to put back into his.

"Okay team once we get to the mountain Amara will be the lead climber and I'll be the belayer.", Captain instructs us. "Does anyone need me to run them through plan A and or plan B?" We all shake our heads no. "Move out."

A lead climber is the person who goes first and puts the bolts into the mountain or cliff for everyone else. The Belayer is a device or a person. In this situation it is the person who stays at the bottom giving the slack needed on the rope and is the last to go up. Following his instructions, we head towards the mountain. We are getting close and should reach the mountain soon. The closer we get the more excited I get for the climb. An Arkan Sonney runs pass my feet while Willa, Malan, and Captain set their weapons and backpacks down to try to catch it. This is the funniest thing I have seen in a while. The Arkan Sonney is a type of fairy animal that takes the form of a white pig and is supposed to bring good fortune to anyone that catches it.

All they get is ending up in a mud puddle. Captain lands face first in a mud puddle, Malan trips over him and lands on his ass in the same puddle. Willa slides into a puddle on her stomach as she fumbles the Arkan Sonney, and it gets away. Once we have quit laughing, we continue hiking through the overgrown field. We have made it a little over halfway when something flies across the sky. Shading us from the sun for a split second. Soon the one creature flying above us turns into five. Squinting as I look up into the sky, I try to make out what the creatures are. To the right of us one by one the creatures land in the field.

"Malan what are those?", I ask in wonder as I gaze at these weird creatures. They have the head and wings of an eagle but the body of a horse. Each of their coats are an assortment of colors. One is black with white spots and there is one that is solid white. Another is white with brown spots and one that is a blend of black and brown, the last one to land is the biggest out of all of them and its coat is a golden color.

"Hippogriffs.", Malan answers me in awe. "I have only read stories about them as a kid."

They did not stay on the ground long. Shooting off into the sky they disappeared just has fast has they had appeared. About three hours later we are standing at the bottom of the first mountain looking up. We cannot see the top that disappears into the clouds. I have been excitedly waiting this climb since I heard about the mission. I just wish we would be repelling down but instead we will be picked up on the mountain by a plane. Climbing feels like a puzzle that I am solving with my body, makes me feel invincible and is one hell of a workout.

I pull out my rope, carabiners, and harness from my backpack. Then I step into my harness tying a figure eight knot connecting the rope to the harness. Next, I hitch my rope to all my carabiners then clip them to my harness. I step up to the mountain to find holes for me to put my feet and hands. As well as spots strong enough for me to hold on to while I slam the bolts into the mountain. After the first step up, just to the side of my hand I slam the first bolt into the mountain then clip one of my carabiners to it. I repeat these steps as I scale up the mountain. Captain is releasing slack as I need while keeping the rope tight. As I make it to the last ledge before the top. I look down checking to make sure everyone is following. Several feet between each other my team scales the mountain. I pull myself over the mountain ledge. When I get to my feet, I suck in a deep breath of air then exhale it. Not only do I feel like I just conquered the world from that climb. The scene that lays before my eyes is mesmerizing!

CHAPTER 2: THE COLLECTOR OF SOULS

Collector of Souls' POV

I cannot believe it has been six years since she just disappeared. It still tears at my heart like the day I found out. I refuse to believe that she is dead! I have this feeling deep in my gut that she is still out there somewhere. I think to myself as I stare at the picture of my love, my twin brother and me. We all grew up together in the Underworld and we had always been inseparable. I had been in love with her since I can remember. Instead of telling her I always acted like I had no other feelings for her other than friendship. I mean who could love the God of Death? Especially someone with such a big heart. I should have told her how I felt even if she did not feel the same. A knock at my office door brought me out of my thoughts. I wipe the few tears from my eyes that had escape and put the picture back into the inner pocket of my black suit.

"Come in.", I call out.

"Sir, Mel is here. I insisted that you are busy. But she will not leave until she sees you.", grumbles my demon assistant Lucas.

"Let her in.", I reply with a big sigh. What does this woman want now? I grew up with her as well and she has tried even harder to date me since my Love's disappearance. Mel is the name she goes by now. After the rise of Christianity and then The Company all the old goddesses and gods that are visit or live in the Mortal Realm gave themselves different names. Some of them like Mel just shorten their names to a more modern name. Her name is Melinoe, the Goddess of Ghosts, bringer of nightmares and madness. Her right side is pale and chalky as if the whole side of her is drained of all its blood. Melinoe's left side is as black as the depths of hell and hardened like a mummy. Her hair is divided the same right-side pale and chalky white where her left side is as black as the depths of the Underworld and her eyes are black voids. She is sexy in a dangerous sense.

She was thought to be Persephone's and Hades' daughter. However, it turns out that Zeus appeared to Persephone disguised as his brother Hades and impregnated her. Hades never really did bond with her before he knew. After he found out he did everything to avoid her. She became very resentful and vindictive especially if you were standing in the way of what she wants. Her powers make it all that easier for her. She has all the normal goddess powers, can appear as whoever she wants and can manipulate mist as well as use it to transport. I have a gut feeling that she might have something to do with my Love's disappearance. Mel did resent her for . . . .

"Hey sexy. I brought you lunch since I knew I wouldn't be able to get you out of this office.", Mel greets me. Swaying her hips as she walks over to my desk.

"Thank you, but you didn't have to do that.", I reply as she brings me out of my thoughts.

"I don't mind it's the only way I can get time with my favorite guy. You are always working.", she pouts. While taking a seat on the corner of my desk. Then Mel sets the bag of fast food beside her.

"Being the Second in charge of the Underworld comes with a lot of work. Especially with the King and Queen being in the Mortal Realm. Which you should know being their daughter.", I add while pushing my chair back to put some distance between us. She has really been there for me through it all. I am sure for her own selfish reasons. I do love her. I am just not in love with her, she is like family. Which I am trying to get her to see. Yes, I am that asshole that slept with her a couple of times then realize she has stronger feelings for me then I do her. Now I am trying to let her know without breaking her heart and losing my friend. Luckily there comes another knock at my door.

"Come in.", I voice.

"Sir there is a group of six that have made it through the forest and are making their way up the mountain with good speed. And Sir the word is they are coming for you.", Lucas informs me without revealing to much in front of Mel.

Which I can tell there is more by the way he came in and is waiting patiently. I pull up all the cameras on my holographic screen as I laugh at the thought of them coming after me.

"Mel I . . .", I start to state.

"I know. You have work to do.", she wines with another pout. She comes over kisses me on the cheek and walks out.

"Sir, Sean one of the Council members at The Company wants to speak with you about one of the team members he has dispatched to peacefully bring you in for an important meeting. He is on line one and will only tell you what is so important.", Lucas continues once he is sure Mel is gone.

I have small drones fly around the whole island and some that stay up here around the castle. I pull up the feed of the two drones that are near the ledge of the mountain. Standing on the mountain is a Woman. I move the drone's angle and zoom in to get a better look. My mouth falls open, I cannot believe my eyes as I pick up the phone.

Amara's POV

I stand there for a little bit admiring the scene before my eyes. There is this beautiful green grass that is painted with splashes of distinct colors of flowers. From blue, purple, red, white to pink, black, yellow, and orange. I did not recognize a single flower. There is a dirt path that leads to the medium grey stone castle that is carved into the side of the snow dusted mountain. Hearing someone grunt I turn to help my team mates up and over the cliff. Once everyone makes it up the mountain, we step out of our harnesses, pack the equipment back up and then stash our backpacks. We all nod at each other and the first team, which includes Captain, Aspen, Malan, and Ace, breaks off. While we wait for them to create a diversion. Willa and I are crouching behind an enormous Austras Koks until they all make it into the castle. An Austras Koks (Tree of Dawn) is an exceedingly rare tree that is said to grow from the start of the sun's daily journey. It is so beautiful setting next to a small light blue pond.

They are about to walk up the last step of the front porch when twelve red eyed demons in their demonic form come running out. Working together my team sends head after head rolling with their swords, until there are twelve heads on the ground. Blood is spraying out of their necks in various directions as the bodies slump to the ground. Then they all turn into black mist. They are able to push the second wave of demons within the castle and down the hall. The second wave is two times as many as the first wave of demons. Our swords, knives and bullets are also magically infused to send a demon back to the Underworld. Seeing how we are near the Underworld's gate we have about forty-five maybe fifty minutes before all the demons they have killed will be back with vengeance. Willa and I creep up the stairs to the master bedroom. If are assumption of the Collector of Souls is correct, then this is where he keeps anything of value to him. He should be in his office at this time of day. At least that is the Intel we got from our Commander. With my luck he is going to be wearing the stupid ring. We find the master bedroom easily with the printed layout. Once in his room I walk into his massive walk-in closet as Willa is looking through his nightstand drawers. Then grabs something off the top of it.

"Amara you might want to see this.", Willa announces as she is staring in shock at something in her hand.

"What do we have here?", a deep voice question.

Willa and I both jump before we search the room for where the voice came from. There is no one in the room with us. We hear a deep sexy snicker then in a blink of an eye standing in front of us is the most gorgeous man I have ever seen! I pick my jaw up off the floor and wipe the drool off my chin. My heart flutters at the sight of him like it has unknowingly been longing for him for a long time. But why? I do not know him. So why in the hell do I feel this way towards him? Shaking those feelings off I glance at Willa who is obviously into him as well. I cannot help but chuckle to myself. Maybe he just has this effect on beings.

"Makaria are you really going to stand there like you don't know me. After getting caught trying to steal from me?", he angrily demands.

Slowly I turn my head to look at him because I can feel his gaze radiating off me. "I'm sorry but . . .", before I can finish my sentence, he has picked me up in a bear hug.

"Put me down.", I stammer out. "I'm not who you think I am. I have never met you before."

He sets me down and stands there in shock. I can see his heart breaking as he searches my eyes for hints of me lying or even joking. He did not want to believe his ears. My heart aches for him and I felt oddly comfortable in his arms. Like I fit into them perfectly. He tries to wipe a tear away without us noticing.

"Then tell me who you both are and why you are going through my private bedroom.", he commands with a hint of heart break before clearing his throat.

My mind is spinning with everything that has just happened let alone how my heart is reacting towards this man. A man I have never met before. Well as far as I can remember. Thankfully, Willa speaks up.

"We come on behalf of The Company and have to bring you in. We would like to do it peacefully but will use force if we have to.", Willa announces.

"I like your courage.", he says with a chuckle. "I will go peacefully if she agrees to answer my next questions honestly. Keep in mind I can kill you both with a single touch. Also, I have the rest of your team locked up in my dungeon. In case you want to try something.", he informs us.

"Please don't hurt any of them. I will answer you honestly.", I plead with him.

"Who are you and what are you trying to steal from me?", he asks in a powerful tone.

"My name is Amara, and she is Willa. We were looking for that ring on your left middle finger.", I honestly answer him.

"What does The Company want with the Ring of Gyges?", the Collector of Souls questions.

"Well, umm The Company doesn't. I need the ring because I made a deal with some powerful ass creature.", I respond. No wonder the creature wants that ring. The Ring of Gyges with just a twist will turn whoever is wearing it invisible.

"The Creature you speak of is it a moose tree man looking hybrid creature?", he inquires.

"Yes.", I answer as I see Willa slip something into her back pocket out of the corner of my eye. I really hope he did not just see that. I have a gut feeling something bad is going to end up happening.

"That's Schrat, he is a waldschrat. He is also older and as powerful as me. I am surprised he let your team out alive. There are only a few that still exist, and they live to kill especially if you have invaded their home. I do not know him personally, but Makaria knew him and trusted him. Which means you can trust him.", he tells us as he takes the ring off his finger. As he hands it to me his hand slowly brushes against mine. I yank my hand back. When his hand brushed mine, I felt a zap of electricity. The Collector of Souls has a sad longing, heartbroken look in his eyes. "That's yours to do with as you like, just please have a conversation with me once this mess with The Company is taken care of.", he pleads with me while placing the ring in my hand. Left speechless from the zap of electricity I just nod. Did he feel that as well? I slip the ring on my finger as he motions for us to follow him out his bedroom. As soon as the ring is on it magically fits to my finger. I walk out first with Willa behind me. He stops her and whispers something in her ear before following her out and closing his door.

I let him walk pass me so I can follow him to the dungeon to get the rest of our team. We follow the Collector of Souls down the stairs, to the right and down to the end of the hall. In complete silence. Willa's face expression is that of someone who just got caught doing something bad. Shit, I hope that whatever it is was worth taking. I think to myself. He opens the door revealing a caramel-colored room with a 65-inch TV, two black leather theater seats, a matching black leather couch, a small dining table and its own bathroom. Aspen is sitting on the couch with a towel rapped in her hair. She is sharing a big bowl of popcorn with Ace and Malan while watching The Ring. I let out a deep breath I did not realize I was holding. When I saw Kaden walk out fully dressed drying what little hair he has with a towel. I rush into his arms as the Collector of Souls looks away like a wounded puppy and shuts the door not saying a word. Kaden clutches me tightly as he places a bunch of little kisses on my lips. A few minutes later a charming demon comes in with a buffet of food on wheels. He keeps looking at me like he wants to hug me. The demon has slick back jet black hair with black eyes. His hair reminded me of Jonny Depp's hair in cry baby. I wonder what his demon form looks like.

"Hey I'm Lucas. After everyone has time to eat, shower and has been healed by our nurse Demitri wants to have a meeting with the Captain of this team. The nurse will be in about fifteen minutes. If any of you need anything let me know.", he adds with one more heart-breaking glance at me before walking out and shutting the door.

I do not think today can get any weirder. We all dig in immediately, it is the best meal I have had in a long time. I pile my plate with brown sugar pineapple ham, mash potatoes smothered in butter with green beans cooked in sugar and bacon grease. There is a knock at the door about fifteen minutes later and I cannot believe who is walking in.

"Hey guys. Sorry for interrupting your meal, but I'm supposed to check you four out before leaving for the day.", the Celtic Dryad from the forest greets us as she points to Aspen, Captain, Ace, and Malan. "O and by the way I'm Sylvia", she tells us as she gives me a small smile.

I elbow Captain and Malan before I tell them, "See I'm not crazy. She is the one from the forest." Malan's jaw drops as he is unable to stop staring at her. "You might want to close your mouth. You are drooling all over yourself.", I whisper to him with a chuckle.

Why are so many beings around here acting like they know me? I must really look like this chick. She heals the other four without letting me help. Even after telling her, I have healing abilities. She is using homemade ointment on their wounds. She felt familiar to me like the Collector of Souls and Lucas does. I think Lucas said his name is Demitri. Man, he is the yummiest man I have ever laid eyes on. He must be around 6"4', lean but muscular, dark brown almost black faded hair with honey gold eyes. As well as a strong jaw line with a goatee covering his chin with a small soul patch. I call them flavor savers but that is too much for some people, ha-ha.

"I'll be back.", Kaden notifies me as he kisses my cheek.

I mentally slap myself. I feel guilty for daydreaming about another man. Especially since Kaden is in the room with me. I nod at him as he turns around and leaves. What the hell, I have never thought of another man like I do Kaden. Now I cannot get Demitri out of my head. I am going to have to quickly get my heart and libido in check.

"Amara, can I talk to you for a bit?", Willa asks.

"Sure.", I respond as I walk over to the couch where her and Aspen are sitting. I can use a distraction from my thoughts of Mr. Sex God and everything else that has happened today. Willa looks at me and then looks at Aspen. "It's cool. What are you wanting to talk about?", I ask.

"I thought you might want to see this. He had this on top of his nightstand turned facing his bed in a frame.", she says as she pulls a picture out of her back pocket. "Also, I know you would want to know that he seen me take it and told me to give it to you. Dude I don't know what is going on, but that guy is clearly head over heels for you or whoever is in this photo.", Willa mentions handing me the picture.

Fuck! I cannot believe my eyes as the blood rushes out of my face. There standing squashed in the middle of two sexy looking guys is a girl. A girl that looks like a younger high school aged me. She has a huge smile on her face that you can see shining in her eyes. The girl has her arms tightly around both guys. The more I look at the guy on the right the more I can tell it is Demitri. The other guy looks so much like Demitri it was hard to tell which one was which at first. My mouth falls open as my mind goes blank.

"What is it?", Aspen inquires a little worriedly as she takes the photo from me. Her chin drops as soon as she sees the girl standing in the middle. Willa sits there not knowing what to say. Which is something because that girl can talk.

"I could be her doppelganger. It doesn't happen a lot, but it isn't unheard of.", I note in denial. The picture tugs at my heart. But I dismiss it. I did not want it to be true, none of them came looking for me and there is no trace of my existence since before the day I woke up. If you know where and how to really dig into someone's past. You will be able to find that even my identity started that day.

"You could be a descendant of hers. You are powerful, one of the most powerful beings I have ever met but her aura screams power in this photo.", Willa expresses.

"She does look just like you. Willa is right though she radiates the aura of a goddess even in a photo.", Aspen finally speaks.

"Hey sorry to interrupt what looks like girl talk.", Lucas notes as his words trail off when he sees the photo in Aspen's hand.

"Hey Lucas, do you know this girl?", Aspen asks seeing the look on his face.

"Yes, she was a beautiful, amazing soul and an enormously powerful goddess. Even at an early age. Her name was Makaria.", Lucas tells us as Willa, and I lock eyes at that name. "We lost her a little over six years ago. She was loved around here more than she knew.", Lucas adds as he makes eye contact with me. "That's all I can say on the matter. I had a couple of the guards retrieve your backpacks. Your Captain and Demitri are about done with their meeting. The Company has sent our ride and it will be here shortly. Amara, he would like a word with you.", he informs us as he hands me my backpack. A couple of demons brought in the other backpacks and places them by the table. I think about it for a moment before nodding. Setting my backpack on the floor I follow him to Demitri's office. Captain is walking out as I stroll up to the door.

"What's up Babe?", Captain asks.

Before I can open my mouth, Lucas tells him that Demitri wants to speak privately with me. A growl echoes through the hall as Kaden grabs my arm. Pulling me into himself he asks if I am okay to go alone. I kiss him on the lips and walk into Demitri's office. After informing him I will be fine. I need answers that Demitri might have. Rather I liked them or not. Do I really want to know? I think as I pause just inside the door. Should I turn and run? No.

Shit it is too late. Slowly I make my way in the room scared of what the answers to my questions might reveal.

"Thank you for joining me. I'm sure you have a lot of questions so I will let you start.", Demitri begins giving me enough time to take the seat in front of his desk.

"I don't even know where to start or how to get my thoughts straightened out. I do not believe I am this woman. Maybe I am her doppelganger or a descendant of hers?", I question.

"You can't be a descendant of hers because she didn't have any kids before her disappearance. It is not impossible that you could be her doppelganger. But I have known that you are her from the moment I saw you through one of my drones at the cliff. Let me ask you this. Do you remember your childhood, where you came from or your parents?", he questions.

"No.", I answer while looking at the ground playing with my fingers. "I woke up one day about six years back not remembering anything. Except that my name is Amara Stone and that I am not human. Strangely I also knew that where I woke up was my apartment."

"Six years, four months and two days ago my best friend disappeared. You see she is the Princess of the Underworld. Therefore, a lot of beings have been looking for her. Some friendly and some not. I have every magical being I know trying every locator spell out there. Even have my best trackers looking as well. Including the God of Hunt, her brother. Yet not a single being searching for Makaria over the last six years can find a single trace of her existence.", he informs me after I sat there silently for a moment.

I continue to sit there taking in what he is saying. After pausing for a little bit, he continues.

"Something definitely happened you are quite a bit weaker, and I can only sense a sliver of your goddess essence. You are heavily cloaked with powerful magic, even your smell is different. But I know without a doubt you are Makaria rather you do or not.", he sadly voices.

I do not know what to think. I have a thousand questions, but I am not able to get my thoughts straighten out before there comes a knock at the door. If I am this woman does that mean I do have people who are looking for me? Or is all this a dead end like every other time.

Lucas pops his head in the door. "Sir the plane has arrived", he informs us. We stand there in silence for a little bit neither of us knowing what to say. He did not take his eyes off me once.

"I guess we need to go meet up with everyone else.", I finally say even though my heart did not want to part with him.

He nods his head as he walks over and holds the door open for me. Then I follow him to the roof. Where my team has already started climbing the rope up to the plane above. After they are all up, I climb up with Demitri and then Lucas following behind me. While everyone is chit chatting among themselves, I sit there quietly. Captain must have notice because he comes and sits beside me. He has no idea of everything that as came to light since getting caught in Demitri's bedroom. Just the thought of being in his bedroom has dirty thoughts trying to sneak into my brain. Just as fast as they tried to sneak their way in, I push them out.

"You okay?", Captain asks as he grabs my hand squeezing it.

"We need to talk when we get home. I learned somethings that could be linked to my missing memories.", I notify Kaden as I look up at him. Captain looks into my eyes reading me for a minute then turns his attention to Demitri, who has not taken his eyes off us.

"Okay we will talk when we get home.", he notes as he kisses my forehead. He talks to Ace for a little bit before getting up to touch base with the pilots. While I once again sit silently thinking about everything.

The next thing I hear is a huge explosion while the plane is roughly jerked. Something hits the side of the plane causing a big enough crack for a substantial portion of the side to be sucked into the sky. In turn sucking out all the oxygen causing the oxygen masks to drop down in our faces. I scan the rest of the plane, Kaden nor Demitri are anywhere in sight. Everyone else is buckled in and putting on their oxygen masks. The plane jolts upward and then starts to descend quickly. My heart is in my stomach as I hope my men are alive. The huge hole in the plane is trying with great force to pull me along with everyone else out. We all brace ourselves for a rough landing except for Lucas, who is just setting back watching me without a worry or an oxygen mask on his face.

The landing is rough but not near as rough as it should have been. One by one we all unbuckle and jump down out of the plane. Ace is the only one that had to worry about the jump since he is the only human. Casting a levitation spell, he lowers himself down. As I search our surroundings, Demitri lands in front of me. I have no words to describe the enchanting beauty of his wings and the way his aura radiates with power. I walk up and feel a few of the feathers. I am mesmerized by his massive dark purple and black wings as well as seeing his true form. That it takes me several seconds to realize that laying limply in Demitri's arms is Kaden's lifeless body. Sinking to my knees as he lays Kaden at my feet. Moving Kaden's head on my legs, I start running my hand through his hair. It takes a few second for the tears to start to fall. But once they did, I cannot control them. My heart is breaking. I cannot believe my Kaden is dead!

"Amara look at me.", Demitri says trying to get my attention in a loving voice. I shake my head no not taking my eyes off Kaden. His head is busted open, his face is burnt, and he is covered in glass.

"Amara look at me.", he exclaims again with more authority in his voice. I cannot help but look up with tears streaming down my face. "With just a touch you can bring him back. Be warned there will be a price that must be paid. You must reach deep down and find the suppressed powers within yourself. You have to accept that you are Makaria, Princess of the Underworld, Goddess of Blessed Death.", he conveys as he begs me with his eyes to accept that I am her.

"I'm not who you think I am.", I snap at him with tears continuing to stream down my cheeks. "I am not that powerful. I faint if I heal a life-threatening injury or heal to many people at one time. And I sure as hell am not the Princess of the Underworld. Let alone a goddess. Please save him.", I cry out as I plead with my eyes. When Demitri does not move I howl, "Demitri save him!"

Every second another piece of my shattered heart is crumbling away. Without a word he places his hand on Kaden's chest. After a few minutes Kaden's heart starts beating and lungs start filling with air. His color is coming back as the blood spreads through his body and his eyes open. Sitting up he takes in his surroundings, wipes the tears from my eyes, and then embraces me tightly. After holding me for a while he lets go. Then pulls us up off the ground and upon our feet. Before greeting everyone else. As he is talking with the rest of our team, I look around for Demitri. I did not notice that he had walked off. I spot him over talking to Lucas by the plane. Our eyes meet and I mouth thank you. Demitri gives me a sad small nod of his head as his response. The look on his face hurts me. I then notice Lucas has a gremlin by its pointy ears in one hand. They finish their conversation and make their way to us.

"This vermin was snacking on the wires of the plane causing the panel to blow up lighting the pilots and Kaden on fire, killing them. Before causing the engine to blow up. Luckily, we landed seven miles from The Company's headquarters.", Lucas informs us. Without a word Demitri reaches out his hand towards the gremlin. My gut is screaming at me. I know what he is about to do.

"Demitri please!", I beg as I grab his hand. Causing us both to gasp when sparks shoot up from where our hands came in contact. It was stronger this time.

"I messed with the balance of life and death already for you. A life spared is a life owed.", he informs me in a deep voice. It is hinted with anger, hurt, rejection and love. He pulls his hand away from me, which rips at my heart. Making me want to reach out and hug him.

"An innocent life should not have to pay the price for something I asked of you. He was just hungry, and I can tell he is a young one. I will take a life to replace Kaden's. If I do not trade a life in two weeks then I will surrender my own life over.", I offer. Sticking my hand out to seal the deal with Demitri.

"The sooner the better. The Fates are already pissed off. But I will deal with them. You have two weeks.", he conveys as he shakes my hand.

Everyone is still shocked over all the events that has happened that no one has really said a word.

"I'm going to call you Grim.", I note as I am taking the gremlin from Lucas and cuddling it like a baby as the others join us. "You have been really bad Grim, but I will give you one more chance. If you endanger innocent lives again. I will take Demitri's advice and take your life to spare Kaden's.", I inform him. Sitting him down I tell him he is free to go. He stands there for a little bit. Then asks if he can stay with me. I nod my head yes as everyone just stands there watching us have a conversation in Grim's native tongue.

"Hell no Amara! I know that look. It's not happening.", Captain wines while rolling his eyes. He knows this is an argument he is not going to win.

"What? I was thinking he could stay with Demitri.", I playfully tease Demitri and Grim.

Everyone busts out into laughter except Grim and Demitri. Captain calls base with Lucas' phone while we start our hike. Sean sent two Rhinos to pick us up and dispatched a cleanup crew. Rhinos are a type of ATV. The ones Sean is sending can hold up to four people each. We get to base in no time. Captain and Demitri are going to Sean's office for a meeting. To update him on everything that has happened. While the rest of us turn in our weapons and equipment. Grim and Lucas are following not too far behind us. Sean is our Commander and a Tuatha De' Danann as well as one of the four Higher Ups. He has been like a father to me, and I am the daughter he never had. Which causes his son, Connor to hate me even more. Connor blames me for his Mom's Death that happened a year ago. If he were not Sean's son, I would give his life to the Underworld. He has become so evil and uses The Company in any evil way he can get away with. Connor's Mom was human so that makes him only half Tuatha De' Danann. The Higher Ups also known as The Council includes Elijah, Dean, and Balthazar as well.

They are all centuries old, and all seem to be on the Council for the right reasons except Balthazar. Elijah is a blonde and blue-eyed lycan vampire hybrid. He only has access to his wolf. Elijah had a powerful witch make his vampire side dormant until his death. I am the only one besides his mate that knows that. Lycans have a wolf and human form while werewolves are a mix between a human, beast, and a wolf. They have a human form but only the strong can control the madness allowing them to shift into it. Alphas and mated pairs are usually the only one strong enough to shift into their human form. Dean has shaggy light brown hair and eyes. He is a dragon. Dragons have two forms their dragon form and their human form. They can master one of four elements. Which is Fire, Earth, Air, and Water. Only an alpha can control more than one. Its unheard of for an alpha to control more than two. Or for a dragon to have spirit element abilities. Dean is one of the alpha dragons. Rumor has it there are very few dragons left and even fewer that are purebloods. Then there is Balthazar, who I do not trust at all. He is a Magician that is fifty times more powerful than Ace. Balthazar looks like all those old wizards in the movies. Well without the beard. He has shoulder length white hair with white stubble and hazel-colored eyes.

Once everything has been checked in, we say our goodbyes and part ways. Aspen and Willa hang with us for a little bit. They ask if I need anything and then make small talk. Both let me know they are here if I do end up needing anything. Aspen is saying bye while Willa begs to take Grim home with her. After several minutes of her begging Grim agrees and leaves with her.

"Shit.", I mumble out loud after noticing the golden ring on my finger. I had forgotten about Schrat and one thing I did know about myself is I will always keep my word. Forgetting that Lucas is still lingering around. I rip open a shadow of the tree next to me. Before I can jump in, I feel a hand on my shoulder.

"Do you mind if I tag along.", Lucas asks.

"Sure.", I respond as I step in the shadow and hold it open for him. Before letting it close. Then opening a portal to another shadow. Stepping out of the second shadow Lucas looks around realizing we are back in the forest on the island. He eyes me curiously but does not say a word.

"Schrat.", I call out as I mess with the ring. It could not hurt if I try it out once. With that thought I twist the ring.

"Well, Hello Ancient One. Rumor has it that you were bailing on our deal.", Schrat voices. As he steps out from behind a tree. He looks around before nodding his head towards Lucas out of respect. "My apologies I thought I heard someone else.", he begins to say with a confused look on his face.

"Schrat.", I whisper in his ear still invisible. He turns around to where he is facing me. "Nah I'm not the type.", I respond playfully as I twist the ring so they can see me. I pull the ring off my right ring finger handing it to him. Getting a smirk from Schrat in response.

"You held up your end and I'll do the same. You as well as everyone on your team has free access to my forest unharmed. If none of you spill innocent blood of the forest. Do not think I do not know about the deer your friend killed. Before you say anything, I am not going to hold it against you. It would have been dinner for something else if not you guys. As for the favor, once you have accepted who you really are, come find me and I will tell you the second key to undoing this powerful curse that was laid upon you. Acceptance of who you are is the first key", Schrat informs me. With a twist of the ring, he disappears.

"Wow, what an exit.", I giggle as my phone rings. My caller id tells me it is Sean.

"Yes Sir.", I answer. "Yes Sir, he is. Yes Sir, we are on our way.", I reply as I hang up.

"Looks like we are in trouble, we better head back.", I jokingly tell Lucas, who just laughs as he follows me back through the two shadows.

"You know Amara that is a badass power. I miss shadow jumping with Makaria.", Lucas remarks before passing me and going up to Sean's office. Once we are both in his office Sean motions for me to sit down in the chair in front of his desk.

"Amara how are you doing?", Sean asks in a fatherly tone.

"I'm holding up.", is my response.

"I have called you in because I have a confession to make. I sent you to the island under a false assignment.", Sean claims as he slides a file my way across his desk. I grab it holding it against my stomach. Not wanting to know the info that it contains.

"I came across this information just recently. The only way you as well as I could know if it is a true link to your past. Was for you to meet Demitri. He would know if you were her or not. Knowing that you would refuse because of all the other times that were let downs and just unearthed more questions. As well as the fact I wanted your team to be there to have your back. I set up the file on the fake assignment. As you were pulling yourself onto the cliff, I was on the phone with Lucas informing him that I had a particularly important matter that I need to speak with Demitri in person about and that I had dispatched a peaceful team to bring him here.", Sean confesses.

I am sitting there in silence. I knew from the moment we got on the cliff until we boarded the plane everything was to easily going our way. As I continue to sit there in silence for several minutes, Sean speaks again.

"There is another matter I wish to speak with you about.", he continues. I look over at Captain who is at the opposite side of the room from Demitri. He has his pissed off, I want to bust shit up look he gets. "Demitri and I feel it would be in your best interest to spend some time on the island. After your vacation of course, I know you all have been planning it for a month. It's up to you."

"If you come stay a couple of weeks, that will give my team the time to find a way to break this curse and restore your memories.", Demitri starts to say.

"She isn't going! You think that because you are a god you can come and kidnap Amara. Taking her way from her home, her family and everything she knows. Just because you like what you see. How is that going to help her? I am not stupid. I see the way you look at her. Not to mention the look, you get when we have any kind of physical contact.", Captain spits out angrily.

Well now Sean knows there is something between Kaden and I if he did not already, I think to myself.

"You will watch your tongue with me. I brought you back for her but don't think for a second, I won't send your ass straight back to the Underworld.", Demitri's deep voice booms back. "At least then her life won't be on the line for yours."

They are in each other's faces now and I am not sure who is going to throw the first punch. Stepping between them I push Captain backwards with my back creating space between them. "Boys calm down. Captain I am a big girl and will make my own decisions. Now let Demitri finish what he was saying.", I command.

"You won't just be coming out to break the curse, if that is even what you want. It is just resources I am offering to aid you. I acquire your assistance as well as anyone you wish to bring. I ask that you stay until the matter is taken care of. Afterwards you can stay for as long as you would like. I will not force you to come.", Demitri continues pleading for me to agree to come with his eyes. Those eyes are so hard to say no to.

"Send me the information on the assignment, give me time to look over both files and I will give you guys my answer when I get back from my trip.", I tell everyone in the room.

"I'll have Lucas get your number and send you a text with my personal number that way you can either get with Lucas or myself with your answer.", Demitri says in agreement.

Captain starts to walk out angrily behind Lucas. I grab his arm pulling him into a kiss. "You go home and calm down. I need a few minutes with these two and then I'll be on my way home.", I tell him. He looks over at Demitri clearly not wanting to leave me with him. He sighs and kisses me back and tells me he will see me at home.

"Sean I am a little pissed that you lied to me. I do understand why you did it though and I know you are right. I would not have gone. I still don't believe I am who he thinks I am.", I voice as I point to Demitri. "I will however try to read both files with an open mind. Only because you are sure it can lead me to answers."

"There is one more thing. I did not want to say this in front of Kaden. Whoever left the file on my desk. Also left a note telling me that it is important for you to meet Demitri. Just know all this was out of love.", he discloses before hugging me.

After Sean hands me the keys to his cabin in a southern town near some mountains. He asks me to lock up before leaving his office. I stand there for a moment in silence soaking up the way Demitri's presence makes me feel. I grab the photo Aspen gave back to me before she went home out of my pocket and hand it to him. Demitri takes it and looks at it with a smile on his face.

"I thought you might want it back.", I confess.

"No keep it. I have two copies.", he says handing it back to me. "Maybe it will spark a memory."

"Okay thank you. I'll let you know my answer as soon as I have one.", I remark as I'm heading for the door.

"Amara, I don't want to overload you with everything. So, I am going to give you space. I want you to know that I am here for you no matter what you choose. And I want to tell you something I have never said out loud before. I feel I need to, or I might never get another chance. I am and have been madly in love with Makaria since I can remember." He declares as he walks up to me grabbing my hands into his own. "The way my heart reacts to your presence and to your touch is the way it reacted to Makaria and only her. That is how I know without a doubt you are her.", he expresses.

I know he wants to kiss me, and I want him too just as badly. But I am with Kaden, and I am not a cheater. With a reluctant sigh I tell him good night and head home. By the time I get home Kaden is in bed asleep with nothing but his boxers on. That is how I like seeing him best. I cuddle up next to him as I slip into a sweet dream happily forgetting about the events that have taken place. Around two in the morning Kaden gets a call about an assignment. So much for a full night's rest after everything.

Demitri's POV

My phone ringing brings me out of a deep sleep. Grabbing it, I clear my throat before answering the call.

"Hello.", I say sleepily.

"Hi. I'm sorry to wake you up. Can you please watch Grim?", she asks. "We got a call about an underground club in Oregon full of vampiric beings that are draining humans."

"Yes.", I answer her. I cannot tell Amara no.

"Thank you so much. I will bring him to you. See you in a bit.", she says before hanging up.

Within two minutes she is at my door holding Grim's hand. Looking as gorgeous as always. After she kisses Grim on the head, she shadow jumps to I am assuming the club in Oregon. The last time I seen Grim he caused our plane to crash, and I was going to trade his life for Amara's boyfriend's. This should be fun I think as I walk back inside. Grim has completely destroyed my kitchen by the time I make it in there. He obviously is not going to be going back to bed. What can I do to keep him busy while my housekeeper can clean this mess up?

"Hey Grim follow me.", I command.

He hesitates for a minute before following me. I lead him towards the back of the castle. Where I just had this built and have not had time to try it out. If this does not wear him out, I do not know what will. As we enter the room, I grab a gun and vest off the wall. Then motion for Grim to do the same. We walk further into the room where I have a pirate ship built for laser tag. Grim says something in his native tongue and then runs towards the ship. We play laser tag for two hours before that little gremlin finally starts to wear out. The little guy is surprisingly good. We stop a couple of times to munch out on some snacks I had one if the housekeepers bring in. With some bottles of water. After taking him to one of the spare rooms. I tuck him into bed and then return to my own bed. Couple of hours later I get a call from Amara. I check the camera in the room Grim is in and he is still sound asleep. I inform Amara that to try to get some rest and I will get with her when he wakes up. I get a good three or so more hours of sleep before Grim is in my room begging for me to get up and call Amara. At least that is what I think he is telling me while holding my phone out to me. I call Amara letting her know he is up and missing her. Within five minutes she is here to pick him up. Grim runs and jumps into her arms as soon as he notices her. Seeing them together makes me fall even more in love with her.

"I hope he wasn't too much trouble.", Amara conveys.

"He was an angel.", I tell her. I cannot take my eyes off her. I want to ask her to stay awhile. That is just not a good idea. I do not want to cause any problems for her or her relationship.

"I know that isn't true but thank you again.", she says after laughing.

She stares at me for a couple of minutes before telling me bye then shadow jumping away. I cannot believe how stupid I was to lose her.

CHAPTER 3: AMARA'S GET AWAY

Demitri's POV

I sit back thinking about everything that has happen. I cannot believe she is back in my life. Even if she does not remember me or want to remember. She is just as enchanting as I remember even without her goddess essence present.

"Demitri it's Saturday night and you are working. You should really get out more.", Lucas chides me as he sits next to me and start sorting the papers into piles of importance.

"Back at you.", I playfully scold him as I elbow him in the arm. There is a knock at the door then the click clack of high heels is echoing off the tile floor.

"Dimitri.", Mel calls out as she walks into the living room wearing a tight red mini dress. "Of course, you are working. Why don't you take a break and come out with me?", she all but begs as she slides herself onto my lap.

"I have too much work to do.", I reply.

"We were just talking about how you needed to get out of the house.", Lucas comments with a laugh as an ornery smirk is creeping up his face.

I reach over punching him in the arm before telling her, "I'm sorry you are going to have to find someone else to go out with."

"We could just go up to your bedroom for some fun.", she purrs as she slides her hand up my other leg.

Grabbing her hand as I stand up, I tell her, "Mel, stop this nonsense. I have told you we can only be friends."

"You don't have to be such an asshole Demitri. Plenty of guys would love to have me.", She sneers before walking straight out the front door.

Lucas bust out in laughter as soon as the front door shuts. "So, what are we going to do to bring Amara back to us.", he asks as he finishes sorting through the papers.

"Nothing. I am not going to force her to do anything. When or if she wants to, she will find a way to break the curse. Even with the curse broken that does not mean she will come back. She has lived a completely different life for a little over six years.", I state with a sad sigh. I want so bad to fight for her. I cannot though, she is already with someone. All I can do is wait and see if she comes back to me.

"Speaking of her curse. While you were having your meeting with Sean. I went with Makaria to deliver the ring to Schrat. He confirmed there was a curse casted on her and he knows how to break it. Even told her the first key to breaking it. Good thing you gave her the ring. From what I gather he will only tell her how it can be done.", Lucas informs me.

"At least she has the means to break it.", I respond.

"Can we at least get rid of that disrespectful and possessive shifter? I still don't understand why you brought him back.", Lucas remarks.

"I can't be the one that brings her pain especially that kind of pain. The way she howled my name ripped my heart apart. I had to do what I could to ease that pain for her. No matter how much it hurt me. You know as well as I do that there is nothing, I would deny Makaria.", I confess.

"Yes, but now her life is hanging in the balance for that douche bag.", Lucas voices angrily.

"Amara is smart she will figure something out and if by the smallest of chances, she doesn't. You should know me well enough to know I have something up my sleeve to make sure it's not her life that is going to be traded.", I assure him.

"Well then that just leaves Mel to deal with.", Lucas says. "I however have an idea on how to get Mel from up your ass if Makaria does come. You will ask her for help on an assignment that will send her to the Mortal Realm. I also advise that we use an illusion spell to mask Makaria's appearance as a backup measure. Demitri, I have no doubt that Mel is the one responsible for what happened to Makaria, and I have a feeling her plan has only just started.", Lucas confides in me.

"I agree completely with you. If she does come, we will have to get use to calling her Amara. I better call the King and Queen. Hades will never forgive me if I keep that his daughter is alive from him.", I say picking up my phone and dialing Hades number.

"This better be important.", Hades answers with frustration in his voice.

"There is an important matter we need to discuss. I have found Makaria, but she has had a powerful curse laid on her. She does not remember anything past the last six years. Except her name is Amara and she is not human. I could only feel a whisper of her goddess essence. She doesn't have access to all her powers and what access she does have is limited.", I disclose. I can feel Hades' anger radiating through the phone.

"We will head back straight away.", Hades informs me barely giving me time to respond.

"No disrespect Sir but I would like to keep this quiet until I find out who did this. I have a gut feeling its someone close to her. Lucas is the only one beside myself that knows.", I mention.

"I will only tell the Queen and I will express the need to keep it to herself for now. She is not going to be patient with not being able to see her daughter. So, work fast and I want an update every day. Demitri find the Bastard that did this to my Baby Girl!", Hades commands before hanging up. Lucas hands me the pipe and lighter as his phone goes off. He stares down at it with his arm stretched out even after I take the pipe.

"What is it?", I inquire.

"Amara just text me asking if I will come out to the cabin tomorrow.", Lucas utters as his phone goes off again. "She said, pretty please I think it would be good for you to get to know Aspen as well as the rest of my team."

"She is trying to set you up with her friend.", I say with a chuckle. "I think you should go. It will do you some good to get off this island."

"I'll tell her that I'll come but I am bringing you with.", Lucas states.

"Don't do that, she needs space and time to figure everything out. She just had her life turned upside down again. Go and have fun, you deserve it.", I remark.

"Okay, so which one is Aspen?", Lucas questions.

"She is the pretty pixie haired energy vamp.", I note as I raise my eyebrows a couple of times.

"She is sexy.", Lucas comments. "Demitri your bond with Amara is stronger than you think, even with her memories gone. I have seen how she keeps reacting to your touch. As well as how her eyes always find you.", Lucas tells me as his phone goes off again. "Amara is definitely playing match maker. She wants me to talk Sylvia into coming.", Lucas chuckles.

"It's probably for Malan who would be a good match for Sylvia. The other two seem like they have something going between them or will soon.", I mutter.

"Alright I'll text her and see if she wants to go.", Lucas tells me as he is texting both women.

We pass the piece back and forth for a little bit before the both of us head to our rooms. Lucas is my oldest friend besides Makaria. I walk up to my bed, strip all my clothes off but my boxer briefs and start to crawl in. When I notice Mel is laying in my bed butt ass naked with only her heels on.

"Mel how the hell did you get in here.", I hiss as I jump out of my bed.

"You know Dimitri you should really close your window.", Mel notes as she winks at me while starting to crawl my way on the bed. "Seriously I can manipulate mist."

"Mel, I have already told you we aren't doing this anymore. I do not feel for you the way you do me. How can you not see all the signs I have been giving you? I have told you multiple times now. We only had sex twice and it has been six months since the last time.", I declare.

"Exactly it has been too long. Cum on Demitri why fight it.", she purrs as she stands in front of me trying to kiss me on the lips.

I pull away before her lips can land on mine and yell, "Mel out now!" Without another word Mel grabs her clothes, runs out of my house slamming my bedroom and front doors on her way out.

"What the hell?", Lucas asks as he breathlessly bust into my room.

"Mel snuck into my bed and was waiting for me naked.", I tell him.

"Damn that girl doesn't quit. You better watch out. She does not take rejection well. Demitri she cannot find out about Amara. She is not strong enough to win a fight against Mel right now. This is the only chance against Makaria that Mel would ever have, and she knows it.", Lucas worriedly expresses as he turns to go back to his room.

"That's why I'm going to assign you as Amara's assistant if she ends up coming.", I inform him as I walk back over to my bed and slip under the covers. It takes me a while to go to sleep. I cannot keep my mind from spinning with thoughts of Makaria and Mel doing something horrible to her. If she is the one that did this there is a lot more to come. I am not going to force Amara to do anything, but I am not giving up on her. I will show her our bond rather she gets her memories back or not. If she still does not choose me, I will be in her life anyway I can. That is my last thought as I drift into a deep sleep.

Mel's POV

Storming out of Demitri's castle I shift into mist and transport myself to New York city. One thing this city is not lacking is young hot men. If Demitri will not give me the attention I need there are plenty of guys that will. Why can't he love me like I do him? I walk into the first bar I come upon. Scanning the crowd, I make my way to the bar. Two guys instantly are asking to buy me a drink. I knew this ruby red spaghetti strap mini dress was an excellent choice. After a few shots with them I grow bored. Excusing myself to the bathroom I head to a supernatural club near here. Humans bore me quickly. The club is just as packed as the bar was. I make my way to the bar and order a fruity drink. Sucking it down I walk along the dance floor eyeing my choices.

As I spot a table in the back corner, I notice a tall sexy man surrounded by women pining over him. He looks like a fun challenge. Lucky for me I must go through them to get to my table. Swaying my hips, I make my way through the crowd to my table. I squeeze through him and a couple of the women. Letting him catch me checking him out before meeting his eyes. Once I am at the table, I slowly sip my drink while pretending to be lost in my own little world. When I finish my drink, I walk out onto the dance floor.

Feeling his eyes on me the whole time. I can tell he is not human, but I have no idea what he is. Then again, I do not know much about anything that has to do with the Mortal Realm. Seeing how everyone from the Underworld is forbidden to cross realms. I do not want to know what Hades will do to me if he catches me here. Which makes that man more intriguing and this so much more thrilling. At least then Hades will have to acknowledge my existence.

On the dance floor I sway my hips as I get lost in the song. Still feeling his gaze radiating off me. As the next song starts to play two women from his group walk over and start dancing on me. The girl behind me is the first to walk up. She is a pretty blonde with short hair wearing a bright pink sleeveless mini dress with black spots all over it. The other girl that is in front of me has turquoise colored hair and is wearing a black blouse that is v cut. Which goes down to her navel and a pair of light-colored jeans. When that song is ending, I act like I do not notice him walking up. A slow song starts to play, and the women leave just as he reaches me. He grabs my hands placing one on his shoulder an intertwines his fingers with the fingers of my other hand.

"My name is Jet Sexton. What is yours? I haven't seen your beautiful face around here before.", he says as he pulls me closer into him. Jet has black hair long on top with the sides buzzed, a thin beard and grey eyes. He is around 6ft tall. He puts some of the gods to shame with his looks.

"I'm Mel and I'm passing though.", I respond.

"Just Mel?", Jet asks while he spins me around the dance floor.

"Yes, just Mel.", I respond.

The group of women that were surrounding him are all giving me the death glare. Except the two that were dancing with me. They are both grinding on the same guy. I flash the group of glaring women a big smile as he gracefully leads us across the dance floor. As the song ends, I lean into his ear and ask him if he wants to grab a drink. After grabbing drinks from the bar, we make our way back to the table I was sitting at. We talk about random things as we sip our drinks. The more I talk to him the more I like him. Too bad I will never see him again. Once our drinks are gone, I suggest we get out of here. He stands up and offers me his hand. Grabbing it I let him lead me out of the club.

"I do not have a room here. I wasn't planning on staying the night.", I express giving him my most innocent smile. "So, do you want to go to your house?".

"And here I thought I was the one doing the hunting.", he says after a chuckle. "Sure, I just have to give my cousins a ride home."

He pulls his phone out and makes a call. Five minutes later the two women I was dancing with earlier come walking out both wrapped in a cute guy's arms. By the way he is treating me I would say he thinks I am human, how cute. I can tell that they are all the same beings I just do not know what kind they are. To explain Sups bonds with beings like them to humans they call them their cousins. My glamour is hard to see through and makes me appear like I have honey brown hair with dark blue eyes. Hiding both my halves making me appear human. Also, it cloaks my essence and scent. Jet has his hand on my leg the whole drive to his house. We sit in silence while the music blares drowning out the noises coming from the back seat. The three of them disappear off into the condo as soon as we get there. I do not see much of the condo myself because Jet leads me straight to his room. It has a simple black and white theme to it. A queen size bed, 80-inch TV, a dresser and one night stand are the only things in the room.

As soon as he shuts the door behind him, I push him up against it and start kissing him. Instantly he is kissing me back as his hands explore my body. Jet deepens the kiss as he backs me up against his bed. Before pushing me onto it he slowly strips my clothes off. Taking every inch of me in he then slowly lays me back as he starts to kiss me again. Jet is being too gentle. Pushing him off me I turn around and get on my knees. Before I can completely get on my knees, he has all the clothes he was wearing in a pile on the floor.

"Fuck.", he says in a tone full of lust as he thrusts into me from behind.

"Harder.", I direct since he is still being too gentle. I want to get fucked not make love to him.

That is the only confirmation he needs. His thrusts become harder and faster.

"God, Mel you feel so good.", Jet moans out.

Just as he is about to meet his orgasm he pulls out and lays on his back. I crawl on top of him then slide down his shaft as hard as I can. Before twerking my ass on him. It feels so good a moan escapes out of my mouth. Keeping him deep in me I spin around to where my back is to him. Bouncing hard on his rock-hard dick I bring myself to an orgasm. Pulling his legs out from under me without pulling out he positions himself behind me again. He is rougher this time than last. Jet slams into me from behind as he pulls my hair. Bringing me to another orgasm before he meets his. Pulling out he spills his seed all over my back. Walking to the bathroom Jet grabs a towel, wets a corner of it, and then comes over to clean my back off. Before I jump in the shower.

"You want some company?", he asks.

"Sure.", I answer as I get an eye full. He could make some good money as a model. I scoot up giving him room to join me.

"So Jet, what are you?", I inquire.

"I am an Incubus. The question is what are you? At first, I thought you were a mere human. If that were true, then you would still be in bed right now in an orgasm coma. Even with Sups it takes them almost an hour to be able to get up. Let alone go more than one around without meeting the same fate as a human.", he informs me.

"Interesting. You are a Mortal Realm Sex Demon. Not surprising since Sex Demons have always been my go-to for some reason. Which would make you a descendant of Lilith's.", I voice more to myself.

"Yes, I feed off lust and I am actually her son. Not all Incubus and Succubus feed off lust though. Some feed off one of the seven sins. What do you mean Mortal Realm? Do you know demons from the Underworld?"

"First generation huh. You are a fascinating one, aren't you?", I say trying to avoid answering his questions. The less he knows the better.

"I have told you about me. Will you at least tell me what you are? A demigod perhaps?", he questions. "I can see the faint shimmer of your glamour now that we have had sex. But cannot see passed it. That is an immensely potent glamour. Most Sups are not even powerful enough to see it. Not to mention I have never felt this powerful before."

"Something like that.", I answer before closing the distance between us. "I have an idea. How about we break your record."

"I'm down, if you think you can keep up.", he teases with a sexy smirk.

Yep, I would definitely end up falling for this one. If we would have had the time to really get to know each other. I leave a trail of kisses down his neck as I slide my hands down his defined abs. As my response. Reaching around me, he turns the water off before leading me to his bed. After round four or maybe six we both end up passing out. I startle awake not remembering where I am. When I turn and see Jet naked asleep beside me, I remember all the fun I had last night. I check out his sexy body before quietly slipping my clothes on. Then head out the door, pausing before shutting it. Maybe if I lived a completely different life this might have had the chance to be something. That was the best night I have had in a long time. I take one last look and close his bedroom door. Once out of Jet's huge condo I transform into mist and transport myself home. I must get back before someone notices I am gone and tells Hades.

Amara's POV
{Saturday morning}

"Hey Baby, it's time to wake up.", Kaden voices as he gently shakes me.

"Five more minutes.", I wine without opening my eyes while I roll over to my other side.

"Lucas is here, and I have everything packed in the Trailblazer.", he informs me.

"Okay, okay, I'm up.", I mumble as I sit up, slip on my shorts, and walk into the living room.

"Morning sunshine.", I playfully yawn to Lucas. If he can even understand my words through the yawn.

"Sorry to wake you sleeping beauty.", Lucas teases back. "I wanted to drop off the file with the job information before you left this morning. Dimitri also wants me to remind you that if you do decide to come that you are welcome to bring whoever you wish. There is more than enough room. Also, I sent you a message with Demitri's personal number. If you have any question or need anything do not hesitate to get ahold of either one of us.", he conveys with hope in his voice. Lucas tells me he will see me later as he winks at me before leaving.

"Damn, you have all the guys from the castle trying to get in your pants.", Kaden comments. As he is making his way back from making sure the kayaks are strapped down securely.

"Kaden, he was just being friendly. Stop getting jealous over nothing.", I warn him as I walk into our bedroom. Stripping off my clothes I am about to jump in the shower. Kaden's voice stops me. "That is a sight I want to see for the rest of my life.", he confesses as he walks over to me.

Spinning me around to face him. He runs his hand down my jaw then down my neck. Slowly moving his hand down my body until he reaches my breast. Massaging it he bends down and sucks on one of my nipples, making me moan. Slowly he leaves a trail of soft kisses up my neck until he reaches my lips. As his lips meet mine, he lifts me up and I wrap my legs around his waist. He carries me to our bed. Laying me on my back, he leans down to where his head is between my legs. Kissing my thigh before he takes my clit into his mouth sucking and teasing it with his tongue. Causing my back to arch in pleasure as little moans escape out of my mouth. He stands up stroking his cock after pulling it out and pleading with his eyes for me to take him in my mouth.

I crawl over then tease his tip with my tongue before taking him all the way into my mouth. Sliding it in and out as I twist my hand in sync with my mouth for a while. I then stand to the side making him turn to face me. Pushing him onto the bed I crawl up and straddle him, his hard cock rubbing against my clit. I press my lips against his as he kisses me back, he opens his mouth inviting my tongue in as I rock my hips on him. Flipping me over on my back he strips all his clothes off. When he is in position, he slides deep into me. Both of us let out a hiss of pleasure.

For the next thirty minutes he puts me in all kinds of various positions, before pulling me on top of him. I ride him fast and hard until an orgasm explodes inside me. Flipping me over on my back he then positions himself on top of me. Slamming into me hard as he pulls out and does it again. I hiss in pleasure as he rubs circles on my clit while pausing for a minute. Not being able to take the pleasure I thrust my hips up and down. Causing him to start pounding into me again. He starts to get close to reaching his own orgasm.

Kaden pulls out before his release, stroking his cock he spills his seed all over my stomach. I lay there breathless as he gets a towel to clean me off. He cleans my wetness from between my legs before cleaning his mess off my stomach. I take a quick shower then throw on a purple tank top and jean shorts. Before slipping on a pair of black sandals that wrap around my ankle. Brushing my teeth and hair next. Kaden is already in the Blazer waiting for me. I hop into the front seat, light a joint as we take off and then pass it to Kaden. We pass it back and forth until it is gone. Kaden drops the roach in the ash tray.

"We have both avoided this conversation as long as we can, Kaden.", I begin the conversation I dreaded to have. "Willa found a picture of a girl that looks like me but a lot younger, like early high school age. She is standing in between a young Demitri and his twin brother. That girl is Makaria the Goddess of Blessed Death, Princess of the Underworld. I could be that girl under a powerful curse.", I disclose. Then I sit there waiting for Kaden to say something.

"I know.", is all he mutters after a few minutes. Not taking his eyes off the road.

"Wait, what do you mean you know?", I question as I try to keep my temper down.

"Demitri told Sean and me who he thinks you are. Then Sean told us about the file but would not say what it held or how he got it. Just that it contains information that could possibly be linked to your past and to Demitri. I asked him not to give it to you.", Kaden confesses. He tightly grips the steering wheel making his knuckles go white.

"Why didn't you tell me? What in the hell makes you think you can make decisions for me?", I remark as I am getting more pissed with every word.

"I also asked Demitri to leave and not to contact you again. To let you continue living your life you have built for yourself.", Kaden adds. "If they cared, why didn't they find you? You had been in Edisto Island in the same apartment for years and even work there. Until we moved into a place together on the same island. Instead of you accidently stumbling upon them years later. After you built a life for yourself from scratch. I don't trust the Collector of Souls.", he voices in a mocking manner.

"You mean you didn't want me to leave you. So, you made a selfish decision about my life not caring how it would affect me. Demitri brought you back from the dead. Then you turn around and disrespect him. Over what, Jealousy? I thought you were better than that.", I add. "I seriously can't believe you!

"How am I supposed to compete with a god?", he finally asks after driving silently for an hour or so.

"You're not competing for me. You already have me.", I assure him. I spend the rest of the ride looking through the two files silently still mad at him.

We are pulling into the cabin's driveway when I get a text.

Aspen ➔ Malan just picked Grim and I up. Willa is riding there with Ace. O and I think Grim really misses you.

Me ➔ Willa and Ace?! Awe I miss him as well.

They have seemed to be getting closer. Good for them I think as a smile spread across my face and I slide my phone into my pocket. I think they will be good for each other. Kaden and I unpack the car not saying much to each other. Before Kaden takes the last few bags to our room, he wraps his arms around me, kisses me lovingly and tells me how sorry he is. Then asks me if I will please forgive him. Walking into the kitchen I grab the two tubs of food to put up. Only leaving out the ingredients needed to make a homemade pizza. I am preheating the oven when my phone buzzes.

Aspen ➔ Yeah looks like it.

I smile to myself as I knead and toss the dough after putting my phone back down. Then I add the sauce on top of the dough with cheese, pepperonis, and thin steak pieces. As I am putting it into the oven, Willa followed by Ace walks in. A few minutes later Grim comes running up and jumps into my arms. I hug that little gremlin tight. Malan and Aspen walk in a minute or two later. I give everyone a hug before the boys go to unload the vehicles. Then I go to the kitchen to check on the pizza. Which has five or so more minutes left to cook.

"So, what's the deal with McDreamy?", Willa asks before she even sits down on the stool.

"Dimitri confessed his love for Makaria for the first time to me. Then tells me he knows I am her because the way his heart reacts to me is the way it reacts to her and only her. Sean sent us to the island under a false assignment hoping the information in this file would be true. Dimitri wants me and whoever I want to bring to stay with him while doing a job for him.", I inform them. Filling them in on what they have missed.

Once she gets me talking, I cannot stop. I need to get it all out. I tell them how Dimitri and Kaden almost get into a fist fight in Sean's office. About the fight Kaden and I got into on the way here. Once I get everything out, I hand them the first file without the letter that was originally in it. Giving them time to look through it while I grab the pizza out of the oven.

File 1:

Page 1: Makaria Goddess of Blessed Death, Princess of the Underworld

<u>Appearance</u>: 5'8" tall with raven-blue black hair that falls in ringlets almost to her waist with beautiful violet eyes.

<u>Powers</u>:
- Immorality
- Super strength

- Super speed
- Super senses
- Healing
- Death's Touch
- Ghost Vision
- Fire manipulation
- Shadow manipulation

Info: She is the oldest of three, grew up in the Underworld and is immensely powerful.

Family:

- Mother - Persephone, Goddess of Spring and Queen of the Underworld
- Father - Hades, God of the Dead and King of the Underworld
- Sister – Melinoe aka Mel, Goddess of Ghost, Bringer of Nightmares and Madness. She is the middle child. It turns out she is Zeus' daughter. He disguised himself as his brother Hades and she was made. Resents her big sister for being their Dads favorite.
- Brother – Zagreus aka Zack, God of Hunting and Rebirth. Prince of the Underworld. Youngest of the three and close to both sisters. Makes sure no one escapes Tartarus or the Underworld.

Friends:

- Thanatos – aka Demitri; God of Death
- Hypnos – aka Harper; God of Sleep
- Lucas - Demon
- Sylvia - Celtic Dryad

Page 2: Amara, Unknown

Appearance: 5'8" tall with raven-blue black hair that falls in ringlets almost to her waist with beautiful violet eyes.

Powers:

- Strong and more powerful than most beings, but not quit as strong and powerful as a goddess.
- Super speed
- Super senses
- Healing
- Fire manipulation
- Shadow manipulation

Past: Unknown
Family: Unknown
Boyfriend: Kaden, Shifter, 2 years

<u>Friends</u>:
- Aspen - Energy Vampire
- Malan - Llewyrr
- Willa - Huldra
- Ace – Magician

<u>Info</u>: Works for The Company under Sean. Her friends also make up the field team she is second in command of. Known in the Mortal Realm as the Death Squad.

<u>Picture 1</u>: Dimitri's twin, Makaria, Demitri, and Lucas with a pretty girl on his arm. They are all dressed up for a ball. Hypnos, Makaria, Thanatos, and Lucas. Senior Prom is written on the back.

<u>Picture 2</u>: Demitri and Makaria dipping their toes in the pond at the base of the Tree of Dawn. On the back it has a date that is ten years ago, and the names Thanatos and Makaria written on it.

<u>Picture 3</u>: Kaden and myself. It is the day of our first kiss out at the lake. I do not even have a photo of this moment.

<u>Picture 4</u>: Me looking at the camera while walking with some woman I do not remember into my apartment. It is time stamped with the date of the day before I woke up with no memories.

We hear the guys coming in so Aspen puts everything back in the file. Willa then slides it under the center piece on the island. I grab a plate adding a few slices of pizza onto it and encourage everyone to grab some as well. We all visit for several minutes in between bites. Before the guys take off to gather wood for the bonfire.

"Coast is clear ladies.", I notify them once the guys are out of ear shot.

"Holy shit Amara. Who the hell has been close enough to collect all this info on you?", Aspen questions.

"Yeah, I'm with Aspen. I am also starting to think you might be her. You look too much like her to not be. Also, you have all but two of the same powers.", Willa adds.

"Besides the fact I'm nowhere near as powerful as a goddess and I don't have three of her powers. I'm fairly sure I am not immortal", I note.

"The curse could be affecting all that or it could be feeding off your energy to maintain its power. Which would make you weaker. Ace and I have been talking about it all.", Willa discloses honestly.

"While we are on the subject of you and Ace.", I mention raising an eyebrow.

"Yeah, yeah. So, what if we are getting a little close. It is not a big deal. I mean we aren't having our first date until we get back.", she says shyly before giggling. I like seeing her happy.

"What about you Aspen I seen you checking out Lucas?", I inquire.

"What, can you blame me. That man is sexy.", Aspen replies.

"O really Aspen, I'm going to invite him out.", I tease her as I am sending Lucas a couple of texts.

Me → Hey Lucas, you should come out to the cabin and go kayaking with us tomorrow.

Me → Pretty please I think it would be good for you to get to know Aspen as well as the rest of the team.

"Don't you dare Amara!", she declares a little embarrassed.

"Too late, don't be embarrassed. This is the first time I have even heard you show any interest in a guy after Dickwodd. What kind of friend would I be if I let you just pass up this chance?", I tell her as I look at my phone that is buzzing.

Lucas → I am down.

Me → Awesome. You should talk Sylvia into coming too.

"He said that he is down.", I inform them as a big smile grows across Aspen's face. "And I asked him to bring Sylvia. We cannot leave Malan out. Let's go out and see if the boys have the fire started yet. They might need my help getting it lit.", I say before giggling.

We all spend the rest of the night under the stars in front of the fire. Relaxing, roasting marshmallows, and making s'mores. Just letting go of all the stress. Grim sits on my lap the whole time. The air has a fresh crisp feel to it and the stars are tinkling around the bright full majestic moon shining down on us. As the fireflies light up the sky trying to find their mate the river is roaring over the rocks. It is so peaceful out here. This is what I needed! I cannot stop the thought of how tonight would be perfect if Demitri was here, from running through my mind.

The morning sun is shining brightly through the window waking me from a restful sleep. Grim is snuggling up between Kaden and I. Slipping out of Grim's hold I walk down the stairs. Following the delicious smell. Ace is in the kitchen cooking eggs, sausage, bacon, and waffles. I wash my hands and help him finish cooking. Grabbing some of the cooked bacon I dip them in the waffle batter. Once they are coated, I place them in the waffle iron. Then pour more batter around it and repeat until the was no waffle mix left. I set the table before making my own plate. As I sit down to eat everyone is slowly shuffling in. Filling the dining room with their chatter. Having finished my breakfast, I wash my plate and kiss Kaden on the forehead. Before going upstairs to our room. Texting Lucas on my way up.

Me → Meet me with Sylvia at the Tree of Dawn in thirty minutes.

Lucas → See you then.

I then enter my room throwing my phone on the bed. Stripping off all my clothes I am about to jump in the shower when Kaden walks in. He grabs my ass telling me how sexy I am. Then spins me around kissing me as he plays with one of my breasts. His other hand slowly makes its way between my legs. Before lightly moving his finger in a circular motion on my clit. A moan escapes my lips causing him to pick me up and carry me to the bed. Not breaking our kiss until he throws me on the bed. He lowers his head between my legs teasing my clit with his tongue.

"Kaden, I have to get ready.", I gasp out as my back arches with pleasure.

He stays down there teasing me for a least five more minutes. Before getting up, kissing me on the lips then walking out the room. I sit there for a moment. O hell no, he did not just do that. Pay back is a bitch Kaden, I say to myself as I take a quick shower. Once done with my shower I wrap a towel around my body, brush my teeth and my hair. I then walk to my bag pulling out a nude pair of bra and panties, a black tank top and jean shorts. Once I am dressed, I slip on my sandals then I head downstairs and out the door.

I rip open the shadow closest to me as I step in it. I pictured the Tree of Dawn before stepping out the second shadow. If I can picture the thing I want to go to. I can jump from a shadow near me to the shadow of the thing I am picturing. I am so happy that they both decided to come. I step out and instantly wrap them both in a hug before shadow jumping us back to the cabin.

When I get back everything from breakfast is cleaned up except two plates. One for Lucas and the other for Sylvia. While they eat, I pack the cooler with Ham, Hot Dogs, Waters, and Soda. Along with Ketchup, Mustard, and Miracle Whip. Kaden drops some beer in there as well. I had let the girls in on my little plan to get Sylvia and Malan around each other as much as possible. I grab the bread and two bags of chips placing them in the dry bag and then placing it on the cooler. Carrying them out to my Blazer I load them in the back. Grim comes up to me asking if he can stay behind at the cabin.

"I know what you are doing Amara.", Malan states as he walks up behind me. While I tell Grim that he did not have to go with us.

"Then do us both a favor and ask her to ride with you.", I respond with a smile on my face.

We take two vehicles, Kaden, Aspen, Lucas, and myself are riding in my black Chevy Trailblazer. Malan, Sylvia, Willa, and Ace are riding in Malan's silver Jeep Commander. Along the way we stop for a couple bags of ice to put in the cooler. I only had one at the cabin to put in it. We drove eight miles upstream from the cabin. The river is walking distance from there, so we will just float down to the bank by the cabin and walk the stuff back. We untie the kayaks from the vehicles and carry them to the water. Kaden ties the cooler to his kayak, and I clip the dry bag to mine. After everyone puts what they need to in it. Getting our oars, we launch off the bank.

We hit the first rapids about five minutes after launching. Then I lite up a couple of joints. Most of us had brought party favors. Including Pot, Shrooms, Beer, and Tequila. I am not much of a drinker, so I just stick with smoking some Weed and eating some Shrooms. I ate just enough Shrooms to get this intense happy body high. After floating for about an hour we find a spot to paddle ourselves to shore to swim and eat. It is getting too hot not to be in the water and of course I am always hungry. After eating two ham sandwiches with chips in it, I go for a swim. Sylvia says something to Malan before diving off into the water. Malan paddles both of their kayaks to shore as everyone else is getting into the water.

The water is waist high as I am heading out even deeper. A group of five humans in a raft are coming our way. It is a real shame they cannot see the beauty of Sylvia's true form. Ace casted a glamour illusion on her before we left the cabin. She is the only one out of us that does not appear to be human. We swim out of their way. Once they pass us, we continue playing in the water.

Out of nowhere there is this toe-curling shriek that sounds like it is coming from two different beings and then we hear the humans screaming in fear. By the time we make it to where they are. One of the humans is being dragged under the water by this horse like creature. The creature is black with the top of its body is that of a horse with its mane full of slithering serpents and a long fish like fin for its bottom half. It drags the first human under water until the human drowns. The water demon then devours the human boy. Then throws his bones upon the edge of the river.

We are trying to get the other four humans out of the river when a beautiful melody flows along the wind. I turn to look behind me. Standing on the water is a beautiful white horse, its mane is continuously dripping with water. The white creature's melody is enchanting the humans as it is extending its back to make room for all of them. Malan and Lucas are swimming two of the humans to shore. While they fight to keep ahold of them. Aspen is pulling the raft to shore that the humans were in before jumping out to get to the white horse like creature.

Willa and Sylvia are calling upon the water element's power. Kaden is fighting against Ace keeping him from going to the creature. When Lucas sees me struggling to get the human girl off the water demon. He passes the human he has to Malan. Then treads back through the water towards me. Even together we are unable to pull her off before the horse like demon dives into the depths of the river. Taking Lucas and myself under with it until the human girl drowns. Giving us no choice but to let go and swim back to the surface. As we are coming up the black horse like creature charges at us. Before it could ram into us it is hit with a wave of water that Sylvia has sent its way. Willa slams a wave into the White horse creature as it is throwing the Human girl's bones on the edge of the river. Then Sylvia freezes it buying us some time.

"Amara, Aspen get the silver rope out of my bag.", Sylvia calls to us as she slams another wave into the black horse like creature.

Without a word we both swim as fast as we can to our kayaks. Grabbing the rope, I cut it in half with the knife I have clip to my bathing suit bottoms. After clipping my knife back and handing one of the pieces of rope to Aspen. We swim back as fast as we can. Good thing I do not go anywhere without at least one knife on me. When we get back to them, the boys are keeping Ace and the other humans on the shore. The white horse demon is just breaking out of the ice as Willa throws a wave over the black horse like creature and Sylvia is freezing it. Without missing a beat, I tie a noose then twist it above my head before tossing it around the white horse creature's neck. Pulling the noose tight I slowly reel it in. As soon as the black horse like creature breaks free from the ice, Aspen has a noose tied and is wrapping it around the water demon's neck. Slowly she reels it in. Both the white and the black creatures are bucking and plunging. Doing everything they can to get free. Malan takes over reeling in the white one while I pin it to the ground and hog tie its legs. The white creature feels like a seal as well as feels colder than death. Sylvia runs to me yanking me as hard as she can off the white horse. She is barely able to pull me off. Slowly I was being glued to the white-water demon. Aspen is hog tying the black one with Lucas' and Willa's help. Once they both are hog tied there is enough silver in the white horse like creature's system that the trance on Ace and the other humans is broken.

"They are kelpie or at least the black one is. I have not heard or read about a white kelpie. They are also known as water demons or water spirits.", Malan informs us being the first to speak.

"The white one is also a kelpie. I have only heard a story about it. Legend has it that there has only been one white kelpie. It was one of the very first two of its kind. It lures humans to get on its back with a melody, then secretes an adhesive making it impossible for them to get off. Taking them to the depths of the water to drown then devour them. It can extend its back to fit multiple humans.", Sylvia add

"Most Sups do everything they can to stay off The Company's radar. Not devour a group of humans out in the open.", Willa states.

"Do their eyes look wrong to you?" I question them both. Their eyes are glossy and clouded over with a greyish-blue color. I know I have seen eyes like that somewhere. I just cannot remember where.

"I have never seen eyes like that before.", Malan answers with Sylvia nodding her head in agreement.

"The Company is dispatching a cleanup crew our way.", Kaden notifies us after hanging up his call, putting his phone back in the dry bag and swimming back over to us. "Once they take our statements, transport the beings and clean everything up we are free to continue our float.

Those two deaths sadden me, but I cannot let it consume me. I have to look at it like we saved three lives. Death is a part of this job, but innocent deaths still hit me hard. In a few days, bodies that will be identical as the two humans will wash up on shore. They will be blue, beaten, and swollen like they have been in the water for days. The bodies will also be made of clay and magic. Kind of like a golem, but they will not be magically brought to life. There will be some cover up story about a float trip gone wrong on the local news. The surviving humans will have their memories wiped and false memories implanted before they are released. I get lost in my own thoughts until I hear Kaden let out a growl wrapping his arms around me in a protective manner. Demitri then lands right in front of me with all his gorgeousness. I must stop myself from running my hands through his wings.

"Are you okay?", he inquires before his feet even touch the ground. I can hear the worry in his voice and can tell he is wanting to embrace me.

"Yeah.", I tell him after taking a few seconds to be able to find my voice. I am still in awe every time I see him in his true form.

"What are you doing here?", Kaden asked in a pissed off tone.

"Have you had time to look over the file Lucas gave you?", he questions before turning to Lucas to have a conversation with him. Not even acknowledging Kaden.

"The file.", I mutter out loud to myself.

Everyone but Demitri and Lucas is looking at me questionably. I hear two voices and the splashing of oars moving in and out of the water getting closer. While the scent of humans float by along with the wind.

"I'll explain later.", I insist. "Ace can you cast an illusion spell? There are two humans coming this way in a canoe."

"I got this.", Ace states confidently as he casts the spell causing the scene before us to appear as it normally would. Just as the cleanup crew is showing up.

The humans pass as the cleaning crew are loading the kelpies and the bones of the humans in the helicopter. While others get our statements. After giving mine, I look around for Demitri. I want to talk to him about their eyes. I find Lucas who tells me that Demitri has already left. My feelings are kind of hurt that he did not say bye. He did say he is going to give me space. I do not know if I want that. There is no denying that there is a strong connection between Demitri and I. No matter how hard I try. I still have not told Kaden that Demitri had confessed his love for the woman he thinks I am. I am going to tell him. I just need time to figure everything out first. He is going to want answers to questions I do not know the answers to. The others finish giving their statements and we swim back to our kayaks. We all sit on the bank when we get back over there.

"Damn guys we can't even go on vacation without finding an assignment.", Ace says with a laugh.

"It's not over yet.", Malan adds as he picks up Sylvia while running into the water.

Sylvia is playfully screaming, "Put me down."

Ace, Lucas, and Kaden all get the same look in their eyes then sprint after

Willa, Aspen, and me. We are in the water before they can reach us. Once they do, they pick us up, then dunk us and themselves under water. I push out of Kaden's arms swimming further into the river's depths before coming up for air. The river is such an enchanting place. The cool water feels so good on this especially muggy day.

"Are you doing alright Babe?", Kaden asks as he swims towards me.

"Yes.", I insist as I swim towards him like I am going to kiss him. When our lips are inches from touching, I use his shoulders to dunk him under the water.

"Okay we are even.", he surrenders after he comes up for air.

"O no we are not. I haven't forgotten about your little stunt earlier.", I comment with a smile on my face.

We swim for a bit, and I eat again before we launch off the bank to finish our float. The rest of the float is so peaceful. I wish Grim could see this, but he said he does not like water. I cannot help thinking how it would be nice to have Demitri here. What is wrong with me? Why can't I get him out of my head? Hours later we get to the bank by the cabin. We swim for a bit before walking the kayaks and cooler back. Sylvia and I are the only ones that brought a bag. As soon as we get back to the cabin, I drop my kayak in the yard and go check on Grim. He is passed out on the couch with snacks and wires laying around him. I turn off the tv which has Child's Play playing on it then go back outside.

"Hey Amara, do you mind taking me back now?", Sylvia questions.

"No, I'm ready when you are.", I reply.

"Great, let me just tell everyone bye.", Sylvia says. She tells Malan bye last giving him a hug and her phone number.

"Mind if I tag along, so you don't have to make more than one trip.", Lucas adds after kissing Aspen on the cheek. Then walks over to where Sylvia and I are standing. I rip the shadow next to me open jumping through to the shadow of the Tree of Dawn. With both of them following behind me I step out of the shadow after I rip it open.

"Thanks again for inviting me.", Sylvia states before giving me a hug and walking off.

"Yeah thanks, you aren't too bad at match making.", Lucas adds with a wink, before rushing after Sylvia to walk her home.

I jump back through the shadows to the cabin. Grim is still sleeping in the living room. So, I ask everyone to meet me in the kitchen before I go to my bedroom to grab the file. Once everyone is in the kitchen, I fill them in on the job Demitri offered me. It is time I see who I can bring in on this job. Now that I made the decision to take it. Those creatures' eyes and what Willa had said kept running through my mind. When my mind is not wondering to thoughts of the God of Death.

"Do you guys remember how the kelpies' eyes were glossy and clouded over? I knew I had seen them somewhere before. There are other creatures that have the same looking eyes in this file Demitri gave me. He wants to hire me through The Company and anyone who I want to bring. I have not said anything until now because I was not sure if I was going to take the job. Willa what you said makes a lot of since. Multiple beings have attacked humans out in the open and I want to find out why. Then put a stop to it. Plus, the kelpies' eyes tie them to this job.", I inform them. I lay the file out on the counter and then sit on a stool quietly. Giving everyone a chance to look through it.

File 2:
>
> Page 1:
>
> Objectives:
>
> - Stop any future attacks.
> - Uncover what or who is behind the attacks.
> - Then stop them.
>
> Traits:
>
> - Insatiable hunger
> - Glossy, greyish- blue colored cloudy eyes
>
> Beings affected:
>
> - Lycan
>   - Status: Captured and contained
>   - After a few hours, its eyes turned back to normal but is stuck in wolf form. The hunger for humans seems gone as well.
> - Forest Troll
>   - Status: Captured and contained
>   - After a few hours, its eyes turned back to normal. The hunger for humans seems gone as well.

Picture 1: A village painted with blood and body parts. Not a single body is recognizable and from the looks of it no one was spared.

Picture 2: A small town painted with blood and guts. None of the buildings were left standing. From the looks of it there are no survivors.

Picture 3: A captured golden wolf with glossy and cloudy eyes with blood dripping from its mouth. The wolf is coated with blood from head to paws. Even its tail is coated. The wolf is also hog tied with silver.

Picture 4: A captured Forest Troll with glossy and cloudy eyes with blood dripping from its hands and mouth. It looks like she has taken a shower in blood and guts and is trapped under a fire net.

"I'm accepting the job and would like all of you to as well. If you accept this assignment, I want you to know we will be staying at Demitri's castle until the assignment is taken care of. If you do not want to come, I will make sure Sean gets you set up with another assignment.", I voice after several minutes.

"Girl you know I got your back.", Aspen voices excitedly.

"I'm down too.", Willa adds.

"You should know I will always have your back.", Malan claims.

"Let's do it.", Ace states.

Kaden does not say a word as he walks out the kitchen and heads outside. "Kaden wait!", I call after him. He stops but still does not say a word.

"Demitri confessed his love for Makaria to me in Sean's office the other day. I thought you should know before you make your decision.", I say not quite meeting his eyes.

"Amara rather you are Makaria or not. Demitri has feelings for you. I am not comfortable with you or myself staying with him. I can see you guys have a connection and I can smell the effect he has on you.", Kaden divulges before sprinting out the door and transforming into his wolf. Not caring he just ripped through his clothes. Shifting is usually super painful but the more you transform the less it hurts each time until its effortless. Elijah personally trains all the new recruits that have any kind of shifting abilities.

I go back to the kitchen to start dinner, but Malan and Aspen were already cooking Beef and Chicken Tacos. I help slice the tomatoes, onion, and lettuce. Setting them all on the bar in bowls along with the cheese when I am done. Grim wakes up a few minutes before dinner is ready. He cleans up his mess after I have asked him twice to do so.

Once dinner is ready, we all sit down at the table after making our plates. Kaden has not come back yet. We chit chat between bites. I am picking up the dishes off the table as Ace and Willa wash them. Grim is right behind me helping bring the dishes to the sink. I make Kaden a plate and put it in the refrigerator after wrapping it in plastic wrap. Ace and Willa announce that they are tired, so they are going to bed. While the rest of us put in the new IT. I am sitting in between Malan and Aspen with Grim on my lap.

"Hey Amara, I like Kaden don't get me wrong. But you need to figure out what kind of connection you have with Demitri. Then figure out which guy you have a stronger bond with. I have seen how both men look at you. While they both obviously love you. Demitri's feelings are stronger and deeper than Kaden's.", Malan informs me just before the movie starts.

Leave it up to Malan to have my back when I did not know I needed it and for leaving me speechless. After the movie I carry Grim to bed. As I slide him under the covers, I hear Kaden come in the back door going straight into the kitchen. Then I slide between them. After cuddling up to Grim I drift into a deep sleep. Everyone sleeps in until around lunch time. By the time I get up Kaden and Grim are in the kitchen making French Toast. Nothing wrong with brunch with a side of ass kissing. Kaden never cooks. I eat about four of them then wash my plate. Since it is our last day here after brunch, we spent the day fishing, swimming, and hanging out on the riverbank. We take a little walk from the cabin finding a spot along the way. When we start getting hungry, we head back to the cabin. Once all of us make it back and eat lunch I check my phone.

Demitri → How are you doing?

Me → Good. I am accepting the job offer.

Demitri → I will have Lucas get with your arrival date and time. As well as how many rooms. Lucas will be your assistant while you are here and will help with anything you may need.

Me → Cool. Thank you. How have you been?

Demitri → Good.

Not knowing what else to say I go help pack up. I get sidetracked when I run into Aspen and Willa. We end up gathering in my bedroom. Aspen thanks me for inviting Lucas, talks about how sweet and sexy he is, and tells us about how he had asked her out on a date. Willa embarrassedly tells us how she lost her virginity last night to Ace. I tell her she has nothing to feel embarrassed about and that I think it is sweet. We ask her how it was and for details. After gossiping about it like girls for a bit we get started packing.

As I am packing up our stuff that is in the bedroom and the kitchen. I cannot help but think about Demitri. I know I want him in my life and that I did not want to lose Kaden. Could Demitri accept that I do not want my memories back and that I want to be just friends? What about if I turn out not to be that woman, is he just going to forget about me? Maybe Kaden is wrong. Maybe Demitri's feelings are just for the woman he thinks I am. I mean he does not really know me. What about the sparks I feel when Demitri and I touch? Then there is Kaden, can he handle me having Demitri in my life? My mind then goes to the first file and all the information it holds. Maybe I am Makaria. I cannot find any differences in the pictures of her or the ones of me. Then I start thinking about the letter. That no one knows about except Sean. I pull it out of my back pocket reading it for the fourth time.

Page 3:

Amara,

You asked me to gather all this information and pictures. Then to keep it safe, only giving it to you if the circumstances are dire. You said that it will help you with the first key to breaking the curse laid on you. I am sorry my friend that you only got six years of peace, even though I have been missing you like crazy. It is imperative that you come back to us! I will reveal my identity in time. Remember to watch your back, you have enemies with plans in the work that are out in the open and some that are hidden in the shadows.

With Love,

Your Dear Friend

After reading the letter again I fold it up and stick it back into my pocket. I know that I need to quit being stubborn and running from the answers I used to seek. Even if I did not want to be her. Someone who might be close to my past self, needs me. Maybe even more than just one person. If whoever typed this letter is right, then I have enemies out there. I am going to need to be at my full strength to not only protect myself but everyone who needs me and my team as well. I cannot stop thinking about how the letter kind of makes it seem like I might have had something to do with my memory loss. I wonder if that picture of whoever and myself entering my apartment meant that I did have something to do with it. Or maybe I at least knew the person. My mind is swirling with thoughts as I bring out the last bags then put them in the Blazer. Kaden comes over wrapping his arms around me.

"You have been really quiet today.", Kaden utters as he is kissing my neck.

"Just a lot on my mind.", I reply.

"Want to talk about it?", he mumbles in between planting more kisses on my neck.

He is such a tease and I still have not paid him back for the other day. At that thought I spin us around pushing him up against the Blazer. I start by kissing a path up his neck to his lips as my hand slowly moves towards his dick rubbing it through his basketball shorts. When our lips meet, I open my mouth as he deepens the kiss. I continue to kiss him while drawing a circular pattern on his bulge for a few minutes before breaking contact with my lips and hand at the same time. Then I walk off to go inside to tell everyone bye.

I hug and tell everyone that I will text them what time to meet at headquarters tomorrow. After everyone has left Grim, Kaden, and I do a once over. Making sure nothing was forgotten as well as checking to make sure everything is clean and locked up. I take one last longing glance before shutting and locking the door. I would love to live out here!

We fell into a peaceful and comfortable silence on the way home. I lay my head on the window while getting lost in my thoughts. Kaden holds my left hand as he drives. Grim soon falls asleep in the back seat. When we get home, it is late. I carry Grim to my bed. We really need to get him his own bed. We can put it in the spare room that I sometimes use as an office. As I wait for Kaden to come up to the room, I check my messages. I have a couple from Aspen and Willa, two from Lucas, and one from Demitri.

Demitri → I hope you had a good time. I cannot wait to see you tomorrow.

Me → I did thank you. Maybe next time you can come?

I cannot help the smile that quickly spreads up my cheeks. At the thought that Demitri cannot wait to see me.

Lucas → Thank you for inviting me and introducing me to Aspen.

Lucas → I'm glad you decided to take the job. How many rooms are you going to need? Also, I have been assigned as your assistant for the duration of your stay with us. So, do not hesitate to get a hold of me if you need anything.

Me → Your welcome. If you hurt her you will have to deal with me.

Me → I will need 6 rooms.

I hope Kaden understands we are going to be on an assignment. So, we need to keep it professional while we are there. Like he is always telling me when giving me my own room key or telling me that all the girls are sharing a room.

Aspen → Thanks for the much-needed weekend. I love you.

Me → You're welcome. I love you too.

Willa → OMG that was the best weekend ever.

Me → I am glad you enjoyed it.

Lucas → Your rooms will be ready at 11am.

Me → Great. Thank you. We will be there around 11:30.

After getting it all worked out with Lucas, I send a group text to my team. There is no need for them to come in early. Since our rooms will not be ready until late morning.

Me → Meet at headquarters at 10:30.

Aspen → See you then.

Ace → Yes Boss.

Willa → Cool. I'll be there.

Malan → Okay.

Kaden walks into our room as I finish reading all the replies from the team.

"This is the file I got from Sean. It seems to be a link to my past which means that if it all is true. Then I do not just know Demitri, we grew up together. I have made up my mind that I am going to follow this lead. But I want you to know that this will not change how I feel about you. I love you.", I inform him. I hand him the file as he sits on the corner of the bed. The letter is tucked in my back pocket still.

"I'm glad to hear it Babe and I want you to know that I have your back on the assignment. No matter how much I do not like it.", he says kissing me lovingly. The kiss deepens until Grim groans and tells me we need to get a room. I laugh as I throw a pillow at him. Then I inform him that he is in our room in his native tongue. Kaden has a puzzled look until he realizes what Grim must have said.

"Good to hear. We are meeting up at headquarters at 10:30.", I inform him.

"Okay I'll be there. You know we should enroll Grim in the school at headquarters. He would be able to learn English and make some friends.", Kaden comments.

"I like that idea. He is a little mess maker.", I agree as I crawl up to my pillow and pull the blanket up to my neck.

"I don't think so. You still owe me for earlier.", Kaden playfully expresses into my neck while sitting the file down.

He picks me up carrying me to the couch in the living room. Laying me on the couch he slides my tank top over my head and kisses a trail up to my breast. After sucking on each one he makes his way to my lips. He pulls away to unbutton my shorts. Then pulls them and my panties off tossing them on the floor with my shirt. He positions himself above me sliding his dick in my wet pussy. Every thrust getting faster and harder as I rotate my hips in sync with him. After I meet my release, he pulls out spilling his seed on my stomach. He jumps up, grabs my shirt, and cleans up his mess he just made. I jump in the shower before once again crawling into bed and pulling the covers up to my neck. Kaden is looking through the file as I walked out the bathroom. So, I leave the light on for him. I am out as soon as my head hits my pillow.

CHAPTER 4: A LIFE OWED FOR A LIFE SAVED

Amara's POV

The sound of my alarm going off wakes me out of my sleep. I turn it off then lay there for a bit as I wake up all the way. There are a few things I want to check in on before leaving. So, I am going in a bit earlier than everyone else. I get dress in office appropriate clothing, a blue button up blouse with black slacks. Letting my long ringlets flow around my face. After packing my bags for the next two weeks I grab a few granola bars for breakfast. Then put my bags in the Blazer after leaving a note.

Kaden,

I went into the office a little early to check on some things. Please bring Grim with you.

Love

A

I head to the office after grabbing my keys. Not going to lie, it makes me nervous that I am going to be staying in Demitri's house. I go to Sean's office first, but he has not made it in yet. Wanting to see how the kelpies are doing I go in search of them. I finally find them both locked in the same tank as each other. It barely has enough room for one let alone two beings.

"Why did you attack those people?", I question them in their native tongue.

"We had a hunger for humans that we could not control.", the black kelpie replies.

"We have never felt hunger like that. Even during the first time we shifted.", the white kelpie adds.

"What do you mean shift? You have more than one form?", I inquire.

"Yes, we have two.", the white one responds.

"Shut up idiot. You talk too much.", shushes the black kelpie.

"I just want to help you. You're not the first that this has happened to.", I inform them. How can I get them to trust me? I am thinking through everything I know that has to do with this assignment. I get an idea and I hope it works.

"Give me a little bit and I'll be back. With proof that I just want to help you.", I express before walking off. Calling Aspen on my way down the hall.

"Hey, I know its early. But I need your help with something. Meet me at headquarters as soon as you can.", I command in a polite tone. She sleepily agrees then I go back to Sean's office. He is finally here so I get down to business.

"Commander I would like to ask to have the kelpies released into my custody. They are tied to my case.", I voice as I enter Sean's office.

"Sure, I'll get the paperwork started.", he replies as he starts typing on his laptop.

Just as he is finishing up my phone buzzes, so I pull it out of my back pocket to check it.

Aspen → Here. In the lobby.

I scoop her up on my way back to the kelpies after putting my phone back. Three employees are standing around Connor laughing. Connor is shocking the water that is in the tank holding the kelpies. My blood instantly starts to boil as I clench my fist as hard as I can. Using everything I have not to go over and just beat the shit out of him. Aspen must have sensed my anger. Or maybe she is having the same feelings as me about it. Whatever her reason is she places her hand on my arm. Trying to sooth the anger rising in me.

"That's enough Connor!", I shout. Everyone with in ear shot turn their heads towards me. "We don't torture. You should all be ashamed of yourselves. They are helpless!"

"Bitch! Maybe you should be the one ashamed, seeing how you are the murder in this room.", Connor says as he sends another wave of electricity through the water again. Shocking the water longer this time than all the times before.

Those words hit hard. How could he talk to me like that? We loved each other like family once. Or at least I did. His Mom became like a mother to me. I tried to save her, but I was not then and still am not powerful enough to bring her back from the dead. His Mom and I were out having a girls' day. When we got T boned by a Ford F150. It hit her side causing the door to bend inward trapping her in the car. I tried hard to get her out. The car caught fire as she begged me to leave her. I try to tell her the fire will not hurt me. Just as someone was pulling me out of the car. I fought them with everything I had. It took four of the firefighters to pull me out of the car. The smoke got to her before they could pull her out. I held her for two hours trying to heal her. Connor never forgave me for not being able to save her. He pushed away from his Dad as well.

I punch Connor square in the jaw knocking him out. How dare he go there knowing damn well I loved her to! How dare he just stand there torturing those helpless beings! As his consciousness fades, he lets go of the device he was using to electrocute the kelpies with. I snatch the device out of the air before it could fall into the water with them. Connor hits the ground with a thud. He is knocked smooth out. I laugh to myself at the thought of him feeling every bit of that hit when he wakes up.

"See we can trust her.", cheers the white kelpie weakly to the other one.

I had filled Aspen in on my plan as we were walking back to the kelpies. She did not think she could pull it off but agreed it is worth a try.

"Try to feel the difference between their powers and the spell laid on them. Then focus on the feeling of the spell, only drawing in that feeling.", I encourage her. Aspen takes a deep breath then she nods as she closes her eyes. She places her hand in the tank on the black kelpie. At first nothing happened.

"It should have worked.", Aspen states as she looks at me confused.

"Try to shift.", I suggest to the black kelpie in its native tongue.

The black kelpie shifts into her human form. Aspen did the same thing with the second one and then she shifts into her human form as well. They are twins and look just alike even their eye color is the same ocean blue. The only difference they have is one has deep black hair and the other one has snow white hair.

"Let us get you guys some better accommodations and clothes. Don't worry none of them are going to get away with torturing you.", I declare as Aspen and myself help them out of the tank. I heal their wounds as quickly as I can before calling Lucas.

"Hey Lucas, can you get me an extra room set up for the two kelpies from the river please. I'll explain more later.", I ask in a rush as soon as Lucas answers his phone.

"Of course, anything else I can do for you?", he asks catching on to my tone.

"It's not safe for them here so I'll will be bringing them there shortly. Since their room is not ready, they can hang out in mine.", I offer.

"No need there is plenty to keep them entertained until their room is done.", Lucas informs me.

"Awesome. Thank you. See you in a couple of minutes. O and Lucas, they are going to need some clothes.", I inform him.

"Amara you did it this time. You are being called in front of the Council.", Balthazar barks with a grin on his face.

Making his way over to us through the crowd of people. I knew I would be in trouble but figured I would have at least enough time to get these two out of here.

"Aspen I need you to stall for me just long enough to get them to Lucas. Will you also please get the paperwork I need from Sean?", I state as I hang up on Lucas and shove my phone in my pocket. I turn to the twins as I tell them, "Follow me and keep up. We don't have a lot of time."

I start running down the hall towards the back doors. Making sure not to outrun the kelpies. On one assignment we were sent to deal with a succubus. That was feeding off people until she killed them. Aspen is using a power she got from her that will persuade him into forgetting about me. Balthazar's only thought will be of her for now. As the three of us make it outside. Ripping open the shadow of the back of the building I then pull the twins in with me. Just as Balthazar's team comes busting through the doors. The rip starts to close as I picture the Tree of Dawn and open its shadow. Lucas is already there waiting for us.

"Is everything okay?", Lucas asks with a worried tone. He politely keeps his eyes up as he hands the twins each a t-shirt and pair of shorts.

"It will be. I have just gotten myself into some trouble.", I note with a laugh before reopening the shadow.

I jump back into the shadow of the back of headquarters. Time to face my consequences. I think to myself as I walk into the building and down the hall. After taking a deep breath I walk into the conference room. As the council calls it, I call it the judgement room.

"Glad to see that you are joining us and not running off like Balthazar said. Take a seat.", Elijah commands in his business tone. All four of their eyes are on me as I take a seat.

"Explain yourself.", Sean directs with disappointment clearly present in his tone and facial features. He is clearly upset with me.

"Connor was torturing the unarmed kelpies while his team was standing around them laughing. They are in my custody, so it is my duty to protect them. I asked him at least twice to stop before I punched him in the jaw. He was going to kill them.", I divulge. Trying my hardest to keep eye contact with Sean. Instead of looking down at my hands like a child getting scolded by a parent.

There is a knock at the door. Freias a Goblin who is also Dean's assistant walks in with an USB port and a small stack of papers in her hands. Hopefully, those are the papers proving they were in my custody.

"Sir here is the camera feed on the kelpies you requested, and Aspen insist that I give these to you guys as well.", she is saying as she hands them to Dean. Before walking out the room she glances at me with a remorseful look. They watch the video feed, look over the paperwork and talk among themselves before turning back to me.

"Your story matches the camera feed. Connor and his team will be dealt with.", Dean assures me.

"Amara you know just as well as I do that you could have dealt with this situation without knocking him out, you are highly trained. We do not tolerate torture, but we are also against employees using physical violence against other employees.", Sean voices with disappointment in his eyes.

Elijah and Dean are sitting there nodding their heads in agreement. Balthazar is getting increasingly angry by the second. I am surprise steam is not coming out of his ears.

"As for her punishment I vote she gets fired and memory swiped.", Balthazar all but hisses out with a wicked grin on his face.

I do not know exactly how I lost my memories. But here when you get memory wiped, they use a glawackus or also known as the Northern Devil Cat. This creature looks like a mixture of a bear, lion, and panther. Capturing one for The Company was my teams first mission together. Its cackle like screech busted all our ear drums. One look into its blind eyes and your memory is wiped. Then they have a few vampires who can use compulsion to implant memories. That way if something happens and the compulsion breaks you still do not have your memories.

"She is the best agent we have and was not only sticking up for helpless creatures. Which is one of The Companies foundations. She was also protecting the integrity of The Company.", Elijah states.

"Balthazar if you push for her to get fired and for her memories to get swiped. Then I will push that you be held accountable as well. For it was one of your teams that was torturing those unarmed beings. Not to mention the fact this is not the first-time one of your team members have gotten away with stuff like this. I will also push that you receive the same punishment.", Dean promises.

"What example are we setting for the other employees if we just let her walk out of here with no form of punishment?", Balthazar hisses not acknowledging Dean's promise.

"Amara if the other three are in agreement your punishment will be a month suspension with no pay.", Sean asserts as the others agreed. Balthazar did not dare push the matter further. "You are dismissed.", he spoke without looking at me.

My team is sitting outside waiting on me when I walk out. Aspen must have told them what had happened.

"So?", Aspen impatiently asks before I have made it all the way to them. Grim is reaching up wanting me to hold him. I pick him up and love on him.

"I'm suspended for a month without pay.", I inform them.

"That little weasel deserved what he got.", Willa conveys.

"What about the assignment?", Kaden questions.

"I don't . . .", I start to say. Before Sean comes out telling us that since I am suspended that Demitri will no longer be working with The Company on this case. He did not even glance my way once. Sean has never been this upset with me. I wait until Sean is out of sight before telling my team that I will take care of this. To just give me a few minutes. I step away to make a phone call putting down Grim to do so.

"Hey Demitri, its Amara, please don't punish my team for my stupid decision.", I plead with him.

"I will still use your team on one condition.", he informs me.

"What's that?", I question curiously.

"That you come work the assignment through me personally and with your team.", Demitri offers.

"Deal, thank you so much.", I reply before hanging up and walking back over to them. "Sean will be getting a call any minute. You guys are going to work with Demitri on this assignment without me.", I comment with a wink once I make it back to them.

"But that's not fair.", Willa starts to protest. Not getting what I meant by my wink.

"Willa it will all work out. Trust me.", Ace comforts her as he looks around to see who is listening.

"Captain, Sean would like to see you in his office.", Sean's assistant tells him.

"I'll see you soon. There is some paperwork I have to take care of with Dean before my suspension starts.", I inform them before going to Dean's office.

"I got Grim for now.", Malan assures me. I mouth thank you to him before turning the corner to head to Dean's office. He is sitting behind his desk with his nose in some papers. I knock on his open office door before entering.

"Come on in.", he voices without looking up as he finishes what he is reading. "Amara, I get why you did what you did. But you are our best agent. We need you to set a good example for everyone else. So that one day you can have my seat on the council. All I ask is for my daughter to take over when she is ready. If she even wishes to follow in her old man's footsteps.", he remarks.

"Yes, sir.", I reply shocked that he wants me to take over his seat.

"Now, with that being said, that was a hell of a punch and catch I must say.", Dean states before laughing to himself. "Just sign these papers for HR. Try to enjoy these next four weeks. You work way to hard anyways."

"Good, Amara you are still here.", Elijah comments before shutting the door and walking up to me. "Watch your back Amara. Balthazar is up to something big!", he whispers in my ear. "Now if you need anything don't hesitate to reach out.", he speaks in a little louder tone than before.

Elijah all but pushes me out of Dean's office. Weird I think to myself before walking off. Zoning out I walk down the hall, lost in Elijah's words. An annoying high-pitch girly voice brings me out of my thoughts when I hear my name.

"Look at Amara's face, I bet she got fired.", one of Connor teammates spits out.

"That's what she gets. Who does she think she is hitting Connor?", a male being on Connor's team hisses.

They are just newbies that are not even field trained. I tell myself as they keep talking shit. I walk out the front door as quick as I can. It is best I do not try my luck twice today. I look down at my phone as it goes off.

"Hey.", I answer the call.

"There will be a black Lincoln pulling up to pick you up.", Lucas informs me as one stops next to the curb in front of me.

A young male demon gets out of the driver's side. Coming around to my side the demon opens the back passenger door for me. I climb in, his scent hits me before my eyes find him. Demitri is sitting on the other side looking devilishly sexy.

"Hey Trouble.", he greets me in his sexy deep voice with a smirk spreading across his face.

Ha! I am trouble, the way he is looking is going to get me in trouble. I thought before chastising myself. He is in a black pin striped suit with a light purple shirt and little bit darker purple tie. It is fitted perfectly showing off his muscles without being too tight.

"Hey.", I respond. Not saying what I am really thinking.

"I figure we could grab some food while having a business meeting. You can catch me up on what's going on and I can answer any questions you might have.", Demitri proposes.

We pull into a restaurant not too far from headquarters. It is fancy but not too fancy. Before we get out Demitri hands me a jewelry box.

"Demitri I can't accept this. I get we have a connection, and I cannot deny I feel like I need you in my life. But we can only be friends. I'm with Kaden.", I express handing it back to him.

"You aren't even going to look at it before saying no.", he replies before raising an eyebrow with a hint of sorrow in his voice.

"Yeah, I would rather not know what I'm missing out on. I'm sure it's beautiful.", I remark.

"This bracelet is magically infused with a powerful illusion spell. As long as this stays on your wrist you will appear to be a red-haired, blue-eyed demon to anyone who has any ill will towards you. It is not exactly safe for you around the castle with us not knowing who laid this curse on you. It is also part of the deal.", he confesses as he pulls the bracelet out and clasps it on my wrist.

I stare at it like a deer caught in headlights. It is gorgeous with blue benitoite and black hematite square gems all throughout it. Getting enchanted by the beauty of the bracelet I did not notice Demitri had gotten out. Until he was standing with my door open, and his hand stretched out to me. As soon as we walk in, we are greeted and seated right away. They have us at a table off in the corner by itself. We order our drinks while flipping through the menu. I get a Dr. Pepper of course. Demitri tells me to order whatever I wanted. So, I order an 8oz medium-rare steak with a baked potato and steamed veggies. What can I say? I like to eat. Once we have placed our ordered Demitri gets straight to business.

"What did you do to get suspended from The Company?", he inquires.

"I punched another employee, Conner. Knocking him out on headquarters' grounds. He isn't just an employee he is one of the Higher Up's kid.", I honestly reply. "I'm sure you had no problem finding that out though."

"Why?", is all he asks.

"Because you're the Collector of Souls. I am sure it is easy for you to get info out of people.", I note.

"No, I was asking why you punched him?", he questions.

"He was torturing the innocent kelpies. It is not even the second time I have caught him doing something cruel to an unarmed or innocent being. Balthazar always keeps him and others out of trouble somehow. Of course, there is always some excuse for why there is not any video feed. Except this time. Also, if I am being honest his words hit me hard.", I explain as our food arrives at a perfect time.

"I didn't ask because I wanted to hear it from you.", Demitri conveys before taking a bite of whatever fish dish he ordered.

I take a few bites and a drink before changing the topic to the assignment. "I would like to be able to interview the other two beings. Sorry, I did not have time to explain before dropping the twins off on you. Those twins are the two kelpies from the river. They were trapped in that form by some type of spell. Aspen was able to siphon the spell, allowing them to transform back into their human form. I think it could also be a spell that is causing these beings to have an unquenchable hunger for humans.", I divulge.

"Lucas actually covered for you already and so did the kelpies, Phoenix and Nixie. I have a huge library you and your team can use for research.", he states. "If you are going to continue on this assignment promise me that you will not take that bracelet off for any reason.", he pleads.

I look into his eyes as he is looking into mine with so much unspoken emotions. I do not remember Kaden ever looking at me with this much intensity. I promise that I will keep it on. We then fall into a comfortable silence as we finish eating. After we are done, he pays for our meals. Demitri has his driver drive us first to my Blazer to get my bags. Then to his little passenger plane. Demitri, yes Demitri flies us in a plane back to his castle.

"I wanted to fly you back here myself. Seeing how your boyfriend would not like me holding you like that, and I am not sure how you would feel about it. I settled for flying you in my plane for now.", he comments through the headset as he lands the plane on his landing pad.

I thank him for the ride before going and checking in with my team, filling them in on everything and putting my bags in my room. Grim is on my bed chewing on some wires while watching the Priest. As soon as he sees me, he runs up and jumps in my arms. I hold him for a little bit before placing him back on the bed. I inform him I still have some work to do. But promised him that when I am finish for the day, we would tour the castle finding fun things to do together. Kaden seems pissy after I show up with Demitri. He is going to have to get over it. Right now, we have work to do. Not to mention Demitri is technically my boss until we solve this case. I will talk to him about it later.

"Hey guys.", I greet everyone. "I need Aspen to come with me and the rest of you to help Ace find any spells that keeps a being trapped in one form and that gives beings a gluttonous hunger for humans. They might be two different spells.", I inform them. "Kaden are you going to be okay with me taking lead on this assignment?"

"You act like you don't boss me around at home.", he playfully responds. Even though I can tell he is still pissed with me.

Aspen and I walk down the hall to find Lucas, but he is already heading our way. With a smile spreading across his face as soon as he sees Aspen.

"Hey beautiful ladies, follow me to the dungeon.", Lucas praises us as he holds out both of his elbows. We wrap are arms through them and off we go. The dungeon is dug deep into the mountain with walls made of stone. It is heavily guarded with demons in demonic form. Most of the demons I have seen were in their human form. The Forest Troll and Wolf are in the first two cells.

"My friend and I are going to come in your cell. We are here to help.", I communicate to the wolf as I kneel to its level. The wolf slightly nods its head as I open the door to its cell. It is a beautiful golden color with amber eyes. Judging by the wolf's size it is without a doubt an alpha or a luna. They are the only ones that get this big.

"Aspen, do the same thing to this wolf as you did to the kelpies.", I encourage her.

"Okay now try to shift.", she commands the wolf after placing her hand on him and siphoning the spell. The wolf shifts into a dark blonde hair pretty boy with amber eyes, who of course is butt naked. I am not going to lie I looked, there is no rule against looking. Lucas throws the guy a pair of clothes that he had a demon bring down.

"You women are just as bad as you say men are.", Lucas mumbles as he shakes his head.

Busted! A blush colors my face red, and I am sure Aspen's as well. Wolf boy just smiles and raises his eyebrow. "Tell me everything you know", I politely demand to both the lycan now in human form and the troll. Trying to get out of this awkward situation. And the image of how good looking he is out of my mind. Damn that boy is fit.

"There was this warmth that started in my stomach growing into this ravenous hunger for humans throughout my body.", The wolf boy informs us.

"Once it started to spread through my whole body, I lost all control and could only watch the horrible acts I was performing.", cries the female forest troll between sobs. She has pear green colored skin, ears pointing to the side, a bright red mohawk, and orangish yellow eyes. With two small tusks coming out from the bottom of her mouth and white troll paint on her face.

"Lucas is Demitri available?", I ask.

"Let me check.", he responds.

"I'm going to get you guys out of these cells. You cannot go home yet, that would not be safe for anyone. If you remember anything else let me know.", I promise them both before following Aspen and Lucas out.

"Aspen that's a badass power.", I applaud her.

"It is, isn't it. How did you even know that would work?", she inquires.

"The idea of it being a spell that was trapping the kelpies was just an educated guess. And then I wondered if you would be able to siphon a spell like you can powers and energy.", I state.

"Well, it was a really smart idea Amara. Please wait here.", Lucas politely orders as he knocks and sticks his head in Demitri's office. "Amara you can go in. I will take Aspen to lunch with me. If she wants to go?", he nervously voices as he turns to Aspen. She excitedly agrees to go with him.

"Hi.", I greet Demitri as I walk in his office.

"Hey." he replies in that deep sexy voice of his. As he looks me up and down with a look that is promising dirty things.

That look and the thoughts that followed causes me to bite my bottom lip. A blush spreads through my cheeks when I notice Demitri had seen me. "I want to discuss moving the troll and wolf who is now in human form out of their cells.", I voice after clearing my throat.

"And what is your plan?", Demitri questions still staring with that intense lustful look.

"Move the wolf boy to a room. As for the troll is there any caves in this mountain? They were under a powerful spell and are not a threat anymore. However, I would like to keep them close just in case.", I inform him.

"Sounds like a good plan to me.", he says as he gets on the intercom telling someone to take the lycan to a room, the troll to the back of the dungeon where it is like a big cave and give them anything they need.

"Thank you Demitri.", I mutter as I exit his office and head to the library to see if my team has made any lead way. Why can I not get the image of how he was looking at me out of my head? What the hell did I get myself into?

Not even Kaden has this kind of effect on me. I think to myself as I head to the library.

"Hey Ace, have you guys come up with any leads on spells?", I inquire as I approach the table off to the side of the library. Everyone is piled around with maps, books, two laptops, and notebooks with notes scribbled in them.

"We have come across three that will cause someone to be stuck in whatever form they are in when it is casted on that person. But we have not come across a spell to cause a being to lose control.", Ace informs me.

"Have you looked into blood magic. A spell that strong will need some type of sacrifice.", I note.

"No, I haven't but I will get on that.", he communicates as he starts searching for books on blood magic.

"You guys should go take a break and get something to eat.", I politely command. I find the librarian who is a purple haired pixie. She is the size of a bottle of water. Yellow pixie dust floats to the ground behind her as she flutters in the air in front of my face. I ask her if Dimitri has any books on blood and sacrificial magic. Telling Ace that a spell that strong would need a sacrifice. Got me thinking about how sacrificial magic is the second strongest form of dark magic.

"That would be in Demitri's personal library. Only Him, Lucas, and yourself have access to it. Follow me.", she announces as she walks to the back of the library. "It has a security system that is unlocked by two fingerprints. All you have to do is pulled that blue book which will read your thumbprint and index fingerprint then the wall will open.", she instructs me.

"How would he have my fingerprint?", I inquire as I hesitate to touch the book.

"That's a question for Demitri. Go on and give it a try.", she encourages sweetly.

I pull the blue book and the wall opens. "Makaria", I whisper to myself as I walk in with the door closing behind me.

There is all sorts of magical objects and books that line the shelves or are in display cases. There is the Hand of Glory, Chain or Lasso of Truth, Book of Thoth, Spear of Destiny, and Cintamani Stone to name a few. The Hand of Glory is some powerful dark magic. It is the hand of a condemned murder and has the power to unlock any door as well as freeze people in place. Chain or Lasso of Truth will make whoever it is wrapped around tell the truth or see the truth. The Book of Thoth is ancient god magic and is said to contain two spells. One to understand the minds of gods and one to understand animals.

When I come across the Spear of Destiny, I cannot help but pick it up and admire it. It is a sacred relic that is said to have pierced Christ's side causing it to be imbued with unique powers. This weapon is one of vary few weapons that can kill anything, and I mean anything. Even a god or goddess, sending their essence to the void. I have no clue how I know that. Continuing my tour, I come across some boots. If I am right, they are the Seven-League Boots. The legends says that they allow the one wearing them to move three miles in one step. I have read a French fairy tale about them. The enchanting Cintamani Stone's beauty is unmistakable but very few have been fortunate enough to have seen it. It is said that it fell from the stars landing in Tibet and is also known as the Elixir of Life. It can grant wishes and immortality as well as symbolizing enlightenment, perfection, and heavenly bliss.

There is one big book about blood and sacrificial magic. I pull it from the shelf and sit at the only table in the room. Grabbing one of the notebooks and pens from the table. I start taking notes as I read. I must have been in there for over an hour because I get a text from Kaden.

Kaden → Hey we are back. Where are you at?

Me → Following a lead. We will meet up when I'm done here.

I stay for another forty minutes before marking my spot and putting the book back on the shelf. Above the button to exit the room is a screen that is showing video feed of the whole castle. I wait until the coast is clear before exiting out into the library. While folding my notes then putting them in my pocket. I have learned quite a bit from just that one book. I send my team a text asking them to meet me in the library as soon as they can. To touch base on what information everyone has gathered so far.

"Ace what have you guys found out", I ask once everyone has arrived.

"Not much, I haven't found anything on a hunger for humans. And the transforming spells we did find. None of them are powerful enough to work for an extended period of time on anything other than a human. We think you are right about them being blood or sacrificial magic. But haven't been able to find any books on those kinds of magic in this library."

"The hunger spell last too long and would be too powerful to be anything other than sacrificial magic.", Willa notes. "As in sacrificing a life for the power to cast the spell."

"I did some research on the locations of the two massacres. I have the next hit narrowed down to two locations.", Malan adds.

"I found a pattern in the attacks and have narrowed it down to two possible locations for the next attack.", Kaden informs us.

"Whatever trapped the lycan, and kelpies was definitely a spell. Since Amara's idea to try and siphon the spell from the beings worked. I have been doing research as well as homing in on this power of mine. I have learned to tell when there has been a spell casted, what it is casted on, and how strong the spell is. That spell was a dark magic spell.", Aspen discloses.

"I haven't come across any spells for a ravenous hunger, but I have come across information on that type of spells. They all require a sacrifice of life in trade for one use of the spell. Also, the stronger the being that is sacrifice the stronger and longer the spell last. O and for the spell to work you have to have the person you are casting it on in your sights.", I inform them on what I have learned. I send them all off to get ready to head out. Pulling out my phone I shoot Lucas a text.

Me ➔ Will you set up a meeting with Demitri for me please. After the meeting I will need a ride for my team and myself to all three of the crime scenes.

Lucas ➔ Meeting with Demitri is in fifteen minutes.

"Amara, can we talk?", Kaden insist in an upset tone.

"Yeah, what's up?", I respond as I put my phone back in my pocket.

"What's going on between you and Dimitri? You seem to be getting closer to him. Not to mention how you keep spending more and more time alone with him.", he all but growls out.

"He is my boss until we complete this assignment. How do you think you guys are still working on it? Which you know. He picked me up and we had a business lunch in public to work out details. You have nothing to worry about.", I try to reassure him trying to keep my anger down and be understanding. His pissy possessive attitude is not helping.

"So, what I'm not allowed to be upset that you are working and staying under the roof of someone who has feelings for you. Especially when you will not even stay in the same room as me.", Kaden keeps on as he pisses both of us off more.

"Kaden don't, you know damn well we have to keep it professional since we aren't married and on an assignment. How many times have you done and said the same thing to me?", I question as I am trying not to punch him in the mouth. No matter how tempting the thought is.

"This is different, and you know it. If that is true, then explain that expensive ass bracelet you have not taken off since he gave it to you on your so-called business lunch.", he spits out the words with venom.

"It's always different when it comes to something being done to you not by you. As for the bracelet its magically infused with an illusion spell that glamours my appearance from anyone that has any ill will against me.", I explain with attitude. "Someone did take my memories remember."

"Sorry to interrupt but it's time for your meeting with Demitri. As for you Shifter I would show more respect when in the presents of the Princess.", Lucas voices without taking his eyes off Kaden.

I can see the anger growing in Lucas's and Kaden's eyes as they stare each other down. So, I tell Kaden to go take a run to help him calm down. While I get back to work. I stop by my room grabbing the file before going to Demitri's office. I knock on the open door as I walk in and shut it. After realizing that my fingerprint worked on his hidden library on top of the file and everything else. The only explanation I am able to come up with is that I am Makaria. He was her best friend so maybe he can help me piece the puzzle together with what is in the file.

"Miss me already?", Demitri playfully teases.

"O yes. I couldn't stand another second away from you.", I sarcastically respond. "Actually, I was wanting to pick your brain about something that has to do with Makaria."

"Sure.", he responds as his head springs up at the mention of her name with a shocked look in his eyes.

"First I want to ask. Did we, I mean Makaria and you ever have sex?", I inquire nervously. "I'm just curious. I was able to access your hidden library. Which makes it even harder to deny that I'm her and makes me wonder how deep your relationship with her was."

"No, we didn't ever have sex. She was, I mean you are my best friend. I thought that could be enough for me. After losing you I found out how wrong I really was.", Demitri confesses.

I hand him the file letting him look through it for a moment. He stops to look at the picture of Makaria and all of them before continuing. Stopping again on the picture of the woman and me going into my apartment the day before my memory loss.

"That is your Sister Mel in her glamour. Be careful around her. She cannot be trusted.", he claims before I can ask if he knows her.

"So, she wouldn't be the one that wrote me this letter then?", I question as I decide that if I want answers about this letter, he is the best person to confide in. I hand him the folded-up letter I pull out of my back pocket. Sitting down in the chair I watch him open and read it. Anger and hurt flash through his eyes as he scans the page.

"If I am Makaria that letter makes it seem like I did this to myself. I don't understand why I would do that.", I mention before he can say whatever is on his mind.

"I have a feeling that you found out Mel's plan and just went with it. So, you did not have to be the Goddess of Blessed Death and Princess of the Underworld anymore.", he conveys with a sad tone. "You wanted to experience the realms beyond the Underworld among other things. You wanted more in your life than just death. You took your responsibility seriously so you could not bring yourself to just walk away. This picture shows me that Mel was up to something, and you knew. Or you at least knew the person taking the picture was there. You are looking directly at the camera."

"Well, isn't that ironic.", I say out loud to myself before laughing.

"What is ironic?", he questions.

"You say Makaria wanted to get away from death and that I am her. Yet here I am second in command of the Death Squad.", I answer him using my fingers to make quote marks as I say Death Squad. That is the name the Sups gave us. Demitri chuckles as he gets the irony of my situation.

"Thank you Demitri. I am going to take my team to all the crime scenes. Can we continue this conversation later?", I question. He just nods his head yes, lost in thought. I hate to leave him after unloading everything on him like that. But I can also see he needs some space to process. Plus, I did not want to know anymore right now. All I have wanted was to know my family and my own sister was most likely plotting against me. I left his office meeting up with my team to head out.

The first crime scene is a blood bath, the village is in the middle of a forest and a river. It was home to thirty or so humans. There was not a sole survivor. I made up my mind right then. Whoever was behind this is going to have their life traded for Kaden's. Which I only have nine days left on my deal. Why has this place not been cleaned up? I was not expecting to find it still looking like this.

"Kaden and Ace collect evidence, Aspen search for where the spell was casted, and Malan track the wolf please.", I direct my team. I liked being Captain, but I am not going to let it go to my head. It feels weird to call Kaden Captain when I am the one leading the assignment. But that doesn't mean I cannot keep our two lives separate.

Malan tracks the wolf to one of the nearby cabins. It is destroyed from the inside out. There is no doubt he shifted in there. From the look of how the door is busted off the hinges and is laying on the floor inside the building. Means he started shifting out in the open and ran in for cover. The back door is also ripped off the hinges but from the inside like he was trying to make it into the woods behind the cabin. It laid outside on the ground not too far from the door frame. I walk out the back door heading towards the woods stepping on the back door.

"The blood spell came from somewhere over here at the edge of the woods. The sacrifice is a little further into the woods somewhere. I can only feel very faint traces of the spells since it has been so long since they were casted. There were definitely two spells casted though.", Aspen states.

"Guys we found where the spells were casted.", I yell to inform them stopping at some droplets of blood on the ground. Looking up and out into the woods, I see the place the sacrifice was performed. I slowly walk closer not being able to form any words. On the ground laid an Angel, even in death she looks majestic. Her beautiful copper-colored wings were cut off and tossed to the side like trash. With her wrists and throat cut. The Angels hands are tied above her head. Her body is positioned where her feet are at an angle higher than her head on some dirt formed into a small alter. There are small trenches dug from her wrists and neck meeting together in a pool below her head.

Symbols I have never seen were drawn in blood on the tree trunk next to her. I have a hunch that it is her blood. We will evaluate samples we collect against each other to know for sure. I can tell one is a wolf but have never seen any of the other symbols before. I can understand the symbols enough to know it is an old dark enchantment spell. After I take pictures of the scene and the symbols. I call Lucas letting him know we need a cleanup crew. I also tell him half of my team need a ride to the town the troll attacked. Then I send the pictures I had taken to him and Demitri.

"Holy shit!", Aspen says as her and the others join me.

"We need to get to the other crime scenes now. If the next attack is happening tomorrow. We are going to have to split into two teams. Aspen and Malan are with me. We will go to where we captured the kelpies. Kaden you will take Ace and Willa to where the troll attacked the town.", I direct.

Dimitri's cleanup crew shows up a lot faster than The Company's. Come to thank of it they did take longer than usual when we found the kelpies. Once the others' ride shows up. I shadow jump us three to the cabin. From there we take Sean's little motorboat to the spot where we captured the twins. I let Aspen take the lead since she can feel out the left-over traces of the spell. They should be a lot stronger here since it happened only a couple of days ago. She finds the spot quickly this time. There are two qalupalik that were sacrificed. There is a male and female, they had to be siblings.

"Amara, I feel some type of magic all around this scene. I felt it at the last location as well.", Aspen expresses.

"It's a time freezing spell. I suspected as much when we found the Angel's body. She should have turned into dust. These beings have confirmed my suspicion. There are still drops of water all over their tails.", I convey.

Qalupalik are descendants of mermaids, but their dark magic changed them from Mermaids into evil looking water creatures. Some believe that it was a curse laid upon them as revenge for killing a witch's lover that turned them into what they are now. They only live-in freezing waters and are aquatic humanoid that have human like qualities, green scaly skin, with long hair and fingernails. They also have a fin that comes out of either the top of their head, torso, or their back. These qalupalik fins are coming out of their backs, and they look young. The scene is the same as the village. Their necks and wrists are sliced open, body angled so their feet are above their heads. With trenches dug from their wrists and necks to a pool below their heads as well as symbols on the tree trunk next to them in their blood.

I take pictures and forward them to both Lucas and Demitri as I did before. Kaden calls informing me that the scene is the same as the one before and the being that was sacrificed is a Banshee. I ask him to take pictures, send them to me, collect as much evidence as they can, and meet us back at the castle before hanging up. I call in two more cleanup crews and we collect as much evidence as we can find. Honestly, there is not much at all that gives us any kind of lead. I shadow jump us back to the Tree of Dawn. Once we get back to the cabin and locked the motorboat back up.

This is definitely a two or more-person job. There is no way one person can simultaneously cut two beings' throats and wrists. The chance of someone using a cloning spell did cross my mind. I dismiss it because Aspen would have felt the magic. When we get back Lucas has two sets of the pictures printed out that I sent him. He gave one copy of each to Demitri and put the other copies in the file for me. Dimitri wants an update as soon as we arrive. I update him on all the information we have. Including Aspen being able to sense the spells, the horrible scenes of the sacrifices, the two possible hit locations and that the next hit is tomorrow. As well as the fact that the sacrifice scenes were spelled to be frozen in time and no cleanup crew was dispatched to the scenes. He gives me a key to what he calls his, tech room. As well as tells me that he might know someone that might have information on the symbols. We come up with a plan as well as a backup plan. Before ending the meeting.

After my meeting with Demitri I have dinner with Kaden, Grim, and my team. It is a nice relaxing dinner. My plate is filled with delicious beef, chicken, shrimp, and fried rice. Kaden did not seem as upset until I want to go to bed instead of staying up and watching a movie with him. He gets all grumpy and storms out of the room. With the long stressful day, I have had, I just need a hot shower and a comfy warm bed.

Demitri's POV
{Earlier that day}

Amara just walked out of my office leaving me shocked stupid. There is a good chance that she let her memories be taken. A chance that she wanted to forget me and her whole life. I did not know how to let that sink in. That thought breaks my heart. Especially since I had started to push her away a few weeks before her memories were taken, and then she disappeared. So, I did not blame her for feeling that way. Part of me wants to send her off to let her live the life she has been living the last six years, she seems happy. My selfish side wants me to find a way to bring her memories back and show her what she really means to me. Then my protective side knows she needs to be at her full strength for her safety. From the sound of that letter, it was not just Mel plotting against her. The question is how many others? It is time all of this gets brought out into the open before something bad happens.

"Hey Brother, its time you come home at least for a little bit.", I communicate to my twin Harper, or Hypnos God of Sleep when he answers my call. He is also known as the Sandman in some cultures.

"Already ahead of you brother. Finishing up a few things and then heading that way. Might take a couple of days.", Harper assures me then pauses. "How is she?"

"Good and stubborn as ever. See you then. Love you.", I state.

"See you then. Love you too.", Harper replies.

Harper is the only other being that was close to Makaria beside myself,

Lucas, and Sylvia. Mel and Zack were the popular ones. Where Amara lived in her own world. She loved to read and train. Him asking about Makaria proves he is the writer of the letter. Or should I say typed the letter. He might also have some information on those symbols. They look faintly familiar. Hopefully, Harper at least has some insight as to what the hell Mel has planned. I bury myself in work to push out the thoughts and emotions swirling within me.

Amara's POV

We are all up at the crack of dawn the next morning gearing-up. We are going to split back up into two teams to cover both locations. Demitri is sending three demons with each of our groups for extra muscle. I cannot believe all the tactical gear, weapons, and tech he has. I have my boot knife and my 8" knife already on me, so I grab a Glock 19 and one of Demitri's bad ass Viking swords.

Kaden, Willa, and Ace were getting dropped off at location one. While Malan, Aspen, and I are getting dropped off at location two. We were not there long before a Lamia comes out of the nearby woods. She has long black hair with her top half of a human and bottom half of a green and yellow snake. I have always wanted to see a Lamia in the flesh. Her eyes were just starting to gloss and cloud over. Meaning we only have a few minutes. I rush into the woods. Getting stopped by two more Lamias. One's bottom half is a black snake with auburn hair on her human head. The other one has dirty blonde hair on her human head and a red colored snake bottom half. Two of the three demons jump in to fight them off. Giving me a window to get through. I do not waste the opportunity as I race through the woods. Coming to a complete stop as my heart hits my stomach like a gut punch. Laying on the ground in front of me is Sean's, Dean's, and Elijah's motionless bodies.

Their bodies are position to where their feet are above their heads. Their wrist and throats are sliced open. Trenches were dug from their wrists and necks causing their blood to pool below their heads. Just like the other three sacrifice scenes. Silent tears stream out my eyes as I take in what is happening in front of me. With my body being locked in place. I focus my hearing on their heartbeats but there is none. That realization hit hard enough to almost knock me to my knees. Standing over Elijah is who Demitri said is my sister Mel, Connor is standing over his Dad Sean, and Balthazar is standing over Dean. All three chanting in sync.

"Who the fuck is that demon bitch?", Mel hisses out to the other two breaking me from my trance.

Hearing her calling me a demon snaps me out of it. How can she not recognize her own sister? Then I remember the bracelet Dimitri had given me still on my left wrist. Her not seeing me but a red-haired demon means that she has ill will against me. Balthazar is the closest to me, so I lunge for him first. He slashes at me as I punch him hard in the face. Hearing the crunch of his nose breaking is not as satisfying as I thought it would be. So, I land a few more punches before the other two began circling us waiting on an opening. Mel is brave enough to come at me first. I hit Balthazar hard enough to send him tumbling back and then swung at Mel as hard as I can. Knocking her to the ground. I kick Connor in the chest as he comes at me next. I pull out my sword as they get up and start enclosing in on me all at once. Balthazar and Mel are slashing at me with their ritual knives. Connor goes for my throat but gets tackled by Aspen. They are fighting on the ground while I dodge the slashes from the other two. Mel knocks my sword out of my hands in the process. Landing punches and kicks when I can I send Mel to the ground again with one of my kicks.

Balthazar takes the opportunity to charge at me going for my heart. Sidestepping to the left just enough I cause him to miss. I slam my knee into his stomach knocking the knife out of his hand. Then taking his head I slam it into the same knee a couple of times. Tossing him aside like trash he hits the ground hard. I do not stop there. All I can see is red, all I can feel is the pain of my heart shattering. There is an echo of a want for death that I have not felt before. Whispering for me to continue, to send his soul to the Underworld. Kneeling by him I lift him up by his shirt and then start punching him repeatedly. I cannot feel any of my hits connecting so I hit harder each time I connect with his face. Until someone pulls me off and pins my bloody hands between us as they hold onto me tightly from behind. The comfort that is radiating from them flows through me. Calming me enough to where I can gain control. Demitri spins me around once he notices I have calm down a little.

He hugs me tightly as he assures me, "It's okay I got you."

After getting my sobs under control. I look around for Connor and Mel, but they have disappeared. I push away from Demitri to kneel between Sean and Dean. Two demons are taking the now bound Balthazar to be transported, he looks savagely beaten and bloody. Three of the demons are coming this way each with a body bag with Malan in front of them. He was making sure the three Lamias were captured and secured. Demitri motion for them to not come any closer. I start to walk towards Aspen where she is kneeling by Elijah.

"Elijah is . . ." I start to say to Aspen as I feel a knife slicing through my vocal cords cutting off my sentence.

Blood streams down my neck and over the hand holding the knife. A loud growl is heard behind Demitri as Kaden, Willa, and Ace come running up with their guns aimed at Mel's head.

"Now, now you wouldn't want me to slit the arteries in your little friend's neck, would we?", she questions them. Daring them to take another step closer. "So Demitri this red-haired demon is your new plaything.", Mel sneers as Kaden lets out a snarl. "Here I thought you cared about me.", she mutters angrily with a frown pressing the knife deeper into my throat. Causing the healing wound to reopen and blood to trickle out.

"Let her go or I swear I'll rip your head off.", Demitri demands. His deep voice booming through the woods.

Just as she is opening her mouth to say something snarky. Aspen uses the arm holding the knife against my neck and flips her onto her back with a swift movement of her hip. Then pulls out her sword and slams it down into Mel. Just as it slides through Mel's chest, she turns into mist. Disappearing she then reappears behind Aspen slitting her throat open. Before turning back into mist and disappearing for the last time. I grab Aspen as she falls to her knees. Pressing both hands as hard as I can on her neck while tears are streaming out of my eyes causing my vision to blur. I try healing her, but my healing powers are not strong enough. Aspen's Life force must already be slipping away.

"Stay with me Aspen! Stay with! Shit, shit, Aspen no, no!", I sob out as she takes her last breath in my arms and her blood gushes out around my hands. Her eyes remain open even after the light has faded out. I let out an earth-shattering scream shaking the trees around us. Causing birds to fly off and animals to run in the opposite direction as fast as they can. The world around me starts to fade into nothing as the pain intensifies. Spreading through every muscle in my body. All I can see is Aspen lifeless eyes looking up at me.

Demitri's POV

I run with every ounce of speed I can muster towards Mel. Barely missing that bitches throat as she materializes into mist and disappears again. I am going to rip her head off with my bare hands the next time I see her. Amara catches her friend as she slumps to the ground pressing her hands against Aspen's neck with as much pressure as she can. I can tell Amara is trying to heal her. Aspen's life force has already started to leave its body. Which means she will not be able to heal her. I look towards my friend Lucas who has fallen to his knees. He was starting to fall hard for Aspen.

As Aspen takes her last breath, Amara let out a scream that is shaking the trees around us. Birds fly and animals run off as quickly as they can at the sound. It instantly shatters my heart and I start to sprint towards her as tears start to blur my vision. Tears I am trying to suppress. I stop inches away when Amara starts glowing like a goddess when they are in their true form. Her eyes are a solid blazing vibrant violet. I have never seen her like this, but there is no mistaking who she is. She is Makaria in her true form. There are no words describing how gorgeously divine she is!

"I am the Goddess of Blessed Death, Princess of the Underworld, you will heed my command and awaken!", Makaria commands as she places her hand on Aspen still heart.

Being the God of Death one of my abilities is the sight of ghost. Which gives me the ability to see Aspen's soul leave and return to her body. Aspen gasps for air as her eyes open quickly. Amara brings Aspen back to life quicker than I have ever been able to bring anyone back. She instantly becomes enchanted by Makaria's true form as does everyone else. Just as fast as Aspen's eyes open, Amara slumps to the ground unconscious. I rush to her with Kaden and Lucas on my heels.

"Don't fucking touch her.", Kaden barks at me as I bend down to pick her up. Pushing his way around me he picks her up and walks off with her in his arms. Having him around is a lot harder than I thought it was going to be.

CHAPTER 5: ACCEPTANCE

Amara's POV

"If it were not for you, she wouldn't be like this! How could you have invited her to stay here knowing she was in danger from her own fucking sister. A sister who is a goddess.", Kaden hisses.

"If I would have known that before I invited her, I wouldn't have. When I found out she had already been staying here. She chose to stay. When are you going to learn she will make her own decisions and trying to force her to do what you want does not work with her.", Demitri says as his voice echoes down the hall.

"Would you two shut up already. I'm trying to sleep.", I groan pulling the blanket over my eyes to block the sunlight. Shit my head is pounding so hard and my whole body is aching worse than the flu. Both rush to my side.

"How are you feeling?", Kaden asks as Demitri stands back a bit. "Is there anything you need?"

"Darkness with some peace and quiet. I feel like I have been hit by a train.", I reply as I try to stand up. As I start to fall, they both catch me and set me back on the bed.

"Take it easy Amara you have been out for two going on three days.", Kaden adds with worry in his voice.

"Wait what, two days, how the hell have I been out for two days?", I mumble trying to figure out what I remember last. "Aspen is she really dead?", I weakly ask as all the events from that day come rushing back.

"She is fine. Amara you brought her back to life. There is no denying that you are Makaria I saw your true form. Which is beyond amazing. Plus, you said I am Makaria Goddess of Blessed Death, Princess of the Underworld heed my command and awaken as you placed your hand on Aspen's heart bringing her back from the dead. Before falling to the ground unconscious.", he informs me. "You have been unconscious ever since."

"What about Elijah?", I question. "He has a vampire side that he had a witch make dormant until his mortal death."

"He is fine, it did take us by surprise and a couple of demon nurses got hurt but once he was given blood. He was able to gain control. After you eat something, you can see whoever you want.", Demitri announces speaking for the first time.

I nod too weak to push the fact that he is being bossy. He leaves the room then comes back with a demon pushing a cart with a bunch of food on it. I eat two cheeseburgers, a bunch of fries and drink two glasses of water before having to pee. I try to stand up for a second time. Both guys catch me again as I start to fall. They were about to sit me on the bed when I tell them, I have to pee. They help me steady myself then Kaden helps me walk to the bathroom. Demitri turns walking out the door. I am back sitting on the bed as Aspen, Malan, Elijah, and Grim comes in. Aspen and I both cry like babies as we hold each other for a little bit. She keeps thanking me. I tell her she does not have to thank me. I love her and would do anything for her. Malan chastises me for once again pushing myself to hard before hugging me. Grim did not leave my side the rest of the day. Elijah thanks me and I try talking to him about their plan to take back The Company. He just shuts it down and would tell me to save it for tomorrow. After we all chat for a while Elijah, Aspen, and Malan leaves so Willa, Ace, Sylvia, and Lucas can come in. I hug and talk to all of them for a little bit. No one is letting me talk about the assignment or anything that has happened. Once I start to get tired, they leave.

"Can I talk to you alone for a minute Amara? Then I will leave you to rest. I can tell you are getting tired.", Demitri asks.

"Kaden, Grim will you please give us a couple of minutes?", I question. I can tell he is not happy about it, but Kaden walks out and shuts the door without a fight. Grim does not move but I am too weak to fight him on it.

"I'm so glad you are okay. We underestimated Mel and you almost got severely hurt. Your Mom and Dad are on their way. After spending the day with them tomorrow, they want you to go back to your life with Kaden, and Grim of course. Let your Dad and I deal with Mel. She is no match for you at your full potential but at your present weakened state you are no match for her.", he speaks as he tries to hide his pain.

"I will spend some time with them. Honestly, I would like to meet them. But I am going to stay here and face whatever happens. I was not seriously hurt I just exhausted my energy level.", I state. "I had a flash of a memory when I first woke up. When Kaden and you were arguing in the hall. At first, I thought it was a dream, but I know now it was not", I disclose as I paused for a minute. "It was the first day I met you and Hypnos. I have known who I am since I woke up a little bit ago. I do not have any other memories surfacing. But soon I will have all of my memories as well as my strength and all my abilities back. Whatever happened started to unlock something in me."

Not knowing what to say he wraps those strong arms around me. I snuggle into the hug while laying my head on his chest. His sent fills my nose as the sparks spread through my body. I lean back enough to see his eyes. When he looks down our lips are just inches apart. Both of our breaths get stuck in our lungs at the closeness. Just when I think he is going to kiss me. Demitri places a loving kiss on my forehead then walks out of the room. Kaden walks in without saying a word, climbs in beside me cuddling me as I drift off to sleep.

Only to get woken up by nightmares throughout the night. Kaden nor Grim are in the room when I finally wake up for good. The sun is shining through the window meaning it must be mid-morning or early afternoon. As I am following the laughter Ace stops me to tell me I should be resting. I inform him I am starving and start to head towards the kitchen.

I hear a woman say, "Makaria!" As three people rush to hug me as I turn around.

"Hi", I breathe out.

"Amara this is your Mom Persephone, your brother Zagreus he goes by Zack, and your Dad Hades.", Demitri states as they set me down.

"Nice to meet you all.", I greet them not knowing what else to say. It seems too crazy to be real. My Mom and Dad are not just a goddess and god. But the Queen and King of the Underworld.

"I'm so sorry Baby girl.", my Mom says as she strokes my cheek. I am going to have to get use to calling her that. "Mel will be punished for this."

"I have set out some food in the kitchen if you guys would like to continue this reunion in there. I'm sure Amara is hungry.", Demitri conveys as he directs us toward the kitchen.

"Yes, I'm starving.", I respond following him. Pausing before I enter the kitchen, I ask Demitri, "Where is everyone?"

"I let them know your family is coming, they just want to give you time to meet them. Kaden said he has Grim and that they are just a text away.", Demitri responds before walking off and letting me have time with my family.

My Mom, Persephone's beauty is so alluring. She has a youthful and curvy look with long medium brown hair with beautiful green eyes that are speckled with brown. My Dad, Hades has pitched black hair and a beard with just as dark of eyes. He is almost as tall as Demitri. My younger brother Zack looks a lot like me. He is about 6'2" with pale skin, shaggy curly raven black hair with blue eyes that have white slits in the middle and the same heart shaped face as me.

We spent most of the day in the kitchen getting to know each other. They ask about my life, job, and my boyfriend. They want to meet everyone. Hades especially wants to meet Kaden. So, I text Kaden telling him to come meet my family and to bring Grim. While Zack and Hades talk to Kaden. Persephone is cuddling Grim and talking to me. After a little while I text the rest of my team so they can meet my family too. Everyone seems to be getting along. Zack is hitting on Willa until Ace walks up and wraps his arm around her. He apologizes, then comes over to talk to me. I cannot help but laugh. Zack and I decide to go on a little walk outside. We both talk like long lost friends. Nixie has her nose in her phone. Not watching where she is going, she runs right into Zack. The way they are stammering around for words I can tell they like each other. I excuse myself as I walk back to the kitchen. Being lost in thought I did not notice when Aspen started heading my way. Saying she needs to talk to me alone, she pulls me into the closest room. It is a game room with a grey couch on one side of the room, a pool table, rocket hockey and foosball tables. As well as a fully loaded bar and an eighty-inch flat screen tv with black leather reclining theater seats on the other side. I am sure there are surround sound speakers throughout the room as well. Half the room is painted apricot orange, and the other half is white. Giving it a happy vibe without there being excessive amount of the orange color.

"Alright Aspen, what's up?", I question.

"Yesterday when I was hugging you. I felt a powerful dark sensation. At first, I was not sure where it was coming from. It did not take me long to figure out that it is coming from your necklace. I want to try to siphon out the curse. Curses feel different than other spells. They feel darker and this feels dark, old, and powerful. It feels stronger than sacrificial magic.", she discloses.

I rub my finger on my necklace dumbfounded. How could the answers to getting back my memories be right under my nose this whole time? I take the necklace off handing it to Aspen. She tries four times but is not able to siphon the curse out.

"It's too strong. Maybe killing the caster will fix it.", she implies with a smirk as she hands me back my necklace.

"Sacrificial spells are set with the sacrifice, and we have no clue if it's the same for an even stronger spell. One thing I do know is every curse can be broken. Figuring out how to break it can feel impossible though. We should head back to everyone. But first I want us to find Demitri. Thank you for figuring it out and trying to fix it. You really are a great Sister. I don't know what I would do without you.", I declare to Aspen as I hug her.

"I haven't completely figured it out. But it is the least I can do after you saved my life.", she discloses.

Demitri is of course in his office, he is almost always working. I walk in asking, "Can we have a minute?"

"Of course, I can always make time for two pretty ladies.", Demitri playfully responds.

"Aspen has figured out that my necklace is what's enchanted with the curse. But cannot siphon it.", I inform him.

"Lucas send Sammy in.", Demitri commands through the intercom as he walks up to me. "Can I see the necklace?", he questions me. I hand him the necklace without a word. "I gave you this necklace when we were younger. I picked this charm because you are the sun in my world of darkness.", he confesses. "When I gave it to you the center was empty."

The necklace has a silver chain with a golden yellow sun with the center is holding a light blue stone. The sun has two different sizes of rays coming out of it. The long rays are squiggly, and the shorter ones are straight. Dimitri lays it on the desk when Sammy comes in, she is a blue haired demon.

"Sammy was a powerful witch before becoming a demon. This is Aspen and Amara.", Dimitri introduces us to each other. Handing Sammy, the necklace while filling her in on what we knew.

"This necklace doesn't contain the curse, the stone in the charm does. The curse has siphoned almost all her goddess essence and memories trapping them in this charm. With each passing day it will trap more of her essence until she is completely human. The stone is also laced with a strong cloaking spell strong enough to even change her sent and hide her from any kind of tracking spells.", Sammy divulges as she examines it.

"Holy Hell, so how do we break the curse?", Aspen asks.

"I have no clue this is Ancient Norse magic and the stone if I am correct is from Asgard. But that is just a guess. I do know for certain that it is not from Earth.", Sammy explains still staring at my necklace in awe.

"Lucas, I need you to get Hades now.", Demitri orders through the intercom. "Sammy and Aspen, you are dismissed."

Within minutes Hades or my Dad is in Demitri's office. Where I find out that Hel who goes by Holle. Daughter of Loki, God of Mischief, and the Giantess Angrboda wants my crown. She might even be the mastermind behind all this. She has wanted to rule our Underworld after Asgard was burnt down. Which means Mel, Connor, and Balthazar are just pawns. Not to mention that while we are trying to stop a war between Sups and Humans from starting. A war between gods and goddesses is brewing in the shadows. I bring up how if she is after my crown and thinks that I am out of the picture. That means the three of them are still in danger. I suggest that they all go back to the Underworld where they will have protection. Of course, my Dad denotes he does not run from anything or anyone. But does think it is best to get my Mom back there. Dad also said that Zack is a man and needs to stay to fight. He even tries to talk me into going with them. Dimitri updates him on everything we have learned about the curse. Then I ask Demitri to put my necklace that contains the essence of my soul in a safe place before going back to the kitchen. My Dad shows up about twenty minutes later.

Once I am back in the kitchen, I suggest we go to the game room. I have Phoenix and Nixie show my Mom the way with Grim. While I fill my team and Zack in on everything. We all end up spending the rest of the day in here. We are even eating dinner in the game room. It seems something is blossoming between Nixie and Zack. This is nice. Everyone seems happy and relaxed. I excuse myself first, I am getting tired. I say good night to everyone then walk to my room with Grim holding my hand. My Dad pulls me to the side so he can beg me to please return with Kaden. Since I refuse to go to the Underworld with them. I assure him not to worry. Promising that I will be back to my old self soon. As well as that I have this and to trust me. He agrees reluctantly and tells me that they will be leaving first thing in the morning. That he has business to attend to in the Underworld before he can come back. But he will be back as soon as he can. Then kisses me on the forehead and lets me go to bed. I go to sleep that night feeling happy and genuinely loved! I have never thought that I actually had people from my past that sincerely cared about me.

Kaden's POV

Amara has been having nightmares night after night for almost a week. Last night however was peaceful. Thanks to Demitri's brother. Since Amara's nightmares are gone, I will be able to get a decent amount of sleep tonight. I think to myself as I walk to the gym. To let out some steam while we wait for Balthazar's ghost to run to Mel. I cannot shake the feeling I am going to lose Amara to Demitri. I punch the bag and exercise for a couple of hours before going to my room for a shower. Amara is sitting on my bed. She did not say a word just walks over to me and starts kissing me with so much desire. I let my hands explore her body as hers explores mine. Stripping off each other's close she then starts kissing me again as she strokes my cock. Amara kneels to where she can put me in her mouth. She sucks on my dick for a little bit before pushing me on the bed. She positions herself over me before slamming down on my rock-hard dick over and over. I flip us over to where I am on top kissing anywhere, I can reach. As I start to get close, I start sliding in and out harder and faster. This is the best sex we have ever had, and I have no clue why. I look into her eyes right before I am about to cum. Amara materializes into Mel. I stop thrusting not sure of what is happening.

"Don't stop, it feels so good.", Mel purrs as she is rotating her hips beneath me. "I have wanted you inside me since I saw you that day in the woods. I knew this would be the easiest way. Come on you were getting me so close.", She confesses between moaning and nipping my ear.

God, she feels so good I cannot help myself. I start slamming into her again until she meets her release. She holds on to me tightly with her legs not letting me pull out. I cum inside her as I choke her with force. She is like a drug I cannot get enough of. Every touch makes me horny all over again. I fuck her three or four more times as herself, cuming in her every time. Then passing out butt naked right after. When I wake up from a little nap she was gone. I set up and run my fingers through my hair. I wonder if Amara is asleep. At the thought of Amara, I am hit with a wave of guilt. What the fuck did I just do!

Ace runs into my room with a panicked look on his face. "Something is wrong with Amara.", he informs me.

I race to her room after putting some clothes on. Where she is laying on the floor unresponsive and cold. I pick her up placing her on the bed smoothing the hair out of her eyes. "Please be okay.", I beg in a whisper. Lucas brings Sylvia in to check her out.

"She is under some type of sleeping potion or spell. She will be fine when she wakes up. If I knew what kind of spell or potion it is, I can most likely counteract it waking her up sooner.", Sylvia informs us. "There is no telling how long it will knock her out for."

"This Bitch might know.", Demitri says as he drags Mel in by her arm. Demitri has anger radiating off him. By the death glare he is giving me, I can tell he knows I slept with Mel. Great now he can use that to break us up and try to take my place at Amara's side.

"I don't know what was in that vile, why don't you ask Mr. Pretty Boy.", she sneers as she points and winks at me.

"How the hell am I supposed to know.", I question her.

"Kaden, It's the sleeping potion we made for Demitri the first time we came here.", Malan replies picking up the vile from the ground not too far from where Amara was at before I put her on the bed.

Amara's POV
{Two nights before}

I get woken up for the sixth time tonight by my own screaming. Every time I close my eyes I am being dragged into another nightmare. This time I must have woken up the others because they all are piling into my room to check on me. After reassuring them I am fine and to go back to bed, I walk down to the kitchen to bake something. Since I am obviously not going to get any sleep tonight. This is night two of these nasty nightmares all ending with me about to die in every horrible way imaginable. The two days before that were the same dream over and over. Or should I say same day. It starts with me running up on Dean's, Sean's, and Elijah's lifeless bodies to the part where Mel slices my vocal cords and Aspen's throat. Then repeats itself over and over every night until the nightmares of my death started. I guess that is what I get for pissing off the Goddess of Nightmares and Madness. Even though in reality I did not do anything wrong. She is just a jealous psycho.

"Can't sleep either?", Demitri asks as he walks in the kitchen.

"Nope, are you having nightmares as well?", I question. He nods in response running his hands through his hair. "What did you do? Fuck and then dump her?", I comment without thinking. I look up from mixing the ingredients for a chocolate cheesecake when he did not say anything. "O shit Demitri you little slut. Sleeping with your dead loves sister.", I tease. I have hit the nail on the head by the look on his face. "I just got the most brilliant plan", I interrupt him stammering over his words trying to explain and apologize at the same time.

I go over my plan with him. Deciding to fill my team in on it when they wake up in the morning. I inform him that I will need Haemorrhois venom, the Spear of Destiny, and how my plan will require me to break the promise I made to him. After I finish explaining my plan, Demitri stays to bake with me the rest of the night as we get to know each other. By the time the sun comes up we have a chocolate cheesecake, a regular cheesecake topped with strawberries, brownies, and two dozen chocolate chip cookies made.

"Go get some rest. The housekeepers will clean up the mess.", Demitri remarks as I start to clean up and wash the dishes. "Sweet dreams Amara.", he calls as I walk out the kitchen with a nod of my head as my response.

"Sweet dreams.", I call back.

I did not want to sleep alone, and I cannot go slip into Demitri's bed like part of me wants. That would not be right to do to Kaden. So, I go climb in bed with Aspen. Kaden and Grim had been up and down with me most of the night already so I want to let them get some sleep. Once everyone is awake and gathered, I share my plan on how to end this bullshit and get The Company back. No telling the havoc they have caused already.

"Amara, Demitri wants to see you in his office.", Lucas tells me as he strolls in on the end of our meeting.

As soon as I walk into his office I am snatched up and hugged tightly. At first, I thought it was Demitri but once I get a better look, I know it is his twin Harper. He is 6"4', same honey brown eyes, muscular and looks like a sex god just like Demitri. The only difference is that Harper does not have any fascial hair and his deep brown hair is in a medium fade cut.

"Gods, I missed you Beautiful.", he chides me before placing a peck on my cheek then sets me down. "I know you don't remember me yet. I just could not help myself. O and I can help you two with your little nightmare problem. Demitri told me all about it."

"Amara this is my brother Harper and the writer of your letter.", he informs me. Thanks, and Amara has a plan to deal with Mel.", Demitri confidently informs Harper. "You can however fill Amara here in on everything you just told me.

I am still stunned by this sexy Demitri look a like's display of affection.

Harper places his hands on mine and Demitri's forehead then chants something under his breath before removing his hands telling me, "You came to me a few months before you lost your memories. Telling me that Mel has plans to lay a powerful curse on you and then kill you while you are weak. You were under the suspicion that Mel had teamed up with someone powerful. There is no way Mel had the power by herself to pull this off. You informed me that you had a plan of your own. You were going to confront Mel and make a deal to willingly let her lay the curse on you. That you would leave and never return instead of you killing her right then. She would have had no choice but to agree. You had me put together that file in case she went back on her deal or formed another plan that will harm someone you love. Unfortunately, Mel worked faster than we thought, and we were not able to find out whom she is working. Well, she has a new plan or whoever she is working with does. Maybe you were just the beginning of the plan. I am not quite sure what it is. All I do know is it's going to be bad!"

"I realized their plan when I saw all three council members lifeless bodies at my feet. Also, how it was done in the open and then left for everyone to see. They are taking over the council to use The Company to start a war between Sups and Humans. They do not know that Elijah is still alive. As well as the fact that once my suspension is up, I can claim beneficiary of Dean's seat. Which leaves Connor with only one seat. Let's let them get a little more comfortable and we will start my plan tomorrow.", I disclose.

"What I don't understand is why you quit researching into who Mel had been working for?", Demitri question his brother angrily as he pinches the bridge of his nose. "Or why you did not tell me that she is alive, and Mel was behind it."

"I was trying to keep you and Amara safe. While giving her some freedom to make her own choice about her life. She never was given that. Plus, she made me promise to not tell anyone. Especially you.", Harper discloses. "Not to mention I wasn't sure if you would believe me. Seeing how you and Mel were getting close."

"I also showed Harper those symbols. They looked familiar but I could not place them. They are Norse Symbols this is some old dark ass magic they are messing with. So, we are right to have the suspicion that Holle is running the show.", Demitri adds turning his attention on to me. Not saying another word about it to his brother.

"Just because its Norse Magic does not mean its Holle.", Harper states.

"No but the Asgardian stone in Amara's necklace plus the Norse Symbols point in her direction.", Demitri notes. "This wouldn't be the first time she has gone after the Underworld's Crown."

"Can I see the stone?", Harper requests. Demitri lays a picture of my necklace with the stone in the middle of it in front of him. "Fuck. Holle is back around, great. She is far more vicious than Mel as well as more powerful.", Harper notes.

"Holle definitely fits. How else would Mel have access to Norse magic? Not to mention a war between Sups and humans would be a good distraction to use while trying to conquer the Underworld.", I add. "We will figure that all out when we get to it. Right now, we need to focus on Mel, Connor, and Balthazar. Since there is nothing else do today let's go swimming. I haven't had a chance to check out the pool and hot tub of yours.", I encourage them to come. I did not give them the chance to answer as I walk out the door towards the indoor pool. My team is already there waiting on me along with Sylvia, Zack, Lucas, Elijah, Wolf Boy, the Forest Troll, the kelpie twins and the three Lamias. Demitri sure did have a full house. I had not realized it before now with how big the castle is.

"Come on Demitri.", Harper says as he tries to persuade him while trying to shove his brother out of the office.

"You want me to die of a heart attack?", Demitri whines.

"Don't act like you haven't seen her in a bathing suit a hundred times before.", Harper replies.

"No, I haven't. Not since we lost her for six years and I realize having her as just a friend is not enough. Not to mention the fact that she is already taken.", Demitri declares sadly to his brother.

"O shit dude you finally admitted you have feelings for her. Damn took you long enough. Well, you are still going swimming. Even if I have to drag you into the water. You are all work and no play.", Harper adds.

I am not that far from his office, so I hear the whole conversation between them. I cannot help the smile that instantly spreads across my cheeks. As I walk down to the pool. I strip off my clothes with my bathing suit underneath. I had planned to take a swim this morning but have not been able to get the chance until now. The brothers walk in play fighting. They both stop as their jaws fall open at the same time. Demitri is looking me up and down meeting my eyes last. I am wearing my black halter top bikini. Harper on the other hand stops upon seeing someone else.

"Demitri who is that over there talking to Amara.", Harper asks.

"That's Phoenix, she is one of the kelpies I was telling you about. I knew you would like her.", Demitri informs his brother.

Nixie is blonde-haired with blue eyes in her human form, her other form is a white kelpie. She is sweet, bubbly, and can be a little oblivious at times. Phoenix on the other hand has a great sense of humor, is down to earth but is not very trusting. Her kelpie form is black and her human form she has black hair with dark green eyes. These twins are rare. There have been only one other set of twin kelpies. Which were the very first two of their kind. The very first ones were a male and a female. The Female one is the only white kelpie heard of until Nixie. Turns out Wolf boy, whose name is Jax is next in line for becoming the Alpha of his pack. The troll's name is Aloe. Tiffany, April, and Winter are the names of the Lamias, which they mostly sunbathed. The best thing about this indoor pool is it has an enormous skylight. We play chicken, which Kaden and I are winning against Nixie and Zack. Then we swim and chill in the hot tub until around midnight. Grim sits on the side of the pool the whole time with Aloe. Harper and Phoenix did not leave each other's side until we all go to bed. Neither did Zach and Nixie. Demitri looks damn good with his shirt off, I shake that thought and image out of my head while I continue to stroll to my room. I take a hot shower then crawl into bed next to Grim once I reach it.

The next morning after breakfast I walk down to the dungeon with Kaden by my side to where Balthazar is being contained. Demitri protested that he comes along as well. Since we need Balthazar to think he has a chance to get me Demitri needs to stay back. Kaden cannot help but smile as I explain to Demitri why he cannot come. If Demitri did not agree I know no one would have been able to stop him from coming with. I began my plan by interrogating Balthazar. Trying to get what information I can out of him. I start by punching him hard or slicing him when he would not answer. Thanks to Demitri's camera we know Balthazar had been making a shank. So, we give him time to finish making it as well as give Connor and Mel time to get comfortable in thinking that all the council members are dead. Before initiating my plan, we wanted Mel and Connor to have the impression that they have all the control of The Company. I turn my back to Balthazar letting him think he has a chance to get one over on me just like I planned. Or the demon that ruined his plan that he does not know is me turns her back to him. As he sees it. Allowing him enough time to strike.

"Die you Demon Bitch.", he hisses as he lunges at me.

I sidestep causing him to miss me then hit the ground instead. As he is getting up to attack again, I turn around taking off the bracelet. He gasps in shock when he realizes that the "Demon Bitch" is me.

"You little Cunt.", are the last words he utters. As he lunges at me, I effortlessly twist his neck snapping it. Then letting him sink to the floor lifeless.

"A life owed for a life saved.", I chant like I have done it before. "Now we just wait for the bastard to run to Mel to tell her who the red haired-demon really is. I am going to take Grim bowling while we wait for her. Good thing she is also the Goddess of Ghost.", I mention to Kaden as I step over Balthazar lifeless body to go get Grim. One debt paid one to go.

"I'll meet up with you later. I'm going to go to the gym for a bit.", Kaden tells me as he pulls me in for a loving kiss.

It gets a little heated before I pull away to go find Grim. Aspen, Willa, Grim and I bowl against Lucas, Malan, Phoenix, and Ace for a few hours. We start to get bored bowling, so we decide to go swimming. We are trying to find things to do while waiting on Mel to show up dramatically to raise hell. I am ready for her. However, I was not expecting to have Connor sitting on my bed with a bottle of Sleeping potion. When I walk into my room dripping wet with a towel around me. It is the potion we made for Demitri as a backup plan to get the Ring of Gyges from him.

"What the hell did you do to Kaden?", I question knowing he was the one that had the potion and would not just willingly give it up. "Drink this and Mel won't slit his throat. Like she did Aspen's. Do you really want to push your luck even more with the fates? I'm really surprise they haven't come after you already.", he arrogantly says. "I still don't get why you would save a useless energy vamp, but you refused to save my mom."

"Fuck You!", I state before I take the stupid vile out of his hand downing all of it. I slump to the floor within minutes.

Demitri's POV

It has been a long day, with Balthazar dead that means Amara has one more life to trade and only has two days left to do it. I have to say it is a damn good plan. I am sitting on my bed trying to watch a movie, still not being able to get the picture of Amara in her bathing suit out of my head. God, it makes my dick hard just thinking about it. Amara walks in with tears in her eyes without even knocking. I pull the comforter up enough to cover my hard on.

"What's wrong?", I question. I want to get up to embrace her. I also do not want her to know how hard I am.

"Kaden and I got into a huge fight. Can I hang out with you I don't want to be alone?", she innocently asks.

"Sure.", I say as I start scooting over to give her room. I must make myself swallow the saliva building in my mouth. She is only in her bathing suit. As she slides under the covers her hand touches my bare leg since I am only in my boxer briefs. I jump out of bed forgetting about my friend standing at attention only cover by a thin layer of fabric. "I'm going to go get us some snacks.", I mumble. While I fight the desire growing with every second as she sits half naked and wet on my bed.

"Was it my touch that got you so hard?", she purrs.

Never seeing this side of her I am barely able to resist it. But I respect her if we are going to have sex then her and Kaden are going to be completely done. She is going to be all mine. There is no way Amara could ever be a one-night stand. Also, I do not want her to regret it the next morning. I did not know how to respond so I just stood there like an idiot.

"Come here.", she half wines half purrs seductively rubbing the spot next to her. "I won't bite unless you want me to."

She had me since she walked in still wet from the pool with all most nothing on. I did not even question what made her change her mind. I just go sit next to her. She starts rubbing my thigh working her way slowly up to my rock-hard cock. She grabs my dick and I grab her hand.

"Amara we shouldn't do this. I don't want you to regret it later.", it takes everything for me to say those words. I wanted. No, I need her right now. Not saying a word, she kisses me with such passion. All my resolve fades away as she strokes my dick. She leans me back as she deepens the kiss. Not being able to stand not being inside her any longer, I flip her over ripping off her bathing suit. My dick hardens even more. As I take in her sexy naked body. If that is even possible from all my blood that has already rushed to my dick. I think before I start to kneel to taste her as I step out of my boxer briefs.

"Dimitri, I need you in me.", she begs in a secuctive voice before I can taste her.

I position myself over her looking into her eyes to make sure she has no doubts about this. Then I slowly slide in and out letting her adjust to my size as I moan in pleasure.

"Harder.", she moans.

I start slamming into her bringing myself so close to the edge. As my gorgeous Amara materialize into Mel.

"What the fuck Mel!", I yell as I pull out then jump off her and the bed. "Pulling a page out of your father's book I see."

"Nice trick she pulled with the bracelet and that's a low blow with the Daddy comment. Come back over here so we can finish what we started.", Mel replies.

"The hell I will.", I growl back.

"The shifter didn't mind that I wasn't Amara. He even fucked me a few times as myself afterwards.", she confesses.

"What the fuck is wrong with you?", I question her wanting to rip her head off.

"You could have had me all to yourself and a seat at the council, but you just had to find Makaria. Guess I should have killed her after all.", Mel pouts.

"If you touch her, I swear I'll rip your head off with my bare hands.", I promise her.

"Demitri something is wrong with Amara!", Lucas says as he runs in taking in the scene of Mel and me both naked. He did not say a word just raised an eyebrow.

"It's not what you think. Lucas, grab Mel so I can put some clothes on.", I order as I grab a shirt and throw it at Mel. After I am dressed, I drag Mel by the arm to Amara's room following Lucas. I can feel the pain of my heart being ripped into pieces through my whole body, at the sight of Amara cold and almost lifeless on the bed. The shifter is sitting next to her. I can hardly stop myself from ripping his head off. Amara's heart is going to shatter when she finds out.

Amara's POV

I woke up with everyone standing around me and naked only wrapped in a towel. Demitri has Mel by the arm, and she is in just a t-shirt. Looks like we hit a little bump not expecting Connor. But my plan can still work. "Connor is somewhere in the castle someone needs to go find him.", I tell them. Demitri, Kaden, and Grim are the only ones that stayed. Ace castes a spell trapping Connor and Mel in the castle before going to help the others.

"Seeing how I can't go anywhere until he dies or lifts the spell, you can let go of my arm.", Mel sneers yanking her arm free as she goes to sit on the edge of the bed furthest from me.

I cannot figure out why Demitri is looking at Kaden like he is going to murder him. Mel gets a pissed off look when Kaden scooted closer wrapping one arm around me and holding my hand with his other hand.

"So, Makaria you want to know a juicy secret?", she questions getting up and walking over to me.

"Shut up Mel!", Demitri says in a threatening tone.

Kaden does not say a word but stiffens beside me as his hand tightens a little around mine.

Before I can answer she continues, "While you were having your little nap, I fucked both your men. Neither one minding when I showed them, I was not really you. In fact, pretty boy here came back for more a few times after knowing it was me.", Mel discloses as she massages Kaden's shoulder with one hand.

"Kaden?", I question wanting him to deny her words. When he did not say anything or even look up at me. I yell his name louder. He just shrugs her hand off his shoulder and stays silent while not meeting my eyes.

"I", he starts to say before his words are cut off by my fist connecting with his mouth.

My connection with his face had so much force it slung his head back hitting it against the headboard. Causing a crack to split down it. How could he do this to me! My hands start blazing with a blue fire as I am losing control of my anger. I jump off the bed lunging myself at Mel. I throw a right hook landing it on her eye and a left hook landing it on her nose. Leaving burn marks from my flaming fists. Her hands fly up around her nose instantly as blood runs out and down her lips. Not missing a beat, I then bring my knee up into her stomach as I push her down on it with my hands on her back. The force doubles her over knocking her to the ground by my bed. I roll her on her back, getting down on her I punch her repeatedly. Demitri starts to break us up, but I growl at him to back off. She flips me over landing a couple of hits before I flip her onto her back. Getting up I go for the Spear of Destiny that I have hidden under my pillow. Unaware of what is in my hand she lunges at me. I pull my hand out from under the pillow, spinning to face her as I embed the spear as deep as I can into her gut. She moves backwards to get away, only to hit the wall.

"Nice try. I can feel the Haemorrhois venom spreading through my body. But it will not kill me. Not for good anyways, I am a goddess.", she sneers as blood starts pouring out of every hole in her body, she slides down on her ass with her back against the wall. As she grabs the hilt of the spear and pulls it out.

"No, it won't but it's still painful as hell. O and I'm sure the Spear of Destiny can give you a true death.", I inform her as she looks down at the spear in her hand.

Shock fills her eyes as she realizes she is holding the Spear of Destiny and that she is dying. She howls in pain and is slowly dying when Zack brings Connor in. Zack rushes to her side grabbing her hand.

"I'm sorry it had to come to this Sis. But you brought this fate on yourself. If it had not been by Makaria's hands it would have been by Fathers. You cannot try to kill your family and you cannot start a war between the Sups and the humans. You had to be stopped.", he denotes sadly as he holds her hand and tears run down his face.

I kneel by her and hold her other hand as she takes her last and final breath. She is evil and did need to be stopped. That does not change the fact that she is also my little sister even if I did not remember her. With Mel dying no one is paying attention to Connor since he cannot escape out of the castle. He grabs a knife out of the back of his pants tucked behind his shirt. Then stabs Demitri as deep as he can embedding the blade in Demitri's kidney.

"Demitri!", I scream having to just watch it all happen unable to stop Connor.

A warmth spread through me as I start to glow bright like a star. I walk over to Connor, put my hand to his forehead and he slumps to the ground lifeless. I watch his soul leave his body as I chant, "A life owed for a life saved." A black smoke claw like hand comes up out of the ground grabbing Connor's spirit dragging it to the Underworld. Both debts have been paid now. I quit glowing while the room starts to go black. I stumble over to the bed before sitting down. It takes me a few minutes before I can shake it off and go pull the knife out of Demitri's back. Since I am the only one in the room that he will let touch him. I try to heal the wound. But it is useless, the wound will not heal, and it is turning the area around it black as it spreads. Lucas runs to get Sylvia. I almost lose consciousness again while trying to heal Demitri. I do not leave his side as I try to slow down the bleeding with pressure. The only thing I can do right now. I try to keep tears from escaping but I am slowly losing that battle.

"He is a god Amara it's not going to kill him.", Kaden tries to comfort me.

"Don't talk to me.", I sneer.

"Don't be like that we need to talk about it.", he pleads with me.

I did not say anything or even look at him. Just rolled my eyes and put as much pressure as I can on Demitri's wound.

"I don't think it needs that much pressure.", Dimitri winces.

"I'm sorry.", I apologize letting up on the pressure just a little.

"Amara just hear him out. He was tricked and having sex with a goddess or god is addicting to most mortals. Just as addicting as heroin.", Demitri states.

"I'm not talking about this with either of you right now.", I command as Sylvia walks in. How can he be on his side about this?

"There is poison spreading through his blood stream. Without knowing what kind of poison, I cannot treat it. Without treatment he will not die but it will take a long time for him to heal.", Sylvia discloses after looking the wound over. Black ooze mixed with his blood starts streaming out of the wound again. "Shit every time the wound tries to heal it rips back open. His body will have to work all the poison out before the wound can start to heal.", Sylvia adds.

"Could it be caused by a spell? I just siphoned a spell from this.", Aspen voices holding the knife Connor embedded in Demitri's back. She walks over placing her hand on Demitri. After a minute or so she falls to the floor glowing. Not like the glow of an aura like how goddesses and gods glow when in their true form. But like she is going to explode. It looks like this white light is beating against the walls of its prison trying to break through her skin from the inside.

"You have siphoned too much power you have to let it out. Or you will combust.", Demitri warns.

"Aspen did you store the air bending powers from when we had to capture that rogue Air Bender?", I hint to her.

She cannot talk but understanding what I am trying to tell her. She lifts her hand and shoots a big gush of wind out of her palm. It was so strong it blows a hole all the way through the wall. With an apologetic look she gets up, kneels back by Demitri, and siphons the rest of the spell out.

"Let Sylvia do it. You have used up enough of your energy.", Demitri demands as I go to heal his wound.

"I'm fine I got this.", I try to assure him.

"I saw you about to faint after using Death's Touch to kill Connor and then again when you tried to heal me.", he remarks.

Without another word I let Sylvia rub her magical ointment on him. Demitri is healed in about a half hour or so. Once Demitri is completely healed I go to my room and lock the door. Not wanting to be around anyone. I even tell Grim that I need some quiet time and to find something to do for a while. Ace informs me that he would keep him over night. There were several knocks at my door, but I did not answer a single one. I lay there crying my heart out. How could he do this to me? I get that at first, he was tricked. But he went back for more than seconds. Without a single thought about me crossing his slutty mind. My blood starts to boil and all I want to do is beat the shit out of him. I let myself cry until I cannot cry any more. Feeling the pain of my heart breaking through out my whole body. As well as the physical exhaustion from being so overwhelmed with emotions. After the tears stop, I make a promise to myself that I will not cry over this again. Then I get up, take a shower, and get dress in a black t-shirt with blue shorts. I look in the mirror telling myself that I am beautiful, I am strong, and I will get through this. Despite my red puffy swollen eyes. Throwing my hair in a ponytail I go for a run and yes, I go running barefooted. My blood is still boiling after my run, so I go to the gym. I am hitting and kicking the punching bag when Zack comes up behind it holding it in place. I continued to beat on it.

"Working out some aggression? You, I mean Makaria and I use to spar when one of us got like this. You want to give it a try?", Zack asks.

"Sure.", I reply.

We get into the boxing ring that Demitri has in the middle of his gym. He is surprisingly good. I am taking it easy on him until he gets a few good face hits in. So, I step it up a little. I did not want to hurt him. It would be awesome to have him on my team. We spar for a good while. Until I get lost in my head like I do sometimes. Muscle memory takes over when I do. This time my mind goes to dark thoughts about Mel and Kaden.

"Take it easy on him. He hasn't had the training you have had in the last six years as well as on top of the training you had before the memory loss.", Demitri voices.

I look down, I have Zack pin on his stomach with his arm bent back and my knee on his back. Blood coming out of his nose and several swollen spots. "Damn Zack I'm sorry.", I apologize while I heal him before letting him up.

"We are good I was just about to break free anyways.", he says with a wink. You have some bad ass moves Sis.", Zack proudly states.

"Want to spar against someone with more training.", Demitri questions as he gets into the ring.

"Enter at your own risk. I won't take it easy on you.", I tease him throwing the first punch. He blocks it effortlessly.

"Thought you weren't going to take it easy on me Princess.", Dimitri teases back. "Seriously Amara let it all out. I can take it.", he encourages me.

I can see it in his eyes that he is serious and that he is hurt that I am hurting. His words and action touch my heart, he knew what I needed. I let him have it. Putting all my strength into every hit. Releasing the anger and heart break along with it. He blocks every hit except for a few. When I land a right hook to his jaw, he flips me over. One of my legs is between his and the other leg is wrapped around his waist. My mind starts flooding with dirty thoughts of us. I can see the fire of lust in Demitri's eyes as well. We are looking deep into each other's eyes. Just before I kiss him, I flip us over to where I am on top of him. This position is not any better I think to myself. As the desire in Dimitri's eyes deepens. My clit rubbed on his dick when I flipped us over causing me to feel how hard he is. It is getting tougher and tougher to be around him without giving in to my desire.

"Well, you two didn't waste any time, did you?", Kaden hisses. "I thought you were better than that Amara."

"Chill man, Amara was just about to make Demitri submit. You ruined all the fun.", Zack informs Kaden as he walks out the room to avoid the drama. Patting Kaden on the back of the shoulder harder than necessary on his way out.

"I guess we were both wrong about each other.", I lie as I am helping Demitri up and then walking off.

"Hey man, we were just sparring. Amara is hurting bad right now. Give her a break. She is just going along with what you say to make you mad. Give her some time to calm down and she will come talk to you.", Demitri tries to reassure him.

"Just sparring huh?", Kaden voices as he nods towards Demitri's rock-hard bulge.

"Hey, I can't help that she has this effect on me. You of all people should understand that.", Demitri responds with a chuckle as he starts to walk off.

"I'm just supposed to believe you have my best interest in mind? The one coming in between us.", Kaden inquires.

"No, I don't have your best interest in mind. I have Amara's. Personally, I want you gone. Have from the second I met you. Your own actions are what is coming between you guys. Not me! Yes, I have made my feelings clear to her, but I have respected your relationship. She deserves better, you will never be good enough for her.", Demitri discloses.

"Ha and you are?", Kaden arrogantly responds.

"Never said I was.", Demitri adds before walking off.

I know I am not supposed to hear that conversation, but I cannot help the smile that is growing from knowing that I have that kind of effect on both of them. I go straight to my room and do not come back out. Finally, I let Grim, Willa, Sylvia, and Aspen in. After they continuously keep beating on the door one after another. We watch a mixture of scary and funny movies while eating a shit load of junk food. All of us ended up passing out on my bed.

CHAPTER 6: A BROKEN HEART & CURSE

Amara's POV

I wake up smashed in between Willa and Grim whose legs were laid over me on my left side. Aspen and Sylvia on my right. There is snack trash littering the floor all around my bed. I successfully sneak out of bed without waking anyone up. I decide to take a morning swim. I am right down the hall from the pool room when I run into the last person I want to see. Yep, Kaden and guess what? He wants to talk.

"Amara wait, will you please talk to me?", Kaden ask with a hurt tone.

"I have nothing to say to you.", I state coldly.

"Will you at least hear me out?", he questions as he pleads with his eyes.

"I guess.", is my response before walking into the pool room, sitting on the side of the pool, and dangling my feet in the water. As I wait for him to sit down and speak.

"I am so sorry Amara! The last thing I wanted to do is hurt you.", he tries to express.

"But you did. Kaden you hurt me really bad.", I answer with tears that I am trying to suppress pushing their way out of my eyes and down my cheeks.

"Please forgive me and give me another chance. I can't lose you Baby!", Kaden begs.

"I don't know. I don't know if I can ever trust you again.", I state. The worst thing about this whole situation is he did not just cheat on me. He cheated on me with the woman that sliced my vocal cords. My sister!

"Just think about it and please don't ice me out.", he asks as he plants a kiss on my cheek then walks out.

I let out a deep sigh as I slide into the pool. My mind is racing faster than I can swim laps. So, after about forty-five minutes to an hour of trying to swim some peace into my mind. Which is obviously not working. I decide I need a joint, realizing I was out. I text Lucas.

Me → Hey where are you at?

Hopefully, he does not look down on me for my habit. If you want to call it that. You know what who cares, I think to myself.

Lucas → In my room. I took the day off. What's up?

Me → Great, see you in a few.

I walk to my room first and throw on a green tank top and black shorts. Then I walk to his room and knock on the door feeling a little nervous. Pot still is not completely legal in every state yet, so I keep that I smoke to myself. He opens the door for me, Aspen is sitting on his bed. I give her a look that says I know what you have been up to. She just giggles in response. I was just teasing her I am not sure if they even have had sex or not.

"What's up?", Lucas voices bringing me out of my own head.

"You got anything going on at the moment?", I ask not wanting to interrupt anything between him and Aspen.

"Girl your fine. What are you needing?", Aspen says eyeing me suspiciously.

"Lucas can you get any smoke.", I blurt out after clearing my throat.

"Let me text my dude.", Lucas says before laughing at me.

"Stop laughing at me.", I playfully pout. Picking up a pillow I throw it at him. "We can hit up Demitri's personal bar in his office while we wait.", I offer. I need to forget the world and all I have access to is booze so it would have to work for now.

"You are a bad girl Amara. I like this side of you. I'm down.", Lucas chastise me playfully.

"Let's do it. It will be like when we snuck Sean's bottle of Crown out of his desk. He walked in on us drinking it. Ha-ha, he made us double our training that day and the next.", Aspen utters between laughs.

"Hell yeah, we set records well drunk and hung over.", I reply. The thought of Sean saddened me, but the memory made me smile. Another thing I want to forget for at least a little bit. Too much has happened in too little time. I need to find an outlet especially before I tried to use Demitri as one. I am not going to lie the thought has crossed my mind a few times. I am not going to be that kind of person and I am sure as hell not going to just use Demitri. I want to be a better person than that and he deserves better. A girl can fantasize though. "So where is Demitri?", I ask as we walk into his office shutting the door behind us.

"He is in a meeting until two so that gives us an hour.", Lucas responds as he opens the liquor hutch bringing out some Silver Tequila. "Do you ladies want me to make you a mix drink?"

"Shots!", Aspen and I say in unison.

"You girls are trouble.", Lucas confesses.

"You're partying with the big girls now.", Aspen jokingly conveys as Lucas pours us all a shot.

"Let's play shots for shots.", I mention.

"Yes girl.", Aspen replies

"Aspen will you find a trash can. Lucas, help me find some useless paper. We need one to three pieces.", I politely order. "We will rock paper scissors to see who will go first and second. Then we take turns making the paper ball into the trash can. Each time we all make the shot we will take turns making the next shots harder to make. If you miss you drink.", I explain to Lucas as Aspen finds the trash can. She takes the bag out and sets it to the side. I won to go first, and Aspen won to go second. We all make it every time in the first few rounds. Once we start putting tricks into the shots and throwing shots from different spots in Demitri's office. We start missing enough baskets that we all three have a good buzz going on. We are having so much fun we lose track of time. I am standing on Demitri's desk with my back to the door and trash can. Preparing for my shot.

"What are you doing?", I hear Demitri say in his serious tone as I throw my paper ball over my shoulder landing it in the trash can.

"Drink up Bitches.", I state excitedly. "They both bet that I couldn't make that shot."

"Tell me why you are drinking my booze in my office in the middle of the day. Lucas you . . .", Demitri starts to say before I interrupt him.

"Because I didn't have any. Plus, it was my idea not Lucas' or Aspen's. So, if you are going to punish someone it should be me.", I assert before sticking my tongue out at him and taking a shot, slurring my words just a little.

"I'll have to come up with a punishment for you.", Demitri replies with an ornery smile as he sits in his chair and digs in a drawer.

"You are a perv Demitri.", I inform him playfully.

"I didn't mean it like that, I was just playing.", Demitri says fumbling through his words. "Here just light this and shut up.", he embarrassedly commands.

Aspen and Lucas have been standing there quietly waiting to get in trouble. Before they burst out laughing. They are laughing so hard they have tears coming out of their eyes. Lucas' and Aspen's laughter is so contagious I am having a hard time lighting the joint before passing it to Demitri.

"I guess you guys don't want to hit this then.", Demitri playfully chastises them as he puffs on the joint. "Kyle will be bringing by that ounce you want here in a couple of hours.", he says to me.

"The fuck Lucas.", I state.

"What?", Lucas asks clueless.

"She doesn't like people knowing.", Aspen informs him.

"We three have been smoking together for centuries.", Demitri says as they burst out laughing.

"So how about we move this to the game room, invite the whole house and turn this into a real party?", Aspen suggest.

"Come on man I know that meeting was the only thing you had to do today.", Lucas tries to encourage Demitri to come. Unspoken words are being said with his eyes.

"You know there is a bar in the game room that's completely stocked right.", Dimitri informs me. Not giving Lucas an answer.

"I know but it's more fun to sneak into your office and drink your personal stash.", I playfully taunt him.

I did not look back to see his facial expression. Instead, I link arms with Aspen as we go round everyone up. This will probably be the last time we are all together. Before everyone goes back to their own lives.

We make everyone come and hang out. It is up to them how hard they want to party if at all. Except Elijah, he left early this morning to see his family and get things straightened out at The Company. Kaden would not get out of bed until Aspen and I made him. He needs this too. Aspen went to hook up her phone to Demitri's sound system. While I grab a couple of platters filling them up with food to snack on. As I set the platters on the end table Aspen grabs me, pulling me in to dance with her. We continue to dance through the songs as everyone shows up and starts mingling. Until a slow song comes on, guess who asks me to dance.

Demitri's POV

Lucas and I come to a complete stop after walking into the game room and seeing the girls dancing. Amara is so alluring. I cannot take my eyes off her. I am brought out of it when everyone starts to show up. I am not used to having this many beings in my castle. Today is the last day they would all be here. So, I sit back and enjoy the chaos. What can I say? I have come to enjoy the peace in my old age. A slow song comes on as Ace and Willa followed by Zach and Nixie go to dance. So does Harper and Phoenix as well as Malan and Sylvia. Lucas walks over to Aspen and asks her to dance. Tiffany and April are playing foosball against Aloe and Jax. Grim is racing against Winter on Need for Speed. Everyone seems to be having a good time. Amara looks at me pleading for me to save her just as Kaden walks up asking her to dance. Before I can make my way to interrupt their dance. Malan whispers something to Sylvia then walks over to Kaden asking to dance with Amara.

I walk up to Sylvia and start dancing with her. She thanks me for saving her from that awkward situation. As I spin Sylvia by Malan and Amara, I realize Amara has tears in her eyes. It makes since now why Malan had quit dancing with Sylvia for Amara. Since I have met Malan, he has been very protective of Amara and treats her like his little sister. Thankfully, only two slow songs play. After the last slow song Amara hands out shots, to those that want one. Amara is taking another shot when Kyle shows up. Amara, Kyle, and I convene in the Living room. I pull my bong out of the enclosed shelf in my end table as Kyle laid three different strains out on the coffee table.

"Sir these are the strains that were just harvested and there will be three more to be harvested this coming week.", Kyle informs me.

"Thank you, Kyle. If you do not need anything else. Your free to go.", I state as I am loading a bowl.

"Or feel free to join the fun.", Amara chimes in.

"Thank you for the offer but my wife just had our first born. I should get home and check on them.", he thanks Amara and then leaves.

"So, is selling drugs your side gig?", she teases me before hitting the bong.

"O yeah, didn't you know I was the first OG.", I tease back. "I have about four different farms in different states across the US and several different dispensaries. Kyle is one of my main farmers, he is a garden fairy and has powerful plant manipulation powers.", I inform her before taking a hit. "You and Harper are actually partnering in it all.", I add after exhaling the smoke. Passing the bong back to her brings back memories of before all this mess. A time when we were teenagers sneaking around smoking because we had to hide it from our parents.

"Partners?", she chokes out between coughs after blowing the smoke out of her lungs.

"Yes. It's something all three of us started together.", I inform her. I load three bowls one from each bag. One of the strains is named White Queen, it is white like snow. Another of the strains is a sativa dominant hybrid called Black Poison, which is purple with green hairs and has a strong high. The last strains is called Blue Mystic which its DNA is unknown and is hard to come by. I let her pick out which one she wants. Of course, she cannot choose just one and wants an eighth of each. I eye out about a quarter and a half of weed then give it to her. She would not stop insisting on paying for it, saying she has done none of the work to deserve to get it for free and did not want to take away from any of the workers. I charge her half price since she is obviously being stubborn and is not going to let it go.

"Thank you. This was fun.", Amara states as she heads to her room.

I slip the money into her back pocket as I stand behind her to put everything up. Then I head back to the party just in time. Malan has Kaden in a head lock. Lucas fills me in on how Kaden was going to go find Amara to get her away from me. Then Kaden got mad at Malan when Malan would not let him. Kaden drunkenly swung at Malan and that is why Malan put Kaden in a headlock while he is walking, half dragging Kaden out of the game room. Amara walks in as Malan and Kaden are leaving. She rolls her eyes as she takes a shot. Then turns around and takes one with Willa, and Aspen. Damn she can hold her liquor for someone who does not really drink. Those three girls together just scream trouble.

The party dies down, and we all just hang out until dinner. After dinner everyone but Amara's team, Harper, Zack, Phoenix and Nixie leave. Once everyone left Willa talks Ace, Aspen, Amara, and me into relaxing in the Hot Tub. Amara went to roll a couple of joints first then is going to meet us there. Harper and Zack inform us they are taking the twins on a mini vacation. Since they have not been able to leave the castle until now.

Amara's POV

I roll a couple of fat joints then head to the hot tub. Since I still have my bikini on under my clothes from earlier, I make my way back to the pool room.

"You look beautiful in that dark green.", Kaden voices slurring his words as he steps in front of me.

"What do you want Kaden?", I ask impatiently.

"I was just wondering if you thought about what I said? I miss you Baby!", he drunkenly states as he is backing me up against the wall.

"I still don't have an answer for you. Why don't you come hang out with us in the hot tub?", I mention.

"How about a kiss? Man, you have no idea how much I have missed those lips of yours.", Kaden conveys as he tries to kiss me.

"How about not.", I reply turning my head to the side, but he keeps trying. "Kaden stop!", I command. When that did not get him to stop. I put both of my hands on his chest shoving him hard into the wall across the hall. Everyone must have heard the commotion because they come rushing out when he hit it leaving a Kaden size hole. Before he can say anything, I tell him, "Just don't! You are making a fucking ass of yourself. Go sober up.", I exclaim.

I walk past everyone not saying a word. As everyone except Malan and Ace turn to walk back into the pool room. They both join us after taking Kaden back to his room. I can feel Dimitri's eyes full of desire on me as I strip down to my bathing suit. This one is the same style as my old one, but a royal blue instead of black. Seeing how Mel decide to still mine off my unconscious body. I figure it was a good reason as any to get a new one. I really did not want that one back. I look at him trying to catch him in the act. Demitri makes eye contact and winks at me after he is done checking me out. Aspen lights up one joint and Malan lights the other. We just chill in the hot tub for the rest of the night getting baked, laughing, and taking turns telling stories. Ace and Willa were the first to turn in. Then Aspen is ready, so Lucas walks her to her room. Malan kicks it with Demitri and I for a bit before heading in. We sit in silence for a little while. I am leaning back with my eyes closed enjoying my high. I can feel Demitri watching me.

"I have a question.", Demitri states.

"Okay?", I respond with my eyes still closed.

"Were you really going to use a sleeping potion on me?", he asks as he raises an eyebrow.

My eyes pop open and I sit up as I honestly tell him, "Yeah, sorry about that. The plan was to use it if we could not persuade you to give us the ring if you happened to be wearing it. That was before all this mindfuck of a mess."

"O, you would have been able to persuade me.", he says in a deep sexy voice.

"Demitri!", I playfully chastise him. "Have you and my Dad gotten any leads on Holle's location?", I ask once I quit laughing.

"We have had a few but all of them turned out to be dead ends.", Dimitri informs me.

"Well, I have a plan to find her. I will go over it with you and the team tomorrow. Okay? I'm exhausted.", I express.

"That's fine get some rest.", he tells me as he stands up helping me out of the water. He is still in the hot tub, so I am standing a little taller than him.

"Thank you for today. I really needed it.", I say before leaning over and kissing him on the cheek. Then heading to my room.

I wake up the next morning with a wicked headache. I heal myself then jump in the shower. After throwing on a black tank top and grey shorts. I go to Demitri's office first to get my necklace from him. Informing him that I have something I need to take care of. Then I will call a meeting to discuss my plan. I head for the Tree of Dawn. It is time I cash in that favor. Once at the Tree of Dawn I shadow jump to the shadow I trapped Schrat in.

"Schrat.", I yell out for him as I step out of the tree's shadow.

"Hello Ancient one.", he says appearing before my eyes. He seems a little happy to see me.

"I'm glad you are putting that ring to good use.", I tease.

"I am indeed. What can I do for you?", he inquires with a smirk.

"I would like for you to enlighten me on the second key to breaking my curse.", I state. "I know this charm contains my essence and I am weakened more every day until the curse is broken, or I die as a human. Aspen wasn't able to siphon it.", I reveal everything I know.

"Who are you?", Schrat questions.

"I am Makaria, Goddess of Blessed Death, Princess of the Underworld, but I'm also Amara, Agent for The Company. I would be lying to myself if I said I would come out of all this just one or the other."

"Very good. That is the first key. The Second key to unlocking your essences and breaking the curse is true love's kiss."

"Are you shitting me?", I ask a little rudely.

"Yes. I couldn't help myself. You should see your face.", he conveys before laughing so hard he almost has tears coming out of his eyes. "To break the curse, you have to blast the charm in sync with five of the elements.", Schrat discloses once he is done laughing and catches his breath.

"Thank you.", I tell him before shadow jumping back to the Tree of Dawn. When I am in front of Demitri's office I send a text to my team.

Me → Meet me in Dimitri's office asap.

"I know how to break the curse but it's going to take all five elements. I have access to Fire.", I announce once everyone including Kaden has shown up.

"I got you on Air.", Aspen informs me.

"I can access the Earth and the Water Elements. My Earth powers are the strongest though.", Willa adds.

"So, that leaves Spirit and Water.", I note.

"Sylvia can call on the Water Element. I'm sure she wouldn't mind helping.", Malan assures us as he sends her a text.

"Amara you and I both can tap into the Spirit Element's power being God of Death and Goddess of Blessed Death. Your spirit abilities are a lot stronger than mine. But since you also wield the Element of Fire which I do not. I will step in to call on the Spirit Element. First, I want to know if this is what you want?"

"Part of me is missing and I want it back. Just keep in mind I am not going to be the Makaria you knew. I'm going to be a combination of Makaria, Goddess of Blessed Death and Amara, agent for The Company.", I inform Dimitri as well as everyone else in the room.

I go over my plan to locate Holle with my team, and Demitri while we wait on Sylvia. Once she shows up and agrees to help. We all go outside to perform the ritual. That way we do not accidentally end up destroying Demitri's office. I place the necklace on the ground as we all gather around it in the shape of a star. Aspen, Willa, and Sylvia are on my left and then Demitri which put him to my right. We wait until everyone has called upon their Element's power. Then at the count of three, we let the power lose on the charm in sync as I focused on who I am. The reddish orange, deep sky-blue streams, shamrock green, sapphire blue, and soft pink streams of magic coming out of our hands are all captivating. A bright azure blue light explodes out of the charm knocking me not only on my ass but knocking me out for a few days as well.

Mel's POV

I wake up chained to a concrete slab. It is pitch black and I can barely see my hand in front of my face. My body feels like I died. At that thought I remember that I had died or maybe I am being tricked into thinking I had. Why else would I be chained here instead of being in the Nothingness? Also known as the Void. Unless this is a part of the Nothingness? It feels like weeks have gone by before someone comes around besides the demon who brings me food and water. The demon makes me think maybe I am in some part of the Underworld I have not seen. If so, then what the hell happened?

"Hello Lil Sis.", a voice comes from a person hidden in the dark. I did not have to see them to know who that voice belongs to.

"Makaria", I hiss. "You seem to have gotten your memories back. I must say touché. I really thought you killed me. Tell me how you did it?", I convey.

"Well, I'm not a cold-blooded killer like you are my little sister. Plus, I could not break Mom's heart even if I did not remember her at the time. I could however feel that her and I had a strong bond. You did need to be taught a lesson though, so I had to do something. I made a fabricated copy of the Spear of Destiny. Those 3D printers are something. Then I dipped it in Haemorrhois venom mixed with a sleeping potion. The same potion that Connor made me drink. Causing your body to feel like it was dying. You were out for several days. I used the fact that Balthazar would run to you and tattle. When he found out who the red-haired demon really was to get you to come to me. Somehow, I knew you would not be able to control that temper and would show up here.", she lays it all out for me.

"What are you going to do with me?", I ask fear making my voice shake.

"That's up to you. Help us take down Holle and I will let you go. Yes, I know about her. In fact, I knew about her before I allowed you to take my Memories. If not, I'll hand you over to Father.", I convey.

"You will let me go that easily?", I question suspiciously.

"Yes, you will just have to sign a blood binding contract. If either of us breaks the contract we will burn in the deepest depths of the Underworld.", she adds as she slides the contract and a small knife towards me. I prick my finger with the knife and sign the contract with my blood. After I slide them back over to her along the ground, she does the same.

"Thank you.", she states coldly before walking off.

"What about releasing me?", I ask pulling at the chains.

Not saying a word, she turns around and walks off. It felt like forever has passed before two demon guards come for me in their demonic form. They unchain me as they inform me that Amara is allowing me to shower, eat and then I must leave. Both demons walk on either side of me out of the dungeon into a spare bedroom. They have me pretty far back in the dungeon. Further than I have ever been. I kept my mouth shut on the way to the spare room until we walk upon Kaden. He turns the opposite way and starts to walk off as soon as he sees me.

"Kaden please hear me out.", I plead with him. He did not turn around and look at me, but he did stop walking. "I meant what I said. I wanted to be yours since the moment I seen you in the woods. I should not have trick you to get back at Makaria. I really am sorry. Please forgive me and give me a chance. I know you feel our bond.", I beg him.

He just walks off not saying a word. I go to the spare bedroom with tears in my eyes. I take a long hot shower before putting on the clothes that were on the bed. It is a red plain shirt and a pair of jeans. I eat until I am full before letting the demon guards lead me through the portal. They did not leave my side except when I showered. Even then they stood right outside the door. Not until I walked through the portal into the Underworld. I use some mist to transport myself to my apartment. Once there I fall to my knees and cry, letting everything out.

Amara's POV

"It worked.", I state to my team and Demitri. While laying the contract on Demitri's desk so he can put it in his safe.

"Now what?", Kaden questions. It is the first time he has talked to me since the other night.

"We will give her the rest of the evening. You will call her tomorrow telling her to come in. Where we will find out what she knows then go from there.", I answer.

"Why am I the one that has to call her?", Kaden questions me.

"She will respond to you the best out of all of us. Plus, you want me to give you a chance. So here is your chance to try and prove I can trust you.", I comment. "You guys go have fun on your double date.", I address Ace, Willa, Aspen and Lucas.

Lucas tried to talk Demitri, and I into going. But a couple's date is the last thing I wanted to do right now. They tell us goodbye as they are walking out the door. Kaden follows them out not saying a word.

"Makaria are you really back?", Demitri inquires.

"Yes, and how many times are you going to ask me that?", I question him.

"Until I can believe it.", he replies as he scoops me up embracing me in a tight hug. Before setting me back down on the floor.

"What was that for?", I ask after giggling.

"I have missed my best friend.", Demitri confesses.

"I am her but I'm not her. I don't think you nor Kaden has really grasped that or can accept that.", I honestly express.

"Even when you didn't remember who you were. I could see you were still Makaria. Also, I could see the changes in you. You have grown and been through a lot. That changes you, there is nothing wrong with that.", Demitri conveys.

"Thank you for stepping in to help break the curse. Will you please let your brother know that I am back? So, he needs to get his head out of Phoenix's pretty ass and come see me for a bit.", I playfully state before walking out of his office.

I go to my room to grab Grim on the way to the kitchen to cook us something. Grim wants chicken so I end up cooking garlic cheddar chicken with baked beans and fried potatoes. It is so delicious, not to mention cooking has always been therapeutic for me. We are on our second plate when I get scooped up out of my chair mid bite.

"I've missed you.", Harper confesses as he pecks me on the cheek from behind and sets me back down.

"Make you a plate. I know you are hungry.", I tell him before I take another bite.

"Holy shit this is good. Man, I have missed your cooking almost as much as you.", Harper tells me as Demitri walks into the kitchen. "Have you talked to him since getting your memories back."

"We have talked, but we haven't had the talk. I need to figure things out between Kaden and I first.", I answer before grabbing Grim and I the last two pieces of chocolate cheesecake out of the refrigerator.

"Demitri dude you have to try this food.", Harper voices between bites as Demitri rummages through the refrigerator.

"Damn this is good.", Demitri exclaims in between bites after making his plate.

"I'm all yours for the rest of the day.", Harper informs me as Grim, and I are washing our plates. I keep forgetting Demitri has housekeepers. The boys are both on their second plate. "Demitri, you coming? We haven't gotten to murder you at zombies in a long time.", Harper challenges him after finishing his last bite of food.

"I figured you guys would want to catch up.", Demitri responds.

"Come on dude it has been forever since the three of us have played together.", Harper adds not giving up.

Demitri gives in to Harper and the four of us spend the rest of the day killing zoms. Grim ends up passing out first, Harper offers to take him to my room. I know exactly what he is doing. He is giving Dimitri and I some alone time in hopes something happens between us. Now that I have my memories back, I recall a shit load of times he has pulled something like this throughout the years. I did not think Demitri cared so I just took it has Harper being Harper.

"Are we going to talk about everything Amara?", Demitri implores breaking the silence.

"Yes, and soon. I am not trying to drag it out. But I need to figure out what is going to happen between Kaden and I first. You know.", I respond after setting the controller down on the coffee table.

"I understand.", he tells me.

"I do have a question though. How many times did you sleep with Mel?", I inquire.

"Two and unless you count the time, I thought she was you. But I swear as soon as I knew it was her, I stopped. I'm sorry I should have never slept with her.", Demitri pleads for my forgiveness.

"How long ago was the last time before she tricked you?", I continue the questions.

"Six months or so ago.", Dimitri responds.

"Give me some time to figure things out and we will continue this conversation soon. Okay?", I assure him.

"Okay.", is his response.

I did not think he would drop it so easily, but I am glad he did. We fall into a comfortable silence while we slay Zoms for a couple more hours. Before Dimitri walks me to my room. Kaden is leaning against the wall by my door. Demitri tells me good night. Then kisses me on my forehead before walking off towards his room.

"Have you made a decision about us?", he questions me right off the back before I can even get in my room.

"No, I haven't.", I respond. I honestly have thought a lot about it but did not know what to do.

"Looks like you have. You keep spending more and more time alone with him.", He hisses out with a distaste look on his face.

"You can't tell me who I can spend my time with. Especially after what you did!", I loudly state.

"Have you fucked him yet?", Kaden continues questioning me.

"Kaden!", I yell out.

"Well, have you?", Kaden inquires.

"No, I haven't. Not that it matters. If you are just going to accuse me of shit because of your own guilt. You can leave.", I voice with annoyance. Which is growing into anger with every second that is ticking by.

"I'm sorry Baby. I'm just so afraid of losing you.", Kaden confesses.

"Yeah, real afraid. I'm sure all you could think about was me when you had your dick in my sister.", I scoff.

"She tricked me.", he pleads with me to believe him.

"And the other however many times?", I spit back. "just leave!", I order him after he sits there silently for a bit. He tries to kiss me before he leaves. I turn my head so his kiss lands on the side of my head. Once he leaves, I snuggle up next to Grim and go to sleep. Good thing Grim is a deep sleeper. I did not want him to be woken up to us fighting. Thinking of Grim gets me wondering how this situation with Kaden is going to affect him.

My day started early with a call from Elijah asking me to come into the office. I take a hot shower trying to wake up. I did not get to bed until at least 2:30 am. I get dressed in pin stripe black slacks and a purple button up with a black tank top under it. Then grab a white Monster on my way to headquarters.

"Thank you for coming in so early. I would like to introduce you to Bruce he is Sean's lawyer and Maria who is Dean's lawyer.", Elijah introduces the humans to me.

"Sean left you his seat on the council, his cabin and half of his money. Connor was to receive the house, the other half of the money and all other assets. Since he has passed away as well and does not have a wife or any children that he has left behind. That leaves you the only living beneficiary. You just need to sign on the X.", Bruce discloses as he hands me a pen. Taking the pen, I slide the legal document closer and sign by the X after reading it. In shock at what Bruce just revealed.

"Dean left you his seat on the grounds that it is temporary. Unless Robyn refuses to take over the seat. Everything else is left to his wife and daughter. He asks that you always keep a team on them. Even if it must be in the shadows. To only bring Robyn into the council when it is safe, she is ready, and only if she wants to.", Maria tells me as she pushes the papers my way. Which I read and sign as well.

Dean's wife Cora wanted to keep their daughter away from The Company and the supernatural world. But Dean did not. He wanted her apart of our world and The Company to train her to protect herself. It is too dangerous for dragons especially purebloods like him and his Family. Dean taught her how to hide her dragon from the humans. After I sign by the X on both legal documents, they put the documents in their briefcase then shake Elijah's and my hand. Before telling me, I will receive a copy of both documents in the mail and walking out of the office. Elijah explains that having two seats would be an excruciating amount of work. He advises me to find someone to take over one of the seats or to help with the workload. Also, that he is putting me in charge with finding someone for Balthazar's seat. Elijah is keeping The Company going by himself right now. Since he is the only Council member left until all the legal documents are finalized and I am off my month suspension. Which he has HR working on loopholes. That way he can bring me back on board faster. On top of trying to weed out Balthazar's and Connor's followers. I can see how much stress he is under on his face and in his posture. I cannot believe how this day is going. I had just recently found out Dean named me the temporary successor of his seat on the council. But I cannot believe Sean named me his, left me the cabin and half his money. Tears trickle out of the corner of my eyes. Sean leaving me the cabin means so much to me. He knew how much I loved it out there. I had even tried to buy it off him a few times, but he would always tell me how he cannot part with it. I express how thankful I am and head back to Demitri's castle to face my sister. This will be fun! I think sarcastically to myself.

Kaden's POV

I call Mel like Amara wants me to, she said to give her an hour and she would be here. Amara left for headquarters early this morning. Of course, I had to find out from Ace. Guess I got drunk and acted like an ass a couple of times pissing Amara off even more. I am so lost in thought I did not see Mel appear.

"Penny for your thoughts?", Mel inquires.

"I'm good.", I respond coldly.

"Can we please start over?", she pleads.

"I guess.", I agree reluctantly. Is this not what I am trying to get Amara to do for me?

"So, what do you guys need anyways?", Mel questions as she sits down next to me.

"We want all the info you have on Holle. We are just waiting on Amara to return.", I inform her.

"I will tell you guys everything I know, but it's not much. She isn't very trusting.", Mel implies as she reaches out grabbing my hand. "I have never met someone who makes me feel the way you do.", Mel continues as she flips my hand over to draw patterns along my palm with her fingertip.

"I'm working things out with Amara.", I insist as I pull my hand away.

"It will never work. The way you make me feel is the way Amara would describe how Demitri made her feel. Before she lost her memories anyway. A bond like that is never broken. No matter how much either one denies it.", she discloses while giving me a knowing look.

"You mean before you took her memories.", I remark. Not bringing up her double meaning in those words.

"Yes, before I took her memories. Holle wanted her dead, I just wanted her out of the picture. You have no idea how hard it was to talk Holle into not killing her. Or what is it like always living in Makaria's shadow and nothing you do is ever good enough.", she divulges to me.

My eyes shoot to hers, I love Amara, but I cannot deny this electric feeling that is spreading up the leg she is now massaging circular patterns on. This woman is bewitching. I quickly stand up almost knocking my chair over. Not being able to take my eyes off her or form the words to tell her to stop.

"I'm going to go see where Amara is at. She should be back by now.", I voice as I stumble over my words. Then try to rush out the kitchen.

"Are you sure that's really what you want?", she purrs as she forms out of mist in front of me. Bringing her hand up to my cheek pulling me into a kiss.

I try to fight with everything I have in me until her lips meet mine. After that I lost all will to fight. I am addicted to this feeling I get from her and am at its mercy. I open my mouth letting her deepen the kiss as she slides her hand down into my pants. Then she starts stroking my cock. Causing a moan from me to escape into her mouth as we continue to kiss. I lift her up as she wraps her legs around me. She quickens the pace of her hand sliding up and down my shaft as I lay her on the table. I move my hands up her dress to pull her panties to the side. My dick hardens at the realization she is not wearing any.

I did not care at the time that it meant she had planned this whole thing to push Amara and I further apart. All I can think about is having my hard dick inside her. I signed my soul away the first time we had sex and this devil is not going to let me go either. As she frees my rock-hard member from my pants, I slam it into her. I am fucking her so hard the table is making noise as it is being scooted along the tile floor. She is thrusting her hips upwards as I am slamming into her bringing us both into an orgasm. Our moans and swears of pleasure fill the room. Her legs are wrapped tightly around me keeping her pressed against me. Rubbing her clit on me with ever thrust into her. I am overcome with the pleasure that is pulsing through my body as I cum.

"What the fuck!", Amara hisses before running out of the kitchen.

"Amara wait, I . . ." I call after her as I pull out and pull my pants up from around my ankles. Zipping up my pants I run after her. I make it out of the kitchen but cannot tell what way she went. I pause for a minute thinking of what I can possibly say, she is right she cannot trust me. Hell, I cannot even trust myself around Mel. All I could think about is being in her from the kiss until I pulled out. No, I am lying. I am still thinking about it. There is no way I can fix this. With that thought, I head to my room to pack my shit and leave. I cannot face Amara. Demitri is right, I am not good enough for her.

CHAPTER 7: VILLAIN IN THE SHADOWS

Amara's POV

Mel walks in to Demitri's office smiling from ear to ear. The audacity of that bitch! Without saying a word, I walk up to her knocking her on her ass with one solid punch to the jaw. Everyone just stands there speechless with their eyes on me. I walk back over to my spot, not saying a word. As I will myself to not continue hitting her.

"Where is Kaden?", I coldly ask Mel as I notice everyone else is here.

"I haven't seen him since you interrupted us and he chased after you.", Mel says after spitting out blood while rubbing her jaw.

"Well then we will just have to get started without him. Ace, please go fill him in on everything when we are done here.", I state. I did not let Mel know he never came after me.

"Mel no games. What do you know about Holle?", Demitri sternly questions her.

"She is Queen of Helheim, one of the nine realms of Asgard. Also known as the Realm of Hel. It is the opposite of our Underworld. There it is icy and cold. Well, was before Asgard was burnt to nothing. She is divided vertically, like me. She is an unbelievable beauty with blonde hair and a blue eye on one side of her. With nothing but her bones showing on her other half with black hair and eye. Holle's plan is to get Makaria out of the picture, marry Zach and kill Hades.", Mel reveals.

"And what, she is just going to graciously spare Mom? The Queen of the Underworld.", I add sarcastically.

"She promised to not harm Mom or Zach.", Mel adds.

"You can't seriously be that dense, to think she is going to keep her word. Especially if her plan fails. I have done research on her. This bitch is not just cruel she is vicious and greedy. She will stop at nothing to get what she wants and won't hesitate to kill anyone that might be in her way.", I convey.

"She promised to curse Mom like I did with you. Giving her a new life where Holle rules the Underworld with Zack at her side. As for Zack she has a love potion she is going to give him and will curse him if needed. I just don't know when.", she replies.

"Anything else?", Demitri asks.

"No, she isn't very forth coming on information.", Mel informs us looking bored. "O wait I do know one more thing. She has to possess a dead body to walk on earth and the body has to be specially prepped for it to hold her Essence.", Mel discloses.

"After my Dad and Demitri told me about her I started researching her. Well, when I can find time. I found a lot of useless facts but did come across a couple of things that could help. One she has the power of ice and two her weakness is fire.", I inform them. Got to love and hate the internet. We do not really have to worry about having a bunch of information on my team and myself. The Company regulates information on all its employees that is put on the world wide web. We form a plan before Ace goes to find Kaden to fill him in on everything.

"You are all dismissed, enjoy the rest of your night we start phase one of the plan tomorrow. Amara, please stay behind.", Demitri announces.

"You're in trouble.", Mel sneers. "I knew he wouldn't just let you get away with hitting me like that."

"Mel shut up and get out.", Demitri demands. "Are you okay?", he asks lovingly once everyone including Mel is out of the room.

As soon as I open my mouth to tell him, tears start streaming out of my eyes. The only sound I can make are sobs. He reaches for me pulling me into a tight embrace. Dimitri just stands there holding me until I can gain control. It feels so right being in his arms making it easier for me to gain control.

"I walked in on Mel and Kaden having sex on your kitchen table.", I sob out fighting back the tears that are trying to escape.

"Those Bastards, I'll break both their necks. Just because he is addicted to her does not mean they can keep hurting you like this.", Demitri voices as he storms out the office towards Kaden's room.

"Amara, I have looked all over the castle there is no sign of Kaden. His room even looks like he was never there.", Ace tells me as he walks back into the office within seconds of Demitri walking out.

I did not want to believe it, so I run to Kaden's room. As I walk into what was his room my mouth drops open. That coward just up and left. He has hurt me so bad, but I did not know how to let go of him. Even after everything. Before now, this is the last straw. We are done!

Aspen's POV

I am getting ready for my date with Lucas. I have been seeing him ever since the float trip. I cannot get enough of him. We have not had sex yet and he does not push it when I stop during our make out sessions. Tonight, is a different story. I am sure I want to take things further with him. He thinks we are going for dinner and a movie. Unknown to him I have a different plan. I have put my hair in a high ponytail and am doing my makeup. I have on matching red lace lingerie. The bottoms are small tight booty shorts, and it has a thin strapped top that meets at a point right above my navel. Showing off my piercing that dangles in my belly button. The back is completely open except one strap across it. I finish my makeup just as there is a knock at the door. I holler out for him to give me a minute while I slip on my black with red bottom high heels. Walking over to the door I open it. His mouth drops open as soon as he sees me.

"I think you have some drool on your chin.", I tease him as I pull him inside shutting the door behind us.

"I thought we are going to go get something to eat and see a movie?", he finally stammers out.

"We are.", I continue to tease.

"Now I appreciate how stunning you look in this outfit. But I do not think it will meet their dress code.", he responds.

"Shut up and just kiss me.", I command as I pull him in

He kisses me with so much desire. Then picks me up as he tosses me effortlessly onto the bed. Kissing his way as he climbs up me. His hands and mouth explore every inch of me before he goes down between my legs to taste me. After pulling my panties to the side Lucas lets out a moan as he sucks and teases my clit with his tongue. I moan out his name from all the pleasure as my back arches. Not being able to stand not being in me anymore he pulls his shirt off, then his pants and boxers as his hard dick springs up. Then positioning himself back over me he slides into my wet pussy. Moaning out about how wet I am as he dips his hips with every thrust into me.

I thrust my hips upward in sync with his rhythm. Making him moan out. That sound makes me want him even more. I start rotating my hips from under him causing him to stop and enjoy the way it feels. Lucas pulls out and rolls me to my side as he gets behind me. Sliding back into me from behind. I let out a hiss as he changes his thrusting pattern. He is so deep I cannot help but moan for him not to stop and to go harder. Lucas makes me meet my orgasm before he pulls out spilling his seed on his shirt as he reaches his orgasm. Getting up he walks to the bathroom to clean himself off. I cannot move as waves of the most intense orgasm I have ever had continues to pulse through me. When he comes back, he brings a wash rag, cleans me up and pulls me to him wrapping me in his arms. After kissing me on the forehead we both drift off to sleep. Unaware of the events happening outside of this room.

Amara's POV

The next day we set our plan in motion. We all put ideas into this plan until it was perfect. First, we have to get Harper and Zack here. Then get Zack to go to the Underworld. Demitri called them last night, they are arriving shortly. I sent Grim to the Underworld with my parents early this morning. There is no way I am going to take a chance on him getting hurt.

"Phase one consist of Demitri/Our parents throwing a ball for Zack to find his future wife. Mel will spill the news of the ball to Holle. Mel will also transform into Zack for the ball while Zack is safe in the Underworld.", I fill Harper and Zack in on the plan.

"What about you. If she sees you, we are all fucked," Mel adds with attitude.

"Amara do you still have that bracelet Demitri gave you.", Malan questions.

"Actually, I do. I was planning to go protect Zack and Grim in the Underworld. But I follow your line of thinking Malan.", I respond.

"Wait so I have to hide while you guys get to have all the fun. That is not going to happen.", Zack voices.

"Then what do you suggest?", I ask him seriously.

"I don't know?", is his response.

"We can put a tracker on him. Then he will have to either take the love potion or make it look like he took it.", Ace adds.

"We could cause a diversion and switch the cups. So, he is seen drinking something.", Willa notes.

We spent at least an hour working out the new plan. Then we all leave the office except Harper, Lucas, and Demitri. They are getting to work on the guest list and getting the invitations out. The girls and I start planning the ball. We only have a couple of days to get it all ready. Zack calls Dad to inform him of the new plan. Letting him know that we need them here to make it work. This plan is risky, and I cannot help but worry that Holle will take this as an opportunity to kill my parents. Aspen and Willa are ordering the decorations while I call Bry. She is a Wild Elf we work with at The Company and is also a DJ. She tells me she is down. Bry offers to do it for free, but I am not going to let that happen especially with Demitri and my Dad covering the costs. I will just send them her bill later. They are both loaded.

Malan and Ace are getting the exit strategies set up for our guest if anything goes wrong. As well as stashing weapons all throughout the castle. Aspen tells us how her and Lucas had sex for the first time. I let her talk about it for a bit before telling her and Willa that I walked in on Mel and Kaden. As well as how afterwards, he takes off like a coward. They tell me how sorry they are and how I did not need him while hugging me. Tears are fighting to get out, but I will not let them. I am done crying over someone who cares so little for me. Or so I tell myself. After dinner, my team and I gather for a meeting in the game room.

"So, Sean left me his seat on the council and Dean left me his until his daughter is ready to take on the responsibilities. If she wants to. He also wants me to keep an eye on his wife and daughter. Elijah wants me to find someone to take Balthazar's seat. I want to keep this team intact continuing the work we do. But if you want that seat then I want you to apply for it. You will be given a fair chance. To get a seat on the council without being a beneficiary you must pass the assessment.", I divulge not getting a chance until now with everything going on.

"You're not going to get rid of me that easily.", Malan states.

"I'm not going anywhere. I have everything I could ask for.", Aspen responds.

"The council isn't my style, but you are the one that can bring The Company back its integrity.", Willa comments.

"Those offices are too stuffy for me.", Ace adds.

"That means so much to me you guys!", I tell them as my phone rings.

Elijah is calling to inform me that Kaden asked to be reassigned. He is going to give Kaden a new team and put him in charge of weeding out Balthazar's followers. Elijah also informs me that I will be leading the team for now on. But needs my vote to be able to proceed. I let Elijah know that he has my vote, and that Kaden would be a good man for the job. After I hang up my phone, I inform my team about Kaden. Also, I talk to them about having my brother join the team since we are one man down now. He is God of Hunt after all. We chit chat for a little bit before we all turn in for bed.

People have already started showing up as I am up in my room getting ready. Demitri has sent a demon to do my hair and make-up. She also brought a box with a gorgeous long midnight blue halter top evening gown. The dress matched the bracelet perfectly. We spent all day yesterday decorating for the ball and getting everything else in order. My Mom comes in and she sees me, telling me how enchanting I look. We go down to the ball together. I must make it look like I am one of the Queen's bodyguards, so I do not raise suspicion. Gives me the perfect excuse to carry my knifes and sword on me. Malan tweaked the spell on my bracelet to glamour my appearance the whole time not just for when someone has ill will against me.

Demitri's POV

I am talking to the demigod Helen. Yes, Helen of troy is a demigod. She is the daughter of Zeus and the mortal Leda, whose beauty is legendary. I catch a glimpse of Amara descending the stairs out of the corner of my eye. Neither Hellen nor her mother compares to Amara's beauty in my eyes. I have to look through her glamour to see her true self and not the demon. The way the dress hugs her curves and the dark blue with the blue-black raven ringlets make her violet eyes stand out even more. I must remind myself to breathe. We still have not had our talk. I am not going to push it though. She always keeps her word. I will give her time to heal, and she will come to me when she is ready. Even though not knowing exactly how she feels is tearing at my heart.

Everyone is in place. Suddenly, the front door flies open, and I take my eyes off Amara. Standing in the entrance is Mel and who I assume is Holle. Always having to make a big entrance. The woman standing next to Mel is a short mahogany brown hair human with brown eyes. Mel did say she has to possess a dead body to be able to walk on Earth. Holle walks right up to Harper slapping him before walking to the bar. That is definitely Holle. Let's just say they have history. Zack is dancing with a goddess in the middle of the dance floor. Everyone else is scattered in teams throughout the room.

When that song is over Zack walks up to his mother and father. They start talking amongst themselves. Holle approaches them as Mel approaches asking me to dance. When I decline, she informs me that Holle knows about us. That I have no choice to dance with her if I want to keep up appearances. I remind her that we were never anything as we walk out to the dance floor. That being true there is still no telling what Mel has said. When the song is over Holle leads Zack to the bar. Willa jumps into action as soon as Holle pours the potion into Zack's drink without him seeing. Acting like she is drunk Willa bumps into Holle spilling her drink all over Holle's dress. Catching the signal, the bartender switches the cup out.

After getting hateful with Willa, she encourages Zack to finish his drink. He throws the drink back and Holle heads to the bathroom as Willa follows her apologizing. Mind linking us Willa informs us that Holle is freezing the liquid on her dress. We all took a mind linking potion before the party that Ace made. It only lasts for about four hours. Holle comes back to the bar and Zack starts acting like a lovesick puppy not leaving her side. I must admit he is rather good at acting. The ball starts to wind down and the guest start to leave. Zack takes Holle by the hand and leads her to his parents. Where he tells them, he has met his soulmate and they want to get married right now.

Amara's POV

Phase one goes smoothly and it is now time for phase two of our plan. We quietly get the rest of the guest out. Having some of Demitri's demon employees take their place. Our Dad agrees to marry Zack and Holle. They both say their vows and just as they are about to say I do, Holle pulls out the Spear of Destiny and shoves it into my Dad's stomach. How the fuck did she get that? It is supposed to be locked in Demitri's office. The plan was to capture her right as they are about to kiss. Then she would either surrender or leave us no choice but to kill her. My Dad collapses to the floor as I rush to him. Malan and Lucas grab him on either side carrying him to Sylvia. As soon as they see Dad go down Demitri and Zack take my Mom to the room we reinforced yesterday with weapons and magic. Mel of course turns into mist and disappears. I turn to Holle, taking off my bracelet before slamming a right and a left hook into her face. Wanting her to know who is about to beat the shit out of her.

I catch the punch she throws at my face. Bending her arm backwards behind her back. Using it as leverage I push her down bringing a swift knee to her stomach twice. Causing Holle to double over for a couple of minutes. After she stands back up, she throws a punch, kick, and another punch. I block the punch and kick. She gets me good with that second punch though. I can feel blood running out of my mouth. The next moments are a haze of punches, kicks and blocks coming from the both of us. Holle and I are both healing as fast as we are causing damage to one another.

With a solid right hook from me, she hits the ground. Reaching up she pulls me down with her. I land on top of her getting in a few good hits. Before she flips us over to where she is now on top of me. Holle lands a couple of punches to my face before I am able to flip myself back on top of her. I connect several hits before Holle's meat suit goes cold and lifeless. Coming out of the girl's mouth is Holle in the form of red mist like smoke before disappearing. I use my goddess speed to get to my Dad. Mel is on the opposite side of the room. I will deal with her later. When I look over at my Dad he is up and changing his shirt like nothing happened with not even a scratch on his body.

"I gave Holle the Spear of Destiny you stab and tricked me with. I knew that copy would come in handy.", Mel tells us full of pride. "She was getting suspicious and was questioning my loyalty to her. After I disappeared for a few weeks Holle wanted me to prove my loyalty."

"Why not just tell us?", I question.

"It had to look real, and I was trying to keep my cover. That way we could know if she changes her plan and so, she will not kill me. That is out the window now. She may be gone but she will be back seeking vengeance. Once she finds out Hades is not actually dead. She will come to kill me and take the throne.", Mel answers.

"Thank you, Mel.", is all my Dad says.

Those three words were a big step in their relationship. One they will start forming, hopefully. I am sure Mel is just as shocked as I am. My Dad never spoke to her let alone said her name. He could not handle how she was conceived and that she was not his. But was his brother's child. Demitri and Zack come running in behind my Mom. Looks like they could not keep her from coming in and checking on my Dad. She runs into his arms hugging him tight before looking over the spot he had been stabbed. He tells my Mom and the others how Mel tricked Holle by giving her a copy of the Spear of Destiny. My Mom pulls Mel in a hug thanking her for saving his life. My Dad calls in some warrior demons to guard the castle while he takes Mom home.

"May I have this dance?", Demitri asks me with his hand out as we walk out of the hospital wing of the castle.

"Sure, but there is no music.", I start to say while placing my hand in his. He leads me to the basketball court, where we held the ball. Just as we enter music starts to play.

"I told her I would pay her extra for one more song.", Demitri confesses as he pulls me in closer. Then runs his finger along the necklace he gave me sending shivers down my spine.

I deeply inhale his scent then he twirls me around the dance floor before dipping me. My breath catches as he stares into my eyes. He looks so good in the black-on-black suit he is wearing. I just notice his tie is the same color as my dress. I thought he was going to kiss me with the intense look in his eyes. But he just pulls me up, spins me out and then spins me back into his arms. Holding me close through the rest of the song. As the song ends, he leans down and kisses me on the cheek. We are staring into each other's eyes, our lips only inches away from each other.

"Sir, we have a huge problem.", Lucas says as he is running up.

Demitri goes off with Lucas as I go to my room to change. I had just enough time to slip into something more comfortable before Malan runs into my room.

"The castle is under an attack by an undead army!", Malan discloses.

I strap on my knives then follow Malan to the weapon room as Kaden and I am assuming his new team are walking up.

"I heard you guys might need some back up.", Kaden says as he voids my gaze.

"Just in time.", Mel responds reaching for a shot gun and extra bullets.

"Here.", Malan voices to me as he hands me a rifle called the Spartan along with a couple extra loaded clips. It is a clone of the M4 carbine with some added features. I sling it over my shoulder as I go to grab one of Demitri's Samurai swords.

"Amara this one is for you.", Demitri tells me as he hands me a sword. "I had the Spear of Destiny melted down with Hell fire and foraged into a sword for you."

Hell fire was given its name by the mortals it is a black flame, comes from the Underworld and is the hottest flame on earth. I put the sword in my hand down. Then pull my new sword out of its sheath running my hand along it. This sword is so magnificent, I can feel the power radiating off it. "Thank you. It's beautiful.", I respond to Demitri.

"You should name it. All the greatest swords have names.", Demitri informs me.

"Alright then I will name it….", I say while trying to figure out something to name it. "Reaper."

Is there a better name for a blade that can kill anything on earth? Reapers are the symbol of death after all in the Mortal Realm. After grabbing our weapons, we go outside to join the fight. Aspen, Ace, Willa, Lucas and even Mel are already out fighting. Not to mention the demon warriors my Dad has guarding the castle. There are piles of bones upon bones at their feet. Everyone is fighting with everything they have. But they are still being pushed back by the undead army as they are shooting as many as they can. What we are fighting are not exactly zombies. They did not want our brains but were undead beings from Asgard here to kill us. Basically, they are killer skeletons that are being controlled by Holle. Those of us that are just now joining the fight unleash a blaze of bullets. Dropping them left and right. Demitri, Kaden, his team, several of Demitri's warrior demons, the warrior demons my Dad sent, Zack, Mel, Harper, Lucas, my team, and myself are no match for how big this army is. There is just too many, we would drop a hundred and a hundred more would pop up. We still continue to fight with everything we have. Holle is in a blonde girl's body this time. There is no way I can get through this mass of undead to get to her. I look around as I try to slay my way to her having ran out of bullets. I cut through a bunch with Reaper and set a bunch of others a blaze. I start getting closer to her only to get pushed back. I look around everyone is holding their own by either using swords, their abilities or both. But we are slowly being overpowered. Everyone is beaten and exhausted. It is time to even the score.

Demitri POV

I look for Amara as I slash through the undead that are charging at me. I send two of their heads flying off their shoulders with one powerful swing as I see Amara. She is hovering a few feet above the ground and her eyes are the same solid violet that they turned when she brought Aspen back to life. A second later a ton of undead along with additional demons start to pour out my castle doors to join the fight. It is just what we needed to even the fight. Holle parts a sea of undead as she charges for Amara. I start slashing my way through Holle's undead army with everything I must get to Amara. Body after body slumps lifelessly to the ground. Heads are flying then rolling across the ground. Decapitating them is the only way to stop them.

With a raise of Holle's hand I am encircled. I stab and slash as more undead keep surrounding me. Just as Holle swings her sword Amara blocks it. Then sends a kick to Holle's chest making her stumble back a little way. After shaking the hit off Holle charges at Amara again. Throwing ice shards as she does. Amara effortlessly dodges the shards and hits Holle with a couple of blue fire balls. Leaving big circular burns on Holle's meat suit. Sounds of swords clashing and thuds rang out through the air of the battlefield. I manage to break through the circle with Malan's help. Getting close to where Amara is, we are hit with another wave of undead.

Holle embeds her sword in Amara's stomach then pulls it out. Amara is doing her best to fight off a group of undead and Holle at the same time, as she is starting to be overtaken. In a blink of an eye some of the undead are being wrapped in vines by Willa. One by one the others slump to the ground as Aspen slices through them. Bodies fall lifeless to the ground left and right. Lucas and Ace are trying to get to Amara as well. Harper, Zack, and some of the demon warriors are pushing back the undead from getting into the castle. I cannot tell who belongs to our undead army and who belongs to Holle's. As more undead come running out of the castle mixing in with the others. I just stick to only attacking the ones that attack me. Amara stands back up after doubling over, raising her sword and slashes Holle's left arm almost off. Causing Holle to drop her sword. Holle's arm is only hanging on by a few tendons as it is gushing out blood. The battle is raging on all around me but all I can think about is getting to Amara.

"Pick it up.", Amara commands.

Not saying a word Holle throws four spears of ice at Amara. She effortlessly dodged three out of the four. The fourth ice spear lodges into her shoulder. Amara's hands instantly turn into flames. Without bothering to touch the ice spear she sends three fire balls at Holle. Two out of the three hitting their target.

"Pick it up.", Amara commands once more.

Holle bends down picking up her sword. Then she gets hit in the nose hard by Amara's elbow after blocking the swing of Amara's sword. Blood is oozing out of Holle's nose running down her lips. She also has two big scorch marks that are still smoking on her chest and stomach. Dodging Holle's swing of her sword Amara slams her sword into Holle. Spinning around Holle with Reaper still embedded in Holle's stomach as blood runs out her mouth. Amara cuts Holle horizontally in half. The top half of the dead body Holle is possessing slides off the bottom half. Both pieces are falling towards the ground. Before either piece of the body can hit the floor, Amara has them in flames. Not giving Holle time to escape and making sure to end her for good this time. Her undead army is gone as soon as the body turns to ash. Even the ones that are in pieces or are just a lifeless pile of bones.

Several demons and undead from our side were lost in this battle. Two of Kaden's teammates were killed. Everyone from Amara's team survived including Zack, Harper, and Lucas. They were all savagely beaten though. Mel is on the ground in front of Kaden, she has her head in his lap. Blood is gushing out of her neck. She had jumped in front of a sword that was meant for Kaden. I have never seen her do something so selfless she must really care about him. Amara walks over then lovingly holds her little sister as she heals her. Then commands the surviving undead back to the Underworld after thanking them. She tells them they will be rewarded for their help. They vanish with a single swipe of Amara's hand. She then commands the demons to take the injured to Sylvia and informs everyone that tonight we will honor the fallen. I am completely mesmerized by her. She is going to make an amazing queen.

Amara's POV

After the feast and bonfire, we had in honor of those that had fallen. I lay in bed thinking about today. Things had taken a turn for the worst, but we were able to still come out of it on top. Mel made me proud today helping Dad and for sacrificing herself for Kaden. Even though I do not want anything to happen to her. I still am not able to forgive her but that does not mean I want her hurt. I hope this can help them have a relationship. Everything that has happened in such brief time is crazy. I start to think about Demitri. What am I going to do? I love him, I have for a long time even though I thought he did not feel the same. Now I have a chance with him. Except I need time to heal before jumping in a relationship with him. Or I will lash out taking this pain out on him. How does that mortal saying go? O yes, hurt people hurt people. He deserves so much better than that. He has really been there for me and has been so patient with all this.

My mind then just takes off and will not let me sleep. Maybe a walk will clear my head. I end up walking by the basketball court which is spotless. No one would have been able to tell there was a ball held in here just hours ago. I find a basketball and start with layups then three pointers. After a bit I just walk around throwing shots from wherever. Demitri catches one of the shots I missed. I have no clue where he came from but glad for the company. He asks if I want to play one on one. I agree even though truthfully this is not the one on one I am wanting to play with him. Man, I really need to calm myself. Demitri has been way too good to me to deserve being a rebound. Plus, rebounds are just distractions they do not heal you. I need to heal.

For two hours we play one on one. I am definitely going to be having a dirty dream about this tonight. Of course, he ends up winning by one basket. We head to the kitchen to get something to hydrate us as well as something to snack on. Demitri grabs two bottles of Gatorade while I grab popcorn, chips, and Skittles. We make our way to the theatre room to watch a movie. Malan and Sylvia are in there watching the new Men in Black, so we join them. Halfway through the movie I must have fallen asleep because I feel myself being laid in bed. Demitri covers me up then kisses me on the forehead.

"Sweet dreams my love.", he lovingly voices as he walks out shutting the door.

Demitri's POV

That naughty dream I have just woken up from has me so hard it is painful. Jumping into the shower I think about that dream as I stroke my rock-hard dick until I reach my release. I hang my head in the water for a bit. It is not what I need but it will have to do. Once I am dressed, I call Lucas to see if he is up for a sparring match before work. He is going to meet me there in ten minutes. I start warming up while I wait. We spar for a good hour. Lucas is my best fighter, and this helps work out some of the built-up frustration. After my morning meetings I notice I have a meeting with Amara in forty minutes. I work on paperwork until then. Amara walks in looking stunning in a white blouse and black pin stripe slacks.

"Morning, I want to start picking up my slack and earning money from the companies I'm partnered in.", Amara greets me.

"Harper and I setup the companies to be run by others. Also, we set up a bank account that every two weeks your shares are deposited in.", I disclose as I hand her the debit card and a piece of paper with all her bank information on it.

"Thank you so much. I would still like to go see the farms and dispensaries sometime. Also, my team and I will be out of your hair tonight.", she discloses.

"Are you sure you can't stay a little while longer?", I inquire.

"That would be nice but unfortunately I have a lot of stuff I have to take care of back home.", she responds reluctantly before telling me bye. Smiling that beautiful smile of hers. I cannot help imagining her bent over my desk as I take her from behind.

Amara's POV

I walk out of Demitri's office shocked by the fact my boys made sure I was taken care of without knowing if I was ever coming back. Demitri did not even know if I was alive. I love them both even more for it. I call Harper to thank him and let him know I want to check them all out. After hanging up I shadow jump to the shadow of my Blazer and drive to my lawyer's office. Last night I had a few clever ideas come to mind. Now I am going to make those ideas come to life. I head back to the castle after getting all the legal documents finalized and signed that I needed. We are going to all hang out together before we leave. It only takes me about twenty minutes to pack my stuff. Leaving a little over four hours until our helicopter will be here. I know I do not really need a helicopter. But my team does, and I like doing things like that with them. If I am being honest, I also enjoy the peace that comes with doing certain mortal activities.

I am going to miss this simple black and silver themed room with the sky light just above the bed. I walk to the kitchen where almost everyone is already here. The smell filling the room is amazing and is causing my mouth to water. I sit in between Demitri and Harper with Zack across the table from me. Everyone that is not here yet are randomly showing up. A big plate of coconut chicken, mash potatoes, and corn is placed in front of me. Digging in I am too busy eating to talk. Once we finish dinner and dessert, which is a chocolate cake with vanilla ice cream. We hang out at the pool, hot tub, basketball court, and the Bowling Alley waiting on our ride.

Demitri stays close to me all night. It was nice, I am really going to miss him. Before boarding I give Zack, Harper, and Lucas a big hug. Walking over to Demitri I hug him tightly before leaving a peck on his cheek. All my stuff is still at Kaden's and my town house. Except what I brought to Demitri's with me. Our town house is the last place I want to go right now. Luckily, I have enough with me to get me by for a couple of weeks and that Demitri's housekeeper had wash my clothes yesterday. So, I have the pilots drop Grim and I off at the cabin. I will worry about getting my stuff later. I have always wanted to live out here and cannot wait to start this new chapter of my life living in this cabin in the middle of the Ouachita Mountains.

Sean's wife redecorated the cabin about a year or so before she died. So, I will not need much. Opening the door, I am hit with that familiar scent. Grim went from room to room until he found his favorite one. Of course, I take the master bedroom. The cabin has six bedrooms all decorated differently. The master bedroom is painted a light blue with a couple of landscape portraits and a picture of the four of us. Grabbing a lavender bath bomb, I go into the bathroom to have a nice hot bath. After the relaxing bath I climb into bed finding Grim snuggling my pillow fast asleep. My phone dings with a message.

Demitri ➔ Good night and sweet dreams.

Me → Sweet dreams, good night.

Then sliding under the covers, I drift off to dreamland as soon as my head hits   the   pillow.

CHAPTER 8: SURPRISE!

Amara's POV

It has been a couple of weeks since the battle outside the castle. Today I stop putting off moving my stuff out of Kaden's town house. I turn my key in the lock for the last time. Opening the door, I then reach down grabbing the boxes I set down next to me. Since the cabin is already beautifully decorated and furnished, I am not taking much with me. So, I pack my clothes, books, and the other few belongings I have. Tears escape down my cheek as I close and tape the last box. Then I leave my key on the coffee table. Kaden pulls up in his new light grey Altima while I am loading the boxes in my Blazer.

"Hey.", he says as he walks over to me.

"Hi.", I reply.

"I'm really sorry for everything Amara. You were right you cannot trust me. Hell, I can't even trust myself around Mel.", he confesses.

"There is no need for you to try and explain. You lost that chance when you took off like a coward. I can't believe I'm saying this, but Mel really does care about you.", I state as I turn to leave.

"Will you ever forgive me?", Kaden pleads.

"I don't know.", I convey. I know I need to for me, but I do not know how to forgive either of them.

"Congratulations on getting a seat on the Council. If anyone deserves it, it is you.", he informs me as he walks into his town house.

I load the last box then head home. My nose is filled with a familiar aroma as soon as I open my front door while Grim runs to greet me. This place still smells like Sean and his family which brings me a sense of peace. I miss them so much, even Connor before he changed. This cabin makes me feel like they are still with me. Walking in I set two of the four boxes down before going to get the other two boxes out of the Blazer. I see a fruit bouquet sitting on my counter. It is full of delicious chocolate covered strawberries. I knew who it was from before I look at the card. Demitri had asked me if I needed help moving, this is something I felt like I needed to do myself. It is not like I had a lot to pack anyway. I pull the card off the holder and read it.

> Amara,
> Congratulations on your new home.
> Love
> Demitri & Harper.

There is a knock at the door and Zack walks in. Just as I am taking a bite of one of the chocolate covered strawberries. A few strawberries are missing meaning Grim has already eaten some.

"Hey Sis, nice place.", Zack says as he walks to the couch and sits down.

"It really is. Thank you for coming over. I would like to talk to you about something.", I inform him. "I want you to apply for a seat on the Council. As of right now we are down two people. Harper is helping with Dean's daughters' seat until she is ready to take it over. That leaves Balthazar's seat. I think you are a great fit.", I disclose.

"I appreciate the offer, but I can't accept. I feel like there is someone more suitable for that position. Plus, I am having to help Dad run the Underworld on top of making sure nothing and no one gets out. Mom has decided that she is stepping down. However, I would love to join your team seeing how a spot is available.", Zack voices.

I cannot help but smile at how much my little brother has grown up. I hate that I missed him growing into a man. Zack hangs out with me for a little bit before leaving. We just hang out watching movies, talking about life, and how good his relationship with Nixie is going. Before leaving he informs me that he is not going to push. But if I want to talk, he is here for me.

After I unpack the boxes, I binge watch some Penny Dreadful. The next morning as I am getting out of the shower Aspen calls me. Squealing about how Lucas has asked her to move in with him. I excitedly congratulate her. Getting dress, I then head over to help her pack. She did not really need my help since she is leaving all the furniture for Willa. The three of us spend the morning laughing, talking, and just spending time together. Our lives are changing so much. Willa offers to pick Grim up from school for me so I can help take Aspen's stuff to the castle. After dropping and unpacking her stuff in Lucas's room, we meet Willa and Grim at what is now just Willa's apartment. I wanted to go up and see Demitri. But I know the boys are busy. We spend Aspen's last night in the apartment with Willa. I really needed some time with my girls. Willa informs us that things are getting serious with Ace. Which brought a smile to my face, I love seeing my girls loved and happy.

I wake up early to take Grim to The Company for school before my important meeting. Not to mention all the paperwork and files I must get through today. The Company does not have the resources to really teach the six beings that go. It is more of a daycare for the employees of The Company. I have a little bit of time before my meeting, so I go home, shower, and dress in black slacks with a light green blouse. Grabbing my keys then slipping on my dress shoes I make my way to Sean's. I mean my mansion. I am still not use to the thought of me owning a mansion. I finally figured out what I am going to do with my inheritance. Walking through the huge double oak doors I am greeted by my lawyer and Malan. I have appointed Malan as my adviser and headmaster of this project.

"Good morning Amara, everything is set and moving according to plan. Dustin has our business license. As well as any other legal documents we need to get this place up and going. He just needs you to fill out and sign a few more pages.", Malan informs me as we walk up to his office.

"Congratulations Amara, you are now the owner of Aspire Academy. I'm sure this school will achieve remarkable things.", Dustin says has he shakes my hand after everything is finalized.

Grim is going to be so excited when he finds out I am opening a school for all supernatural beings. It is for grades pre-k to some associate level college courses. There are a few schools scattered out through the United States. The magicians, lycans, vampires, and hunters have their own schools. Their schools are exclusively for their kind only. There are so many other beings out there that need help controlling their powers or a safe place to stay. Getting all the legal documents signed did not take as long as I thought it would. So, I stay a little while longer to help get everything ready to start hiring and unloading the delivery trucks. Once that is all done, I grab something to eat on my way to headquarters. I am so excited I could barely keep my secret. I walk into my office while stuffing my face to find Harper and Aspen with their noses in paperwork. They fill me in on how Kaden's team has weeded out almost all of Balthazar's followers in The Company. It turns out they are still trying to conduct Balthazar's and Mel's plan. To bring down The Company while starting a war between humans and Sups.

I sit down at my desk diving into the huge pile of employee files trying to find candidates for the empty seat on the council. I am so thankful for Aspen and Harper. I did not know how I was going to get everything even close to being done today. A couple of hours in I get a text.

Demitri →Want to come over tonight?

Me→ Yes, but it is going to be a late night.

Demitri → I'll be up.

Me → See you later then.

I am missing that gorgeous face of his. I get back to work getting lost in the files until Elijah walks in. He is checking in to see how much progress I have made with finding candidates. I let him know that I have not made any progress and that once I am done going through employee files, I want to go through our data base. Elijah agrees that would be a good idea before heading out for the day. I look at the time on my phone which reads 8:00pm. Shit looks like I do not have time to go home to change. Sending Harper and Aspen home I turn off my computer. Then head down the hall to get Grim.

After dropping him off at home since he did not want to go with me. I rip open the nearest shadow. Jumping into it, I then shadow jump to the Tree of Dawn. The smell of garlic butter steaks fills my nose as soon as I open the front door. Instantly my mouth starts watering. I walk into the kitchen drinking in that sexy body of his. We have not seen each other since I left, he has been keeping in touch though. Demitri is just setting our plates on the table.

"I see you got a new table.", I state as I sit down.

"The other one needed replacing. I have missed you a lot.", he response.

"I have missed you too.", I confess as I feel our bond pulling me to him. "All of this smells and looks amazing."

Licking my lips before I dive in. On my plate is a juicy Ribeye sauté in garlic and butter with broccoli covered in melted cheese and mashed potatoes smothered in butter. We catch each other up on what has happened in our lives since we last saw each other. I did not tell him about Aspire yet. Malan is the only one at the moment that knows about it. One of the housekeepers brings out a big piece of chocolate cheesecake just as I am finishing my dinner. Wow Demitri is bringing out all the stops. This whole meal is probably my favorite meal. Once we are done with dinner, he takes me by the hand and leads me to the garden.

It is an enchanting garden. It must have been added while my memories were missing. I did not even know it was here. It is laid out in the shape of a swirl pattern. Painted with all kinds of rare, beautiful flowers. Blue Evening Primroses, white and pink Peacock Amaryllis, and purple and white Hanging Naked Man Orchids fill the garden with their vibrant colors to name a few. There are also magical plants like Wolfsbane, Bat-thorn, Aeglos, and Molly. Bat-thorn is like Wolfsbane but for vampires and Aeglos is used for healing. In the center is a beautiful stone waterfall and a couple of benches. The flowers and grass around it make it look even more beautiful.

"Thank you for being patient and giving me time to heal.", I voice.

"You don't need to thank me. I love you Amara.", Demitri response looking intensely into my eyes. "There is nothing I would not do for you."

"I love you Demitri.", I confess. "I just don't want to turn around and jump into another relationship. Even though I have wanted to be with you for so long. I'm still healing."

"My heart belongs to you. We will go at the pace you want. I just want to call you mine."

"I am yours Demitri.", I voice not being able to deny it any longer.

Reaching up Demitri cups my cheeks and stares into my soul. Before bending down to kiss me. It is such a loving kiss. A warm tingling feeling spreads through my body. I wrap my arms around his neck and my legs around his waist as he picks me up. Just as I am deepening the kiss, his wings come out and he takes off into the night sky. Without breaking our kiss. We are above the tree line when I finally break the connection between our lips. It is so breathtaking up here. Demitri flies us around the whole island and out a little way over the ocean. As soon as we land, I continue where we left off. I nip at his bottom lip as he pulls me closer into him deepening the kiss once more. I tease his hair as his hands explore my body with me standing on my tip toes. I have never felt like this from a kiss. I wanted. No, I needed him right now and I cannot get close enough to him.

"If we don't stop now, I will not be able to control myself from taking you right here.", he whispers in a deep voice coated with lust in my ear.

That voice just makes me want him even more. I let him know that by rubbing my hand in a circular motion over the huge bulge in his jeans. Causing him to growl out my name. I cannot tell you how many times I have fantasized about being the one to make sounds like that come out of that sexy mouth of his. Demitri takes my hand continuing our walk as we fall into a comfortable silence. My phone starts to ring but I ignore it. I did not want anything to change this moment. I get two more calls before I finally pull my phone out to check it. Mel starts calling as soon as I see it was her that had called me the other times. I have not talk to her since the battle, probably even before that. I reluctantly pick up the phone to hear uncontrollable sobs. I tell her I will be right there. This must be bad, despite her selfish cruel ways Mel has always been strong. I have never seen or heard her like this. I have not forgiven her, but this is my little sister, and she needs me.

"Demitri, I'm sorry but I must go to the Underworld to help Mel. Something bad has happened.", I inform him after hanging up the call.

"Can I at least give you a ride?", he response.

I nod my head yes as he snatches me up bridal style and takes off towards the castle. He then flies us through the portal and into the sky of the Underworld. In no time Demitri is setting me on Mel's porch.

"Good night.", I say to him.

"You aren't going to just get away with teasing me like that.", he playfully whispers in my ear before leaving a small kiss on my lips. "Good night Beautiful."

Gods that man is delicious. I watch him take off into the night until I cannot see him anymore. Seeing him in his true form will never stop amazing me. I really want to finish what we started. Reminding myself that my sister needs me I walk into Mel's apartment hollering for her. I hear her crying in the bathroom, she is sitting on the floor against the wall staring at the counter. Three positive pregnancy tests lay in a row on her bathroom counter.

"O shit!", I say out loud as I slide to the floor next to her wrapping my arms around her. Then pulling her into my chest letting her cry.

"It's Kaden's.", she is barely able to say between sobs.

Holy fuck! I did not know what to say. I want to comfort my sister, but I cannot lie this hurts bad. Kaden has always wanted kids. We just never had any because I was not ready. I am still not over Kaden or what had happened. Even though Demitri and I are slowly getting serious.

"I tried to tell him, but he won't talk to me. I can't raise a baby especially alone.", Mel expresses as she continues to sob.

"I know without a doubt that once he gets passed his anger. Kaden will step up and do right by his child. Plus, there is no way I am going to let my sister go through this alone. Get up off the floor I'll turn on the shower.", I direct Mel. After running the shower, I pull out my phone and text Kaden.

Me → We need to talk.

Kaden → I just got home. You mind coming over?

Me → No, see you in a few.

I inform Mel that after she gets dressed, we are going to go talk to Kaden together. While Mel is slipping on some clothes. I grab one of the pregnancy tests. After shadow jumping us to the Mortal Realm, I drive Mel's Lexus over to Kaden's town house. She tells me she needs a minute, so I stand outside the car waiting on her. Once she is ready, she gets out then walks up to knock on the door. As soon as Kaden opens the door and sees Mel, he tries to shut the door on us. I slip my foot in the door before he can.

"Kaden, you need to talk to Mel.", I prompt.

"You shouldn't have brought her here.", he spits out. "Now move your foot."

I push the door open which pushes him out of the way. I walk through the door followed by Mel. "Mel tells him.", I command.

"I'm pregnant with your child.", Mel confesses after playing with her hands for a little bit while working up the courage.

"Right.", he angerly responds as I am handing him the pregnancy test. "Doesn't mean it's mine."

"Bullshit!", is all Mel says.

"We all know how big of a whore you are.", Kaden adds.

"I haven't been with anyone but you since I saw you for the first time.", she stutters between sobs before running out of Kaden's town house.

"I get that she has done some fucked up things. As well as that you are angry and hurting. But you will not talk to her like that. It is not just her fault things have turned out the way they have. If you have doubts about the baby being yours, get a paternity test done.", I voice before going to take my sister to my house. I still did not know how to feel about all of this. I did know my sister did not need to be alone tonight. She cries the whole way to the cabin. I feel bad for her even though she did this to herself. I send a text to Demitri before I pull off.

Me ➔ Heading home and taking Mel with me. This situation is fucked!

When we arrive, I show her to one of the guest rooms. Grim that little sweetheart turns a movie on and is cooking them some popcorn. Mel is out before the popcorn is done. I make sure she is covered up then go out front and sit on my porch swing. I check my phone, but Demitri still has not replied. Laying my head back I close my eyes as I get lost in my thoughts and emotions. Out of nowhere I hear a thud, I open my eyes to the man of my dreams standing in front of me. Without a word Demitri sits next to me then pulls me up into his lap. He embraces me tightly not pushing to know what had happen today. Without me having to tell him he is giving me what I need. Uncurling from his chest I sit up looking him in the eyes letting out a big sigh as a few tears roll down my cheeks.

"That bad huh?", Demitri asks not taking his eyes from mine. While pushing a strand of hair behind my ear then wiping the tears away. Still not being able to find my voice we sit in silence for a little bit longer. Looking up at the crescent moon I can feel her power radiating all around me.

"Mel is pregnant with Kaden's child.", I finally blurt out after sitting in his arms for a while.

"Damn. How are you holding up Baby?", Demitri asks pulling me tightly into his chest.

"Honestly, I don't know how to feel about it.", I confess. I did not want to hurt Demitri, but I cannot and will not lie to him. I slide down laying my head on his lap. He runs his fingers through my hair slowly lulling me to sleep. At some point Demitri picks me up carrying me to bed. Opening my eyes as he lays me down in my bed then pulling the covers up over me. "Will you please stay with me tonight?", I plead. Without a word, he climbs in the covers behind me. I snuggle into him where I fit perfectly. Nothing can beat this feeling. He is my home! I drift off to sleep in total bliss.

Grim is snuggled between Demitri and I when I wake up. I did not even feel him climb into bed with us last night. Slipping out of bed I go check on Mel, who is still sound asleep. I step outside to watch the sunrise. It has been a while since I have had the time to just stop and watch the sun paint the sky as it rises for the day. Few minutes later Mel comes out, laying her head on my shoulder watching the sun rise with me.

"Good morning beautiful. Your Mom is calling.", Demitri informs me as he hands me my phone while hanging halfway out of the door.

"Good morning handsome.", I reply before answering the call. "Hello Mom, Yes I'll be there in a bit."

"Mel if you want you can hang out here with Grim. I have to go see Mom and Dad.", I inform her. "Just tell Grim that I'll be back soon when he wakes up."

"I'll give you a ride.", Demitri offers.

"Please give me a couple of minutes to change.", I convey. Running into my room I change quickly. I throw on a pair of grey shorts and a midnight blue tank top. Before brushing my hair and teeth. "Alright I'm ready.", I notify Demitri as I step outside.

He scoops me up, kisses me on the forehead and takes off towards his castle. Once there I go straight to the gates of the Underworld. I pause for a minute before going in. I have not been to the Underworld since I lost my memories. Besides when I came to check on Mel. I was worried about her, and it did not hit me like it is now. Holding my head high I walk through the gates petting all three of Cerberus's heads on my way through. I pass by the Acheron River on the way to my Dad's office. Most know it by the name River of Woe. My Mom, Dad, and Zack are already there waiting on me. My Dad's office is so different from Mom's and simple. It has a black couch, his desk with his laptop, and a filing cabinet. Not one picture hangs on the bare light grey walls. The huge window with the view over the Underworld cannot be beat by anything in my Mom's office.

"Baby Girl, we have asked you here because your Mother and I are retiring. Your brother has been helping to get everything ready. You are my heir leaving you next in line. I do request that your brother helps you with all the responsibilities until you take a King. As well as Demitri stays second in command until he is ready to step down.", My Dad discloses.

Still processing everything my Dad has just said I nod my head. I am not sure how to respond.

"EEK. I am going to start planning your Inauguration Ceremony at once.", my Mom excitedly squeals out as she rushes to start the arrangements. My Dad and Zack have a few things to go over with me before I can leave. Walking out of the gate I am still stunned. I go straight to Demitri's office. Without knocking I walk in and slump into a chair in front of his desk.

"What's up Babe?", Demitri asks me curiously seeing the look on my face.

"My Mom and Dad are retiring their crowns.", I reveal.

"Congratulations.", he voices.

"I'm not queen material.", I remark.

"You will make an amazing queen.", he declares as he walks over to me pulling me up into a hug. "I have seen the growth in you as well has your parents. They would not give you this opportunity if you were not ready."

"Thanks Baby, I need to get back to Mel and Grim.", I add.

"You want me to give you a ride?", Dimitri asks.

"It's fine. I know your workload has just gotten even heavier until the Ceremony.", I note before placing a kiss on his lips. Then walk out and shadow jump to my cabin. My nose is instantly filled with the scent of cinnamon rolls when I walk through my front door. Mel and Grim are smiling while baking them together. They have one pan in the oven while working on filling another one. She seems to be in a better mood. After eating two large cinnamon rolls, I start cleaning up. Mel grabs the plate out of my hands saying that she has it under control. After she is done, she comes in and sits next to me to watch the movie.

"I had made up my mind I was going to get rid of this baby. Let's face it I'm not a motherly person.", Mel confesses. "Now I don't know."

Shit Mel, I did not want her to regret that decision. She might not see it, but I have seen it in her. Only with Zack but it is still there. "What made you change your mind?", I ask her after the long silence.

"Spending time with Grim. I felt cared about in that moment. Then I started thinking about how it would be if that were my little girl instead of Grim. Which gets me thinking how all I ever wanted was someone to love me for me. Here I am determined to throw that chance away because I am scared, I am not good enough. That I am going to screw this kid up.", she confesses.

"Sis as long as you love this child and strive every day to do your best. You will be a good Mom. No matter what happens with Kaden. I will be here for you and this Baby.", I inform Mel as I hug her.

"Thank you.", She tells me as tears are running down her cheek. "I don't know what I would do without you. You have always tried to be there for me, but I could not see that through my jealousy. I'm sorry I let my envy turn me into a vindictive bitch.", Mel apologizes.

"I'm just glad your skin didn't turn green.", I state with a laugh while nudging her with my shoulder. She giggles a little at my attempt to lighten the mood.

We walk down to the water hanging out there until dinner time. After dinner Mel gets a call from Kaden asking to talk. She goes to meet up with him while Grim and I go to bed. Checking my phone after I get Grim snuggled into his bed. I see that I have a text message.

Demitri → Good Night Beautiful

Me → Good Night Demitri

Snuggling under the warm covers I drift off to sleep as soon as my head hits my pillow. Grim comes into wake me up even before my alarm, he is excited about his surprise. Last night I told him that he would be a little late for school because I have something I want to show him. We get ready for the day, eat breakfast, and then head out. I pull up in front of my mansion. Well, what is now officially Aspire Academy. I am so excited! I have secretly been working on this for a while. I fill Grim in on how I have started this Academy and he will be going here starting opening day. He is so excited he rushes out of the car and inside. I let him check out every room before taking him to school. Before he gets out, I see a sad look on his face. I ask him what is wrong, I thought he would be excited. He informs me that he is excited, but he is going to miss me. I pull my little creature into my arms. Telling him that he will always be my son and can live with me as long as he wants to. I also inform him that you do not have to live there to attend. A big smile spreads across his face and he jumps out heading to school. I head back to Aspire where Malan and I spend the rest of the day interviewing various beings. We are so close to being able to open. I still have not told anyone. Instead, I sent out invitations to everyone for opening day.

After picking up Grim I pick dinner up then head home. I eat before taking a long hot shower. My life keeps changing every time I start to get comfortable. I guess I need to be kept on my toes. I dry off, throw on a t-shirt and panties then crawl into my bed. I lay there for a little bit running everything through my head before finally going to sleep. Grim had already put himself to bed. He is growing up too fast. Malan and I spend the next couple of days getting everything ready to open. Aspire Academy is set to open in a week. As Malan sets lunch in front of me my phone buzzes. The smell of fried Chicken Strips and French Fries fill my nose as I check it.

Demitri → Date Night?

Me → Can't wait.

Demitri → I'll pick you up from your place at 6.

Me → See you then. I love you.

Demitri → Love you more.

Once we are done eating, we continue the interviews. By four o'clock our last interview is over. We have a good base to start with. I leave feeling accomplished with a smile on my face. Picking up Grim I get him home, feed him, make sure he takes a shower and get him settled in. After turning the Tv on a timer to go off at nine I take a quick shower, before painting my face, brushing, and braiding my hair. Then I slip on a black dress that hugs my curves. It comes a little above the knees with silver high heels. Just as Demitri knocks on my door. He looks so yummy in those black dress pants and green button up shirt. Catching me licking my top lip as I take him in, he raises an eyebrow. Handing me a bouquet of Forget Me Nots he then bends down and places a kiss on my lips. I take the flowers inside to put them in a vase. Once I am back outside, he wraps his arms around me taking off into the sky. I love this feeling I get when he flies me around.

Demitri lands in a clearing that is somewhere in the forest on the island. It is set up for a picnic. The sun covers the clearing laminating the soft, fluffy, light green grass. Not a single plant other than the grass is growing here. Demitri has a blanket laid out in the middle. Even has a picnic basket sitting on the blanket. I am having such an enjoyable time relaxing, snacking, and talking with Dimitri. Seeing this relaxed sweet side of him is making me fall even more in love with him. Leaning over kissing him, I start it out slow and lovingly then deepen the kiss. Demitri lifts me up and has me straddling him in one swift motion. Deepening the kiss even more as I rotate my hips in a figure eight pattern. Feeling starved for his touch. He moans then flips me over on to my back. Moving his head between my legs he takes turns between licking and rubbing his finger in a circular motion on my clit over my panties. Pulling them to the side he eats me like he has been longing to taste me. Sucking and moving the tip of his tongue in a swirling motion on my clit. My back arches in pleasure as I moan out his name. Trailing his finger down my lips he inserts two fingers in me while sucking my clit. He continues eating and fucking me with his fingers until my legs are shaking. Begging him to put his dick deep inside me, he quickens his pace. I moan out his name as he sucks an orgasm out of me just as it starts to pour down rain. Sitting up on his knees he puts my panties back in place. Before scooping me up bridal style. After taking off into the air he flies us back to his castle.

As soon as he lands on his balcony, I start kissing him as the rain continues to pour down. Screw it we are already wet. This kiss is full of hunger. He grabs me by my thighs as I jump up wrapping my legs around his waist. Walking in his room he puts me against the wall. I run my hand down over his bulge then I unbutton and unzip his pants. Reaching into his boxer briefs I pull his rock-hard cock out letting it spring lose. After pulling my panties to the side I position his dick at my entrance. Rubbing it up to my clit and back down. As Demetri holds me up, I use him for leverage while I put him in me. Moving him in and out with my hips as I quicken my pace. I slam him all the way into me rubbing my clit on him. Dimitri moans out has he grabs me by my ass. Then bounces me against him at a fast pace. Making me take all of him deep in me with every bounce. He moans out my name and tells me how fucking good I feel. As he walks us over to the bed, he does not stop bouncing me against him. I do not stop rotating my hips as he slides in and out of me with every bounce. Laying me on my back he pulls out of me to strip me out of my soaked dress and panties. Before pulling off all his wet clothes. I cannot take my eyes off him. But I hated the empty feeling I get when he pulled out of me.

"You are so sexy.", he growls out as his hands explore my body. Demitri positions himself on me as he slides his dick into me. Flipping him over onto his back I kiss him passionately. Before leaving a trail of kisses down is neck, chest, and stomach all the way to his thigh. Nipping here and there. I take his rock-hard dick into my hand and start stroking it. Then I run my tongue up and down his shaft. Before sliding him into my mouth until it hits the back of my throat. Twisting my hand up the part that would not fit in my mouth I use my other hand to play with his balls. Tears run down my face mixing with my saliva as I keep slamming his shaft into the back of my throat over and over. I suck as hard as I can as I pull him out of my mouth. Climbing on top of him I slam down. Bouncing and twerking my ass harder and faster bringing myself close to an orgasm. I spin around where my back is to him picking up the pace without pulling him out of me. I am bringing myself over the edge. Sitting up he pulls me off him then lays me on my back.

"I'm going to be the one to bring you to an orgasm our first time.",

Demitri breathlessly informs me as he slides into me. The dipping motion he is doing with his hips is bringing me closer and closer. I moan out his name as he is burying his dick into me bringing me to an orgasm. The sound of me moaning his name and his fast pace brings him to his own orgasm. Spilling his seed deep in me.

"Damnit Demitri!", I exclaim jumping up and rushing into the bathroom to push what I can of his seed out of me. Damn I am sore. I have not been with someone this big before, I think to myself.

"It's okay Babe.", he notes after he quits laughing which is pissing me off. "I have a sterilization spell casted on me every few months."

After peeing I clean myself up in the shower and then climb into bed with Demitri. Of course, he is already passed out. I snuggle up to him laying my head on his chest. I am out instantly.

I wake up to Demitri walking out of the bathroom in just a towel. I am dumbfounded by the sight of his muscular almost naked body. Feeling the tingle and wetness starting to pool at my opening. I walk over to Demitri pushing him up against the wall reaching up to kiss him. He pulls me in closer as he kisses me like he needs me and cannot let me go. His hands start massaging my breast as he leaves kisses along my neck. While rubbing my clit with his fingers in a circular motion. No one has ever been able to turn me on like this. Wasting no time, I rip the towel off him as he deepens the kiss. Slowly I kneel as I run my hand down his chest and abs. I take him in my mouth sucking as I slide him in and out of my mouth. Twisting my hand as I slide it out. He growls out as he picks me up by my ass lifting me to his face. I am sliding my legs around his shoulders as he is sliding his tongue into me.

"Fuck Demitri!", I moan out. He continues to fuck me with his tongue while walking over to the bed then lays me on my back. Not lifting his head from between my legs he continues eating me like a dessert.

"Damn. Baby you taste so good, and I love how wet you get for me.", he says between sucking on my clit and rolling his tongue in me.

"Please Demitri, I need you in me.", I beg as I roll over onto my hands and knees.

He slides in me from behind as I inhale sharply, noticing I am still sore from last night. He slowly moves in and out of me. Kissing the back of my neck up to the side of my chin. Turning my head his lips and tongue beg for entrance in my mouth. I part my mouth pushing all my passion into this kiss. He pulls my legs to my chest giving him a better angle to bury himself in me. As he wraps one of his hands around my neck. Thrusting fast and hard he is quickly bringing me to an orgasm. I moan out my ecstasy as I cum all over his dick while my walls tighten around it.

"Fuck Baby you are so tight.", Demitri growls out as he buries his seed deep in me with his orgasm.

I uncurl my legs not being able to hold them up any longer. While my orgasm is still pulsing through my entire body. Laying down for a little bit longer I try to catch my breath before jumping in the shower, which Demitri joins me. I really enjoyed the shower together even though I am in a hurry. I have to get home to get Grim to school and then I have last minute things I need to do to be able to open Aspire on time. Before going to The Company. As well as having two interviews for the seat on the Council. Not to mention all the paperwork I have been putting off.

‹‹›‹‹›‹‹›‹‹›

{Six days later}

Today is the day Aspire opens its doors. I am having a tough time believing that it is finally happening. I have been getting increasingly excited about this project the closer I get to accomplishing it. I am just leaving the lawyers heading over to unlock the doors. I hope the students are going to love it. Sean already had a massive library, several big boy toys, an archery, a pond stocked with fish, and a gun range. Sean and Conner called their four dirt bikes, three four-wheelers, a Rhino, and an Argo their toys. The Argo is pretty badass, it drives in water or on land. They call it an all-terrain vehicle. Sean and Connor loved their toys. There are also plans to add a gym, a pool, a garden and add on to the guest house.

I spent the morning finalizing the paperwork to get all my inheritance money into an account solely for Aspire Academy. As well as the mansion and anything on its property. That way Malan and any other being who becomes headmaster can utilize all of it. I did set it up to where Malan or myself must finalize anything not already included in the budget. The bills are automatically paid each month. I must trust in someone else to run the Academy for me. I still have my responsibilities at The Company.

Not to mention I am about to be the Queen of the Underworld. I honestly have thrown myself into this project that I have not really thought about me becoming a queen. Yes, I was groomed for this most my life. But that also feels like another life. Plus, it does not help that I got a little taste of a mortal life. One that is free of those responsibilities forced on me. I did not ask for this. I never even thought about rather I wanted it or not. I just accepted that it is my destiny.

Before going to unlock the doors, I pick Grim up. The Blazer is rolling to a stop when Grim jumps out running to unlock the door. He would not give up asking if he can be the one to do it. So, I give in. There is already a line. Grim takes off down the hall to get his class schedule. While everyone follows in behind him. By lunch time the halls are full of beings, some are staff, and others are students with their families. We also have beings that have come from all over just to check out the new Academy. It warms my heart to see so many people, I did not think there was going to be this big of a turn out. Of course, the headmasters of the "Elite" schools of this area as they call themselves show up. They are ones to definitely keep an eye on. Everyone that I personally sent an invite is here to show their support. Even Sylvia and Schrat stop by for a little bit. Malan is busy greeting future students and families as Willa and Aspen come running up squealing in excitement. I am greeted and congratulated by everyone else. After checking in with Malan to make sure everything is going smoothly. I head to The Company for the interviews I have this afternoon. It is such an amazing feeling to bring this dream to reality. Once off work and home I start to plan the dinner I am going to have. My team and Demitri already knows about it. So, I call my brother and sister. Leaving my Mom for last. I already know what she is going to say.

"Hey Mom, can you and Dad come over for a Thanksgiving dinner tomorrow?", I ask her once she picks up my call.

"Makaria you know we don't celebrate mortal holidays.", is my Mom's response.

"It doesn't have to be a Thanksgiving dinner. I just want all of my family together for dinner.", I express. When she does not say anything, I try begging. "Mom pretty please. Zack and Mel agreed to come."

"Okay fine. You know as well as I do that when you ask your Dad, he isn't going to tell you no.", she conveys.

"Thank you. Thank you.", I say excitedly. "I love and will see you tomorrow."

"I love you. See you then.", she tells me before hanging up the call.

Since Aspen, Malan, and I found each other we have not only had a thanksgiving dinner together. But we cook the dinner together every year. It is like Friendsgiving, but we are a family not friends. This year I want my family apart of it. Even though things are still rocky with Mel. She is my little sister and I want her here. Plus, she has been trying really hard to do better. Tonight, I am preparing the desserts for tomorrows dinner. I am baking Pecan pie, Pumpkin pie, an Apple Fritter cake, and special adult brownies.

The next morning Malan and Aspen show up to get everything cooked and set up. Malan deep fries a turkey and bakes a ham in coke a cola while Aspen and I make the sides. I start the green beans and mash potatoes as Aspen makes a fruit salad. The meats and last side just finish cooking when everyone starts to arrive. Willa and Ace are the first to show up. They offer to set the table that I had Demitri put up outside. It is a pretty day to eat outside. Not to mention I do not have enough room for all of us in the cabin. Grim is filling the drinking glasses then takes them to the table. Dad and Mom walk in with Zack several feet behind them after all the food is on the table. Mel shows up just as we are all piling our plates. It smells so good my mouth is watering. We all chit chat in between bites. It turns out to be an amazing dinner. We all laugh and share stories. Just relaxing, forgetting all the shit we have and will face day to day. Once everyone has had their fill and dessert we start to clean up. Mom and Dad leave right after dessert. After everything is cleaned up, we all meet up in the living room for movies and THC brownies. I cannot think of a better way to end tonight.

CHAPTER 9: NEW QUEEN OF THE UNDERWORLD

Amara's POV
{Couple of weeks later}

Zack walks through my front door plopping down next to me on the couch. We spend the night binge watching the shows we got behind on while I was having major memory loss.

"You know Sis Aspire Academy is a really great idea. A first of its kind.", Zack states proudly. "Are you ready for your inauguration?"

"Hell no. Are you ready for your first assignment?", I respond.

"Hell yes!", Zack excitedly voices. "You will be a great queen. Don't doubt yourself."

In between episodes we talk about Mel, our parents, both of our love lives and anything else that has happened. Grim is already passed out by the time I am ready for bed. Zack's first mission is tomorrow and then that night is my inauguration. So, I asked him to come over and stay the night. I have really missed my little brother. My nerves nor my mind will still. No matter how hard I try to calm them. I lay in bed for at least an hour trying to get my mind to settle so I can sleep.

"Good morning. This one is a little unusual which is right down our alley. Two bodies have been found completely drained of everything. Both were mothers whose husbands called in their deaths and their missing kids.", I debrief my team once everyone has joined me in the conference room.

"How long ago did this happen?", Aspen questions.

"The first body was discovered three days ago. As for the last body she was found this morning. This assignment was brought to us because these attacks have been linked to others throughout states nearby. The FBI was pulled in before us and they have gotten nowhere. The kids still have not been found and it is not just human children that are being taken. There are numerous species of children missing."

"How many kids are missing?", Malan asks.

"In the town we will be working in a total of three. A three-year-old boy from the first family. The second family has a boy that is six years old and a girl that is two years old. With them and the ones from the other cities there are about ten children missing in all. All the mothers of these children have been found dead from the same cause.", I answer. Gods this breaks my heart. Those poor children and their fathers.

We strap on our Company issued black HK416, black Glock 45, and a black Vulcan Gear Medieval sword. After gearing up Ace packs some of his new gadgets he has been working on. Neither crime scenes really give us much as far as evidence.

The soul of the second woman is running around her house looking for her son and daughter as she screams over and over, "Those aren't my Babies!"

I feel the hunger of my strongest power start to rise. One that I have only used once in an exceptionally long time. It took me so long to master it that I am afraid to use it. Afraid to feed the hunger because it will only want more. With this power comes desire to take a life. It is after all the power of Death's Touch. Demitri's death touch works on mortals while mine works on immortals as well. His Death's Touch does not kill immortals but will keep them down for a while.

When we broke the curse, I got all my abilities back. The memory spell placed on me was no match for my true power. It was broken before I woke up with a horrible pounding headache and my necklace back around my neck. Now I have all my abilities back I can see ghosts. Or whatever you want to call them. They live on another plane where they can see you and everything around but very few can see them. Until the soul is brought to the Underworld by a reaper where their fate is decided. From what my Dad says anything mortal has a soul and the stronger the being the stronger the soul.

Willa is talking to all the neighbors. As Malan is roaming around the house for clues or information we can use. Ace and Zack are trying to track the kids. While Aspen and I are surveying the bodies at the morgue. Both women looked like all their insides were sucked out of them, only skin and bones are left. Aspen informs me that neither of the women died from magical causes. There is not any bite marks or puncture wounds either. Asking the coroner to email me the autopsy reports for both women. We head back to The Company to see what the team has found out. We are coming back empty handed. Hoping at least one of them have something that will help us.

"We have another body.", I inform my team while looking down at the text message I just received.

We have not even been gathered at headquarters for an hour. In no time everyone is gearing back up and we head to the new crime scene. Hopefully, this one will give us a lead and we can stop this thing before someone else dies. She looks just like the first two, the woman is sitting back lifeless on a couch with her children missing. Her husband is sobbing uncontrolledly while trying to answer one of our agent's questions. It is truly heartbreaking. I am not going to let this happen to another family!

"Amara, I would like to try a spell. I get the idea for it at the last crime scene when you saw the ghost of the deceased woman. I wanted to look into it and make sure I was capable of performing it before bringing it to you.", Ace conveys as he approaches me.

"Alright Ace show us what you got.", I encourage him while walking out of his way.

"It will allow us to see an echo of what happened here.", he explains to us as he forms symbols with his fingers. I can feel the magic filling the air around us.

This echo spell is neat. The woman glides out from down the hall to sit on the couch. On the exact spot where the cleanup crew just removed her body from. She looks almost like a mixture of a ghost and hologram but in ways different as well. She sits on the couch cradling an infant as she breasts feeds the tiny thing. As the baby continues to nurse it starts to grow bigger. While the mother is slowly being sucked dry right before our eyes. The mother is starting to look just like she did when we found her. I cannot stop the feeling that I need to do something, anything. But this has already happened. All I can do is stop this from happening again. A little girl no older than two drops down off her mother's lap walking off like nothing had happened. Passing by a mirror on the way out the door the toddlers true form is revealed. The creature stands about five feet tall with blue grey tone skin and solid black as night eyes. Even though you can tell she is a young creature her body is withered with violet medium length hair.

"A changeling.", Zack mutters.

Collecting the extraordinarily little evidence we can find we get out of the Cleanup Crew's way. As we all pile into the black third row seat SUV, we hear shots being fired. We jump out of the SUV then using our supernatural speed we race down the road. Once we reach the house at the end of the street we bust through the front door. A father and son are fighting over a gun while the son has a bleeding bullet hole in his chest. The mother is unconscious on the kitchen floor. She looks drained but it looks like he was not able to finish the job. The little boy cannot have been older than five years old. Ripping the gun out of his Dad's hands the boy goes to sink its teeth into the father's neck. I grab him off his dad a second before he can. I wrap my arms around him tightly keeping him from escaping. The little boy then shifts into a younger version of itself causing my grip to loosen enough for him to get free. Ace throws this round device to Willa who is by the front door. Just as the changeling gets to the door Willa throws the device right in front of its feet. A net made of flames shoots out over the creature.

"That's impressive Ace.", Aspen expresses.

"It gets better. It's coded with every being and their weaknesses that is in our data base.", Ace informs us proudly.

This must be what he has been working so hard on. Ace and the tech squad have been working on a new device to help capture different beings since we got back from Demitri's the first time. The Company sends my team out to hunt down and kill the most dangerous of their most wanted beings. Calling in another cleanup crew I tell them to inform the Interrogator to be ready for us. The Interrogator is a Mutant. They get the name Mutants because in every way they are human except for one mutated chromosome that gives them an ability. She has unicorn color hair with honey brown eyes and is the best interrogator The Company has ever had. As well as having the most ruthless reputation yet is the sweetest person I know. Just a touch from her and a lie from the one she is touching, and that being's soul is burned with a flame almost as hot as Hell fire. As soon as we all get back to The Company we meet in the library. While the changeling is taken straight to the Interrogator. We must find these kids and we are running out of time. Willa and Aspen are researching changelings. Zack and Malan are hunched over the map marking down all the places that have been hit in this town and others. They are trying to find a pattern to help locate a hiding spot or where the next house that will be hit is located.

"Changelings are a type of Fae. The mother changelings replaces children of diverse species that she has stolen with her own children. Making her own children shift into the child they are replacing. The changeling child feeds on the mother until her death.", Zack informs us all.

"It says here that to kill changelings you have to kill the Mother with fire.", Willa adds.

"O and when they shift, they are restricted by the gender they were born. So, it is safe to assume there is at least one female and one male plus the mother.", Aspen adds.

"Also, the Second family had a boy and girl come up missing at the same time.", Malan notes.

"No luck with using magic to track the kids, they must be repelling the magic somehow.", Ace says as he joins us.

We spend the next three hours gathering all the information we can as well as formulating a plan of action. I pick Grim up then head to Demitri's castle to get to the Underworld. I am seriously in need of a long hot shower. Tonight, is my Inauguration Ceremony. When I step out of the shower my mom has three different demons there to help me get ready. I slip into an emerald mermaid gown. Its sleeves are off the shoulders meeting at a V in the middle of my chest. Then flows down and out around my feet while hugging my curves like a glove. My hair is done in a long thick French braid and my makeup has a natural style to it. My blush is a light brown, eye shadow is cream on the outer half of the eye lid and green on the inner half, and my eyeliner is done in a cat eye style. The mascara makes my thick eyelashes look even longer and thicker. I look beautiful. I like how makeup looks on me, I just feel like it is a waste of time to apply it and then take it off every day. Walking away from the mirror I slip into my silver open toe high heels. Taking a deep breath, I walk to the staircase. My hands will not quit shaking and sweating while my stomach is doing summersaults. I have not been this nervous in a long time.

Standing at the edge of the stairs waiting on me is Demitri. He looks so delicious in that solid black on black suit with an emerald-colored tie. My Mom is a slick one, she has tried to get us together ever since we were teenagers. She is one of the few that knows about our relationship. This is her way to show us off as a couple. I do not mind everyone knowing about us. As we are being announced I slide my hand through his arm and smile up at him.

Leaning in I whisper, "To bad this is really important, or I would be pulling you back into that room burying you deep in me.", I whisper with so much desire. Not being able to help myself my eyes sneak a peek at the bulge growing at my words. Making the desire of wanting to pull him into a room deepen.

"O just wait Baby you will be. You look gorgeous.", Demitri replies in a husky voice full of the same desire I feel then escorts me down the stairs.

When we reach the thrones, my parents stand up. Demitri gives my arm a reassuring squeeze then walks off. My Mom and Dad or should I say my Queen and King come stand directly in front of me.

"Makaria do you vow to uphold the law of the Underworld, rule with a just hand and always put our people first. Just as I have before you?", my Dad asks.

"I vow to uphold the law of the Underworld, rule with a just hand and always put my people first. Just as my King has before me.", I vow more confidently than I feel. My Dad slices his palm and mine then pushes both our palms together. Magic swirls around not only us but the whole room, it is so powerful I am sure the others can feel it as well.

"Makaria do you vow to uphold the law of the Underworld, rule with a just hand and always put our people first. Just as I have before you?", my Mom asks as she steps closer to me.

"I vow to uphold the law of the Underworld, rule with a just hand and always put my people first. Just as my Queen has before me.", I vow once again. My confidence in myself is growing with each word. My Mom slices her palm and then slices mine again since it has already healed. Then pushes the palms of our hands together. Magic fills both of us and once again the room. Blood oaths are binding and cannot be broken. Even with the death of the binder, since I made the vow twice with two different people making them both binders to the vow.

"Long live Queen Makaria!", both my parents announce to the room full of demons, goddesses, gods, and everyone dear to me from the Mortal Realm.

"Long live Queen Makaria!", almost everyone chants back as I turn to face the crowd.

The sight of those demons standing there defiantly causes a feeling of dread to creep in my gut. I hope they are not plotting against me. I think to myself as I look out at my people. At the lives I have vowed to protect. My parents have been preparing me for this moment my whole life and it is still so overwhelming. So many lives and souls on my hands. But I will be the best queen I can. At that thought I raise my chin a little higher.

My Dad is walking over to me with my crown in his hands. Just as he is about to place it on my head completing the ceremony and officiating me as the Queen of the Underworld. The door is blown open into the crowd taking out a few demons with it. In walks three beings with a dramatic flair. The first being to walk in is the size of an Amazonian with hair the color of dried blood. If I am correct, she is a giantess. To the right of her is a monstrous wolf that has black fur with splashes of red in it. It has foam spilling out of its mouth with a look of uncontrollable rage in its eyes. To her left is an enormous sea serpent that is a mix of black and green with sharp scales. As well as having one of its eyes black and the other red.

"Angrboda!", my Dad growls. "You are not welcome here!"

"She is not worthy of that Crown!", she hisses out.

Angrboda, Angrboda . . . . Has a monstrous size wolf and an enormous sea serpent with her. I keep saying this over and over in my mind. I feel like I should know who they are and its gnawing at me. I know I have heard that name somewhere. O Fuck! I am dead! It might have taken me a little bit to register who they are, but I know now. They are Holle's mom and brothers. The woman is the Mother of Monsters of an other-dimensional planetoid called Asgard. Fenrir is the wolf, and the sea serpent is Jermungondr. Where the hell is Loki? Wait a second is that bitch challenging me for my crown? I start to panic but that is quickly replaced with anger. The urge for my power to take a life is thumbing in the back of my mind. As it is being fueled by my anger. Trying to break through my barriers keeping it back.

"She killed my daughter in cold blood.", she continues eyes locked on mine threatening death through her stare.

Got to love the fury of a mother that has lost a child. I feel bad for her, I cannot imagine the pain she is in. That does not mean that I am going to sit back while she challenges me for my birth right. Not to mention all the work I put in to preparing for this role my whole life. The anger has taken over the sympathy I am feeling. Remain calm, I keep telling myself. My Dad starts to step forward, but I put my hand on his chest. Before I walk over to stand face to face with her.

"Holle openly attacked us twice trying to take over. She chose her fate.", I announce to not only Angrboda but the entire room. "As a Princess I did what I had to do for my kingdom. As a being to another I really am sorry it had to come to that."

There is no denying the savagery in her eyes. This is not going to end peacefully but that is not going to stop me from at least trying.

Still locked on my eyes with a look promising death Angrboda lifts her ax and then swings it at my head. In one swift motion Demitri catches it. The force of the swing causes the blade to cut through to the middle of his hand. Demitri yanks the ax out of her hands. Then jerks his hand down off the blade of the ax. Just as I am jumping out of the way. Fenrir and Jermungondr leap at my throat from both sides. Zack and Harper wrestles then pins down the enormous serpent. While my Dad catches the monstrous wolf by its throat dangling it off the ground above his head. I can hear the crunching sound of his bones being crushed as my dad tightens his hold on Fenrir's neck. Out of nowhere that stupid trickster god appears behind my Dad with a knife cutting into his throat. Blood is oozing out around the knife down my Dad's neck. Lucas and one of my guards are next to me ready to attack the next being that comes at me.

"I will not lose another loved one!", Loki reverberates angrily.

"And I will not let you take my Husband's life!", my Mom sneers appearing out of nowhere with the dagger she just used to slice our hands slowly digging deeper into his neck. Loki's blood is spilling down around the knife and my Mom's hand. "You guys shouldn't have come here looking for a fight."

"Enough!", my voice booms and echoes through the room. The room has split into three groups of beings. Some are rushing to leave. Other beings are just standing there watching the events unfold and then there are beings ready to fight at my side. "Why have you come to challenge my crown? Haven't you lost enough?"

Then she says the words that I knew where going to come out of her mouth, "I Angrboda Challenge Princess Makaria for the Crown of the Underworld. In tribute to the death of my daughter." Making sure to let me know she knows I have not finished the ceremony yet.

Calmly without breaking the eye contact she has held this whole time I walk over to where my Dad had dropped the crown to save me. The crown is an enchanting piece of work. It is made from fulgurite formed with the flame of hell. Decorated with green emeralds, blue sapphires, and black obsidian stones. I break eye contact just long enough to pick the crown up. As soon as I am up right, I fix my eyes back on Angrboda lifting the crown placing it on my head.

"I Queen Makaria accept your challenge for the crown.", I respond with no emotion. Gasps and whispers can be heard throughout the room. What she did not know is that the crowning is for show. The ceremony was sealed with my vow and all three of our blood.

"Makaria what have you done!", my Dad and Demitri cry out angrily in unison.

"See you in two days Princess.", Angrboda says refusing to call me by my real title as an evil smirk creeps up her face. With the promise of death still in her eyes.

Holy Hell! What did I get myself into? I make a call to have everything reschedule for the next three days, including today. Which I spend training with my Dad, Demitri and Zack. The next two days pass way to fast. I walk to the center of the ring after choosing a sword and Angrboda chooses an ax off the wall of weapons. It is against the rules to use magic or enchanted weapons. Once we are both in the center of the room, we are enclosed within Hell fire. She circles me as I wait for her to attack first. I know she is strong and fast, but I need to see how strong and fast she is as well as get to know her movements. If I am going to walk out of this alive. She attacks fast and without mercy. The ringing of my sword clashing against her ax can be heard in every corner of the room. As she keeps making advancements on me. Angrboda kicks me in the stomach after I block her ax again. Then in the next second, she has her ax swinging over her head and brings it down towards my shoulder. Threatening to take my arm off.

I roll out from under it, but I am not quite fast enough. It slices open my left shoulder exposing the muscle and bone. I can feel the blood rushing out like a river down my arm. Sucking in a deep sharp breath from how bad it stings as the air is hitting it. Fuck it hurts! She blocks my advancement giving me the opening to elbow her in the nose with my right arm. With a crunch blood gushes out her nose and down her lips. Giving me enough time to land a kick to her chest sending her into the flames. The smell of burnt skin fills my nose. Every movement sends pain shooting down my arm. Jumping out of the flames with a scream Angrboda licks the blood off her lips. Then charges at me, swinging her ax towards my stomach. Only dodging the ax by seconds, I did not have enough time to completely dodge her second swing. Which split my cheek wide open all the way a cross my face. Causing blood to spill down my neck. I can tell by how bad it stings that its deep.

Recovering quickly, I block her ax from taking my head off. The sound of sword and ax clashing against each other rings throughout the room once again. Angrboda is starting to wear down which is good because I am healing fast and still have most of my stamina left. Sinking her ax into my leg I embed my sword into her stomach then pull it out with a twist. Angrboda sinks to the ground blood spilling out around her. Dropping her axe next to her as she does. In a flash she shifts into a massive chestnut brown wolf then launches at me. I slide under her huge form just in time. Blood is oozing down my leg for the wound left by Angrboda's axe helping me slide better.

Spinning around I advance on her as her tail comes at me to wipe me out. I duck it as I slice her hind leg. There is not much room to move around with the size of her wolf form. Come on Amara think, I cannot overpower this beast. But maybe I can out smart her. With a whimper Angrboda spins around quickly flinging me into the flames with her snout. Then my body falls to the ground with a loud thud. Knocking the wind straight out of me. Fire does not hurt me, but Hell fire is the hottest fire in the Underworld. So, I can feel the heat even though it does not damage me. Blue flame fire is the second hottest. I can conjure all the colors of fire except black. However, when in the Underworld I can draw power from it allowing me to conjure Hell fire. It is still difficult for me to do even with the extra boost.

While I try to catch my breath, I hear voices begging me to get up. The beast is stocking its prey getting ready to tear me apart. I lay still gathering energy as well as my breath. Angrboda launches at my throat with the intent to rip my head off once and for all. Just as she is landing on me, I lift my sword. Using her weight as she lands on me. I embed the tip to the guard of my sword into her chest barely missing her heart.

"Submit or die.", I command from under her still holding the hilt of my blade. She snaps then growls at me. I twist my blade causing a whimper to escape out the wolf's mouth. I give her one more chance. Who says I would not go to these lengths if I lost a child? "Submit and I'll allow you, your boys and Loki to walk out of here with your lives."

I summon Death's Touch as my eyes fill with a blinding violet light. Displaying my strongest power. My hand is glowing just like my eyes as I reach towards her. We both can hear Fenrir, Jermungondr, and Loki begging her to please submit on the other side of the flames. If they were any closer the flames would be burning them. Then Angrboda did the last thing I thought she would. That massive wolf laid on its side and exposes her neck. I cannot believe she submitted, I really thought she would force my hand to kill her. Dooming my people to a blood bath. I have no doubt we would win. The numbers are in our favor plus we are on our own territory. But we would have lost a lot of lives in the process. Pulling my sword out of her chest. I point it at her as her blood drips off the tip. As I step back giving her enough room to transform.

"Shift", I command Angrboda. The flames disappear as she shifts out of her wolf form.

My Mom is the first to reach me. Embracing me tightly she tells me between placing kisses all over my cheeks, "Makaria that was so stupid and brave! I am so proud of you though."

"Okay, Okay Mom. Enough with the kisses. I love you too", I tell her. She stops kissing me but starts checking all my wounds to make sure they are healed or at least almost healed. My left arm is still hanging limply at my side a little over halfway healed.

"That was an honorable thing you did. If given the chance Angrboda would not have offered, you the same option. She would not have hesitated to kill you.", my Dad expresses with hints of different emotions under the serious tone as he embraces me.

"I know Dad. But that is not who I am or who I want to be.", I inform him as I hug him back.

Demitri was just a second behind my Mom and Dad. Stepping back to let my parents have their moment with me. As soon as my Dad lets me go, Demitri has me in his arms picking me up off the floor.

"Your parents are right. Please do not do anything like that again. I will not make it if I lose you a second time.", he whispers as he tries to hold back the tears.

"Baby I love you, but I am queen now. I will do what is needed for my people!"

"I know.", is all Demitri says.

Grim, Zack, and Mel are the next to grab me in a tight embrace telling me what they thought about what I did. Pretty much the same as my Mom. Then it is my teams turn. Once I am able to make my way through everyone. I walk up to the throne taking a seat as my team and followers that have stayed are chanting my name. Everyone goes silent as my Dad walks up placing the crown on my head. Applause and chanting erupt throughout the room once more.

"Long live Queen Makaria. Long live Queen Makaria.", they chant.

I hold up my hand bringing silence to the room. "You are banished from the Underworld. Violating this banishment is punishable by death.", I declare looking down at the four of them.

Loki swoops Angrboda up who is still healing from her wound. Caused from my sword almost going completely through her wolf form. He leads the other two out the door without a word. Once they are out of sight my eyes sweep the crowd. I cannot believe everyone I hold dear from my old and new life are here to support me, even Schrat, my team, Elijah and Kaden came. Which is an even bigger deal since they had to astral project here. It still amazes me that I have some many people in my life that love and support me. While I did not have my memories all I had for the longest time was Malan and Aspen. Then once I joined The Company, I gained Sean, his family, and the rest of my team. I can feel the changes in me, I am not that young girl anymore. Ha I am a lot older than I thought. Also, I am not lost, not knowing who I am or feeling unloved and unwanted. The biggest change is I finally love myself completely. Something I did not have even before I lost my memories. After a few more rounds of cheers, I dismiss everyone.

"Hey Amara, will you join me for lunch?", Demitri asks after everyone has left.

"I would love that.", I reply while taking his hand and letting him lead the way.

Demitri takes me to a diner in the Underworld. When I look through the window Sean and his wife Nancy are sitting at a table.

"Aspen told Lucas how much they meant to you and what had happened with Nancy. Lucas of course told me. I hope you enjoy your lunch with them.", Demitri tells me before taking off into the sky.

I stand outside for a while as I go back and forth on the decision to go inside or not. Finally working up the courage I make my way inside the diner. As I reach their table, they both stand up and give me a hug. She is just as pretty as I remember. Giving both Sean and Nancy a hug I then take my seat. Neither one of them seems upset or pissed at me. Nancy tells me that there is nothing that can make them stop loving me. Sean seems to feel the same and I have not seen him this happy in so long. He asks about The Company and everything that happened after his death. I start with Elijah being half vampire and how he just informed me the other day he is retiring. I also tell them about how we stopped Balthazar, Mel, Connor, and their plan to start a war between humans and Sups. There is an awkward silence after I mention Connor's hand in it all. I apologize that he died at my hands and that he cannot be with them. Nancy grabs my hand and tells me that it is okay. She said that Connor chose his path and that even though it breaks her heart it is no one's fault but his own. Then she congratulates me on becoming Queen of the Underworld. We chit chat like schoolgirls for the next half hour before I must go. Sean did not talk much. No surprise there he never has been a big talker. We are so busy catching up that we barely touch our food. After getting a to go box and piling my food in it I make my way back to my office to finish my work for the day. I am so glad I did not chicken out of that lunch date. Man, I have missed that woman and her beautiful soul. I have never in all my centuries met a being so compassionate.

{One Month Later}

It has been a month since I was inaugurated as queen, and my workload still has not lessened even the tiniest bit. Grim has been dorming at the Academy during the week and coming home every other weekend. Demitri and I are doing great! Malan and Sylvia are about to be parents. I have narrowed the list down to eight possible candidates to fill the two seats. Which the limit is six. I still cannot believe Elijah is retiring. I am so happy I got to work alongside him. We still have not been able to locate the mother changeling. Every lead turn into a dead end and we are about out of options. The Interrogator could not get much information out of him. All she managed to find out was the mother does not give out the location of where she keeps the children. However, they have a spot that they meet at when he has acquired a child. He also told the Interrogator that she does not care the species of the child. I called Kaden's team in on this as well, we cannot let any more kids go missing.

"It's reckless.", Ace voices rejecting my idea.

"What other choice do we have?", I question both mine and Kaden's team. "Does anyone else have a better idea?"

It is a reckless and, in a way, a cruel plan. Who is to say it would work, that the mother changeling would not see right through it? We are left with no other options. No one else said a word so we get to work. Willa takes the changeling to get his memories wiped making him forget he was captured. Then she will take him to have memories implanted making him think he had been hiding out until the coast was clear. After Ace casted a spell knocking him out. Aspen injects him with a tracking chip behind his double pointed ear. Malan and Zack rough him up a bit making it look like he put up a fight trying to escape. I heal him just enough to make his wounds look like they are old wounds. Then we set him free leaving a gift he can use to get back in his mother's good graces. The fact he has been gone a month is one of the things that makes this plan so risky. She is going to be suspicious. Ace and Willa make a golem child making sure to put a tracking chip in it. Guess we will see if this plan is a total failure or not.

While waiting on a location I go back to my office to continue to comb through the data base. I heard of this legend of a powerful being that has the strongest connection to the water element seen in a long time. She just vanishes one day. Only to reappear here and there until she stops reappearing or maybe she changed what she looks like. They call her The Sea Witch no one knows what kind of being she is. My theory is she is the same being of the legend of this mermaid who was captured by a group of qalupalik. They cursed her to walk the earth for eternity to get back at her parents for not agreeing to an arrange marriage. Her parents are the Mermaid King and Queen of the Pacific Ocean. In the mermaid world each ocean has its own ruler. All answer to Poseidon of course.

Most think she is just a really powerful witch. The difference between a witch and a Magician is a witch draws their powers naturally from within themselves and the elements. Where Magicians tap into the Aether Element using spells. Forty-five minutes in I still have not found anything on the Sea Witch. All I keep coming a crossed are legends about her. Ace comes running in telling me that the tracker on the changeling went dead. Shit!

I sent the changeling to its death. I cannot dwell on that right now. I must save these kids. Both teams are suited up in record time. Kaden's team and mine meet at the golem's location. I also sent two teams to the last location of the changeling before his tracker went dead. We arrive at an old farmhouse a mile into the woods with a small pasture surrounding it. I motion for my team to check the house and for Kaden's team to check the barn. Zack, Malan, and I go through the front door while Aspen, Willa, and Ace come in through the back. Every room is clear, standing in the kitchen I look around. Walking over to the stove I notice it is still on. We just missed her. I signal for my team to move out and search the property surrounding us. She cannot have gotten too far.

"Amara, we have cleared the barn, there are thirteen children including the golem. No changelings though.", Kaden informs me over the com.

"House is clear, checking property now. Call in a rescue and a transport team please.", I reply as I enter the woods following the grunts and thuds of a fight.

I am a good distance in the woods from the farmhouse with my team behind me. A big female changeling and two smaller changelings have a female swamp creature surrounded. They are also known as swamp nymphs. She has glowing neon green eyes with hunter green leaves on her shoulders, hip bones, and over both nipples. A hickory brown colored vine wrapped around her neck then flows down and around her waist. Just at the top of a mid-thigh skirt made of the same hunter green leaves. The swamp creature also has gills on the side her neck, fin shaped ears, and her skin is the green-brown color of swamp water. As well as webbed fingers and toes. Holy shit, I cannot believe I get to see a swamp creature in action. Out of nowhere massive hands made from mud spring out at the two changelings dragging and trapping them waist high in the swamp. Leaving just the mother changeling to deal with. I signal for my team to hold their positions. From the looks of it she did not need our help. I also want to see how this plays out. We will step in if she needs our help. In just a few minutes she has the mother changeling hog tied on the ground with light green vines. Walking towards her with my weapon lowered my team follows.

"You guys from The Company?", she asks.

"Yes, I'm Amara Stone.", I answer.

"Sweet. I'm Jazlyn Hale, she is all yours. Saves me a trip to headquarters.", Jazlyn replies as she transforms into her human form.

Without another word I walk over to the mother changeling. Lifting my hand, I push the blazing feeling out my palm. Torching her with a blue flame. Turning her into ash as she screams in pain. Instantly the male and female changelings still trapped in the swamp start screaming as a blue flame engulfs them. Turning them into ash as well. All three of their ashes are blowing off into the wind.

"We would be honored if you join The Company. We could use someone strong like you.", I offer as I hand her my business card. That is spelled to only let the one who I hand it to see what is written on it.

Jazlyn and I talk for a while as the different teams are finishing up their tasks. She has been tracking the changeling mother for couple of months. When I was younger, I did a lot of research on her species. These beings fascinate me. She has a human form and swamp creature form. I have never heard of any nymphs having a human form as well. I wonder if she is a type of hybrid. In her human form she is just a little taller than me with chestnut colored hair with caramel highlights cut in a long bob. Half of her almond shaped eyes is green, and the other half is brown on an oval shaped face and has an hourglass figure. She tells me she will consider the offer and I thank her before we return to headquarters to make sure all the kids get home safely. I really hope she joins. When I get back to my office, I pull out my phone noticing I have a couple of texts from earlier this afternoon.

Grim ➔ Hey Mom be home by six. Dad is cooking dinner for us.

Me ➔ Okay see you then. I love you.

Grim ➔ I love you too.

Demitri ➔ Baby, please don't be late. This is important to Grim. See you tonight at your house.

Me ➔ I won't my Love.

I look at the clock and I have just enough time to clean up my office then head home. Once my office is clean, I walk outside and shadow jump home. I will get my Blazer tomorrow. Getting home with enough time to take a shower. I let the stress of living in two worlds wash off me with the streaming hot water. After I get out and dry off, I slip on a sky-blue tank top with black shorts then brush my hair leaving it down to air dry. Grim walks through the door hand in hand with a female gremlin as I make my way into the living room. She looks like most gremlins with pointy ears and teeth. She is shorter than Grim with yellow eyes, short spiked black hair, and ruby red lips.

"Hey Mom.", Grim greets me as he hugs me.

"Hey Son.", I reply wrapping him in a tight embrace.

"This is my girlfriend, Ava.", he informs me as he grabs her hand pulling her to his side. The smile on his face brought a smile to mine.

"It's nice to finally meet you, Ava.", I greet her giving her a hug.

"It's nice to meet you too.", she replies returning the hug.

"Let's eat.", Demitri calls from the kitchen.

We walk to the kitchen table and have a seat. Demitri sets our plates on the table then leans over giving me a kiss before sitting down. Demitri has cooked Beef and Broccoli on fried rice for dinner. The smell has my mouth watering. He even mixed wires into Ava's and Grim's plates. It touches my heart how thoughtful Demitri can be. He really has been so good to Grim and I. I cannot help but laugh at the thought of how they acted with each other. From the first time they met until now. Their relationship has come a long way. Grim was so ornery when I first started dating Demitri. He even plastic wrapped Demitri's toilet bowl when we came over for dinner one night. In the middle of the night, I get a call from Demitri about how he had gotten up to pee. Leaving the light off and half a wake he ends up peeing all over himself. Because someone plastic rapped his toilet seat. I half wish I could have seen it happen. I chuckled to myself.

Dinner goes smoothly as we chat. Ava tells us about where she is from and how her goal is to become a Guidance Counselor at Aspire. She seems like a sweet being and Grim is falling head over heels for her. I cannot be happier for them. I also cannot believe how quickly Grim has grown up from when he wrecked our plane until now. Or believe what an amazing being he has grown to be. Ava and Grim leave shortly after dessert since they have class in the morning. Demitri and I watch a couple of movies after they leave. I end up falling asleep on his lap halfway into the second movie. When the second movie is over, I wake up a little. As he carries me to my bed then lays me down. Pulling the covers up over me. Before he goes to leave, he bends over placing a kiss on my forehead.

Reaching up I grab his hand pulling him into bed with me. Demitri slides under the covers as I roll to my side facing away from him. Snuggling deeper into him after he gets comfortable. My ass is rubbing on his dick as I snuggle into him. It is growing up my back, the more I move the harder and longer it gets.

"If you don't stop teasing me. I'm going to take you right now.", Demitri growls with so much desire.

I do not say a word I just start swaying my hips in a figure eight. While pushing it into his hard cock. Getting out of bed he turns the lights on, flips me on my back. He has my pants and panties off. It happened so fast I did not know what is happening until they are on the floor. In a playful mood I jump up and act like I am going to escape. Demitri catches me midair as I jump off the bed towards the door. Tossing me onto my back on the bed.

"I want to see that sexy body of yours.", he mutters before sucking my clit into his mouth.

Sucking on it for a few seconds he then swirls the tip of his tongue on it. Nibbling on my clit occasionally. He picks up speed causing my back to arch and my legs to shake from all the pleasure. His fast and unrelenting speed is making the sound of a dog lapping up water. I do not care as the pleasure fills my entire body bringing me to an orgasm.

"Fuck me Demitri!", I utter in a shaky voice.

Demitri does not answer but continues eating me like he has been starved. Sucking my release right out of me. While I ride the waves of my orgasm Demitri slides his rock-hard dick into my soaking wet pussy. Causing me to moan out. Immediately he increases his pace slamming faster and harder into me. As he dips his hips with each thrust. Pulling out to roll me on my side he takes me from behind. Slamming deep into me while he swirls his fingertip on my clit. I am hit with another orgasm. Making me moan out his name just as he spills his seed in me. Meeting his own release. We lay there for a little while with him still in me as he embraces me tightly. Still riding the waves of ecstasy from our orgasms together. We finally tear way from each other and hop into the shower. The hot water pouring down my body is having every nerve send signals of pleasure. After Demitri washes me, I dry off then pull on a t-shirt and crawl into bed. He kisses me on the forehead before sliding under the covers and falling asleep. Curling up next to him I drift off to sleep as soon as my head hits my pillow.

I get woken up at three in the morning by a phone call from the local police. Turns out someone broke into the geek lab at headquarters. As I slip pants on, I call Elijah. Informing him on what is going on and that I have it handled. Then I call Ace and have him gathered the tech squad so we can figure out what all is missing. While I am slipping on some sandals. I make sure to leave Demitri a note before I shadow jump to the office. Once outside the headquarters the alarm is blaring, and the back door is busted off its hinges. After walking over the debris and glass I made my way down the wall to our tech lab. The lab's door was blown off the hinges as well and the cameras had been disabled on this wing. Ace is the first to arrive and the others arrived shortly after. They get to work immediately inventorying everything. Only one thing is missing, Ace's new project he has been working on for at least two years. It was going to be presented to the Council next week. Shit!

After we get the lab cleaned and reorganized, I send them all home for the day. The being that did this knew how to avoid the cameras, exactly what they were coming for, and where it was. If Connor were alive, he would be my first suspect. This is definitely something he would do.

CHAPTER 10: THE NEW COUNCIL MEMBERS

Amara's POV

I comb through the pile of files from beings who have applied for one of the two seats. Elijah knocks on my door before walking in.

"Amara, you have been handling the responsibilities of running two seats really well. I think it is time you learn The Company's secret. Follow me.", without another word he walks off down the hall.

Towards a different wing of the building and then stops at a dead end. I close the file I am currently looking at and quickly followed behind him. Elijah places his hand on the wall causing a door to appear. Following him through the door we step into a big studio apartment. It is dark but not pitch black. A figure stands in the darken kitchen sucking dry a bag of blood. The creature looks like a fresh human corpse with bat like wings.

"Strigoi", I whisper.

Some say they are troubled spirits that have risen from the grave. Really strigoi are the made vampires. They have red rings around their pupils with razor sharp fingernails and teeth. Few have bat-like wings and all of them have an infectious bite. Strigoi are vampires from Hala. The crazy vicious looking vampires you read legends about are actually strigois.

"She is a powerful one. I can smell the power radiating off her.", he conveys as he is smelling me with blood dripping from his lips. With one motion he is in front of me. He is so fast I barely seen him move.

"Samuel, this is Amara. She is the beneficiary of Sean's seat and temporarily Dean's.", Elijah introduces me. "Amara this is Samuel. The founder and fifth seat of the Council. He likes to remain a hidden seat holder. We only bother him when the votes are tied."

"It's nice to meet you", I greet Samuel.

"Like wise.", Samuel replies with a smirk.

I am not sure how to take how he is looking at me. The look says he wants to eat me. The question is how does he want to eat me?

"Well, I'm sure Amara has a lot of work to get back to.", Elijah voices as he steps in saving me from the awkward situation.

"Have a nice evening, Samuel.", I convey as I turn to walk out the apartment.

Once I am back in my office I continue to comb through the files on my desk. Elijah would like me to select six candidates. I already have two spots filled. The trick is getting them to show up to the assessment. One is for Jazlyn, and one is for the Sea Witch. Jazlyn has not sent an answer yet. As for the Sea Witch I have not been able to find a trace of her in the supernatural or human world. There are many legends about the monsters she has killed and stories of her time fighting alongside the witches. After combing through the last file, I have four candidates selected. I check the time on my phone, it is 7:30pm. Cleaning my office I then head home.

Demitri is waiting for me when I walk out the building. He flies us to a restaurant for dinner then my house for movies. I fall asleep at the beginning of the third movie. I should have gone to bed way before that. Demitri picks me up to carry me to my bed after the movie ends. I wake up a little bit when he lays me down. He pulls the covers over me and kisses me on the forehead. I really did not want him to leave, I wanted to protest. But I am not awake enough to make a sound come out my mouth, let alone open my eyes. Rolling onto my stomach I snuggle into the blanket to get comfortable. I am already missing the warmth of Demitri's body. As well as the tingling sensation I get whenever he touches me. I am really starting to hate sleeping without him. I wonder if he will move in with me. I think as I drift off to dream land. The next morning, I am woken up by a phone call. Two hours before my alarm.

"Hey Amara, I know its early, but I can really use your help. I am being followed by five ogres.", Jazlyn conveys as soon as I answer the call.

"Where are you?", I ask.

"Where we met.", is all she is able to say before the sound of fighting is all I can hear. Then the line goes dead.

I shoot out of bed slipping on a pair of shorts, socks, and boots as quickly as I can. Still in the t-shirt I slept in. As I throw my hair up into a messy bun, I walk out the door. I send an SOS message to my team with the location. Grabbing Reaper on the way out. Before shadow jumping to the old farmhouse. Right in front of the entrance to the forest Jazlyn is fighting five ogres in her human form just as five others join the fight. While seven more are making their way to her from within the forest. She is doing well at holding her own, but she is outnumbered.

I jump into action swinging with as much force as I can. My sword cuts through the ogress's leg closest to me. Cutting it clean off right below the knee. As blood sprays everywhere the ogress tries to maintain her balance. I cut her other leg off causing her to tumble to the ground. With one more swing of my sword the ogress's head is flying through the air. Before the ogress's body can hit the ground. Her blood is painting all the greenery around us red. Not wasting anytime, I go for the ogre that is closest to me. Running up the ogre's body I take his head off with a swift swing before he could grab hold of me.

Jumping off his shoulders before he hits the ground lifeless. I roll as I hit the ground and go for the next one. Jazlyn has managed to kill two as well. Now she is working on keeping the seven ogres from reaching us. She is in her swamp creature form now. With a flick of her wrist a tall wall made of roots, shrubs and other plants binds itself together blocking the ogres from making their way to join the fight as it surrounds us. Jazlyn really is powerful, and we need her at The Company. She could do a lot of good. Jazlyn is not fast enough to put up the barrier around us and dodge the ogre that has snatched her up.

"Let me go Fucker!", Jazlyn voices catching my attention.

Ducking the ogress trying to grab me I run to assist her. Charging the one that has her. I jump up raising my sword over my head and then I bring it down on the ogre's wrist chopping it off. Blood is spraying out of the nub where his hand once was. As the hand hits the ground, Jazlyn shifts back into her human form. Giving her the space, she needs to pull herself out. With her Demon Blade still in her hand she runs up the ogre's other arm as he makes a grab at her. She then sinks her blade in the ogre's eye. Jazlyn jumps down off his body as it hits the ground. While the life leaves his eyes. The air is knocked out of me after I am hit in the chest by an ogre's club. The force throwing me back into a tree trunk. I have broken several ribs on both sides, I can tell by how bad it hurts to breathe and to get myself up off the ground. Watching Jazlyn kill the ogre took my focus off my surroundings.

As I am forcing myself up through the pain. The ogre that got me with his club and an ogress charge at me. Lifting my hand, I engulf the ogress in a blue flame turning her into ash. Since she is the closest to me. Then turn my hand towards the ogre that broke my ribs setting him on fire until he is ash as well. Two thick green vines come out of the ground taking out the last two ogres. One of the vines wraps around an ogre's neck then snaps it. The other vine pierces through the last ogre's heart. Well, the last one on this side. Just as that ogre's life fades out my team shows up. The barrier parts allowing them to pass through on the side diagonal from the ogres and ogresses. That are beating viciously against it. Their brute strength is no match for Jazlyn's power. The wall bends in after the impacts but almost instantly spring back with no damage. Giving us both time to catch our breaths. Jazlyn then brings down the barrier with a flick of her wrist.

Unleashing the seven ogres and ogresses. These seven are different from the first group. They are warriors decked out in armor and helmets. Each one carrying a different weapon. Wanting to end this quickly with a raise of my hand I engulf the ogre closest to me in a blaze of blue fire. Burning him into ash that is blowing away in the wind. His club with metal spike burning up with him. His screams echo through the forest as the sounds of battle can be heard behind it. Then I spear my sword into the heart of an ogress. Zack is fighting off an ogress that has a mace. Malan's sword is clashing with a double-sided battle ax. Jazlyn is dodging a Warscythe while a big hammer is being slung at Aspen. Willa has a vine wrapped around a Cane Machete pulling it out of an Ogre's hands. Ace is using a magical shield to block hits from a Goblin Scintiter. Which looks like a machete with a curve in the top of it. These warriors are trained well but they are still stupid and slow by nature. Which makes them no match for my team and Jazlyn. Soon seven lifeless warrior ogress' and ogres' bodies lay on the ground.

I call in a cleanup grew before going to find Jazlyn to find out what that was all about. Those were not just some random group of warrior ogres and ogresses. They were the Ogress Queen's warriors.

"Okay so explain.", I state as I walk up to her.

"I was hired by a mayor of a human community. Her and I have been friends for long time. The job was simple hunt down and kill the ogre that had destroyed their buildings and ate her children among almost all the children of her community. I tracked the monstrous thing down and killed it.", Jazlyn answers.

"And?", I ask.

"Turns out that the ogre I killed was the Ogress Queen's Son.", Jazlyn discloses.

"I'll have Elijah deal with the Ogress Queen and the hit on you.", I inform her.

"Thanks, I owe you big time.", Jazlyn conveys.

"You could pay me back by coming to the assessment this Friday at noon.", I offer.

"Let me think it over.", she replies.

"Alright team. Move out.", I command after giving her a nod.

Once we are back at headquarters, I finish all the documentation on our assignment. Before going home to my empty house. It has gotten so lonely without Grim living here. My phone rings as soon as I walk through my front door. Throwing my keys on the counter I answer the call.

"Hey Beautiful. You want company?", Demitri asks in that sexy deep voice I can't get enough of.

"Depends on who the company entails.", I playfully respond. "I don't think my boyfriend would appreciate me having another guy here alone with me. Especially when I have no clothes on.", I tease.

I am laughing so hard it takes me a little bit to notice he has hung up the phone. Which makes me laugh even harder. Walking over to the refrigerator I start to open the door. Before I can grab a soda Demitri is in my kitchen and has me scooped up in his arms bridal style.

"I thought you said you were naked.", he conveys with a frown and disappointment in his voice.

"Really that's all you heard.", I note with a laugh. I cannot help but laugh at the disappointed look on his face and how fast he got here.

"How was your day Baby?", I asked him after placing a peck on his lips.

"Better now.", he says as he kisses me. "I can only stay for a little bit. I am working late tonight. How was your day?"

"O, you know same old same old. I battled warrior ogres and ogresses sent by the Ogress Queen to kill Jazlyn.", I state.

We talk about everything and nothing until he must go. During our conversation we moved from the kitchen to the couch. Demitri pulls me down onto his lap as I go to sit next to him.

"Well, I hate to. But I have to go.", he declares as he holds me in a tight embrace not moving.

"Demitri?", I ask trying to work up the courage to ask the question I have been wanting to ask him all night.

"Yes, my love.", he responds still holding me tightly.

"Will you move in with me?", I question.

"When?", Demitri asks.

"Umm I don't know. How about tonight?", I respond leaving it open for him to decide when.

"I would love to.", he answers.

After a few more minutes of embracing me tightly he stands up sitting me down on the couch.

"I'll be back tonight as soon as I can, but it's going to be really late. I love you.", he tells me before kissing me on the forehead.

"I don't care as long as I get to wake up next to you. I love you.", I voice.

Demitri kisses me passionately then instantly deepens the kiss. When we finally tare away from each other he heads back to work. Filled with excitement I jump in the shower before going to bed. Tomorrow I am working in the Underworld.

My alarm goes off waking me up. Demitri has me pinned with one arm over my stomach and a leg wrapped around both of my legs. I try to wiggle my way out, but his grip tightens.

"Good morning Beautiful.", Demitri's deep husky voice is music to my ears. He pulls me closer into him. I can feel his morning wood pressed up against my ass making its way up my lower back. Gods he is so long and thick. Not being able to help the desire filling me. I start rotating my ass on his rock-hard dick.

"If you keep doing that, I'm going to shove this dick deep in you.",

Demitri growls out. "I still owe you for last night."

I pick up my pace in response, I am getting so wet. Flipping me over on my back Demitri rips my t-shirt and my panties off as well as his boxers. Then he is deep in me in the next second. As he thrust deep in me slowly, I thrust my hips up wanting more of him. After a while of us moving in sync he pulls out and flips me on my knees thrusting back into me.

"Harder.", I moan out.

He slams into me harder and faster. Making me moan out his name as he moans out mine. His balls are slapping my clit every time he buries his rock-hard dick as deep as he can in me.

"Fuck Baby you are so tight.", he growls out with a husky voice full of lust. He is bringing me so close to an orgasm with every deep thrust.

"Cum for me Baby.", I hiss out in pleasure as I am about to be hit with wave after wave of an orgasm.

Demitri pulls my knees to my chest as he continues to thrust into me. Just as my orgasm hit so does his. Demitri is spilling his seed in me as both of our bodies are flooded with our release. I catch my breath as he pulls out of me then I jump in the shower. After I am all washed and dried, I walk into my closet butt naked. Putting on a thong and bra, I then search for a dress fit for a queen. I choose a simple yet elegant dress. The top is rose gold which fades into a bright white. Spreading down around my feet. The border is rose gold going up the middle of the slit up to the V-neck. The split starts just above my knee and the sleeves are rose gold fading into a bright white cuff. The only jewelry I am wearing is the sun pendant necklace Demitri got me when we were younger. It is the only jewelry I ever wear, and I never take it off. Letting my hair air dry I slip on a pair of open toe black high heels that wrap around the ankle. Walking out of the closet Demitri is looking at me so intensely.

"Damn! You are enchanting.", he informs me as he rushes over and kisses me with so much desire and love. "Are you ready", he questions me after he pulls away. Leaving me trying to catch my breath as I take in all his sexiness. Demitri is wearing a fitted black suit with a blood red shirt under it. He grabs my hand leading us out the door. Wrapping his arm around my waist once we are outside. His beautiful wings gracefully extend out just as he is about to take off into the sky.

"My turn", I state as I rip a shadow open leading Demitri in behind me. Then I shadow jump us to the Tree of Dawn.

"Wow Amara, that is almost better than flying.", Demitri conveys as we walk in the castle to the gate of the Underworld.

Petting all three of Cerberus' heads on our way through. Okay, I must try harder at staying focus today and not zoning out. I get bored when seeing to some of my duties as queen. Then I get distracted easily. It sounds bad I know. First thing this morning a demon does my makeup then I call a meeting to officially announce Demitri's and my relationship. As well as for now he will stay my second in command. Next, I have my monthly meeting where the demon leaders have a chance to voice any concerns, issues, or opinions. Then all the other demons by levels have a turn. Their eye color is how you know what level the demon is. Thank goodness I only have to do this once a month.

The rest of my day is being filled with finalizing a bunch of paperwork. My least favorite of my queen duties. Especially the fact that in both of my jobs, paperwork is an extensive portion of the work. Once I get through the massive stack of papers on my desk. I have my last meeting for the day. A meeting with Demitri and Lucas. We are going through everything that needs to be done in the next two days. Lucas makes a list of what needs to be done tomorrow which Demitri and him will take care of. Since tomorrow I will be working at The Company. I also have a meeting with Malan and the board of Aspire. They want to discuss building other locations across the world. I never thought my school would get this big. As well as branching out and making college level buildings. It really has me excited and feeling accomplished. Its finally time to go home. Not being able to hold in the sigh of relief I head home to get out of this dress. Once we meet outside the castle, I reach up on my tip toes kissing Demitri on the lips. Then I tear open the shadow closest to me.

"Meet you at home.", I tell him with my eyebrow raised.

When Demitri's beautiful wings are out I shadow jump home. I beat him home only by a few minutes. Since it is my turn to cook dinner, I get busy browning the meat. While it is browning, I throw corn, black beans, dry ranch, and taco seasoning into my instant pot. Then I mix everything together. Once the hamburger meat is done, I dump it in with the other ingredients. After stirring everything together I put the lid on and turn it on. Demitri walks up pulling me against his chest. As he tightly embraces me, I lean into him. Us being here, living together still seems like a dream. This is what I have wanted with him since I was a young woman with a crush. I just never thought I would have it.

"Would you want to go on a date tomorrow?", I mutter. Unsure how to ask. "I'll plan it."

"Sure, it would be nice to get out and do something.", Demitri answers.

"Awesome! Let's watch a movie while dinner is cooking.", I voice as I walk into the living room plopping on the couch.

Demitri lifts my legs placing them on his after sitting down next to me. I fall asleep before I even get to eat any of the delicious Taco Soup that I had been wanting all day.

My weeks are spent switching between my duties of being one of the Council members and Queen of the Underworld. Which is now my routine.

Without the help of my team, Demitri, Zack, and Lucas I would not be able to accomplish the things I have. Not to mention Malan and Sylvia for running Aspire for me. Malan has always wanted to be a part of something like that. That is why we only call him in for the assignments we need his help on. Seeing him running Aspire I realized that is where he belongs. Sylvia is switching between being doctor at the castle and doctor at Aspire. Just until she finishes training the nymph that is replacing her at the castle. They really are a perfect couple.

When I have time at The Company, I have been searching for the Sea Witch. Along with hoping Jazlyn shows up to the assessment that is today. Since I have not heard from her. There are two different assessments. One is for employment that everyone must pass to work here. Most of the time this assessment is intertwined into your interview and your first assignment. Which your first assignment is more of a trial and part of your interview is a demonstration of your talents. You do not have to have abilities to work here. But you do have to be able to survive and in this world that means you need to be able to fight. Second part to the assessment is only held to fill a seat on the Council that did not have a beneficiary. I did not have to go through the assessment for the seat since I was named a beneficiary. So, I am curious as to what it entails.

As for my search for the Sea Witch my last leads are both dead ends. Just like all the others. This woman is damn good at making it look like she does not exist. I even sought out Schrat for help, he is off somewhere. Sylvia is supposed to let me know when he gets back. The smell of rich dark coffee pulls me out of my thoughts. Guess it is time to pull my lazy ass out of bed and get ready for the assessment. Elijah made sure this is the only thing we have to do today. So, I did not have to be there until thirty minutes before it starts.

Walking into the kitchen Demitri is whipping up batter while the waffle iron is heating up. I jump on his back wrapping my legs around his waist and my arms around his neck. Making him drop the bowl on the counter to hold me so I do not fall. Even though I can hold myself up without his help. Peeking over to see what contents are in the bowl. Yes, I mentally say as I see chocolate chips. Yummy my favorite. After leaving a trail of kisses down the side of his neck I jump down. Letting him finish cooking breakfast. Getting to wake up every morning to him instantly puts a smile on my face that does not fade.

A part of me always knew that Demitri was my soulmate. I had this whole in my heart when I lost my memories. Now I think that subconsciously I was missing him not being a part of my life. The hole is slowly being filled the more he is around. That shows me how strong our bond is. I know that together we can get through anything.

I sit down at the island as he places a plate of waffles in front of me before grabbing his plate and sitting next to me. After cleaning my plate, I go get dressed for work. I walk pass Demitri in just his t-shirt and booty shorts. He reaches out and slaps my ass. As he is telling me how sexy I look in his shirt. I give him a seductive smile before swaying my hips as I walk off.

Once at headquarters I walk to the arena. This is where we train and do our assessments. Elijah fills me in as we wait for everyone to show up. The assessment is broken into three parts. The first part will be them battling against each other. Giving them the chance to show not only their strengths and abilities but also their weaknesses. The second part is an obstacle course in a sense. It is set up with illusion magic and they all must finish together, or they all fail this part. This will show how well they can work as a team.
In the final part they must beat the Labyrinth. That is what everyone calls it. The candidates will place their hands on this magical stone. Which will send them into their own mind's labyrinth. Where they must face not only their deepest desires and true nature. But their deepest fears. This part is the main deciding factor. They cannot make it out by themselves then they are not worthy of a seat on the Council. Only the strong and good hearted can make it out.

Except Balthazar, I am not sure how he got a seat. That does not mean people's hearts do not darken and get corrupted overtime, Elijah's words echo in my thoughts. Was it a warning or was he talking about Balthazar? I wonder silently to myself. Elijah and I both sit on our thrones as we wait for the candidates. One by one they start to show up. I cannot hide my shocked look when the first one to show up is Jazlyn. Quickly I fix my face like Elijah has taught me. I really need to work on keeping a blank serious face. Not letting my emotions shine through telling everyone around exactly how I feel.

Not too long after that everyone else arrives. There is a nephilim named Malachi, which is a being who is half angel half human. Drake who is a Dhampir, which is a being who is half vampire half human. A jinn named Julian whose family has worked for The Company for three generations. Then there is Celestia, she is a sylph. From what Grim tells me a powerful one at that and the last of her line. Her parents were brutally murdered, and it was clear she was the target. To this day their deaths are still unsolved. Celestia Whitlock was four years old and was hidden in the human world until Aspire opened. Turns out my Dad and Mom were the ones who hid her. When she came into her abilities, she could not control them, and her human parents became afraid of her. They sent her to an insane asylum. When she heard a rumor about Aspire, she broke out with the help of Malachi and Drake. Then took refuge with us at Aspire. Where she learned to control her abilities.

Malachi, Drake, and Celestia are the best of the best at Aspire. Just as we are about to begin Schrat walks through the huge solid oak doors like he owns the place. I rush down the steps to give my old friend a hug. Elijah follows behind at a slower pace.

"It's good to see you too Ancient One.", he says as he returns my hug.

No one can take their eyes off Schrat or hide how scared they are of him. Well except Elijah and me. Not many people have even heard of a being like Schrat. The few that have, know how deadly and unfriendly they are. Let alone they cannot help the feeling of being scared down to the bone at the site of him. I know very few beings that Schrat will let this close to him let alone hug him.

Man, he takes me back to a simpler time in my life. When I was younger on the island. Schrat was teaching me how to control and use my abilities at will as while as training me to fight. It cracks me up that he is still calling me Ancient One when he might be older than my Mom. The first time he called me that was when I had lost my memories and had him trapped in a shadow. After he almost killed my team and me. He has always been like an uncle to me. I am not close with my Dads siblings. Most of them live on Olympus. It is enchanting and all, but I will always choose the Underworld and the Mortal Realm over Olympus.

"Elijah", Schrat greets him with a nod. "I have a candidate for the assessment."

"Luckily, we have an open spot", Elijah replies.

I know that even if I did fill all the spots Elijah would not turn down someone Schrat has brought in himself. He is not just feared he is respected as well.

"Good. Nora Griffon this is Elijah and Amara.", Schrat introduces her to us. "I think you two will really be impressed by her."

"Alright Nora if you will please join the others. We will get started.", Elijah politely commands as we walk back to our thrones.

Schrat follows us up taking a seat next to me. Looking down on our candidates I study all the beings below me. Drake and Malachi are about the same height, and both are muscular as well as looked the part. Malachi the half angel has blonde hair with blue eyes. Whereas Drake, the half vampire has chocolate brown hair and brown almost black eyes. They seem like close friends. Which does not happen often. Them both being half human might be what brought them together. Celestia is 5'4", petite with snow white hair that falls just past her shoulders and innocent icy-blue closet eyes on a diamond shaped face with a star shaped stud in her nose. Both Drake and Malachi seem very protective of Celestia. Nora is 5'7", thick and toned with amazing curves, emerald hair done in a wide surface braid, a square shaped face, deep-set grey eyes, and her septum pierced. Standing at the height of 5'10" Julian has a black mohawk with hazel eyes.

Elijah pulls two names at a time out of a container. To spar them against each other until there is only one left. They are all very skilled and have good control over their abilities. It is down to the last two. Nora and Jazlyn which they are well matched. Even though Nora won. She looks familiar but I cannot remember where I have seen her face. All six of them would have no doubt easily passed the assessment to be employed with The Company.

It is time for part two, which will show us how well they can work as a team with strangers. This Illusion magic is based off one of each of their fears. They must work and fight together to make it through all six rooms. Each room contains a different fear of one of the beings in the group. That is exactly what they did as well as setting a new record for time completed.

Part three, this part is the deciding factor of the assessment. Nora won round one and they each get a point for completing the second round as a team. I am sure this assessment is the fourth assessment The Company has held. Supernaturals do live a long time. If the seats do not turn hands due to death every few hundred years, they will hold an assessment for that seat or those seats.

One by one they touched the Verum Tuae stone. It is Latin meaning your truth. Then one by one they slump unconscious onto the cots they are sitting on. Only the pure of heart can make it through without the magic words to pull them back. Once they are in a deep sleep a magical hologram like screen pops up in front of us. One for each of the candidates. Showing us what the candidates were experiencing trapped in their own minds while fighting their own demons. Two hours has passed, Celestia opens her eyes as she sits up taking in her surroundings. So far, she is the only one to have made it out on her own. Twenty minutes later Jazlyn then Nora pulls themselves out without assistance. We are giving the others forty more minutes before Elijah will speak the word to pull them out.

"Expergisci.", Elijah voices. Slowly the other three open their eyes and sit up. "We will meet Wednesday in the conference room. Where we will inform you on the results of your assessments. Be there at 10am. Thank you, you are dismissed."

All the candidates one by one leave the arena. Schrat disappears along with them. Having not just one but three beings pull themselves out of the labyrinth is another first for The Company. Usually only one if any can make it out without that magical word. Elijah and I cut out early for the day. Picking up burgers and fries along the way I head home to leave the Blazer. Then I shadow jump to the Tree of Dawn. This tree has been my favorite plant since I was a little girl. I would sit against the trunk and read, escaping into other worlds. Or dip my toes in the light blue water at the base of it. Walking up the stairs my super hearing picks up a female moaning, and it is coming from Demitri's office. My mind instantly takes off into all kinds of scenarios. I try to shake off the pain wanting to spread through my heart.

That just is not who Demitri is I tell myself. Pushing the door open I get a perfect view of a blonde-haired being with orange butterfly shaped wings bent over his desk. As he thrust hard and fast into her from behind with his hand wrapped in her hair. No matter how hard I want to I cannot take my eyes off the scene in front of me. Faster than I thought I could move I have him pinned against the wall by his throat.

"Damnit Harper. What the fuck!", I hiss letting go of his throat once I realize its him. "You seriously couldn't have done this anywhere else?"

"Aww Amara your just mad I ruined your fantasy of getting it on with my brother on this desk.", he teases as he pulls up his pants. I do not take my eyes off his. Demitri and him look too much alike that it is tempting to look. But I refuse to give in to it.

"What makes you think we haven't already.", I tease back. This is not the first time I have walked in on Harper giving it to some random girl. I love that Demitri is the opposite of his brother when it comes to women.

"You, naughty girl.", Harper voices with mock surprise.
Demitri and I have not actually had sex on this desk. This desk is new seeing how we broke the original desk that was in here. Harper does not need to know that though.

"Are you really going to let some bitch, talk to you like that?", the blonde human size pixie sneers as she latches on to his arm. Orange pixie dust flutters around her as she beats her wings. Some pixies can grow to human size, but it drains them quickly. Most cannot hold it longer than twenty-four hours.

"Sweetheart I wouldn't push her. She is one that even I wouldn't cross.", he tells her as they head out the door. Before walking out, he places a kiss on my forehead. "I'll call you tomorrow.", he voices before I can ask about Phoenix.

With a look that tells me to not push the unspoken subject he rushes out of Demitri's office. Harper gets around when he single but when he commits to a woman he does not cheat. Something had to have happened between him and Phoenix. Or I would not have found him with that pixie. The next morning Harper and Demitri are sitting around the island. As I walk to the refrigerator to get something to eat, I see the pain hidden in Harpers eyes.

"Awe Harper what happened?", I ask as I wrap my arms around him.

"They dumped us to return home to Scotland.", Harper mutters as he fights the tears threatening to sneak down his cheek. Standing there I hold Harper for a little bit before wiping the one tear that escapes. Last night's events are starting to make since.

"I know things are hard right now. So Just keep in mind what I am about to say is 100% out of love. Okay.", I state. Waiting quietly for some sign of acknowledgement. He nods his head, so I continue. "Sleeping around isn't going to help get over her. They are just distractions. You need time to heal. You are also not going to meet a nice girl that way either."

After giving him a tight hug, I then walk out the room to call Zack. He is off on an assignment so I doubt he will answer, I must try. With no luck at reaching him it goes to voicemail. Hanging up the call I send him a text.

Me → Hey little bro just checking in. How are you?

Putting my phone back in my pocket, I gather all my work stuff and head to the patio. Fridays I work from home unless I have to be at one or the other. It is such a beautiful morning. The sun is a harvest orange color as it slowly rises in the sky. Fog creeps along the luscious grass as the birds chirp their songs. I work outside most the day while the boys go off to cause trouble. Warming up some left-over Taco soup, I grab the chips and flip through the movies. After the movie I head to bed. I am too tired to wait up for Demitri. I still have not heard back from Zack. I hope he is not taking it too hard.

The sun is shining through the curtains urging me to wake up that next morning. The smell of bacon and eggs drifts into the room causing my stomach to growl. Sliding out of bed wearing only a black thong and Demitri's t-shirt that is hanging off one shoulder. I make my way to the kitchen. Demitri is standing by the stove in only his boxer briefs. My mouth waters as wetness leaks into my panties. I am not sure if it is the smell of the bacon, the sight of Demitri or a combination of both.

"Good morning Handsome.", I say softly but loud enough for him to hear.

"Good morning Beautiful.", he responds as he turns the stove off.

Then turns to look at me. His eyes slowly take me in head to toe. When Demitri's eyes come back up they meet mine. They are full of lust. The need for me showing in his eyes intensifies my need for him. Swaying my hips, I strut over to Demitri. When I reach him, I kneel in front of him. I slide his dick out of the slit in his boxer briefs. His dick twitches as soon as my hand wraps around it. I stroke his length watching him grow hard. It twitches again as I slowly glide it into my mouth. Pulling out once it hits the back of my throat. Demitri hisses as soon as it leaves my mouth. I tease his growing member with my tongue. Before gliding it back in and quickening my pace as I bob my head on his dick. Grabbing a fist full of my hair he moans out my name. I start to softly twist his balls with my hand. Demitri's dick convulses then he starts thrusting into my mouth.

"Shit Baby. You're going to make me cum.", he growls out before burying his hard cock into the back of my throat.

I swallow every drop of his seed before sliding his dick out of my mouth. After the last wave of his orgasm hits, Demitri picks me up placing me on the island facing him. He wipes the tears from under my eyes before pulling my shirt over my head. Then kisses me with so much love. As the kiss deepens, we let go of everything. We both let down all our walls and truly open completely to each other. His lips leave mine then start to leave a trail of kisses down my jaw to my nipple. Taking the right nipple into his mouth. He sucks on it while he is massaging my left breast. Then he nips and teases my swelling nub with his tongue. His mouth switches to my other breast as he continues his pleasuring assault on my body. He rubs my other nipple between his thumb and finger. I can feel myself getting wetter with each touch. Sliding his hand down my body he swirls his finger on my clit on top of my thong. As he kisses down my stomach. When his mouth reaches the top of my thong, I lift my ass so he can pull it off.

"Fuck Demitri.", I moan out as he sucks my clit into his mouth and slides two fingers in me.

"Your so wet Baby.", he voices breathlessly before using the tip of his tongue to make a swirling pattern on my clit. While he is gliding and twisting his fingers in my wet pussy.

"Demitri!", I beg him.

"Yes.", he responds picking up his pace. "Tell me what you want Amara."

"Fuck me Demitri!", I moan out going crazy with the need for him to be inside me and the pleasure he is sending pulsing through me.

Right before I am about to cum, I feel Demitri pull back. Opening my eyes, I lean up on my elbows to see why he has stopped. Demitri is standing there with his eyes taking in every inch of me. When he locks eyes with mine there is even more lust flaming in his eyes than before. If that is even possible. There is also something else I am not quite sure what to call it. But in that moment, I know that I did not just love Demitri. I am in love with him, he has my heart and soul. That other emotion shows me that he just realized it himself. Relief floods through me at the realization that he feels the same way. Not hesitating he slides his still rock-hard dick against my wet folds before slamming into me. He starts out slow as he makes love to me. He kisses my swollen lips, and his tongue is begging to enter my mouth.

"Harder.", I moan out as I wrap my legs around his waist. Giving him the access to my mouth he wants.

Demitri picks up his pace and thrust as hard as he can. Every thrust is bringing me closer. As the orgasm hits and pulses through both of our bodies there is an explosion of pleasure as our souls connects as one. I sink down on my back onto the counter while Demitri sinks into me. Keeping himself up on his elbows so all his weight is not on me. My legs barely have the strength to hold themselves up around his waist. Our eyes do not break their connection as our souls dance as one. Until the final wave of our release hits us. That was earth shattering. Our souls connecting like that made the orgasm ten times more powerful. We lay on the island tangled together for a while.

"Ouch.", I gasp out as I rub my hand under the inner bend of my left elbow.

Demitri jumps up to check me out. Sitting up I look down at the spot I am rubbing, and my breath is instantly trapped in my lungs. The spot on my arm is glowing black in the shape of a sun like the charm on my necklace. The necklace that held my essence and fed my curse. I look up to Demitri, he is looking at the same spot but on his right arm. Where a crescent moon is shining black like mine. After a few minutes, the burning dies as the tattoo, brand, or whatever you want to call it stops searing into our skin.

"You are the sun to my darkness.", Demitri whispers the words he told me when he gave me the necklace.

I found out later that Demitri had placed a powerful protection spell on it when he first gave it to me. Seeing how the curse was stronger magic it broke the spell. This time when he had it spelled, he made sure to find the strongest protection spell out there.

"In Fatis Anima mark.", Demitri mutters in amazement. "Legend has it that there has not been a fated pair in thousands of years. The marks are a gift from Gaea, a symbol of their Souls connection. As well as their unbreakable bond. It lets them share each other's abilities and strength. There is a rumor that they also give you the ability to mind link each other as well. Like how the shifters, lycan, and werewolves can with their marked mates. The alpha's that still follow the old ways and mark their pack members can mind link those pack members as well."

I am overwhelmed with emotions. Somehow, I know that I am not just feeling my emotions. But Demitri's as well. A smile spreads across both our faces as our love and desire for each other intertwines. Flowing through our connection. I knew the day that Demitri gave me the necklace we had a special bond. I lean into Demitri kissing him passionately. Releasing all the emotions flowing through me pushing them into that one kiss. After several minutes of the most passionate kiss of my life. Demitri breaks our kiss to pick me up and cradle me against his chest. Like I am the most sacred thing in the world. I snuggle into him as he carries me to the bathroom. Demitri sets me down to turn on the shower.

Once he has the temperature right, he climbs in the shower. I grab his outstretched hand then step into the shower with him. Closing my eyes, I lean my head back in the water. Soaking in the sensation I get when the heat from the water stings my skin as the last ripples of my orgasm fade. He lathers up my hair massaging the scalp has he does. Demitri with a delicate touch washes my lower lips then lathers up the washrag. Using the same delicate touch, he washes my body. After reaching up to grab his washrag and lathering it up. I take it from him and start washing his body. While he washes his hair. A joint would bring this high from my orgasm and the hot shower to an ultimate buzz. I think to myself as I finish washing this masterpiece of a body.

Stepping out of the shower reaching for my towel, I realize how weak my legs are. Holding myself up on the counter with one hand. I wring out my hair with the other. I then try to make it to the bed on shaky legs. Halfway there Demitri picks me up and sets me on the bed. Before I could protest him carrying me. While I sit there in my towel, Demitri reaches into the nightstand's drawer. Pulling out the weed, tray, and papers to roll a joint. If we had not grown up together, I would have sworn he could read my mind. Once he has rolled it, I leave a kiss on his lips as he hands it to me. Scooting up to the headboard I move around to get comfortable. As I light the joint, I inhale filling my lungs with that sweet smoke. While my body sinks into the pillow. After exhaling I lick my lips tasting the hint of fruity pebble flavor unique to this strain. When we finished smoking the joint, I test my legs before completely standing. Then go slip on an emerald tank top with jean shorts. This is my go-to outfit. What can I say it is what I am most comfortable in. Then I slip on a pair of black socks before I slip on my black sneakers. Next, I brush my teeth and hair. Then braid my hair into a mermaid tail as I walk into the kitchen. I eat the cold bacon before throwing the eggs out the back door and then place the plate in the dishwasher.

"Sorry your breakfast is cold.", Demitri conveys as he walks in wearing a dark blue t-shirt, black cargo shorts, and black sneakers. This man can look gorgeous in anything.

"It was well worth it.", I respond as I walk over to him. "Now my fated Soulmate are you ready.", I ask as I grab his hand.

Leading us out the cabin I shadow jump us into a shadow at Untamed Paintball. It has twelve different arenas set up. Malan, Zack, Lucas, & Aspen are on their way here. You can even custom build an illusion in one of the arenas. Of course, that cost extra. This place is better than its reputation. We have it set up where the beings at Aspire come here as part of their training. Or for fun for the younger students. Right now, Aspire Academy is kindergarten through twelfth grade. With some Associate college courses. It is so big we are adding more classrooms and two more housing buildings.

"Amara it is so nice to see you again. Looking even more beautiful than the last time I seen you.", Teryn greets me and places a kiss on my cheek. "Who is this sexy Creature?" He is eyeing Demitri from head to toe with a smile on his face.

"This is my SM Demitri.", I convey.

"SM? Is that some kinky name like Master.", he asks as his grin grows even more.

"Soulmate. Your thoughts always go somewhere naughty.", I respond with a chuckle after rolling my eyes.

"And yours don't enough", Teryn playfully adds.

I laugh at his goofiness as we follow him to custom build our illusion while we wait on the others. I met Teryn back when I did not have my memories. He is about 5'9" with dirty blonde hair and has light brown colored eyes. Teryn is a spirit of the woods. This arena is part of the woods he roams. We were on an assignment to rescue three human children that were taken by a pack of gytrash. They are a ghost that appears in animal form to lead travelers astray. Gytrash are black with red eyes, and they usually take the form of a dog, horse, mule, or crane. They are more often than not malevolent. The kids were taken by the gytrash into Teryn's woods. He helped us find and rescue the human children. Teryn also took them to meet the transport team as we captured the three gytrash. Ace's gadget really makes capturing beings so much easier. I do not remember what name he gave it.

My team has been asking if the Underworld is real. Then is heaven and hell not. Basically, it is all true and not true in a way. Different religions have different names for the same things. As well as get somethings right and some things wrong. Goddesses and gods still do not even know everything. What the humans describe as heaven is what Olympus looks like. When they describe Hell, they are describing Tartarus. Tartarus is where the evilest and most wicked of souls are condemned. The Titans are imprisoned in the deepest part of Tartarus. All human souls go to the Underworld where they are judge and placed accordingly. If you want to call the place good souls go to Heaven and the place evil souls go Hell. Then both heaven and hell are in the Underworld which is one of the four Realms of Earth.

There is the Mortal Realm which we are in now and is the human's realm. The Underworld where mortal's souls go when they die. Then there is Olympus and Hala. Olympus is the goddesses and god's realm. Hala is the realm for all the Fae. Or better known in the Mortal Realm as supernatural beings and creatures. Everything that human's call monsters. Except vampires, ghost, undead, zombies, magicians, angels, demons, mutant, lycans, and some creatures that are fallen angels. The first lycan was a human cursed by Zeus. Apollo and Artemis cursed a human. Then Artemis blessing the same human made the first vampire. Angels were created by the creator of humans and live in a corner of Olympus that Zeus as sealed off from the rest of Olympus. Demons are beings from the Underworld. Ghost of course are mortal souls and Undead are skeletons being control by a necromancer. zombies are created by a virus that only effects humans. It was also created by human scientist trying to make a bioweapon. We have kept the virus pretty much under control and haven't had a global break out. Mutants are humans that had a chromosome mutate in the womb giving them an ability. The ability usually surfaces around puberty. Some of the fallen angels were transformed into monsters.

In the beginning there was Chaos and Order. Or at least that is what we know them by. They only teach gods and goddess about Chaos, who gave birth to the primordial ditties. There must be a balance with everything. So how could there just be Chaos? The only mention of her is that she gave birth to them. I refer to Chaos as female because of how she is described as giving birth to ditties. They did mention something about from the void Chaos birth the primordial ditties. The Void is the place immortals go when they die. Researching in the Mortal Realm I have come crossed more about order in some of the religions. Wanting to separate Chaos's creations from the humans that Prometheus created, Order divided the Earth into four realms. Chaos is the one that built the portals between the realms. After Order realized what Chaos had done, he locked the portals. Not only sealing off all the realms from each other except the Mortal Realm and the Underworld. But also sealing all the other creations off from the humans.

Lost in my own head I did not see everyone showing up. I am so excited! This is going to be so bad ass. They are going to love it. Today they are going to get a glimpse into the Underworld. If a mortal body walks into the Underworld, it claims its soul. If they can even, make it past Cerberus. Humans' eyes cannot even see the portal. I have probably pissed the fates off enough. So, I do not want to chance taking my team down to the Underworld. I wonder if they are going to catch onto the fact the Underworld inspired these illusions.

We set up both illusions for half an hour each. We step into the football field size area. Teryn already has the illusion casted. The first time I came here I thought it was a spell. But the more I come the more I believe he has someone who can create illusions working for him. Because this feels too real to be a spell. As well as it does not have that magic shimmer that illusion spells put off. Plus, this is the only arena that is an illusion. Elysium is the most beautiful part of the Underworld, the place of our first illusion. My Dad created Elysium for my Mom. When she suggested another realm be made for the purest of human souls. It became the Underworld's heaven. With its luscious green fields flowing along the rolling hills and banks of the crystal blue rivers. The clear blue sky has a few fluffy white clouds floating along the wind. In this round it is every man for themselves. I had building structures randomly added in, so we have some cover. For two hours we shoot each other until we were all out and then start again. The last around looks like it is coming down to Demitri and me. Except I do not see Zack on the sidelines. I push that thought out as soon as I see Demitri crouching down. He is barely peeking out around the corner of one of the buildings. I steady my hand, aim, take a deep breath, and then squeezed the trigger. The paint ball splats on his mask right on his left eye. Yes, I won!

"Do you surrender?", Zack asks.

"Never.", is my response as I roll onto my back, shooting Zack right in the chest.

But I am not fast enough. He gets me on my side before I can get my shot in. Even with my goddess speed my back was to him, and he was already aimed at me. I should not have left my back open especially playing with Zack the God of Hunt. Taking a break before the next round, we munch on some snacks and drink our water. This next illusion was harder to design. Tartarus is not just a place it is a deity. Demitri and I agree to design a massive cave that is internally on fire with screams of torment echoing down the tunnels. The last half hour we fight as a team to beat Kronos.

"That was amazing Amara.", Ace says as the others agree.

"That really was a brilliant design of the Underworld Sis.", Zack adds.

All my team member's eyes get big, but no one said much except for wow, cool, or something to what Zach said. I think it is taking them a few minutes to process.

"Was that Kronos in the last round?", Malan asks.

"Yep.", I reply popping the p.

"Badass.", Aspen adds.

"You couldn't have planned a better date Baby.", Demitri notes as he wraps his arms around my waist. "I'm starving want to go get something to eat?"

"Yes!", I answer him.

As I am telling them bye Aspen notices our marks. She asks when and where we got them done. So, I have Demitri explain it all to ever one since he knows more about it then I do. Malan is the only one that has heard about these marks. Sometimes I forget how old he is compared to the others. Grabbing Chinese food, we spend the rest of the night relaxing and watching movies until we fall asleep. Sunday rolls around before I know it. We spend the morning cleaning the cabin. Then spend the rest of the day relaxing like normal mortals. I like to spend my Sundays like this, always have.

Today is Monday which means I work at The Company. I am meeting with Elijah and Samuel to decide who will get the two seats. This is going to be a hard decision. Three out of the six candidates brought themselves out of the labyrinth. The other three did so well we are most likely going to end up not just offering them a job. But a chance to run their own team. I kiss Demitri on the lips then head to work. Before I am out the door, he spins me around and kisses me deeply.

"Amara, I want to start working on making a family.", Demitri confesses.

This is not the first time he has mentioned this. He has been making comments here and there for at least about a month now. I just do not know if I am ready. I have so much going on right now that I can barely manage to get it all done. How am I going to add a baby to all that as well? Not to mention I will have to quit going on field assignments and I am not ready to do that. Also, I am scared as hell to carry and raise a baby. On the other hand, I would love to have Demitri's children and most of the work I would be doing can be done at home.

"Baby that makes me so happy to hear. I just have to much on my plate right now.", I convey as I place my hands on his cheeks. "How about we wait until The Company fills these two seats and they take on their workload. Which will lessen mine. As well as give the sterilizing spell time to wear off and we won't have any more casted."

Demitri picks me up off the floor and spins me around. Kissing me before he sets me back down.

"So, you are okay with waiting a little bit?", I ask meekly.

"At least this time you didn't say you weren't ready to have kids. Its progress Baby.", Demitri replies making me chuckle at how he said it. "I knew I wanted you to be the mother of my children. But seeing you raise Grim like your own reinforced that."

I tell Demitri I love him and kiss him one last time with a couple of tears escaping down my cheek. With a smile on my face that is not going to fade all day I head to work. The meeting is long and comes with a twist I did not see coming. Getting home late I jump straight into my bed. Finally giving into Demitri's teasing and plea to be in me I am able to get some sleep after a great orgasm.

After my morning shower I find a dress to slip into. Once I am ready, I shadow jump to the Tree of Dawn with Demitri. We part ways at the gate as I pat all three of Cerberus's heads. There were rumors that there is a group of demons forming a resistance. They do not believe a woman is fit to rule the Underworld. I am almost done with making my rounds, my last task of the day. When I am encircled by a group of demons. My two guards are at my side with their swords drawn as soon as they started to close in. Ordering them to put their weapons down I then give the demons two choices. They can either vow to follow me or be banished to the depths of the Underworld. Where the evilest of souls are banished. I let them know they will only get this choice once. If they continue their attack, I will slaughter them all. I did not want to have to kill my own people. They are forcing my hand. Their actions have made them traitors to the crown which is punishable by death. But they are still my demons. The beings I vow to protect. I need to make sure a war does not break out. This will be a safe place for the kids and everyone else. I am warming up to the thought of being a mom more and more.

Focus Amara, I think to myself as my mind starts to drift. I am bored of this already. I wonder if the leader is ever going to shut up. He keeps going on and on about how women are weak and are not fit to rule. How he will never bow down to a woman. Word has gotten out, Demitri and Lucas in their true forms push their way through the circle of demons. Sliding in between my guards and me on both sides. Lucas's demon form is beautiful, I wonder if Aspen has been able to see it. Especially in comparison to the demon leading the resistance. There is about fourteen of them surrounding us. Luca's demon face looks almost the same as his human face. Apart from his black as night lips and horns that come out of his forehead. As well as the hunter green eyes, so dark the almost look black on his red tented skin. The demon leading the resistance is a rust color with red horns, yellow eyes, and jagged yellow teeth.

"If you accept my banishment then drop your weapons and kneel.", I command.

Bored of listening to this demon's pathetic speech. Okay half listening. Half of them drop their weapons. The other half raise their swords getting ready to attack at his command. Bad move, I am more powerful down here. There is something here that feeds my power. My anger rises as does the desire to use Death's Touch. Who are they to challenge me? Most of them are lower-level demons. The others are the lowest level of demon warriors. They have no idea what it takes to rule. My parents spent most my life raising me to be a leader, and I still struggle. With the snap of my fingers the demons that were about to attack are engulfed in a black flame until they are ash. With a second snap of my fingers the half that dropped their weapons are banished and teleported to the depths of the Underworld. I take slow deep breaths trying to calm the desire of Death's Touch. That is trying to push its way to the surface as it demands a life be taken. It is so powerful it scares me. With everything I have in me I fight it back down. Once I get it under control, I finish my rounds and go home.

Next morning, I am sitting in the conference room waiting for everyone to join me. Nora, Schrat, and Julian were already here. Elijah walks in with Jazlyn behind him. A few minutes later everyone else arrives a few minutes apart. I sit back letting Elijah take the lead.

"Now that everyone is here, we will begin. We will call you in one by one to discuss your results. You will go sit in the waiting room and wait for your name to be called.", he informs them.

"We are incredibly pleased with the turn outs from all your assessments. This decision was not an easy one to make and definitely was not taken lightly. The four that are not offered a seat today will be offered a chance to join and run their own team for The Company. You can exit out the door behind you. See you soon.", I add not being able to wait until the secret is out. This is huge! Like earth shattering huge.

"Julian, you may go in.", Elijah's assistant calls out. He follows him in and has a seat.

"Hi Julian. We were really impressed with your leadership skills. Unfortunately, I cannot offer you a seat, but we would like you to run your own team of agents. You have trained well, and your determination will take you far.", I inform him.

Elijah is having me take the lead since the next two weeks are his last. He says I need the experience. Julian accepts our offer. I let him know he starts Monday and then I dismiss him. Next Nora and Schrat walk in. I have not seen him help many beings. This only reinforces that this was a good decision.

"Congratulations, we would like to offer you a seat on the Council.", I convey after she has taken her seat.

I go over what she needed to know to be able to start Monday. After she thanks me and accepts the offer, I ask to speak to her in private. Pulling her to the side I asked Nora if she is the Sea Witch. Something about her has my gut believing she is. For only a second, I seen the surprise look in her eyes at that name. She quickly shakes it off and tells me that she is not the Sea Witch. She thanks me one more time before she leaves. I have a feeling she is lying but I am sure she has her reasons. I hope one day she trusts me enough to tell me what she is hiding from. Maybe we can help her.

I deliver almost the same speech to Drake and Malachi as I did to Julian. The only difference in the speeches is what made each of them stand out. Both accepted the offer as well. Even though they were bummed they did not get a seat. But they have always dreamed of working for The Company. Then it is Celestia's turn.

"Celestia you were quite impressive out there. I would be honored if you would take over my seat.", Elijah informs her. Once she accepts the job, he ran her through what she would need to know for Monday.

Jazlyn comes in last. I did not want to deliver this news, but I also cannot wait for her turn. For the twist I do not think neither Elijah nor I saw coming. I wonder how all this is going to affect her. Hopefully, she knows I am here for her.

"I want to start by saying you were amazing at the assessment. You are enormously powerful and well trained. We were only expecting one not three to be able to bring themselves out of the labyrinth. Since we only have two seats, I cannot offer you a seat at this time.", I convey. I hate having to tell her she did not get a seat when I was the one that pushed her to come. "Before you go. Someone would like to speak to you."

Samuel walks in as we walk out. I want to hear this conversation so bad. But this is a private conversation. Samuel is about to drop the biggest bomb on Jazlyn. He is about to inform her that she is his daughter. That before he was turned into a strigoi, he was a Matter Manipulator who fell in love with her Mom. A Matter Manipulator is a name given to a witch that has a strong connection to the Matter Element. Samuel also is going to inform her how he wants her to take over his seat on the Council. Leaving it up to her rather she wants to remain a hidden seat or not. If she even accepts the offer.

CHAPTER 11: THE MISSING DRAGONESS

Mel's POV

I am so nervous this is the first doctor's appointment that Kaden has agreed to come to. Not to mention he has to astral project here to be able to come to the Underworld for the doctor visit. It surprised me that Amara aloud it. Today is also the day that I find out if my Lil Bug is a girl or a boy. I am so excited to see my Lil Bug, but I am so over being pregnant. One and done thank you very much. I think to myself as Kaden walks up and sits beside me. He asks me how I am doing and makes small talk as he keeps distance between us. He has not touched me since Amara walked in on us. Goddess I wish he would just hold me and that I could kiss those sexy lips. I know what I did was a shitty thing I am not saying that. But I feel at home when we are together, and I cannot control or ignore the connection pulling me to him. Awkward silence falls between us as we wait to get called back. The Obstetric Sonographer comes out to get us taking us to a room. She rubs the cold gel on my stomach with the Transducer. Moving it around until she finds my Lil Bug, who is doing summersaults in my stomach. Finally, Lil Bug is still long enough for the Obstetric Sonographer to get a peek.

{Few months later}

The four months of my pregnancy went by way to fast. I am not ready to be a mother. I am a very vindictive being which made me believe I was unlovable. There was a time when there was not anything, I would not do to get what I wanted. Now all I think, or should I say worry about is if I am doing a good enough job with my baby boy. Tonight, is one of those nights I doubt myself and that I am a good mom. I have been up with Chase for hours and he will not go to sleep. If I am not up and walking him, he screams and cries his little head off. I am dozing off while walking him I am so tired. He has done this the last three night since Kaden left on an assignment. Not being able to take it any more without losing my shit I call my big sister. Maybe she will come help before I fall asleep walking him. That will not be good for either of us. Amara picks up on the second ring and will be here soon. Just as I start to nod off again, she walks in then takes Chase from me. Before ordering me to go to bed. Watching her with him I have no doubt she is going to be an amazing mother someday. When even all I saw was my own envy of her I still looked up to her. I watch her spin and toss chase up in the air a few times before making it to my room. Clasping onto my bed I am out like a light as my head hits the pillow.

{Four years later}

I cannot believe that Chase turned four last month. He looks just like his Dad. I never imagined anyone could love me so much. After an hour of fighting a nap, he falls asleep. Getting my chance, I take a long hot shower. Being a mom is tough and I never felt like I had maternal instincts, but my little Chase brings it out of me. Kaden and I were living together, well when he was not traveling for work. He asked for us to move in with him. After Chase was born and the DNA test results come back that he was the father. So, Chase and I moved to the Mortal Realm.

Until a week ago when he moved out. I have a feeling it is because he has met someone. Chase only sleeps for about fifty minutes before getting up and destroying the house. While he is sitting at the table coloring, I cook dinner. Even though Kaden and I have come a long way I know he will never be in love with me. He may have love for me, but I am the reason he lost Amara. He will never forgive me for that. When he is around, he makes sure not to touch me. That way he does not feel our connection as he continues to deny it.

Hades and I are at least talking now. Not the father-daughter relationship I have always wanted. But it is a start. He even comes over all the time to see Chase. Zack and I are back on good turns. As for Amara and me, we are slowly getting there. Which I completely understand. I owe her for not killing me that day. I am going crazy being trapped in this house I need something mischievous to get into. I think as I place Chase's plate in front of him. I make my own plate before sitting in the seat next to his.

"Mommy can we please play hide and seek?", Chase asks in a soft voice as he places his plate in the sink.

"Okay. You better go hide 1 . . . . 2 . . . 3 . . . . 4 . . . . 5.", I count with my eyes closed. Chase quickly goes to find a hiding spot. When I reach twenty, I take off to go find my little man. After taking the last couple bites of my dinner. The door to my room is cracked, so I slip through quietly. I bend down peeking under the bed expecting him to be there. Which he is not. Hearing a rustling sound come from the closet I tip toe over.

"Gotcha", I excitedly exclaim as I open the closet door just as a bat flies over my head before flying around the room and heading into the hall. Spinning around on my heels I run after the bat. "That's cheating.", I state with a chuckle as I leap at the bat. Both of us fall to the ground. As a black Lion lands on me. Reaching up I pet the underneath of his chin as I tell him,

"Okay my Lil Bug it's time to get your bag packed.", I command. "Go get packed.", I say sternly when he does not move.

"Go get packed.", Chase mocks after he transforms from the lion into his Dad.

Seeing Kaden's face made me inhale sharply. I cannot stop the two tears from leaking down my cheek. It hurt so bad that he still denies our connection. "Don't mock me son. You're Dad isn't going to be happy if you aren't ready when he gets here.", I inform him after clearing my throat.

"Your Dad isn't . . . .", is all he can get out before I start tickling him. Chase is laughing so hard that a few tears are slipping out of his eyes and down his cheek.

"Are you ready?", Kaden questions as he walks through the front door without knocking.

Chase transforms back into himself and dashes for his room to finally pack his bag. That voice makes my heart skip a beat and wetness to leak into my panties. Kaden's nostrils flare as he smells my arousal. In one motion he is in front of me with a look of pure desire. His lips are inches from mine. I cannot fight it anymore. I lean in that inch covering those sexy lips with mine. Pouring all the emotions he makes me feel into that kiss. To my surprise he deepens the kiss as he picks me up by my ass. I wrap my legs around him lost in the kiss. The emotions I am feeling from Kaden's lips makes this kiss feel like a goodbye. Kaden plants me on my feet before Chase rushes in the room.

"I'm ready.", Chase yells as he races for me and jumps into my arms. With his backpack slung on his back.

"I'm going to miss you Mommy.", Chase declares as he snuggles his nose into my hair.

"I'm going to miss you more my Lil Bug. But you are going to have so much fun at Dad's new house.", I convey as tears slip down my cheek. This is going to be so hard I do not want to share Chase. I want all of us to be a family so bad. I set Chase down, then he walks over grabbing Kaden's hand. More tears escape out my eyes. I cannot believe how big he has gotten, and I am going to miss him so much.

Kaden clears his throat before telling me, "Um so I'm seeing someone."

I am shocked silent as I feel the pain of my heart breaking as it spreads its way through my entire body. Even though I have had a feeling that he was moving out for this reason. I could not prepare myself for this blow. Yes, he is denying the bond now, but I figured one day he would give into it and forgive me. After a few minutes of silence, I finally ask, "Are you bringing her around Chase?"

"It's not that serious yet.", Kaden answers with a small smile before walking out the door hand in hand with Chase.

I sink to the floor, letting myself cry. He refuses to forgive me for coming in between him and my sister. After getting it all out I walk to my room, I really need to fuck some shit up. There is this warm electric sensation that shoots through us even with the slightest of touches. It makes it so damn hard for either of us to stay away. Which ends up pissing him off even more. He loves me, he just needs some time and space to heal. Were the words he used to inform me that he was moving out and already had a place. All I can do now is accept the fact that Kaden will never accept our bond. Which means he will never be in love with me. I wipe the tears from my face as I pull myself together. As well as off the floor. Kaden loves Chase and is a wonderful dad to him. Which makes me fall even more in love with Kaden. Walking over to the grey stone fireplace in my room, I make up my mind that this is the moment I start to move on. My new hobby will help release some of this stress and raw emotions. Pushing the hidden button on the right side of the mantle the hidden door next to it cracks allowing me access inside. No one can access this room another than myself except Chase and Mom. Since we share some of the same DNA.

After I had it built, I snuck into Olympus and stole some hair from Zeus so I could do a spell where he cannot enter. I snooped around until I learned when he was going to get his hair cut. Putting the demigod that was going to cut his hair to sleep. I then shift into her taking her place. Slipping some of his hair into my pocket as I cut it. This hidden room was originally built for an emergency shelter. Now it also shelters my outfit for my new hobby. At the back wall in a hidden case is a dark purple leather two-piece suit. I am the only one that can open this case. The suit is magically infused to rip off easily and reattach itself for when I shift. The coolest part is not that it allows me to shift and then have clothes on me as soon as I shift back. Or that it fits to the form of the being wearing it. But with a push of a button on the screen on the left inner arm it turns into any outfit in its data base. As well as accessories for your outfit including any weapons in its data base.

I stole the tech from Ace who would have been presenting it soon. Well, if I had not stolen this model. Now he has to build a new one from scratch. They still have not figured out that it was me that broke into The Company's Tech Lab. If Connor had not been babbling on and on about it, I would not have known about this tech. When we took over The Company, he would not shut up about this secret gadget the tech team had been working on. I snooped around and found out what it was. It seemed cool but not worth my time. Especially since it was nowhere close to being done when I found it. When I found out that my big Sis killed Connor before he had a chance to steal it. I decided I wanted it. I slip into the suit then head out to find a little trouble.

Sticking to the shadows I comb the city looking for creatures that want to act on their darkest desires. Twenty minutes later I walk upon a vampire draining a young woman. I pull out one of the daggers I had chosen for tonight. Slicing my palm, I squeeze the blood out letting it slide down my hand. The smell of my blood fills the air getting the vampires attention. Gods' and goddesses' blood is addicting to them. It drops its victim and charges at me in the same second. In two seconds after that its head goes flying while its body hits the ground. Drowning the body in gasoline I set it on fire with a match. Once the body is covered in a blaze of fire, I search for its head. Down the alley a little way I find it, I drown it in gasoline and set it on fire as well. The vamp's head and body turned to ash as it blows away in the wind. Rushing over to the woman I scoop her up using my super speed I run her to the ER. Within a blink of an eye, I have her in a wheelchair and by the front desk. All without being seen.

Amara's POV

I am trying to focus on the giant pile of paperwork in front of me. But my mind will not stop thinking back to that positive test that is still sitting on my bathroom counter. We agreed for Demitri to quit getting the infertility spells casted on him every few months. It is just so surreal, we tried for two years. Then the disappointment of not getting pregnant became too much. I figured something is simply wrong with me and I cannot have kids. I was beginning to accept that and then boom I am pregnant. We stop trying that did not mean we were preventing a chance for it to happen. I guess I am just shocked that I am going to be a Mom. Picturing a little boy running around barefoot has a smile sliding across my face while I rub my stomach.

"Does this say what I think it says?", Demitri inquires as he drops the pregnancy test on my desk. Bringing me out of my thoughts with the smile still painting my face.

"Hey Baby.", I say innocently. "Yes, you are going to be a Dad.", I squeak out as a couple of tears and a sob try to break free.

"Hey, it's okay Baby. What is wrong?", he asks worriedly.

It cannot be hormones this early on, can it? I think to myself before answering, "I'm just so happy but I am also scared.

Demitri wraps me in a tight embrace as Zack rushes into my office. His face is drained of all of its color.

"Robyn Dagon has been kidnapped!", Zack conveys breathlessly. Everything else out of his mouth comes out in an over worried babble. That I cannot understand.

"Slow down and start from the beginning.", I encourage him.

After he catches his breath, he explains how the Dark King kidnapped Robyn's Mom. Then after they kidnapped Robyn, she traded herself for her Mom's freedom. Which is exactly what he wanted. Robyn is a full blood dragon one of the last few pure bloods. If the stories are true, The Dark King is one of the evilest beings out there.

I send out a sos alert to Jazlyn and her team. Telling them we head out in ten minutes. Celestia and her team are combing through satellite and camera feed. From a twenty-five-mile radius from her apartment. When we ran her plates, we found out that her vehicle had been involved in an accident. Both vehicles were abandoned when the police arrived. My team including Zack are patrolling the accident scene on foot. Nora's team is searching for any abandoned houses or buildings in that general area. Everyone is getting called in on this assignment. We must save Robyn from the Dark King. What really scares me about this situation is that her mom had hers and Robyn's dragon suppressed. That way no one would be able to know that they are pureblood dragons. So, how did he know Robyn is the one he is looking for? Not only that but since Robyn's dragon is suppressed, she is not much stronger than a human.

Once I make sure all the bases are covered, I join my team and several others after gearing up. We head off to the warehouse she was spotted walking into on satellite feed. I shadow jump Nora, Jazlyn, and I a block from the building. Demitri arrives a few seconds later and the rest will be here shortly. We have other teams searching through the other buildings. Nora fills us in on some history of Hala while we are waiting on the others. Before the Great War Hala was broken down into four kingdoms on land and four kingdoms under the water. One of the kingdoms on land was ran by Robyn's parents. Another was under the Dark King's and his mate's rule before she was murdered. Dean was blamed for her murder causing a war to break out. The whole realm is said to be nothing but death and destruction now. No longer the beauty it once was. Dean, his family, and his followers fled here to the Mortal Realm with Nora's help.

Arriving at the warehouse Jazlyn's team flanks the building from the back. While my team enters through the front. We clear the building in five minutes. The place is clear, and it looks like there had been a tornado in here. Which is a sign that they opened a portal taking her to Hala. I merge calls to the other two Council members and inform them what we found. Demitri suggests that we open the portal on the castle land. That way we can have a demon army waiting in case something or somethings escape through the portal. That is our best bet, so we are going to regrouped at the castle. Just as Demitri and I are about to shadow jump to the Tree of Dawn the Horsemen come walking up. Jazlyn and Nora are riding back with their teams.

"I would say it is nice to see you Amara. But that would be a lie.", Reggie sneers.

"Awe you are just as sweet as the last time I seen you.", I respond.

"What are you doing here Amara?", Hunter asks.

Hunter is looking good. I dated him before I lost my memories. I broke it off after I learned Mel's plan and decided to go along with it. He begged me not to do it. I do not know if I could live with myself if I had to end her life to save mine. Which would have been the outcome had I not decided to allow my memories to be taken. I also knew Zack would make a great king. My brother and I went to my Dad about forming a team to help protect all four portals. As well as stop anyone that wants to create portals to the other realms. Even though that is a challenging task and requires a shit load of power. He gave us the go ahead. We used humans with reaper blood that did not have enough of it to come back as a reaper. A reaper is a being that is one-fourth or less angel that has died. They are given a chance to come back as a reaper and earn their wings. Then named them the Horsemen. My brother and I created five then hid the fifth until she was needed.

We created Truth, Death, War, Famine, and Pestilence. Then gave them special abilities. When Chaos unlocked the portals all five came together and hunted down anything that escaped. While the Elementals fought Chaos so that they could close the portals. As long as whatever crossed over follows the two most important rules they are allowed to stay. Rule one no killing humans. Rule two no exposing one's true form to humans and no using abilities in front of humans. The Company deals mostly with those beings that break those rules now. Where the Horsemen now mainly protect the realm portals and stop anyone trying to open any of them. No one knows why the portals were not lock but only shut. Or what happened to the Elementals and Chaos afterward. If the first generation of Horsemen knew they took it to their graves. They stay Horsemen until they meet a true death, or they ask to quit. No one has given up on a second life in the Mortal Realm yet.

Hunter is War and has chocolate brown hair with hazel eyes. Then there is Reggie who is Pestilence. He has red hair with light blue eyes. Owen is famine he has dirty blonde hair with chestnut brown colored eyes. Death is Troy, he has jet black hair and amber brown eyes. The fifth is Elethia, she has golden blonde hair with bright green eyes. She is truth and the strongest of all five Horsemen.

"Someone special to me was kidnapped and taken to Hala. I do not have time for this. I must get to Hala to save her.", I divulge to them as I start to leave.

"That is a stupid thing to do.", Elethia states. "That realm is not what it once was. Darkness and evil have overtaken it."

"We can't allow you to do that.", Owen says as he steps in front of me.

"I think you have forgotten who helped create your team. No one will stop me. Have a nice night.", I say as I turn to leave with Demitri on my heals. I must get back so we can save Robyn.

"Amara.", Hunter calls after me.

"Hunter, I don't have a lot of time. I must get back.", I say in an urgent tone.

"You should really rethink going to Hala. Whatever has taken over it almost killed all of us. I don't want anything bad to happen to you.", he discloses as he reaches up to tuck a strand of hair behind my ear. But stops when Demitri clears his throat.

"Baby we are short on time.", Demitri states while placing his hand on my shoulder.

"Thanks for your concern. I must get going.", I voice before ripping open a shadow and stepping inside hand in hand with Demitri. I then shadow jump us to the Tree of Dawn.

Demitri's demon army is ready and waiting. Nora gets to work opening a portal to Hala as soon as we get to the castle. It takes a lot of power to open one to another realm, so she is pulling power from me. Slowly a swirling black hole starts to form. I step through first with Reaper in hand as everyone else follows.

On the other side of the portal is an almost dead world. All the plants are brown and withered. There is an eerie silence hanging in the air. There are no sounds of animals, insects, and beings. Now that everyone including Nora is on this side of the portal, we start marching towards the Dark King's castle. When it comes down to it no matter how things turn out. I am not leaving without Robyn. I promised her Dad I would keep her safe. That girl is damn good at slipping her guards and is not making it easy. But I do not break promises.

An hour and a half later we are walking up on the tunnel entrance. Over half of the town is destroyed and there is not a lot of beings moving around. There are underground tunnels that lead to the castle. They were built for an emergency exit in case the castle gets stormed. Dean has blueprints of both castles in his office. The echoing of footsteps can be heard halfway down the tunnel. Two beings come running towards us with a mob chasing them and ordering them to stop. There has got to be at least sixteen beings in that mob.

"Get against the wall. Let the first two beings past then block the way. Don't let anyone else through.", I whisper loud enough for both teams to hear me.

Once Robyn and the being she is with make it past us we make a wall out of our bodies. Turns out the mob is full of royal guards. The royal guards do not hesitate as they charge at us with all the speed they have. Lucky for us the tunnels are too small for them to shift into their dragon forms. As they get closer, we can tell that a lot of the guards are not even dragons. They are something of which I have never even heard. Zack and Jazlyn in her swamp creature form battle a group. Her five team members are fighting another group, as well as Aspen, Ace, and Willa. Malan, Demitri and I are dropping them as fast as they can get to us. Screams and the sound of blades cutting through flesh echoes down the tunnel. Green and black colored blood is painting the ground and walls as well as anything else in its path. As bodies slump to the ground lifeless. Within an hour or so there is not a single being of the royal guard left standing.

We have a bigger issue than what we had originally thought. At least half of the royal guards are some demonic species. This species is not known to any of the realms of Earth. They look like a killer clown with horns that bend back like a Jester's hat and eyes blacker than the pits of the Underworld. We thought we were going to be fighting just dragons. Things just are not adding up but right now I must get Robyn back to the Mortal Realm. Through the com I notify Nora to get ready to open the portal that we are heading back her way. Once we reach the forest Nora grabs my hand and opens the portal while channeling my power. Robyn and the guy helping her go through first, next Jazlyn and her team. Then my team goes through. After everyone but Nora and Demitri is in the Mortal Realm. I step through with Demitri following me and then Nora steps through. That was way too easy, are the words running through my head as the portal closes.

I run over to check Robyn out. She whisperers my name before pulling me to her and crying in my arms. Letting her cry for several minutes, I then pull her up and take her to the castle. She will be the safest there. Jazlyn promises to wrap everything up at headquarters for me. Aspen calls Robyn's Mom letting her know she is safe and that she will bring her to Robyn if she wishes. The guy that helped her is glued to her side. I have not seen Robyn or her Mom since before Dean died. When Dean was a live, they lived on several acres in a supernatural town. The only humans that live in these towns are ones born from a supernatural, mated to one or a child of a human that is mated to a supernatural. Also, there are human hunters. They usually stick to themselves or with other hunters. Most of the human hunters are pulled into this world mostly due to someone close to them getting killed by a monster. As they call them.

After Dean died, Robyn's Mom had a powerful witch suppressed both of their dragons and moved them to a human city. The Company has their best security team watching them in the shadows. Robyn can evade the best of them it seems. She falls asleep in my arms before we make it to the castle. Demitri and the guy who helped Robyn fly straight here. They touch down as I reach the front door.

The dude shifts out of his dragon form as soon as his four feet hit the ground. His dragon is an enchanting black with forest green eyes, and pointy scales. His spine and outline of his wings are forest green as well. Not to mention he is massive. Dean is the only dragon I have seen in their dragon form until now. Dean was a beautiful blood red and is just a tiny bit smaller than this guy. In his human form Robyn's friend is 6'2" with a baby face, dreamy forest green eyes, manly chin, and full lips with a beautiful smile. That I am sure drives girls crazy. His reddish medium brown colored hair is styled in an undercut giving him a bad boy look. He is wearing black combat boots, a white t-shirt and a black leather jacket finishing off the bad boy look. Along with a tattoo peeking out from under the collar of his shirt.

Once inside the castle I take Robyn to a guest room and lay her in the bed. Then post four-armed demon guards at her door. The dude runs straight into the room Robyn is in. It is a fight to get him to leave her side, so she can rest in peace. I finally talk Robyn's friend into leaving the room when I offered him the room next to hers. As we walk out of the room Aspen and her mom walks through my front door.

Roland's POV

I did not want to leave Robyn's side. Even though she is asleep. I walk out following the lady that was leading the team that saved us. There was no way I could have taken all the royal guards out on my own. Robyn has become more beautiful than I could have imagine. With layered shoulder length dark wine-red hair with a round face and upturned turquoise eyes. Robyn is about 5"6" with an athletic build. Far more gorgeous than any of the girls in Hala.

"Roland? What are you doing here? I knew you had something to do with this!", the woman accuses me.

"It's Prince Roland.", I reply courtly. "Who are you?"

"I'm Queen Cora.", she replies rudely.

Shit, that's Robyn's Mom, I think to myself.

"Cora, have a seat please and give him a chance to explain.", the lady politely commands. "Prince Roland, I'm Amara. Please explain what exactly happened back there. That has got to be the easiest rescue I have ever been a part of."

"A Seer that is close to my family came to see me one night. She tells me the Dark King was going to kidnap a woman and that I had to save her. If I failed to save the Salamander the earth will be the beginning of the destruction of our galaxy. She also told me that on the next crescent moon I was to meet the group of beings from other realms in the tunnels. Those beings would keep us safe. Two days later the Dark King kidnaps her then tries to force me to strap her into this machine he had his minions build.", I inform them. "The machine he had built sucks the abilities out of one being then inserts them into another. He also wants to use her eggs to repopulate our race. Ever year less women are being born and the pure blood females that are born are infertile. He believes she can solve that problem as well as believes she belongs to our family. Since she is my betrothed. I did not know who she was at first. She has grown up so much.", I continue. Isabel, the seer, told me to trust the one leading the team and that is what I am going to do. So, I give them the whole story.

"Lies, you are just as heartless as your father.", Cora hisses.

"That monster is not my Dad. Something has taken on his appearance. My Dad died a few days after my Mom. I was the one that found his dead body. Then the next day he is up walking around like he had not died the day before.", I informed them. "Cora don't act like you know what's going on in Hala. You guys fled eleven years ago. Leaving the few of us that still believe in Hala to fend for ourselves."

"Watch how you talk to me young man!", Cora hisses out.

"Enough Cora! Robyn is sleeping once she wakes up, I am going to persuade her to stay here at the castle. You should as well. Drake and Malachi should be here with their teams to help guard the perimeter and I have my best demons guarding the inside of the castle. Roland you are more than welcome to stay as well.", Amara discloses.

"That's a good plan. The Dark King is going to assume you will be keeping her at The Company. Seeing how Dean was one of the original Council members.", I note.

"How did you escape him?", Amara questions me.

"I embedded an oak table leg into his heart while Robyn had a whip made of black flames wrapped around him. But he will not stay dead long. Don't be fooled he will keep coming after her until he has her or I find a way to end him for good.", I divulge.

"There is all the proof you need to tell he is lying. There is no way Robyn used any powers when her dragon is suppressed. Let alone fire when her ability is ice.", Cora voices.

"Now Cora you know just as much as I do that before we lost Dean, Robyn had grown into her fire abilities.", Amara reminded her.

"It is not unheard of an alpha controlling more than one of the elements." I note. Fire and Ice huh? I always wondered what her dragon looks like and what element she would get her abilities from.

"I have two more questions than you can get some rest. What are the Dark Kings abilities and tells?", she asks.

"When he is weakened, he can't hide his true eyes. They are a solid pale yellow with a triangle shape pupil. No one I have come across has ever heard of eyes like that. As for powers he has syphon so many lives there is no telling what he can do.", I answer. He can only hold one appearance at a time. When he takes on someone's form, he gets their knowledge and memories as well as their powers. He has had a machine built that does the same thing as his ability so that he can create an army to help him take over the world."

During some point of my conversation Cora decided to go to Robyn's room. I try to go set with her until she wakes up. But of course, Queen Cora is not having that. It killed me to see Robyn cry herself to sleep in Amara's arms. Especially with how strong she was during her stay in Hala. I just need to see the rise and fall of her chest. I need that visual conformation she is alive and safe. Every time I open the door to the room Robyn is staying in. Cora starts spouting out some bullshit about how I am lying as well as probably the one behind the kidnapping. O and my favorite, how I am just as evil as my father. How can she talk about my Dad like that? When she knows how much of a good person he was! Wait until she realizes who I am to her daughter. That Bitch is going to lose it. I cannot help but chuckle out loud at that thought.

Biting my tongue, I turn and go into the room I will be staying in for now. Jumping in the shower I wash all the dirt and blood off. I zone out lost in thought as I stare at the mixture of my blood, dirt, and water swirling down the drain. How the fuck do I kill this Bastard for good? Most of my wounds are healed but he really did a number on me. I will die before I let him have her. Stepping out of the shower I dry off and then wrap the towel around my waist. There is a large tray filled with a variety of foods on the desk. Eating until I cannot fit another bite in my stomach, I then put on some boxer briefs and slip under the covers. I am out as soon as my head hits the pillow.

Amara's POV

Demitri did not leave my side the whole time during the rescue or now at the castle. I knew what was going to come. He is going to want me to step down as Captain of my field team while I am pregnant. I still cannot believe I am going to have a baby. Aspen has not said much the entire day and that girl can talk. Once Cora goes to Robyn's room and Roland goes to his. I push Aspen to talk to me.

"Amara I'm pregnant and Lucas is wanting me to either stay home or at least get out of field work.", Aspen finally voices.

"Aww sweetheart how long have you known?", I ask her.

"A few days.", is her reply.

"Well, I found out today that I'm pregnant.", I declare as I look to Demitri for his reaction. He has this stupid grin plastered to his face. "I know it's going to be hard not working in the field, but I think it's smart. At least until we have our babies."

"Fine I want one last assignment before I go into boring desk duty.", Aspen compromises.

"Actually, you would be doing me a favor if you take on Robyn's workload. Until she takes over."

"That is not going to happen.", says Cora as she walks in on our conversation. "I'm her Mother and I know what's best for her. We will be going back to the human city."

"She is safest with Amara and I.", Roland interjects as he walks in the room behind Robyn.

"What makes you think that either of you get to make any decisions for me!", Robyn exclaims with a scratchy voice.

"Robyn how are you feeling?", I ask her before her mother can spout off anything else.

"Better.", is her only response.

"Don't worry about all that just relax, and we will figure it out later.", I inform her. While giving those two a look telling them to back off, especially Cora. She can be overbearing with Robyn. I know she does it out of love, but she is going to have to realize that Robyn has grown up.

"Demitri and Roland see if you can find anything on this being or one close to it. Or the demon clowns we fought. Aspen stay with Robyn. I have to make a quick stop by headquarters.", I voice as I divide up the tasks.

Shadow jumping to headquarters I call a Council meeting. Nora is the only one not at the office. It does not take her long to get here though. Once she is seated, we start our meeting. I lay everything I knew out for them. We worked together to come up with a plan of action. Jazlyn brings up how we used a golem child once and how we should create a Robyn golem. Which is not too bad of an idea. I brought up how we need to destroy the machine he had built. Jazlyn gets started on the golem while Celestia is covering the perimeter, Nora is covering inner security, and I am going back to protect Robyn. After contacting Ace he agrees to build a bomb for us. I am so proud at how well we work together and how amazing these women are. They give me courage that if we work together, we can defeat whatever this Dark King is.

Before I leave, I also put into vote for Zack to take over for me as Captain of my field team. Using that opportunity to inform them all that I am going to be a mother. All four voted in agreement that he will be a good fit. Jazlyn did not think I notice the slight change in her posture. I am curious as to what is going on with my brother and her. I have seen how he looks at her, but I wonder how she feels about him. Pushing the curiosity back for another time I head back to the castle. As I am about to Shadow jump, I receive a text.

Aspen → You might want to get back quickly. The drama has escalated.

Me → Separate them I will be there in a minute.

After replying to Aspen, I shadow jump to the Tree of Dawn. I walk in on Aspen dragging Cora out of the living room. Roland is throwing Robyn over his shoulder to take her into the kitchen. Both women are still running their mouths. Robyn is so much like her mom. I chuckle at the scene before going to talk to Robyn. She has made up her mind she wants to take over her father's seat and to train at The Company headquarters. Of course, Cora does not want that to happen. Hence the scene I walked in on. Once I get Robyn calmed down, I go speak to Cora. Robyn is twenty-one years old now. She needs to let Robyn live her life. I get she is scared. I get it more now than ever. All she is doing is pushing her way. There is some yelling and swearing. But in the end, Cora realizes I am right and calms down.

Dinner is quiet which I do not mind. Demitri sits beside me with his hand on my leg. Demitri and Roland cooked some fall off the bone ribs and mash potatoes with mac & cheese. After eating too much I head for a hot shower. Leaning my head back with my eyes closed I let the water run down my body. Washing the stress away with it. Getting lost in my thoughts I did not hear Demitri step in. When I feel him kiss my belly and then my lips I am pulled out of my thoughts. Opening my eyes, I take in the gorgeous naked man in front of me. I cannot believe how lucky I am.

Demitri's POV

After jumping in the shower with her I start a trail of kisses from her neck to her hard nipples. Massaging one of her nipples between my thumb and finger. As I suck on the other one driving her crazy. I switch to the other breast giving it the same attention. Then continue my trail of kisses down her body. Leaving one last kiss between her thighs. Before taking her clit into my mouth. Gods, she tastes so good! I still cannot believe she is finally mine and she is going to have my child. My dick grows even harder as I lick and suck an orgasm from her. Standing up into the water I spin her around then place her hands on the shower wall. Leaving a couple of kisses on her shoulder. As I position myself at her wet entrance. I love how wet she gets for me. I thrust into her burying my rock-hard cock deep in her. She moans out my name as my finger makes a light slow circular motion on her clit while I increase the speed of my thrusts. She pulls herself off my dick leaving me hungry for more. I am so close.

Spinning around she pins me to the wall. Amara wraps her legs around my waist after jumping up on me. Both my hands are holding her up by that delicious ass as she slides me into her. Working her hips as she buries me in her. It is driving me crazy. Loosening my grip, Amara twerks her ass faster sliding me in and out of her. The faster she twerks the closer we both get. Amara moans my name as her pussy milks my dick bringing me to an orgasm. Our eyes are glued on each other's as I hold her tight. I rest my head against her chest while we ride out our orgasms. The water is starting to get cold, so I set her down and wash her as quickly as I can. By the time I am out of the shower and dried off she is already in bed asleep. Crawling into bed I snuggle her against me as I drift off to sleep with a smile on my face.

Amara's POV
{Couple weeks later}

I am still in awe that I am going to be a mom. The heavy breeze is making this sweltering day bearable. Leaning against the trunk of the Tree of Dawn. As I am dangling my feet in the sky-blue colored water of the pond at its base. I rub circles on my little belly in disbelief of how big it has gotten already. In that moment, my little princess decides to kick the shit out of me. I close my eyes as I focus on feeling her move around. Suddenly I am not on the mountain top I am in a panic room as five beings are climbing down the ladder. The panic room is painted an honest blue. You can tell they tried to make it look like a comfortable bedroom with a 65" smart tv, a black comfy reclining couch, a California king size bed, and an expensive top notch surveillance system. As well as a small kitchen that has a black stove, black medium size refrigerator, and a table that turns into another bed. As four scared girls of various ages climb down into the room it hits me. There is no mistaking that those girls are Demitri's and my daughters. Sure enough, the fifth being that climbs down into the panic room is me. The vision continues for what feels like a while before I am pulled out of it.

"Amara, Amara sweety wake up.", Sylvia says as she gently shakes me.

"Where is Demitri?", I ask as soon as my eyes pop open.

The last couple of weeks we have spent at the castle training Robyn. She is not bad just rusty. I can tell she has not trained since her Dad died. When she was a teenager, he would bring her here to train. It is impressive how she can still wield fire with her dragon suppressed. Robyn does not just have fire abilities she can summon the flame of the Underworld. The hottest of all flames and known as Hell fire. I am only able to summon it when I am in the Underworld. When we are done Demitri, and Roland square off. He is almost as skilled as Demitri. As far as the Dark King goes, we have not come across a single being that can do anything similar to him Not even in the Ancient Texts. I am starting to think that maybe he is not from this galaxy or at least from a distant planet. What other reason is there that even the oldest of gods have not even heard of a being like him. Or the demonic clown creatures he has doing his bidding.

Early this morning The Company is attacked, and the golem is kidnapped. Robyn is back at the castle with Roland as well as a bunch of demon guards and Lucas. Zack is on his first assignment as Captain. After we stop the Dark King, we are all going our separate ways. Turns out Willa and Ace are going to have twins. Willa is put on bedrest for the rest of her pregnancy. Ace is taking over as head of the Tech team. Aspen is taking over Robyn's seat while Robyn is her intern. When she is ready, Robyn will fully take on her birth right. They are working from the castle. Until we either find a way to kill the Dark King or find a way to shut the portal for good. Malan is going to focus his time on his family and Aspire Academy.

It is my day to work in the Underworld. So, by the time Demitri and I reach The Company the Dark King is long gone. It is so cold I can see my breath in the air. The front door is blown off its hinges and laid a few feet from the entrance. Several guards are frozen solid throughout the hall in mid run. While different beings surrounding them are working on trying to thaw them out. A few are knocked over and shattered into a million pieces with a bowling ball size rock in the middle of them. We had a Council meeting four days ago. Where we decided the less beings we have here, the less lives we will lose. Since he has the golem, it is time to strike the Dark King. If we cannot defeat him, we will seal him away in Hala. We lowered the number of guards but not too much that it would look suspicious. Then moved everyone up past the first two floors. Keeping the golem on the first floor in a hidden room in Dean's office. The door to that hidden room is blown off with such force it is embedded in the wall. All the cameras are burnt too almost nothing.

The Dark King knows Dean's moves to well. Dean built this safe room for his family. Which is built to keep dragons and anything else on Earth out. So how the Fucked is the Dark King able to get in it if he is a dragon? Not to mention from what I have seen here he has abilities from at least four of the elements. Yes, it is known for alpha dragons to have abilities from two elements. Which is rare. Having abilities from four elements is unheard of. Even impossible sounding. Another thing pointing to my theory. Jazlyn is taking care of everything at The Company. While I wait patiently with Demitri for Roland, Celestia, her team, and my team to gear up. All I'm taking is Reaper, my 8" blade and my boot knife. Reaper is what I named the sword that Demitri had Hephaestus forged the Spear of Destiny with the flame of the Underworld for me. This is the last assignment we will have as a team. Even if I do decide to go back into the field, the others are not coming back. A tear escapes out the corner of my eye at that thought.

Roland wanted to stay with Robyn, but he must save his people. Zack, Roland, and Zack's team will help get all the beings they can to our side of the portal. Nora steps through but is waiting here to reopen the portal with Demitri's help. Holding it open is too draining, which causes a higher risk of it closing and her not having the strength to reopen it. Demitri of course is going to be glued to my side. Celestia, our teams, Demitri and I will rescue the golem. Letting Roland take the lead since this is his land, we follow behind him. I bet this place was captivating before all the death and destruction. Instead, it looks like something sucked the life right out of the whole realm.

As soon as we enter the town beings start to follow us. The group keeps growing as we get closer. On our way to the castle, we do not run into any of those demonic beings. Once Roland reaches the top step of the castle. He turns around addressing everyone that has gathered.

"I Prince Roland vow to bring my followers from these dark ages into a better life. If you have pledged your loyalty to me already. Or wish to pledge your loyalty to me. Meet me at the entrance of town with your families. Go now we do not have much time. Only bring what is essential for survival.", Roland conveys.

Most of everyone is rushing about, a few have fled into the castle. I am sure to warn the Dark King. Some of the soldiers stayed to help us fight. While Roland and the others get everyone to safety on the other side of the portal. Celestia, her team, my team, and myself barely make it inside the castle. Before an army of those demonic beings is attacking us. I cannot get over how much their faces look like a killer clown with sharp teeth. Mel would lose her shit if she saw these creatures. I laugh to myself at that thought as I glide Reaper into the heart of the one that charged me. Two more were behind it. Still holding onto the handle, I place my foot on his chest. Pushing him back with my foot as I pull my blade out. As thick green blood gushes out of the wound. Its lifeless body slumps to the ground. Getting back into my stance, I wait for the right moment.

Two are charging at me trying to go for my neck with their piranha like teeth. Slicing the first demonic being's head off I splash blood all over the other creature and myself. Seconds later my blade is through the other creature's eye. Poking out of the back of the demonic being's head. It slumps lifeless to the ground as I pull Reaper out. Four more surround me. Where the fuck, do they keep coming from? I reach for my flame. As I feel it flowing through my body, I set the four around me on fire. Screams fill the air, but they still close in on me. The first one to reach me sinks his teeth into my shoulder. Tearing a chunk out when it pulls itself off me. Furry fills me from the pain as a royal blue flame explodes out of me. Turning all those bastards around me to ash. Leaving only three to deal with but not for long. Demitri is at my side checking out my wound. While Zack, Malan, and Aspen each take one out before the ashes of the others drift off in the wind. A little beaten but not defeated we step over the bodies. As we make our way to the room the Dark King is keeping the machine in. The golem is strapped into the machine. Standing next to her is the Dark King with his hand on her shoulder. I want to knock that smug look off his arrogant face. The Dark King has salt and peppered color hair. A goatee the same color and forest green eyes.

"I'm so glad you could make the trip.", he greets us like we are old friends. "Where is my son? I figured he would be the first through that door. Seeing how I have his betrothed."

"I am not his betrothed . . . .", the golem starts to say. This is a damn impressive golem, props to Jazlyn. She not only looked just like Robyn she sounded and acted just like Robyn as well.

"Quit with the games. Do you seriously think I believe you are that stupid", I command in a voice that would make any alpha kneel before me.

"Right. I must say this is a very impressive golem. You had me fooled up until I try to pull her abilities out. Which is quite painful from what I have witnessed.", The Dark King conveys with an evil smirk spreading across his face.

"Bastard.", Malan mutters.

Without a second thought I spear Reaper deep into his chest. He turns just enough for it to miss his heart. The Dark King taunts me as he pulls it out like he is pulling a tack out of the bottom of his foot. Then harpoons it at my head. Reaper slices my cheek as I try to dodge it and lodges in the door behind me. The Dark King claps his hands together twice. Right after he stops dozens of huge creatures drop from the ceiling. Time for plan B. I give the signal, and everyone starts to retreat.

These creatures have a body similar to a werewolf, stand over seven feet tall with a head and wings of a bat. With massive ears and teeth. Once I have pushed everyone out the door. I try to close the door as those creatures try to push their way out.

"Now Celestia. Everyone else get to the portal.", I command.

"Mercy.", with that one-word Celestia pushes the button that was in her pocket.

Then we both run to catch up with everyone else. That word mercy was the command that Jazlyn had put in place in case we could not save the golem. A command that causes the magic that brought it to life to leave its clay form. Making it nothing but clay in the shape of Robyn. An exceedingly number of batlike creatures bust out the door as soon as I take my weight off it. The Dark King's evil laugh echoes throughout the hall before the explosion is all you can hear. As the castle shakes and debris falls around us. The creatures that made it out before the explosion are flying above us. Trying to escape the fire threatening to consume everything. Demitri and my team stop as soon as they see I am not following. Those batlike creatures are following us. There is no way I am going to let them get a chance to go through the portal.

Picking up a rock from the ground I throw it into the sky. It connects with a creature causing it to come after me. Just like I wanted. When it is in range, I throw a royal blue fire ball at it. My team and Demitri follow my lead. Only a few ended up following Celestia and not attacking us. They should be able to handle them. My team, Demitri, and I are surrounded. At first, they come at us one at a time. With our backs against each other we take them down easily. Painting the brown barren land orange with the blood of each creature they take down and black with the ashes of the ones I burn to nothing. Just as more of those bat-like creatures are flying by above us.

Realizing how easily we are taking them down. The rest charge at us all at the same time. I wench every time I lift my arm. The bite I got on my shoulder is not healing and a nasty clumpy purple substance is oozing out of it. Of course, the cut on my cheek is going to heal slow like humans heal since it was done by Reaper. At the thought of Reaper, I wished I would have thought to grab it. I am sure going to miss that blade. Working together we kill the rest of them. Even though we have sustained several injuries none seemed to be serious. Well except maybe my shoulder. After the last one falls lifeless to the ground, we take off running towards the portal. No one is in sight not even Nora when we reach the spot where we crossed realms. Only dead bodies. Few are from our team or are Roland's followers. Most of the bodies are the demonic bat creatures thank goodness. Shit are we to late? Surely, they would not just leave us. As my anxiety starts to pick up. Nora and Roland jump down from a branch in a tree then walk out of the cover of the forest. Nora reopens the portal after grabbing Zack's hand pulling in some of his power. I make sure everyone is safe on the other side of the portal and all the bodies of our fallen are in the Mortal Realm. Before Demitri and I start to step through a loud screeching sound comes from the sky as two of those creatures fly at us.

One is going for the portal, and one is going for Nora. Obviously not smart enough to realize she is the one holding it open. Jumping out of the portal I jump in front of her just as the creature reaches for her. I pull the knife from my boot embedding it in the creature's chest as it tries to take off into the sky with me. We fall with a thud, the creature landing on me. It starts to slash my heart out of my chest. Reaching out I touch the demonic were-bat. Using Death's Touch, I stamp out its life force. I did not think just reacted. Laying there for a bit I will the breath back into my lungs. While trying to keep the desire of Death's Touch under control. Demitri has the creature off me before I can get a full breath of air in my lungs and my chest is already starting to heal. My shoulder however still has not begun to heal. He scoops me up bridal style carrying me over to the portal that is opening back up. Nora is using Zack as a power source like she did to get Roland's people to the Mortal Realm. When I jumped in front of Nora it knocked her down causing the portal to close. This girl is something. She takes out the other creature and reopens the portal in no time. As soon as Demitri steps back into our realm, he takes off into the castle.

"Where are we going? I need to make sure the portal gets closed.", I question.

"I knew you should not have gone.", he utters not telling me where he is taking me.

"Like you could ever stop me from doing something I want to do.", I say back mad at him for ignoring my question.

When he turns down the hall that leads to the hospital wing I knew where he is taking me.

"Demitri really I'm fine.", I wine.

"We are getting our baby and your shoulder checked out. That is final.", Demitri conveys. "Please no more field work until you have our baby."

The look on his face shattered my heart. I have no choice but to agree. Even though I have a feeling it is going to be easier said than done. I have never seen Demitri look this scared in my life. Demitri follows Sylvia into the exam room. Where she does an ultrasound of our Baby. Our Little Tot is healthy and growing. I am about a month along which leaves three months to go. Goddess' pregnancy duration is four months, full blooded Sups' duration is six months and half human Sups' duration is eight months. I notice that my baby bump has grown a little as she wipes the gel off my stomach. Sylvia has to clean and suck out all the purple substance. Then has to put some type of ointment on it before my shoulder starts to heal on its own.

"Demitri some of those demonic beings got through the portal before Nora could get it completely closed. They came out of nowhere.", Lucas says after he catches his breath.

Leaving a quick kiss on my forehead Demitri takes off after Lucas while I'm left here, unable to help them.

Demitri's POV

Grabbing my scythe off my office wall I run down the castle hall and out the door beside Lucas. The demon army I had on standby is fighting the demonic beings that slipped through while Nora is closing the portal. There is no sign of the Dark King, and the portal is completely closed now. Every one that had portal jumped with us is fighting alongside my demon army. Except Roland, him and Robyn are getting his people settled in. Of course, Amara is also setting this one out and any future fight until she at least has our baby. Rather she likes it or not. Swinging my Scythe, I take the huge demonic bats head off as it charges at me. There is a mixed of two different demonic beings that got through. Six are dead and there are at least ten of the creatures left. One of those killer clown looking beings is dropped on me by one of the batlike creatures. Losing my scythe when we hit the ground, I summon deaths touch. With a single touch the demonic being slumps on top of me. My Death Touch only works on humans. All it did was weakened this creature. As I reach for my Scythe it buries its teeth into my neck. Finally grabbing my Scythe, I drive it into the side of the creature and push it off me. It was a bad Idea using Death's touch. It is powerful and is hard to control. Getting up in a trance like state I walk over to the next creature. Putting my hand on its forehead it slumps to the floor. Then I drive my Scythe through this creature's back. The light fades from its eyes as I pull my weapon out of its body.

"Shit! Guys grab him.", Lucas calls as soon as he sees my glowing eyes.

I hear his words, but they sound distant. All that matters right now is that

I give into the desire of Death's Touch. I kill two more creatures before Lucas, Roland, Celestia, and Nora can take me down. While my demon army finishes off the last few creatures. The more you use Death's Touch the stronger the desire is to use it and it will consume you quickly. They all hold me down a little over five minutes before I am able to control it again. Once I am back in control there is still a whisper of desire. I do what I can to push it back. Lucas talks me into going to get checked out by Sylvia. My neck is not healing and just like Amara's shoulder this nasty chunky purple substance is leaking out of the wound. He is threatening to go get Amara if I did not go. She is not going to be happy when I walk in wounded when I made her stay behind.

"Demitri what the hell happened?", Amara inquires as she gets down off the bed to check me over. She reaches out to heal me, but I grab her hand. Entwining my fingers in hers.

"Don't. I will be fine. Several of those creatures got through as Nora was closing the portal. They have all been killed and are being rounded up to be set on fire.", I inform her.

When Sylvia walks through the door Amara gets out of her way. Sylvia looks the wound over. This nasty purple substance is starting to ooze out of my neck at a faster rate than it was. Sylvia sucks all of the substance out before applying her homemade ointment. I can feel the wound starting to heal.

"I am going to do some test on the substances I got from your wounds. If it can stop a goddess and god from healing, then it is even more dangerous for a mortal. Are you sure you got all of them? The last thing we need is a new monster wreaking havoc in the Mortal Realm.", Sylvia questions us.

"I am sure, but I will have a team do a sweep of the island and I'll check every camera myself. If it will make you feel better.", I promise.

"Yes. It would.", Sylvia expresses.

She bandages my neck and sends us both home to get some rest. Rest is the last thing on my mind as I watch Amara's sexy hips and plump ass sway as she walks out in front of me.

Amara's POV

"Are you alright?", Willa asks as we pass the waiting room. While she tries to get up out of her seat.

I cannot believe how big her belly is already. Aspen is the only one who knows why Demitri acted like that. My whole team is gathered in the waiting room to make sure I am alright. This warms my heart so much. I guess this is a good time as any to tell them the news.

"Willa I'm fine. Sit back down and rest.", I voice. "Don't mind Demitri he is being dramatic. We are having a baby!", I inform them as I hold up the ultrasound pictures. "So, this mission is going to be my last."

"Guys I think there is something in the water. I'm pregnant as well and this is also my last week on the field team.", Aspen adds.

"OMG, I'm so glad I don't have to go through this alone.", Willa exclaims.

"Baby don't ever think you are alone.", Ace informs her.

"I know and you have been here for me. It's just not the same has having my girls going through it along with me.", Willa notes.

Everyone congratulates each other. I cannot believe I get to go through this pregnancy and raise my kid with my best friends' kids. Now I have no doubt I can do this whole mother thing. Demitri wants to stay here tonight, so I am close to the hospital wing and Sylvia. There is no telling what kind of aftereffects that nasty clumpy purple substance will have on us. Her and Malan live in her cottage that is somewhere in the forest on this island. As Demitri and I are walking hand in hand down the hall Celestia comes walking up with Reaper in her hands.

"Hey. Glad to see you are all right. I grab this for you.", Celestia says as she hands me Reaper.

"Thank you!", I reply excitedly. I love this sword and thought I would never see it again. "How did you manage to grab it? You were running beside me after you pushed the button for the bomb. I did not see it in your hands.", I question curiously.

"With a little wind magic.", she states wiggling her fingers at me.

"You are amazing.", I praise as I give her a hug before Demitri, and I continue to our room.

Once we reach the door Demitri kisses me goodnight then heads to his office. Walking into the room I slip out of my pants and then crawl under the covers. After slipping Reaper under my side of the bed. I start thinking about how good it would feel to have Demitri in me as I am taken away to dreamland.

"Were you up all night?", I ask Demitri. He is just walking into the room as I am waking up the next morning.

"Yes. I wanted to make sure none of those things escaped. Sylvia is right we do not even want one of those creatures lose. There were seventeen that got through the portal.", he discloses.

"Did we get them all?", I ask.

"All but one. The batlike creature that dropped the demonic clown being on me. It used that as a distraction to take off. I have no clue where it went. It's loose in the Mortal Realm.", Demitri confesses.

"Baby don't stress we will find it. Lay down and rest. I'll take it from here.", I order him. When he tries to protest, I push him back onto the bed making him lay down. "Exhausting yourself is not going to help anyone."

I throw some clothes on using the light coming from the window and skylight. After closing the skylight, I shut the door behind me. Then I send a group text to my team and the Council members.

Me ➔ Meet me at the castle ASAP! Demonic Creature loose in the Mortal Realm.

Within twenty minutes everyone is here. Splitting into teams we get to work. Celestia and her team are our eyes. They are going through every source of video feed there is. Jazlyn, Zack, and their teams are on the ground following up every lead. Robyn and her team are working on a plan for damage control once we find the batlike creature. While Nora's team is working with us to trap and kill this thing. Four hours into searching for this thing Celestia walks into Demitri's office.

"We got a sighting in Wala.", Celestia calls out just as my phone starts to ring.

"Mel I'm in the middle of something can I call you back?", I question after answering the call.

"Actually, Big Sis this is important. I thought you would want to know there is this monstrous bat creature attacking people.", Mel informs me.

"Let me guess you are in Wala.", I state.

"Yes. Chase and I are both here. How did you know?", she questions.

"That is the creature we are hunting. We are heading there now. Get Chase to a safe place. We will handle the beast.", I tell her before hanging up my phone while Demitri walks in. During the call I could hear petrified screams and the rapid pounding of Chase's heart.

"Hey Baby, you up to hunt down that monster?", I ask as I look behind me to meet his eyes.

"Please tell me you were not just about to go hunt this thing without me.", he notes. "You agreed no more field assignments."

"Do I really need to answer that?", I ask. "Without the proper sleep you would not have been any help in a fight. However, I promise I was going to make sure you knew where I was. How am I supposed to set this one out when my nephew is there and scared out of his mind? I promise this is the last one."

"What is he doing there?", he inquires.

"I have no clue. Mel and Chase are both there.", I state. Reaching up on my tiptoes I place a passionate kiss on his lips. Using the moment to send him some of my healing power to make sure he was at his best.

"Amara you did not need to do that I am fine.", Demitri mentions before getting back to the mission without an argument. "Where are we going?"

"Wala", I state.

"Wala as in one of the inhabit islands of Vanuatu?", Demitri asks.

"Yep", I answer.

Ace pushes the button on his device and a teal door appears. Opening the door, I walk through on to a beach with Demitri right behind me. Once everyone is through the door Ace steps through and it disappears. As soon as I am in Wala, I call Mel. She informs me that she is hiding Chase in one of the huts closest to the beach. The creature is destroying everything in its path as it makes its way through the island. I put my phone up and take off running towards the beast. They all follow me and my wordless command. This creature has destroyed almost half of this island.

"Demitri and I will take care of this creature while you guys help the people.", I command as we walk upon the massive demonic bat.

We circle the creature waiting to attack once everyone is taken to safety. It has its eyes locked on Demitri. In a flash of movement, it attacks Demitri without mercy. Just as fast Demitri blocks the creature's attack and kicks it in the chest sending it my way. With one swift movement of Reaper the demonic bat's head is rolling on the ground as its body falls next to it. While orange blood sprays out of the neck. After calling in the cleanup crew I call Sylvia to see if she can come help. Then send Ace with his gadget after her and three of her nurses. While I start healing some of the people that got injured. There are too many wounded for me to heal myself especially while being pregnant. Nora is directing everyone to round up all the people of the island and put them into groups. Ones that need medical attention and the ones that did not. The cleanup crew wipes the memory of the creature from their minds using the glawackus. Then a vampire agent replaces it with the cover up story Robyn came up with. They start with the people that do not need medical attention and then the ones that have already been healed. Until everyone has had their memory wiped and replaced. The reapers are going to have their hands full here. A lot of people did not make it or will not make it through the night. Being pregnant I cannot heal life threatening wounds. Even if I could there is still too many that needs healing. It would be awesome if Ace could invent a device that could memory swipe and plant memories in a bunch of people at once. I am too busy healing people to hear how the story is going to be spun this time. I am sure it is one that will stick. Robyn is really good at that. Once I start getting tired, I quit healing people and let Sylvia take over. When everything is wrapped up, I head home leaving the paperwork for tomorrow.

{Several weeks later}

I am in my office at the castle finalizing some paperwork when the pain hits me. It started as lower back pain about an hour ago. Which I dismissed at the time. It cannot be labor pains I am only two months along. It is too early. I double over when the second one hits only three minutes later. Zack walks in to drop off the paperwork for his last field assignment.

"Amara what's wrong?", Zack asks with big, worried eyes.

"My Baby is coming.", I say through clenched teeth as I am hit with another contraction.

"Shit!", Zack mutters as he scoops me up and takes off running towards the hospital wing.

The nurse hooks me up to the monitor as Zack calls Demitri. After I am hooked up to the monitor the nurse calls Sylvia, they form a plan to stop my labor. They give me a shot of Terbutaline to slow or stop my contractions. It works until about midnight when I am woken up by a contraction. Demitri flies me back to the castle's hospital wing. Where they put me on Magnesium and a Terbutaline shot every few hours for four days. Our little Tot is anxious to come.

It is my second day out of the hospital on bedrest. I am already going crazy not being able to do anything. Believe me, Demitri makes sure the only thing I do is get up to go pee. Speaking of I need to pee I think to myself as I stand up, I notice my shorts are wet.

"My water just broke.", I shout.

Demitri runs into the room on the phone calling Sylvia. As I double over from the pain. They are hitting every two minutes. This baby is going to come before Sylvia can get here.

"Demitri you are going to have to help deliver our baby.", I inform him. He goes ghostly white. "Demitri!", I hiss through the pain. "Grab some towels and meet me in the kitchen. O and we will need a bowl for the placenta."

In between the contractions I pull my shorts and panties off and then waddle my way to the kitchen. The mess is going to be easier to clean up in there. I barely make it to the kitchen with my contractions hitting every minute.

"Demitri! She is coming.", I shout. "Spread all but one of those towels out under me.", I order him as I try to fight against my instincts to push. "Now get ready to catch her as I push her out. Then wrap her in the towel."

Steadying myself with my hands on the table as I squat down. When the next contraction hits, I push as hard as I can. Aspen comes to my left and Lucas is on my right helping to hold me up. By my sixth push Demitri informs me that he can see her head and that she has a full head of hair. Sweat is dripping down my face and body. I am so exhausted. She is almost out just a few more pushes. I think, trying to motivate myself. I push two more times with everything I have in me when the contractions hit. Our baby girl slides into Demitri's arms. She is silent and purple.

Her umbilical cord is wrapped around her neck. My heart sinks into my stomach and I am left speechless. Tears are pouring down my cheek as I beg for her to be okay. Demitri is able to slide one finger in enough to unwrap it from her neck. Just as Sylvia rushes in. She takes our baby and admittedly uses a syringe to suck the liquid out of her throat and nose. Her lungs fill with air and then she starts crying loudly. The best sound I have ever heard. Sylvia then clamps and cuts the umbilical cord. Severing my baby's body from mine. After she cleans and checks her out. Sylvia swaddles her in a blanket and brings her to me.

"What are you going to name her?", Sylvia asks as she places the most beautiful being I have ever seen in my life in my arms.

I had no clue my heart was big enough to love someone this much. This time tears of overwhelming joy slide down my cheeks. This is the happiest day of my life. I cannot begin to explain the joy and love that fills my heart.

"Emery", I say through my tears and a smile.

CHAPTER 12: THE PROPHECY
{14 YEARS LATER}

Amara's POV

Demitri → Hey Babe. You free for lunch?

Me → Yes, at 1.

Demitri → See you then. I love you.

Me → Awesome see you then. I love you too.

The two hours until my lunch break went by fast. I meet Demitri outside the front of headquarters. Reaching up on my tip toes, I plant a kiss on his lips. He deepens the kiss as he wraps his arms around my waist. His beautiful black wings gracefully protrude out of his back. While I wrap my arms around his neck. He bolts into the sky heading north without breaking our kiss. Other than a few rainclouds, it is a beautiful day. Sooner than I would have liked Demitri lands in a valley.

There are about five or so cottages, six different marijuana gardens, a harvest building in the middle, a hydro chronic building, and a garage. It is so amazing to see how much this place has developed. There are even a few cottages built about an acre away from the garage. This is the first marijuana farm that we started a few years before I lost my memories. We started out with one garden, and we were living in tents. Harper, Demitri and I built the buildings ourselves. We have so many amazing memories here. Taking in the scenery around me reminds me of a memory of Demitri and I sitting on his couch. He was getting me some smoke for the first time since I lost my memories. I was supposed to choose what kind I wanted. I realize now that Demitri was trying to spark a memory with the weed we cultivated together from this farm.

I cannot believe how patient he was and how he did not push me to remember. He seen me even when I did not know who I was. I really could not have gotten a better man. Demitri walks up behind me as I am lost in thought. Wrapping me in a tight embrace he pulls me into his chest. Resting his chin on my head he takes in the scenery with me.

"Thank you, my love.", I express.

"For what?", he asks.

"For having patience with me while I didn't have my memories. And for bringing me here.", I state.

"Of course. I would do it all over again.", Demitri discloses.

Leaning down he kisses me passionately as he slides his hand down my back then squeezes my ass. He deepens the kiss as my phone rings. I pull away from the kiss to answer the call, it is the principal of our daughter's school.

"Looks like Emery got into a fight at school. She has been suspended for two months and next time they are expelling her. We need to go pick her up.", I inform Demitri after ending the call.

With a chuckle he scoops me up bridal style and takes off into the air. Those wings and this man are still as beautiful to me as the first time I seen his true form after I lost my memories. I cannot believe how wonderful my life has been. I have four amazing kids and an amazing husband whose also my best friend. He lands in front of the castle's doors. Once through the gates of the Underworld I pet Cerberus. Like I do every time I come through this way. Demitri scoops me back up and flies us to Elysium. This is the same school we went to growing up, it is the only school in the Underworld. Emery is waiting outside with a fucking black eye when we land. She is my mini me all over. Besides her height and some of her attitude she did not take after her Dad much.

"You have got to be kidding me.", I say as I turn her face to get a better look.

"The other person better look worse than you do.", Demitri teases with a wink.

"O, you know Logan does Dad.", Emery replies as she pulls her head out of my hands. "I'm fine."

"Hell no", I say as I march to the front office. No one hurts my Baby! Especially a male.

"Mom please don't. Can we just leave?", Emery whines.

"Babe you have to let her fight her own battles.", Demitri adds.

I do not say a word as I continue my march to the front office. I take a couple of deep breaths before opening the office doors. I bypass the secretary and march into the principal's office.

"What punishment did the young man that got into a fight with my daughter receive?", I question.

"Hello, Amara. He received the same punishment as your daughter.", the principal replied.

"Why was he not expelled for bullying and putting his hands on a young woman? I have informed you quite a few times of him repeatedly bullying her.", I inquire.

"Logan is our star player. If he is not back at school in time for playoffs, we have no chance against the Olympians. Not to mention his father makes a hefty donation every year to the school. So, it is better not to upset him more than I must.", is his response.

"Well, if that is how this school is being ran, I Queen Makaria am removing my daughters from your school.", I voice as I walk out of the office.

The office staff are whispering among themselves trying to figure out if I really am the queen. The principal just shut the door behind me. Not believing a word. That is okay he will be freaking out soon, I think as a grin creeps a crossed my face. He is not going to have that job much longer. Demitri and I decided that we would raise them in the cabin in the Mortal Realm but send them to school in the Underworld. That way they get a little of both worlds. Then come junior high school they get to choose to go to Aspire or keep going to school in the Underworld. Emery wants to stay in the Underworld with her friends.

"Mom what did you do?", she shrieks.

"Be proud. I didn't burn the building down like I want to.", I tease as she glares at me. "Relax I just unrolled you from this school."

"Yes! Does that mean no more school?", she questions excitedly.

"No, you are going to school.", I reply. "You will take the placement test for Aspire.",

"Mom! I don't want to go to school in the Mortal Realm.", Emery says full of attitude.

"Your only other option is online school.", I inform her.

"I don't want to do online school.", Emery whines.

"Then take the Aspire placement test.", I state.

After picking up our other two girls. I call upon Charon to transport us to the gate. When we get home Demitri gets Jade and Grace in the bath while I start dinner. Dinner is quite while we eat our fried chicken, mashed potatoes, and corn. After dinner I tuck Grace and Jade in bed then kiss them on their foreheads before cracking their door. Emery is in her room on her tablet. I tell her I loved her and to get to bed soon. Demitri and I decided to give her a couple days off. Before we have her take the test for Aspire. She is a good kid. She just does not take shit from anyone and not to mention she is a scrappy thing. As I lay down and snuggle up to Demitri I cannot help but be excited for tomorrow.

The next afternoon little kids dressed up as different monsters are playing tag as they chase each other through the cabin. Today is Jade's birthday, I cannot believe she turns six today. She looks exactly like Demitri except she has jade green colored eyes. Emery is fourteen and Grace is ten. Demitri just got back with her monster cupcakes. Life has been peaceful for the most part. The portal is sealed and has not been touched. We still do not know if the Dark King died in that explosion. Hell, we still do not even know who or what he is. I stick the candles in the cake then light them one by one. As we all sing happy birthday. Jade blows her candles out before we can even get halfway through the song. We let her unwrap her presents once everyone is done eating their cake. Then the kids take turns whacking the Frankenstein piñata with a blind fold on.

It is crazy how fast the time has gone. My team has completely split up, everyone has either quit working for The Company or has gotten out of field work. We keep in touch despite not working together anymore. Malan and Sylvia are still running Aspire Academy and overseeing the other locations. Which we have eight other locations in the United States and four locations in other countries. As well as having three college campuses in the United states. They have two children. Ace is running the Tech Squad at The Company while Willa stays home with their three kidos. Aspen is the lead Training Instructor for The Company. She is also about to have their second child. Zack is Captain of his own field team, the new Death Squad. Mel and Kaden still only have Chase. Kaden has finally quit denying his bond with Mel and they seem to be doing better. Chase is eighteen now he is such a smart and loving boy. Demitri remains my second in command. He said I am meant to rule as queen not behind a king. He does help out with a lot of the work though.

Once everyone leaves, we all pitch in to help clean the house. Except for the birthday girl, she really wore herself out. After dinner I put the youngest two to bed and make sure Emery is in the shower. Then I go clean up after dinner. I click on the light to the kitchen. As the lights come on Schrat is sitting at the island.

"Hello Makaria.", he says as he turns to face me.

"Hey Schrat, what's up?", I question worriedly.

Just as all the other Council members are following Demitri into the kitchen. It must be something big. He does not just pop up at my house in the night like this. Or have the others come to my house for a meeting.

"I have come across a prophecy that I believe is referring to the Dark King and the five of you.", Schrat discloses as everyone gets settled in. "The prophecy states that five Elementals will emerge centuries after the last Elementals. With the help of a sixth Elemental from another galaxy, they will defeat the evil trying to consume not only our planet but our galaxy as well.", he continues as he rolls out the prophecy. "The Six Elementals are Gnome, Undine, Sylph, Salamander, Wraith, and Tiger."

"Earth, Water, Air, and Fire. What does Wraith and Tiger symbolize?", Celestia asks.

"Wraith symbolizes the spirit element. I have no clue what Tiger could be symbolizing. I have only ever heard of the five elements", Jazlyn conveys. "Amara you are definitely the Wraith. You are the strongest spirit welder I have ever come a crossed. I mean come on you raised an army of undead."

"Very Good Jazlyn. Though most know about the four elements, some believe in a fifth. Diverse cultures believe in different elements.", Schrat adds. "The truth is there are twelve elements that all magic comes from."

"The Seer from Hala did call Robyn the Salamander. Makes since you are the only dragon around that can summon your abilities with your dragon suppressed. Not to mention you can call on Hell fire.", I note.

"We all know that Celestia is the Sylph. With her ability to not only call on the air element but can control the weather too.", Robyn comments.

"Which would leave Nora as the Undine. I mean there is no doubt that Jazlyn is the Gnome. She is the most powerful swamp creature I have come across.", I voice. "I knew there is more to you then you just having water abilities. You are too powerful.", I disclose to Nora.

"You have been right all along. I am known as the Sea Witch. Except I am not actually a witch at all. I am a Merrow that is cursed to walk on land for the rest of my life. It is a long story and I promise to tell you everything. Just know I kept it from all of you because I am being hunted and the least you know the better.", Nora explains.

Merrow are a type of mermaid. Some believe they are water beings not mermaids. They must have their own cap to transform their tails in the water. Their caps magically appear when the Merrow is born. They are born on land and then once they reach puberty their magic manifest and they usually spend the rest of their lives living under the water. The only way for her to be cursed to walk the earth is if someone stole her cap.

"There is more.", Schrat interrupts my thoughts. "It is told that the Elementals will have two markings. One is the marking of In Fatis Anima just below the right wrist which will allow them to call on their fated soulmate's strength and abilities. This marking only appears when their souls have linked."

"Like these?", Demitri ask as we show him our sun and moon markings in the exact spot the prophecy said the markings were going to be.

"Yes, just like those.", Schrat says with wonder. "The other marking will be a symbol of their element on the back of their necks. It will not appear until all six beings have been united. The translation is vague, I have no clue what the sixth being is, the powers they will weld or what their markings will be. It does say that this being will follow the evil to our planet."

"Schrat, the sixth being is going to crash here. But that is not going to happen for at least a few years. When I was pregnant with Emery, I had a vision about a crash landing. And some of the things in that vision won't come to pass for at least four years from now."

"Interesting. You will have to tell me more of this vision later.", Schrat voices. "I'm having trouble translating this last part."

"May I take a peek?", I ask as I try to translate the text. "We don't have a word to translate into this word. Maybe that's the Evil being's name? It says that if this great evil is not stopped, he will continue to consume galaxy after galaxy until there is nothing left but a Void. I might have translated that a little wrong. It could say that we have to trap him in the void. I am not sure. This language is old and not a language from Earth that I have come across."

"The Dark King does have the power to siphon the live force out of anything. Which fits with the prophecy saying the great evil will consume the galaxy. Why are you so sure it is the Dark King Schrat?", Robyn questions.

"Those beings are called psychic vampires. They are similar to energy vamps except they feed on life forces not energy. Also, where an energy vamp does not have to syphon energy to survive a psychic vampire have to continuously feed to survive. I have only heard of these beings.", Schrat informs us before moving on. "I know the Seer from Hala. Her consciousness visited me as you were making your way back to the Mortal Realm. She told me she is going to seal her side and it would be the last time we would ever see each other. She also informed me that the Dark King is only severely weakened by Amara's blade and the explosion. As well as the fact that he is not Roland's father but an extraterrestrial psychic vampire with extraordinary powers. The last thing she told me was that I had brought five of the Elementals together. Now more than ever I need to help them find the sixth. As well as help them all prepare for what is to come.", Schrat informs us.

"Well Fuck.", Dimitri states. The only thing he has said throughout this whole conversation.

We all sit there in silence for a while trying to process everything we have just learned. After a while we start going in circles because there is nothing we can do until the sixth being gets here. I offer them all a room since it is late. Jazlyn and Robyn take me up on my offer. While Celestia and Nora decided they would rather go home to their own beds. I crawl in bed ready for sleep to take me away to dream land. Demitri on the other hand has another idea. He starts kissing my neck then makes his way down my chest and stomach. Ripping off my shorts and panties he takes my clit into his mouth. Sucking and teasing it with the tip of his tongue he inserts two fingers into my wet pussy. Before I have time to protest, he has me dripping wet.

Continuing to thrust his two fingers in and out of my wet vagina, he devours my clit and juices. Bringing me so close to my release. As I moan out his name he leans up, rubbing his long thick hard dick against my wet folds. Before lifting me up and sitting me on it. Gods it is so deep and feels so good, I cannot help but moan out. Wrapping my legs around him I move back and forth at a fast pace. Bringing myself even closer I lean him back so I can ride his rock-hard dick. I twerk my ass harder and faster bringing us both closer to our climaxes. Demitri moans out my name when I switch to rolling my hips with him deep inside me.

Causing an orgasm to ripple through my entire body. My walls tighten around his rock-hard cock as it pulses while he fills me with his seed. We lay there while the after waves of our orgasms ripple through our bodies. Demitri rolls me off him then goes to the bathroom, cleans up and then brings back a wet wash rag to clean me up. Once he is done, he jumps back in bed. Pulling me into him he embraces me tightly as we drift off to sleep.

Morning comes to soon. I get up and get ready for my day in the Underworld. Demitri has already gotten up and got the girls ready for school. Grim picked Emery up to give her a ride to Aspire. Once we arrive in the Underworld, I take our other two girls to school before going to my office. The morning went by peaceful and fast. There is a knock at my door as I just finish eating my lunch.

"Come in", I call out while throwing my trash away.

"Queen Amara, Tartarus has been breached and one of the prisoners has escaped.", one of my demon guards informs me.

"Do we know who escaped and how they were able to?", I question.

"Not yet. Lucas is trying to find out what he can Ma'am.", he replies as Lucas comes running into my office.

"Amara a lycan we haven't been able to identify yet has snuck into the Underworld, broke into Tartarus and broke out a lycan we know, Jax Hinsen. ", Lucas informs me as he hands me pictures from the security cameras.

"What the hell is Jax doing in Tartarus and how the hell does someone break into the Underworld let alone Tartarus?", I question as my anger grows by the minute. Whoever condemned him to that fate is going to have to deal with me! While he was staying at the castle after having two spells casted on him, we became close friends.

"I comb through our records. It turns out that Morrigan an Irish Goddess condemned him to Tartarus a couple of weeks ago.", Lucas discloses.

"Where are they now?", I question.

"They have almost reached Charon's boat.", Sydney one of my most trusted guards notifies me. She had come in behind Lucas with a few other guard members.

"Syd take a small group and peacefully bring them to me.", I command. "Inform them that Amara Stone wishes to talk to Jax. Shouldn't have any problems from them once you mention my name."

"Yes Ma'am", she replies as she leaves my office.

"Lucas get the word out to all the gods and goddesses that from here on out they cannot condemn someone to Tartarus without either yours, Demitri's or my approval. Also track down Morrigan for me.", I instruct.

Lucas nods his head as he exits. I decide to make a deal with the Fates while I wait. As usual they talk in riddles, but I understand enough to know what must be done. I was not back in my office long before they walk in.

"Jax, it's so nice to see you again. I just wish it were under different circumstances.", I convey as I give him a hug.

"It's good to see you again. Queen of the Underworld huh?", he says teasingly. "Amara this is Zoe Madris, my mate."

"It's nice to meet you, Zoe.", I greet her. "Lucky for you I am", I tease back. As I take Zoe in, she is gorgeous and by her stance I can tell she is feisty. She is probably about 5'6" with midnight blue hair that is twisted back in a French braid. With a diamond shaped face, full rosy, pink lips and monolid shaped golden eyes. Zoe is petite but is more muscular than you would think.

"It's nice to meet you as well.", she greets me.

"So, Jax explain to me how you ended up condemned in Tartarus. Then Zoe can explain how she snuck into the Underworld and broke into Tartarus. As well as how she then breaks back out and almost makes it back out of the Underworld.", I politely command.

He tells me how he was dating Morrigan when he found out that Zoe is his mate. Morrigan was furious when he told her. She killed him and condemned his soul to Tartarus. Zoe is one smart woman. It turns out she made a deal with Charon for passage to and from Tartarus. A deal Charon would have never been able to refuse. She used the ring of Gyges to sneak past the guards in Tartarus. It is safe to say she got that ring from Schrat. I wonder at what price? Once inside she freed Jax from the snakes that bounded him to one of the columns. Then they shifted into their wolf form and overpowered my guards.

"So, let me get this straight you made a deal with Charon that two days a week for a year you will take his place?", I question her.

"Yep, a day for passage to Tartarus and one for passage back.", is her reply.

"Clever", I note before calling on the com for Charon to be brought to my office. "How did you get passed Cerberus?"

"I fed him a cut of steak that was marinated in a strong sleeping potion.", Zoe discloses.

We chat for a little bit while we wait. Zoe could not be more perfect for Jax. I hope they can work through whatever is pushing them apart. They are the first mated pair I have met that act like friends instead of a couple. Either way his life is better with her in it. That woman is going to accomplish remarkable things. Charon arrives not saying a word. My Dad could be harsh with his punishments. So, there is no telling what he thinks is going to happen to him. Charon looks like what I picture Old Man winter looks like. He has a white beard that is just as long as his white hair. He wears a long cloak with the hood up hiding everything, except his eyes that blaze like a fire in a furnace.

"I accept my punishment Queen Makaria.", Charon voices with a bow.

"Tell me Charon what would your punishment be from my father for this type of offence?", I question.

"One year in chains for every living being I allow into the Underworld

Ma'am.", he replies."

"Why help her then?", I question as I nod Zoe's way.

"I can see into the depths of souls. That young man is not evil and did not deserve to be condemned to Tartarus. Plus, how could I turn down a deal of a lifetime your majesty.", Charon discloses honestly.

After Charon finished talking everyone stood there silently. While their fates hung in my hands.

"Here is what is going to happen.", I convey once I have had time to process everything and come up with a decision. "Charon will give Zoe a ride back out of the Underworld. Jax I am afraid you have to stay here."

"Jax is coming with me!", Zoe commands using an alpha tone with her strength and power lacing every word. An ability that would make any alpha I have met submit.

"Let me finish.", I respond while thinking how she is full of surprises. I would love to get to know this woman more. "The deal you made with Charon still stands since he will be giving you a ride out. Jax must remain here. He is a soul with no physical body to exist in. If Jax leaves, he will slowly go mad as a ghost. However, when you find his body calls me on this number and I can bring him back.", I tell her as I hand her my card. "There is one condition from the Fates though."

"Doesn't matter what. I'll do it.", Zoe says.

"A life for a life by your hands.", I inform her.

"That is not happening! Zoe, just go get on the boat with Charon. I'll be fine.", Jax orders her. "Go live your life."

"Jax this is my choice. I am not leaving you here. Do not say another word. My mind is made up and when have I listened to you?", she adds with her arms folded against her chest. "I'll do it."

"Please don't do this. Taking a life will change you in a way you will never come back from.", Jax begs.

"You really think Morrigan is just going to stop with you. I bet you she is already coming up with a plan to come after me. If she has not already. This is how it always was going to end. Her vs Me, either way this goes I will have you in my life. So, she cannot win.", Zoe adds.

"I will help you with Morrigan anyway I can, but she must die by your hands. Here.", I say as I hand her Reaper. "The Spear of Destiny was foraged with Hell fire to make this sword. I call it Reaper. Only one being has survived this blade. I promise you Morrigan will not. Charon will be getting with you on the details of your deal with him. Now you two go with the guards while I discuss somethings with Charon."

Once everyone is out of the room, I informed him that he is to report straight to me. He is also supposed to bring any good soul condemned straight to Demitri, Lucas, or I. My Dad might have quote unquote stayed out of the affairs of the gods and goddesses, but I will be damned if I am going to allow good souls to be condemned. Especially condemned to Tartarus. As for the days Zoe fills in for him, I tell him he is free to do as he please. Also, that if he wanted to explore the Mortal Realm. I would make it possible. Charon walks out of my office after our talk. Feeling like I am not doing enough to help my friend. I pick up my phone to call my brother. I must clean up this mess here and reenforce security. It seems it is lacking when my dear brother is not here running the security team. I am glad she was able to get in and get him out. Being the queen, I have to make sure this does not happen again though. Tartarus is full of the evilest of souls that cannot be allowed out.

"Hey Zack, are you free for a few hours maybe longer?", I ask once he picks up the call.

"I guess I can move some stuff around for my Big Sis. What's up?", he inquires.

"I want you to go with a friend, Zoe to make sure she doesn't run into too much trouble getting her mate's body.", I inform him.

"I can do that.", Zack remarks.

"Awesome thank you. I will have a helicopter pick you up and then you can pick her up not too far from the bottom of the mountain. Also, we are going to need to double the security team training. They really blotched it today.", I tell him.

"You got it. Love you.", Zack says

"I love you.", I note before hanging up the call.

"Thank you for doing that for her.", Jax says as he walks in.

"It is no problem at all. I know how lycans can be. I got some work to do but you are more than welcome to hang out here or go back to the room you are in and watch Tv. Or you can find something else to do while we wait.", I convey.

"Okay cool. I just have one question. Is there any other way than her having to kill Morrigan to bring me back? It doesn't seem worth it to me.", he questions.

"I see it from your point of view. But I see it from hers as well. This is her choice, and she is right. I guarantee you that Morrigan is already got a plan in motion to get her revenge on Zoe and it will not just be a simple death either. You know how cruel our world is.", I voice.

"True. Except Zoe is not like us Amara. She was raised isolated deep in a forest by a creature named Schrat.", Jax informs me.

"Interesting. Well, Jax I can tell you this. If Zoe was raised by Schrat then she is more than able to handle herself. I was trained by Schrat myself.", I disclose.

That little bit of information makes it clear how she was able to acquire that ring from Schrat. Without saying another word, he leaves my office and I try to get as much done as I can while I wait to hear from them. After a few hours Zack calls to inform me that they have Jax's body. I let Jax know and tell him to wait in my office. Before heading to the Tree of Dawn where I shadow jump to his pack house. Once there I jump into the hole, rip off the coffin lid and then I place my hand on Jax's head. With a thought I command his soul to return to his body. Jax's heart starts beating pumping his blood through his veins and arteries. Then his lungs start filling up with air. Jax's body is slowly healing as his color starts to come back. The second I jump out of the hole Zoe is in the coffin with him. She wraps her arms tightly around him and he has to peel her off of him. Then she jumps out of the hole and hugs me. As she thanks me over and over. After making sure Jax is fine I tell Zoe I would see her soon. Before shadow jumping Zack and I back to the Tree of Dawn.

It has been about two weeks since Zoe snuck into the Underworld. Things have only escalated. It turns out that Morrigan found a spell strong enough to knock out Charon and Cerberus without them noticing. Once Charon was knocked out, she stole his skiff that controls his boat. Giving her transportation and access to the rivers of the Underworld. She filled up a magical flask that can hold the water from the rivers of the Underworld and then sold it in the Dark Market. Luckily, she was only able to get water from two of the rivers before Zoe caught her. It was her day to take over for Charon when Morrigan tried it again. This time Morrigan's plan had a different outcome for her.

"Amara, I sent you the video feed from all the times that Morrigan snuck into the Underworld. She was able to get in on three different occasions", Lucas informs me over the intercom.

I pull up the first video feed. It starts out with Morrigan sneaking into the Underworld. She puts Cerberus to sleep first. When Charon's boat comes into her view, she starts singing a melody again. The souls closest to her starts to fall asleep as she makes her way closer to the boat. Morrigan creeps up to who she thinks is Charon as she raises her voice from a whisper. What she did not know is that Zoe had made a deal with Charon. She also did not realize Zoe has EarPods in leaving her melody useless. Zoe notices the souls falling asleep before she notices Morrigan. She lands a superman punch to Morrigan's face without even taking out her EarPods as soon as she spotted her. Morrigan did not even have time to recover before Zoe connects two more punches to her face. The last hit to the jaw sends Morrigan on her ass. Without hesitation Zoe pulls out my sword then detaches Morrigan's head with a single swing. Morrigan's head flies off into the crowd of wondering souls as blood paints Zoe, the ground, and the souls closest to them. Morrigan's body slumps lifeless towards the ground just as Zoe catches it. She tosses it into Charon's boat before going to look for Morrigan's head. As blood sprays everything in its path.

"A life owed for a life saved.", Zoe says as she throws Morrigan's head with her eyes still opened into the boat with her body.

There is definitely more to Zoe Madris than meets the eye. Even if she has alpha blood, she would only be able to hold her own for so long against a goddess. Zoe just beheaded Morrigan without her being able to land a single blow. Morrigan is a Goddess of War. The way she handles herself and her personality there is no denying that she has alpha blood. With the power and strength she has, she is also part something else though. Something powerful. She reminds me of one of my close friends before I lost my memories. It was after Demitri started to pull away and Harper was busy with his flavor of the month. We both were sneaking out of our realms into the Mortal Realm when we met and became instant best friends. Eight months of us meeting up in the Mortal Realm she meets a lycan and falls in love.

The last time I saw Selene she was pregnant and scared that Zeus would find out and kill her baby. Zoe does look at lot like Selene. Rumor has it that Selene made a deal with Zeus to save her lover and in turn Zeus wanted her to go back to Olympus with him. Another rumor is that no one made it out a live that night. Her lover, and their whole pack was murdered in their sleep. I have heard faint rumors about Selene's child being killed that night as well. But I cannot find a trace of Selene's child ever existing. Then I get it on good word from a goddess I know years later. That Selene is indeed trapped in Olympus. If Selene is alive then there is a reason, there is no trace one way or another of her having a child. So, I quit digging. It is better to not know then for the wrong person to find out as well.

After watching the other two videos I have learned that Morrigan stole water from the Rivers of Archon and Styx. I am almost done watching the last video when I get a call from Celestia. There is a small southern town not too far from my cabin that the towns people are attacking and killing each other. I call Demitri informing him that I must take an unexpected trip to the Mortal Realm. Once out of the Underworld and by the Tree of Dawn, I shadow jump to headquarters. Zack and his field team are already gearing up.

"I want Nora and I to come with you. I need to know if this is linked to the waters of the river of Styx getting brought to the Mortal Realm.", I inform Zack.

"Meet you guys there.", is Zack's answer as his team and him head out.

I ran into Nora on my way to her office. "Hey, you want to join me on an assignment?", I ask her. "I need your expertise."

"Sure, as long as we can shadow jump there.", she response.

I debrief her on my call with Celestia about the quiet small town that has been consumed in violence and how it could possibly be linked to water of Styx making its way to the Mortal Realm while we gear up. I shadow jump us near a gas station I am familiar with in the small town. The streets run red with blood from the bodies that are spread out all over the town. As we make our way further into the town screams fill the air around us. It is an all-out war, and it is every person for themselves.

"Since it's the whole town going crazy and attacking each other. Let's go check the main water source while we wait on the others.", Nora suggests.

"Good idea. Will you be able to tell if the water has been altered and will you be able to undo what has been done to it if so?", I question her as I continue to speed walk, moving at a pace that Nora can keep up with.

"Different water sources have different properties which will allow me to know where it's from and if it has properties that shouldn't be there. Allowing me to know if it has been tampered with.", Nora discloses. "I will also be able to tell if all of the water is from this realm or another is mixed in. As for untainting the water. I can try a cleansing spell. That still leaves the town's people to deal with."

"That will help a lot. Messing with the main water source would be the quickest way to disperse anything to the town's people. This rural town uses a water tower to get their drinking water. As for the town's people, I have an idea.", I inform Nora before I pull out my phone to make a call. "Hey Harper, I need a favor."

"Sure, what's up?", he asks.

"I'm sending you, my location. I need you to come put all the humans and animals in this town to sleep.", I inform him over the speaker phone as I am sending my location.

"On my way.", Harper tells me.

I hang up the call just as the water tower comes into view. Nora reaches it first and starts climbing the ladder. I follow her up the ladder, onto the platform, through the metal hatch door and out onto the catwalk. Peering down over the edge of the thin railing we can clearly see the dark blue water of the River of Styx mixed in the clear grey color of the tower water. Nora drops a mixture of herbs into the water as she casts the cleansing spell. Nothing happens so she chants it one more time.

"Damnit!", Nora exclaims.

We are discussing our options when my phone rings. Ace calls to ask what the situation is with the town to see if his Geek Squad has anything that can help. I explain to him how someone has dumped water from a river of the Underworld into this towns water tower. How Zack and his team are dealing with the town's people until Harper can get here. Ace says that he might be able to help then hangs up the call.

"What was that about?", Nora asks as I start to put my phone into my back pocket.

"Ace says. . .", I start to say as Ace and Harper are walking towards us on the catwalk.

"How did you guys get here so fast?", I question curiously.

"This new device I'm working on. It opens small portals allowing you to step through a door into anywhere in this realm. I still have a few kinks to work out and still have to come up with a clever name for it."

"It's pretty cool.", Harper notes. "I was at The Company when you called me."

"Here.", Ace voices as he hands me a green water bottle. "This should be able to hold water from the Underworld. If you can get it to separate from the tower water."

"I'm sure I can handle that.", Nora informs us as she grabs the water bottle.

"Cool well I have a town to put to sleep.", Harper says as he turns to make his way out of the water tower.

"Make sure that includes any animals that could have access to water out of this tower. Not just house pets.", I politely command. "Ace sense you are here will you help Zack and his team get everyone including the animals to the church. From there we can figure out who all encountered the water and how.", I politely direct before turning my attention back to Harper. "O and Harper if you are going to pursue Celestia then no fuckboy shit. I will kick your ass if you hurt her."

There is only two reasons Harper would go to headquarters. I was not there so the only other reason is him trying to get the attention of our pretty snow-white haired beauty.

"You got it boss.", Harper replies with a smile.

"I have a device that will help tell us if someone has come in contact with it.", Ace discloses.

"Awesome.", I say as the boys exit the water tower to help Zack and his team.

Nora holds the water bottle out over the catwalk as she starts swaying her other hand. Several seconds later dark blue water starts swirling up into the water bottle. Once every drop of dark blue water from the river of Styx is in the bottle, Nora stops swaying her hand. There is not even enough water to fill the water bottle. Which means most of it has already been filtered into the town. This situation is a big fucking mess. I pull out my phone to send a text to Demitri.

Me → Hey Babe, I am not going to be done here in time to get the girls. Can you please pick them up from school?

Demitri → Of course. Stay safe. I love you.

Me → I will. I love you too.

I put my phone away to exit the water tower. I did not feel like climbing down so I just jump down.

"Show off.", Nora says before she giggles once she makes it down the ladder. Then we take off towards the town square.

By the time we make it to the church Harper has the whole town and all the animals nearby asleep. The others also have everyone including those animals spread out in the chapel of the church.

"Are you able to pull the water of Styx out of their bodies?", I ask Nora as we enter the church.

"Yes, but only one at a time. This many people and animals will take me hours. And that is if it does not completely drain me halfway through them all.", she replies.

"Amara turn the room into a Sauna with your flame.", Zack suggests. "It will lessen the amount of water she will have to pull out of each of them."

"I'm not sure I can do that.", I confess.

"Just imagine your flame staying the same size but growing in heat.", Harper adds.

"Okay. I'll give it a try.", I respond.

I call on my flame and then command it to grow hotter. The room is growing hotter with every second, soon we are all pouring out sweat. My flame goes from an orange red to a blue and white color. While I focused on keeping my flames lit, growing the temperature in the room, and keeping the flame in my hands. Harper runs to the Underworld to grab water from the River of Lethe. Everyone else is searching the room for people that are not sweating out a mixture of regular sweat and a dark blue sweat anymore. Those individuals are being assessed by Ace's device and removed from the church if they have none of Styx's water in their system. Then tested to see if they are indestructible. The ones that have not encountered the water are asleep in another part of the church. Thanks to Ace's device we were able to sort through everyone quickly.

The River of Styx can turn anything indestructible that is submerged in it and if ingested will drive you mad with hatred. The ones that turn out to be indestructible are being put in a different part of the building than the ones who are not. The plan is to take the humans that are indestructible back to headquarters to debrief them. Then as long as they follow the few rules, they are free to start a new life or go back to their old one. As for the indestructible animals they will be relocated to supernatural communities. The cleanup crew has already arrived and are finishing up. When Harper gets back, he will give the other group of humans a drop of water from the Lethe river taking their memory of what happened. He will then wake them up and Zack will inform them of a blood crazed bear that ripped its way through their town. As a vampire that Harper is bringing back with him is imprinting that memory into their heads.

It sounds like Harper just got back. Good timing, we are down to a couple of dogs, a racoon and ten humans left in the chapel. It is getting harder and harder to hold the flame at this temperature. Something is not right, even though I am not in my realm where I draw power from the Underworld. My power is still draining too quickly. I start to sway as everything around me slowly goes black.

"Shit Amara!", is the last thing I hear out of Harper's mouth before I am pulled into complete darkness.

"Glad to see you are awake.", Sylvia greets me as I open my eyes.

She is checking my vitals on the monitor. Demitri is asleep in a chair with his head on the hospital bed I am in. I ran my fingers through his hair, waking him up. He pops up and wraps me in a tight hug. Then places a loving kiss on my lips without letting go of me.

"Since your both awake now. I have some news. Amara, you have been out for fourteen hours. You overexerted yourself so easily because you are with child. Would you like to know the gender of your baby?", Sylvia informs us.

"I'm having a girl.", I respond. "I can't believe I'm far enough along to know the gender already. I didn't think it would happen this soon.", I think out loud.

"Yep, another beautiful baby girl.", Sylvia voices.

"Babe how have you known the gender for every one of our kids?", Demitri questions.

"In the vision I had of the crash, I may have left out the part where we had four girls and the youngest was around the age of four or five years old at the time of the vision. I am sorry I did not tell you. I did not want to ruin those moments for you. Please do not be mad.", I confess.

"I'm not mad Baby.", Demitri says as he kisses me on the forehead.

"Because of your record of high-risk pregnancies. I'm putting you on bed rest immediately and you will remain on it until you give birth.", Sylvia orders.

"Come on Doc, do you know how hard that shit is?", I whine as her and Demitri give me a look telling me that I have no choice and I know it. "Fine.", I say with a sigh.

Lucas is getting everything set up in the Underworld for me to work at home and Robyn is doing the same for me at headquarters. While Demitri flies us home to start me on my jail sentence. I know I am being dramatic, but bedrest drives me crazy! This is going to be a long pregnancy.

<><><><><><><>

{4 years later}

Today is Grace's basketball championship. She has been a mess all day. More and more she looks like me. Even though she has Demitri's eyes.

"Deep breaths. You got this.", I say trying to calm her down.

After taking several deep breaths she joins her team while I join Demitri, Grim, and our three other girls on the bleachers. The game goes into overtime with the other team having the ball. The other team's player that caught the ball comes running down the court. Dribbling the ball with her left hand. Stopping a little passed the three-point line she shoots the ball. Just as it sails over and is about to sink into the net. Grace jumps up catching the basketball then immediately passing it to a teammate. Staying parallel with her teammate Grace runs down the court towards their basket. Her teammate passes her the ball back and with a layup Grace scores the winning point. To celebrate the whole team and their families are going to go out for pizza and ice cream. Once we get home, I change out the laundry. Demitri comes up behind me. Slowly he moves his hand up my stomach towards my breast. As he leaves trails of kisses on my neck.

"mmmm", I moan. "Let's take this to the bedroom."

Demitri scoops me up and almost runs to the bedroom. Looking around for the girls like we are in enemy territory. I cannot help but giggle at this behavior. I mean it has been a little bit since we have been able to sneak off. But not that long, a couple of days maybe three. Tossing me on the bed he locks and shuts the door. Kicking off his shoes as he makes his way two me. Then lifting off my shirt he starts massaging and kissing my boobs.

"I like it when you don't wear a bra.", he says before taking my nipple into his mouth. Then leans up to kiss me as I start to pull off his shirt.

Bang! The sound of our door slamming into the wall causes us both to jump.

"Mommy, can I have a snack?", Paisley asks making sure to show her puppy dog eyes. I cannot believe how she is a perfect blend of Demitri and I. She has Demitri's hair color, but it is curly like mine. Her eyes are violet like mine but shaped like her Dad's eyes.

"Sure, Mommy will be right there.", I tell her as she turns and runs for the kitchen.

"I told you that you needed to fix that door.". I voice before following Paisley while putting my shirt back on. She is in the freezer trying to get a popsicle.

"Mommy what was Daddy doing?", she questions me as she eats her snack.

Shit I was hoping she did not see anything. "I walked into a nest of sea ticks on an assignment today. Dad was just making sure I got them all off.", I lie to her. I hated to lie to her but what else am I supposed to tell a four-year-old?

I have been on edge for a few weeks now. It has been a little over four years since Schrat told us about the prophecy and we have no clue when the spaceship will crash but it will be soon. I try to shake that thought out of my head and focus on making pizza bites for lunch. The girls had dentist appointments in the Underworld this morning, so I took the day off. Out of nowhere a tremor spreads its way through the cabin. I take off down the hall for my girls as the house shakes violently. Everything on the walls and shelves are crashing to the ground around me. Emery, Grace, & Jade come running out of their bedrooms. Paisley must be in my room. I tell them to follow me as I take off at a pace, they can keep up with down the hall. Once in my room I walk into the back of my closet opening what looked like an armoire. I holler at the girls to step in it and take the stairs that leads to an underground bunker.

The tremors stop just as quickly as they started. The only thing that can be heard is the groaning and creaking of the cabin. Urging the girls to pick up their pace we climb down the stairs into the bunker. I am not sure how long the cabin can remain upright with the force of that tremor. Sounds of glass shattering, wood cracking and busting apart. As well as the sound of stuff busting and breaking fills the air. Just as I close the reinforced door the cabin starts caving in on itself. Paisley and Jade are curled up together on the bed crying. I rush over to them wrapping my arms tightly around my Babies as I try to comfort them. While Emery is bitching about how she left her phone in the house. Grace has not said much but I can tell by the look on her face she is scared as well. The panic room is painted an honest blue color. I tried to make it look like a comfortable bedroom with a 65" smart tv, a black comfy reclining couch, a California king size bed, and an expensive top notch surveillance system. As well as a small kitchen that has a black stove, black refrigerator, and table that turns into another bed. Just like my vision.

After I get them calmed down and preoccupied, I use the backup cell phone that we keep done here. Since I left my phone up in the cabin as well. First, I call Grim to check on him and his family. Fortunately, his home is out of the tremor zone. Before I can get off the phone with Grim, Demitri is calling for the second time. He was catching up on some work in the Underworld. Grace is turning on cartoons while Emery is keeping the youngest two calm. After I get off the phone with Demitri I call Aspen. Then I turn on the police scanner which is buzzing with all kinds of calls. They were getting calls about an UFO crashing, people's homes being destroyed by an earthquake, and people being trapped in the rubble. Grace flips through a news station channel that is saying how a meteor crashed fifteen miles from us and that is what caused the tremors. That is awesome that Robyn is on top of it that fast.

I make one more call while waiting on Lucas and Aspen to show up. I inform the cleanup crew lead to tape off the scene and that no one is to enter for any reasons. Makes since now why I could not shake the thoughts about my vision. Back when I was pregnant with Emery, I had my back up against the Tree of Dawn. Soaking my feet in the beautiful light blue water of the pond, I lay back and close my eyes. Images of this day flashed in front of my closed eyes. The only clue of when this vision was going to happen was that I would have four girls by then and the youngest would be around four years old. After that vision was when I had Demitri build this bunker.

A knock from the door to the tunnel brings me out of my thoughts. The tunnel runs underground and comes above ground in the woods. I got the idea from Roland's castle in Hala. I kiss all my girls on the forehead and tell them that I love them. Before Aspen and I head to the crash site. Lucas and their children are going to keep my girls company until Demitri can wrap things up and get home. Aspen informs me that Jazlyn and Ace are on their way to make the cabin brand new. With some hocus pocus as she calls it. Once out of the tunnels I use a shadow from a tree to shadow jump us to the crash site. Even though I have not been there I knew the area and remembered enough details from my vision to shadow jump us within walking distance.

In the middle of the forest trees and plants are knocked down all around a massive crater. Just like in my vision. Nothing is left of whatever landed here except its destruction. Police alarms were sounding in the background. I shadow jump us to headquarters before they reach the crash site. As I walk through the double doors of our conference room I am suddenly taken to the inside of a spaceship. Sitting on a big fluffy couch is a mesmerizing amethyst colored humanoid with the most beautiful royal blue hair that stops at the middle of her back, two black horns, and a long tail. Her tail looks like a mouse's tail, it is the same color as her skin and the tip matches her hair. The being also has a diamond shaped face with upturned aquamarine & sea green colored eyes. With the height she is sitting down she is around 5'5" in height. She is kicking ass on some video game, and she obviously cannot see me. She turns her head to look out the window as I am being snapped back into the meeting room.

"Our Sixth being has arrived, I know what she looks like and a general area to start looking.", I voice as soon as I gain my bearings after being sucked in and out of a vision.

The End

Glossary

✷ : POV (point of view) change

⟨⟩⟩⟨⟨⟩⟩⟨⟨⟩⟩⟨⟨⟩⟩: Time as passed [more than a few days]

Four realms of Earth:
Mortal: realm made for the humans
Hala: realm made for the Fae
Underworld: realm made for human souls. Ran by Hades and his family.
Olympus: realm made for the gods, and goddess. Small portion that is sealed off from the rest of the realm is where the angels live.

A

Air Bender: A name for someone with a strong connection to the Air Element.

Aligist: The ability to understand and communicate any language.

Amazonian: Race of warlike women noted for their riding skills, courage, and pride. Daughters of Ares.

Ancients: Name for Greek Gods and Goddess after the rise of Christianity

Angel: A spiritual humanoid being with wings, they were created to protect humanity and human souls.

Arkan Sonney: A fairy animal that takes the form of a white pig that brings good fortune to those who manage to catch it.

Asgardian Giantess: An enormous female superhuman being from an other-dimensional planetoid called Asgard.

B

Banshee: A female spirit that wails warnings of impending death.

C

Celtic Dryad: Celtic Forest Nymph whose life is linked to a tree mostly weeping willow and oak trees.

Cerberus: Three headed dog that guards the portal to the Underworld.

Changeling: Human-like Fae creature. A lot of time the children are put in place of the children the mother changeling steals and feeds off the mother. Usually, human babies but can be any species.

D

Dark King: Extraterrestrial physic vampire.

Deity: A god or goddess.

Demigod: The offspring of a god/goddess and a mortal.

Demon: A being from the Underworld Realm.

Demonic WereBat: A massive demon looking bat like extraterrestrial.

Demonic Clown: Extraterrestrial killer clown looking creature with jester hat shaped horns.

Dhampir: Offspring of vampire and a human.

Doppelganger: An apparition or double of a living being.

Dragon: Male being that has two forms: Human form and giant flying reptile form.

Dragoness: Female being that has two forms: Human form and giant flying reptile form.

Dryad: Forest Nymph

E

Elemental: Entity of the twelve elements, a being that as mastered and can embody one of the twelve elements.

Energy Vampire: Also known called an energy vamp. Feeds off begins energy and abilities.

F

Fae: Every Supernatural being except ghosts, undead, zombies, mutants, angels, vampires, demon, magician, lycans and some creatures that are fallen angels. From the Realm Hala.

Fairy: Humanoid being that has magical abilities. Only some have wings.

Fairy animal: Type of fae creature. Has magical abilities can resemble a Mortal Realm animal or a combination of multiple Mortal Realm animals.

Forest Troll: Green skinned large ape like creature with sharp fangs and claws that live in forests. Powerful large arms with three black beady eyes.

G

Giantess: Being like an Amazonian from Asgard.

Garden Fairy: Humanoid being with earth magic abilities that lives in gardens.

Ghost: Wondering Spirit or Soul of a mortal.

Goblin: Type of Fae creature. Usually, mischievous.

God: A male deity that is from Olympus.

Goddess: A female deity that is from Olympus.

God Shifter Hybrid: Male child between a god and a Shifter.

Golem: A creature that is created using inanimate matter (usually clay or mud) then brought to live with magic.

Gremlin: A mischievous animalistic looking creature with a spiky back and strange eyes

Gytrash: A sprit that appears as a horse or a dog that haunts lonely roads.

H

Haemorrhois: One of the many massive Saharan snakes feared for its venom. Also known as the Bleeder. The venom causes its victims to bleed out like massive wounds.

Hippogriff: A creature with the head and wings of an eagle, and body of a horse. Can fly as fast as lighting.

Horsemen: Five beings with trances of reaper (type of angel) blood that die are brought back to protect the portals of the four realms. They were created to stop any apocalypse not to bring them.

Horse Demon: Name for a magical evil horse creature.

Huldra: Seductive forest being with Earth Element abilities. Also known as lady of the forest.

Humanoid being: A being that has human characteristics.

Hunters: Beings that hunt "Monster". Which are supernatural beings and creatures. Mostly humans but can be any type of being.

I

Incubus: Male Mortal Realm demon that feeds off one of the seven deadly sins.

J

Jinn: mighty beings created from smokeless fire. They can take on a human, animal, flame, and smoke form.

Juarogunna: Giant spider that turns into a woman to lure people to its killing ground to drain them.

K

Kelpies: Water being with two forms. One form is a human form. Their other form will either be a white horse that has a mane that looks like it made of dripping water, or the top of their other form is a horse and bottom part is a fish tail.

Koda: Fox like fairy animal.

L

Lamia: Creature with the top half of a human and bottom half of a snake

Llewyrr: Similar to the High Elves. Where worshipped as Celtic Gods before the rise of Christianity.

Lycan: Has a human and Wolf form. Very first lycan was an evil king, Lycaon. He was cursed by Zeus for trying to feed Zeus one of his sons.

Lycan Vampire Hybrid: An offspring of a Lycan and a vampire.

M

Magician: A Human that can tapped into the Aether Element with spells. They have a feeble trance of Fae blood, usually witch.

Matter Manipulator: A being with a strong connection to the Matter Element.

Mermaid: Female aquatic being with the top half of a human and body half of a fish.

Merrow: A type of mermaid or aquatic being that can only get their fin with a magical red cap.

Mortal: A being with a soul and have a soul.

Mortal Realm Demon: A demon born in the Mortal Realm instead of the Underworld. Usually referring to a Succubus or Incubus.

Mother Changeling: An adult human- like Fae creature that steals babies and replaces them with her own children.

Mutant: Human except one chromosome that mutated giving them an ability. The ability usually surfaces around puberty.

N

Nephilim: Offspring of a human and an angel.

Northern Devil Cat: Also known as glawackus. Looks like a mixture of a bear, a lion, and a panther. One look into its eyes and your memories are wiped.

Nymph: Being of nature.

O

Ogre: Male man-eating giant.

Ogress: Female man-eating giant.

P

Pixie: Small humanoid with wings. From far away they look like glowing orbs and pixie dust falls from their wings every time the move. Some can magically grow human size but can only hold for twenty-four hours. They are about the size of a bottle of water.

Plant Humanoids: Human looking plant beings. They can take after any type of plant

Primordial Ditties: The first generation of Greek Goddesses and Gods. Precedes the Titanesses and Titans.

Psychic Vampire: Vampiric beings that feeds on life forces to survive. Not a known species of earth.

Q

Qalupalik: A type of mermaid that only lives in freezing waters. It is said they get their monstrous looks from using dark magic. Or that the first was a mermaid that was cursed.

R

Reaper: A being that is one-fourth or less angel that has died. They are given a chance to come back as a reaper and earn their wings. They are tasked with delivering souls to the Underworld.

S

Sea Serpent: Giant water snake.

Sea Witch: Legend of a powerful being with Water Element abilities.

Seer: A being with powerful time element abilities.

Shifter: Also known as a shapeshifter. Can shapeshift into any being they can picture. Some are restricted to one animal form and a human form.

Spirit of the Woods: A spirit of a being that has die in that forests or woods that now protects the area and the creatures that live in it.

Strigoi: The made vampires. They have red rings around their pupils with razor sharp fingernails and teeth. With bat-like wings and an infectious bite. The vampires from Hala.

Succubus: Female Mortal Realm demon that feeds off one of the seven deadly sins.

Sups: Name for anything with abilities. Shortening of the word supernaturals.

Swamp Creature: Also known as swamp nymph. Swamp, plant, and mud humanoid that lives in or around swamps.

Sylph: An Air Elemental also known as an air spirit.

T

Tuatha De' Danann: Rare race of beings that were casted out of Olympus or the heavens on a cloud of mist for knowing too much. They were thought to be and were worshipped as a Celtic God. Whose worship ended with the rise of Christianity.

U

Undead: Skeleton raised from its grave and controlled with necromancy abilities.

V

Vampire: Blood thirsty born humanoids. The first vampire was cursed by Apollo and Artemis and then later was blessed by Artemis. Which finished his transformation into a vampire. The alphas' bite can turn humans into vampire thralls when they want it too.

Vampiric Beings: Blood thirsty beings. Varies kinds and are Fae beings.

Vampire Thrall: A being bitten by a born vampire alpha. They are blood bounded into service to the vampire alpha that bit them. Speed, strength, and senses are heightened some.

W

Waldschrat: A being that is at least seven feet tall, its face looks like a moose skull with massive antlers, eyes that are glowing like the fury of the sun on a scorching summer day and the body of the creature looks like a combination of man and tree. God like speed and powerful magical abilities.

Water Demon: Name for an evil water being.

Water Spirit: Name for good water beings. Some use it to refer to Leviathan (a massive sea monster. The first sea monster is the fallen angel Leviathan).

Werewolf: Fae creature that is a mix between a human, beast, and a wolf. If strong enough to beat the madness they have the ability to shift into their human form. Usually only alphas, lunas, and mated pairs are strong enough. Also known as lycanthrope.

Wild Elf: Race of elves that mostly lives in isolated forests.

Witch: Human counterpart fae being with abilities from one of the elements. Also, use spells and potions.

Z

Zoms: Nickname for zombies. Undead that crave brains and have to eat brains to not become mindless monsters. A virus created by human that only effects humans turns them into a zombies.

ABOUT THE AUTHOR

H.K. Walker is a mother of five and is a Phlebotomist. She loves spending time with her kids, the outdoors, reading and writing. H.K. Walker's books will take you into a world where anything is possible and will have you on the edge of your seat wondering what will happen next.

www.ingramcontent.com/pod-product-compliance
Lightning Source LLC
Chambersburg PA
CBHW051242250626
47155CB00009B/3127